THE BUTTERFLY DIALOGUES

THE BUTTERFLY DIALOGUES

Postmodern Fables for Kids & Grown-ups

Steven Carter

Hamilton Books
A member of
The Rowman & Littlefield Publishing Group
Lanham · Boulder · New York · Toronto · Plymouth, UK

Copyright © 2011 by
Hamilton Books
4501 Forbes Boulevard
Suite 200
Lanham, Maryland 20706
Hamilton Books Acquisitions Department (301) 459-3366

Estover Road
Plymouth PL6 7PY
United Kingdom

British Library Cataloging in Publication Information Available

Library of Congress Control Number: 2011937794
ISBN: 978-0-7618-5576-7 (paperback :   paper)
eISBN: 978-0-7618-5577-4

In loving memory of Kathleen Stokes Brownell

Book One

The Dialogues

The child is father of the man.

—Wordsworth

[Improvisation on a line by James Joyce]

A caterpillar said to a butterfly,
"Once upon a time you were what I am!"
But the butterfly flew off, giving him no sign of love, or farewell, or recognition.

A beautiful turquoise and black butterfly remarked to a dull brown caterpillar, "Believe it or not, I am what you will be."

"What for?" replied the caterpillar, checking out his fur. "On *me* it looks good."

Two caterpillars implored a butterfly,
"Will we be able to soar like you one day?"
"Yes," replied the butterfly, "but you must be patient."
"How long do we have to wait?"
"Go to Mother Nature for the answer to that question." And the butterfly flew off.
The caterpillars put the question to Mother Nature, who gave them the answer.
"Why, that's too long," said one.
"Why, that's not long enough," said the other.

A butterfly encountered a caterpillar on the same mulberry leaf.

"My goodness," they said to each other in unison, "but you're a funny-looking creature."

"Fools!" scoffed a praying mantis, perched on another leaf, "you belong to the same order!"

"Why, that's no fun," they said in the same disapproving tone. "Wait till Mother Nature hears about this!"

A butterfly lectured to an attentive class of dragonflies.

"Today's talk," she intoned, "will be short and bittersweet. We'll encapsulate the meaning of life in one fell swoop, beginning and ending with a riddle, to wit:

'*Aside from obvious issues of age and maturity, what's the fundamental difference between children and adults?*'"

Silence; then—

"Please tell us the answer," one dragonfly pleaded.

The butterfly cleared her throat.

"The answer is," she replied, "'*Children wish to be adults and adults wish to be children.*' That, ladies and gentlemen and boys and girls, is pretty much it. Class dismissed."

"What do you want to be when you grow up?" a butterfly asked a caterpillar.
"I want to be a butterfly."
"Maybe you should set your sights a bit lower; that way you won't be disappointed."

"What do you want to be when you grow up?" a butterfly asked a caterpillar.
"I want to be a butterfly."
"Maybe you should set your sights a bit higher; that way you won't be disappointed."

Caterpillar to butterfly:
"What do people think of when they see you?"
"Tenderness—isn't that wonderful? What do they think of when they see *you*?"
"Tenderness—isn't that wonderful?"
"There's no accounting for some peoples' taste."

On a very warm day a caterpillar glanced up to see a butterfly flittering and fluttering above him.

"What're *you* up to?" the caterpillar inquired.

"I'm keeping myself cool by fluttering my wings," replied the butterfly cheerfully. "Just look as my colors sparkle gaily in the sun while you, on the other hand, appear to be toasty enough in that fur coat."

"Actually," said the caterpillar, "you're not cooling yourself off at all; the rapid motion of your wings creates friction, warming the air and making you expend more energy. If I were you, I'd settle in the shadow of a leaf and fold my wings until the sun goes behind a cloud. For my part," he added, "what you quaintly refer to as this fur coat keeps my body at an even temperature, rain or shine. Now, don't you remember those happy golden moments when you, too, were a caterpillar?"

And he crawled away.

A few minutes later, another butterfly happened by and saw the first butterfly, motionless and silent, perched in the shadow of a leaf.

"Why, look at *you*," the second butterfly exclaimed. "Why aren't you flittering and fluttering up here with me, colors sparkling gaily in the sun? Actually, you seem a bit down in the mouth. Remember what the poet said, my friend: 'Grow old along with me; the best is yet to be—'"

"Oh, shut up."

As a tribe of Monarch butterflies migrated between Canada and Mexico, one said to another,

"Why in Christ's name are we doing this?"

"To breed, of course; you see, it's all according to what the poet William Wordsworth called nature's holy plan."

"Do me a favor. If you see Mother Nature before I do, tell her this is a hell of a long way to go just to get laid."

A pair of butterflies came to rest on a flower next to the entrance to Our Lady of the Perpetual Sigh Basilica, located in a park near Hyannis Port, Massachusetts.

"What *is* this strange place?" one asked as worshippers filed in for Sunday Mass.

The second butterfly explained that they'd happened upon a house of Christian worship.

"But why aren't they paying any attention whatsoever to *us*?" the first butterfly asked. "We're beautiful to look at, are we not?"

"As a faith, Christianity never had much time for the natural world," the second explained. "Virtually every other world religion did or does, but not the Christians. They're interested exclusively in the next world."

"What is that?"

"It's a spiritual place where Christians hope they'll go after death—provided that it's heaven, of course. Heaven, to answer your next question, is envisioned by many as very beautiful—a kind of park."

"Ah! Where there are flowers and butterflies!"

"Bingo."

Two butterflies fluttered up and down the rows of a cemetery, coming to rest on a gravestone.

Gazing at the inscription, one asked, "What do the words say?"

"'Here lies a hero of the political process."

"Yes."

Spotting a rider-less bicycle dawdling down a country lane, one butterfly said to another,

"Check that out; pretty amazing, huh?"

"Sure is," agreed the other, "and no handlebars to boot!"

"But why is *that* amazing?" inquired the first butterfly. "There's no rider."

Two butterflies, husband and wife, paid a visit to a divorce lawyer.

"I'm obliged to ask you two if, even now, there's something you can do to save the marriage," the lawyer said. "I mean, isn't there anything you have in common?"

"*What did he say? What did he say? What did he say?*" the wife demanded shrilly.

Glaring at her, the husband repeated the attorney's words.

"I'm seeing a marriage counselor," the wife sniffed, "but *he* won't go."

"They don't know anything," snarled the husband.

"Well," the attorney folded his hands, "It's plain to see that you're irreconcilable. Accordingly, my fee shall be—"

"Ah, we were hoping you'd do this pro bono," they said in unison. "You know, in favor of the good."

"I am doing it in favor of the good."

Two butterflies, husband and wife, paid a visit to a divorce lawyer.

"I'm obliged to ask you two if, even now, there's something you can do to save the marriage," the lawyer said. "I mean, isn't there anything you have in common?"

"*What did he say? What did he say? What did he say?*" the wife demanded shrilly.

Glaring at her, the husband repeated the attorney's words.

"I'm seeing a marriage counselor," the wife sniffed, "but *he* won't go."

"They don't know anything," snarled the husband.

"Well," the attorney folded his hands, "It's plain to see that you're irreconcilable. Accordingly, my fee will be—"

"Ah, we were hoping you'd do this pro bono," they said in unison. "You know, in favor of the good."

"Sorry."

The wife and husband left the attorney's office whispering endearments to one another.

In a California wood, two hikers wearing strange robes adorned with stars and crescent moons happened on a colony of Monarch butterflies clustered around the lower branch of a redwood tree.

"Would you care to perch on my finger, little one?" the first hiker said to a butterfly named Jake. Jake did so.

"O look!" the second hiker gushed, "the delicate patterns on his wings surely bear witness to the existence of a Higher Power. How beautiful! And the trees! And the flowers! And the clouds! And—"

"Who the hell are you?" Jake interrupted.

"We belong to the Sierra Nevada Church of the Blessed Asteroids," the first hiker replied, putting Jake back on the branch. "We must be off!"

Singing and chanting, they continued their hike; a few moments later, however, a very large black bear jumped out from behind a clump of poison oak and with a loud growl gobbled them up.

"What was that sound?" Jake the butterfly asked a cohort.

"Darwin taking out the trash."

Jake the butterfly went to a shrink.
"I feel like the whole world is against me," he complained.
"What makes you think you're so darned important?"
"That makes me feel better!"
"Then you're cured."

Jake the butterfly went to a shrink.
"I feel like the whole world is against me," he complained.
"What makes you think you're so darned important?"
"That makes me feel worse!"
"Then you're cured."

A butterfly said to a caterpillar,

"Cousin, they say that happy families are all the same, but unhappy families are unhappy in different ways. How do *you* feel about that?"

"I feel miserable."

"So do I."

In a California wood two hikers wearing strange robes adorned with stars and crescent moons happened on a colony of Monarch butterflies clumped around the lower branch of a redwood tree.

"Would you care to perch on my finger, little one?" the first hiker said to a butterfly named Jake. Jake did so.

"O look!" the second hiker gushed, "the delicate patterns on his wings surely bear witness to the existence of a Higher Power. How beautiful! And the trees! And the flowers! And the clouds! And—"

"Who the hell are you?" Jake interrupted.

"We belong to the Sierra Nevada Church of the Blessed Asteroids," the first hiker replied, putting Jake back on the branch. "We must be off!"

"You got that right."

On a ranch in Iowa, two butterflies lighted on the fence of a hog corral where dozens of hogs were being rounded up for slaughter. All they could see was a mass of porcine rear ends and curly tails disappearing in the dust through a chute at the far end of the corral.

"Everything depends on perspective," observed one butterfly.

"Absolutely!" agreed the other. "No ifs—what is it they say?"

"No ifs, ands, or butts."

"I covet my neighbor's wife," a butterfly said to a marriage counselor, "and I don't know what to do about it."

"Divorce your wife," suggested the counselor, "then talk your neighbor into divorcing *his* wife, and marry her."

"What if my neighbor marries my ex-wife?"

"In that case I'll be happy to offer you a package deal on future visits."

Two lady butterflies were chatting away in a field of lupines.

"If you were a character in an opera," one ventured, "what character would you like to be?"

"Oh, please!" the other rolled her eyes.

"OK, OK, I get it. For my part, *I'd* like to play that lady wearing the Viking helmet and carrying a shield, you know, in Wagner's *Ring* cycle—"

"You don't have the body type."

"Why, thank you!"

"You're too fat."

After the funeral of a particularly disagreeable butterfly, one of his cohorts remarked to another,

"Not to speak ill of the dead, but—"

"Oh, hell," the second butterfly interrupted, "why not speak ill of the dead? If they could, what do you suppose the dead would say about us?"

A very rude and aggressive butterfly was given to tormenting his fellows with remarks such as, "Have you noticed that one of your wings is slightly lower than the other?" and "Your colors look awfully drab when the sun goes behind a cloud," and "Why don't you stop flittering and fluttering aimlessly all over creation and get a life?"

Finally the tribe of butterflies grew sick and tired of this and agreed to beat the miscreant to death with their wings.

"Spare me!" pleaded the rude butterfly. "You see, I had a difficult childhood."

The tribe decided to summon an arbitrator. After reviewing both cases, he declared, "It's imperative that we take childhood into consideration. Spare him."

"Well, he got off," complained one disgruntled butterfly to another.

"Looks like we screwed up big time!"

"What do you mean 'we'? It was your bright idea to ask a caterpillar to arbitrate."

"Check out the intricate camouflage on my wings!" boasted a butterfly to a caterpillar. "Mother Nature has seen to it that the veins imitate capillaries on a leaf, rendering me invisible. But the really cool thing is the ingenious eyespot which appears to *refract* the capillaries passing through it, like a drop of rain water. Bottom line: any passing lizard will think that I'm a leaf, and walk on by—not that lizards think much anyway—"

Prattling on in this vein, the butterfly failed to look where he was going and flew down the throat of a wide-mouthed frog.

As for the caterpillar, *he* slowly crawled under a canopy of leaves, quite sure that he would never die.

A butterfly passed away after a long and successful career in politics. His funeral was planned for a Saturday.

"He'll lie in repose until then," one constituent informed another.

"'Lie in repose'? What other way to lie is there?"

"I'll pretend you didn't say that."

"Do you know the multi-volume work *Remembrance of Things Past?*" one butter-fly inquired of another.

His cohort replied that he did not.

"It's about the infinite ways that the senses, especially the sense of taste, can open the portals of memory."

"I can't remember anything that happened an hour ago."

"Is that a good thing or a bad thing?"

"It's a good thing—that way I can better concentrate on the future."

". . ."

"I'm lonely," said Jake the butterfly to a shrink. "And I suffer from deep-seated feelings of alienation."

"How long have you felt this way?"

"Since I came to your office this morning."

"Are you trying to be funny?"

"Yes."

Jake laughed for the first time in a very long time.

"Well, knock it off," said the shrink. "We need to get serious about curing you."

In a state of euphoria, a butterfly boasted to a caterpillar, "People write songs and poems, even operas about me; but nobody ever wrote anything about *you*."

"'I cannot play the fiddle,'" the caterpillar quoted Themistocles, "'but I can build a mighty state from a little city.'"

"But you're just a lowly caterpillar."

"Am I indeed?" murmured the caterpillar, immediately leaving off spinning the chrysalis he was working on.

Perched on a leaf, a butterfly announced plans to reach for the sun.

"I wouldn't do that if I were you," cautioned his friend the caterpillar. "Remember what happened to that foolish Greek boy."

"His wings were made of wax."

"Same difference, dude."

The butterfly fluttered high in the sky until he approached the sun, where his wings were so badly singed that he plummeted to his death far below. The next day one of his cousins happened by the same leaf where the caterpillar now appeared to be bowing in an oddly reverential manner.

"Are you in deep mourning?" the cousin asked.

"You could say that, yes," nodded the caterpillar. "I'm spinning a chrysalis."

Two species of butterfly prepared to go to war. Two caterpillars, one from each species, attempted to broker a peaceful solution to the conflict. By mutual agreement on both sides, they were immediately put to death.

The opposing commanders expressed identical sentiments to their lieutenants, namely that, as one put it, "It's a crying shame that some people have to meddle in important matters that don't concern them."

"If I may be so bold," a caterpillar said to a butterfly, "what religion do you profess?"
"I profess the Religion of the Sacred Butterfly—the one true faith! And you?"
"I profess the Religion of the Holy Caterpillar—the one true faith!"
"That's right!" exclaimed the butterfly, remembering something. "You *do* know," she went on, "that our mission in life is to convert you to the one true faith."
"Not to worry."

Every year, in Pismo Beach, Calif., tens of thousands of Monarch butterflies migrating between Mexico and Canada make a pit stop, settling in clumps on eucalyptus trees surrounding RV and trailer parks. Hundreds of tourists travel great distances to witness this annual event.

Interviewing one butterfly, a TV reporter asked,

"So—what do *you* think about being here?"

"'Hell is other people.'"

"Why, that's not a very charitable thing to say about those tourists who drove many miles just to see you!"

"I wasn't referring to the tourists."

A white moth and a black and yellow butterfly performed an impromptu aerial ballet over a field of yellow flowers.

"I know what you are," said the butterfly. "You're a myth!"

"Well, I know what *you* are," returned the moth. "You're a flutter-by!"

Thus the moth and the butterfly, neither of them knowing who the other was, became fast friends.

In a deep forest a beautiful flower grew next to a dull gray rock. To pass the long hours, they were in the habit of conversing about everything under the sun and moon.

One day a pair of courting butterflies fluttered by; the first lighted on the gray rock, the second on the beautiful flower.

"You flatter me," said the rock to the first butterfly.

"Thank you," the first butterfly said.

"You flatter *me*," the second butterfly said to the flower.

"Thank you," said the flower.

After a time, the butterflies fluttered off, but returned the next day. This time the first butterfly lighted on the flower, the second on the rock.

"You flatter me," the flower said to the first butterfly.

"Thank you," said the butterfly.

"You flatter *me*," said the second butterfly to the rock.

"Thank you," said the rock.

The courting butterflies, their ardor cooled, fluttered off, never to speak again. And the rock and the flower continued the conversation as before.[1]

---

1. This fable originally appeared in my *The Judgment of the Crows*, published by Hamilton Books in 2009.

Early one August morning a caterpillar and a butterfly were enjoying nectar of dew on the same mulberry leaf.

"'Sometimes,'" quoted the caterpillar, "'one loves life so intensely that tears come into the eyes.' Look at the sky, the clouds, the trees, the flowers, and the yellow and green stones shining in the clear stream below us. And look at *you*," he added, his voice thick with emotion. "You, too, are very beautiful. Well," he went on after regaining his composure, "what'll we drink to?"

"Death in summer."

Book Two

The Strange and Amazing Parisian Odyssey of Alphonse and Alain, or: The Butterfly Effect

We always kill the thing we love.

—Oscar Wilde

A discussion

As traffic on the Rue Cher hummed below them, Alphonse and Alain, husbands both, were discussing the State of Things.

Declared Alain, ". . . Monsieur, in France it's the most insufferably tedious, boring, comfortless, *bourgeois* institution imaginable."

"Don't *I* know it, monsieur," Alphonse sighed, antennae drooping. "Sometimes it seems as though I've been married for a hundred years!"

"I was referring to adultery."

A moment in the Bois

Lighting on the white flowers of a horse-chestnut branch in the Bois, Alain said to Alphonse,

"Monsieur, why is it that, as time goes by, things always seem worse, never better?"

"What are you talking about, monsieur? Look at the French; they never change."

"QED."

Sacred ground

Alphonse and Alain wandered into the Cimitiere Montparnasse, where someone had placed a white chrysanthemum on the grave of Charles Baudelaire.

As they lit on the flower, Alain bowed his head.

"Why the bow, monsieur?" asked Alphonse.

"He made us feel the religious intoxication of great cities," Alain murmured.

Rising into the air, dipping their yellow wings in salute, they continued their sojourn across Paris.

A visit to the Louvre

Late one chilly April morning, Alphonse and Alain flew through an open window on the second story of the Louvre. For two hours they fluttered up and down the great halls, pausing before masterpieces such as "L'ecole d'apelle" by Jean Brocis; "Head of an old woman wearing a bonnet" by Balthasar Denner; "Boy with a club foot" by Jusepe de Ribera; "Pandemonium" by John Martin; "Portrait of Francois I as John the Baptist" by Jean Clouet; "Portrait of the duc d'Orleans" by Ingres; "Interior Scene" by Jean-Jacques de Boissieu; "Poor man wearing a hat" by Francisco Sasso; "The Countess del Carpio" by Goya; "The Lacemaker" by Vermeer; "The Virgin of Chancellor Rubin" by van Eyck; "The Coronation of the Virgin" by Fra Angelico," and, of course, "The Mona Lisa."

Finally they rested on the brass rail in front of Poussin's "Ruth and Boaz."

"It's all so beautiful," sighed Alphonse.

"Yes," Alain returned. "But it's not enough."

"What do you mean?"

Without replying, Alain rose into the air and led Alphonse out through the open window they'd entered; and as they flew in the bright Parisian sunlight over I. M. Pei's Louvre Pyramid in the Cour Napoleon, a little girl holding her mother's hand happened to look up and see them disappear into a canvas of sky and clouds.

The Sacre Coeur

Settling on the lower branch of a chestnut tree near Montmartre's cathedral of the Sacre Coeur, Alain and Alphonse watched as an elaborate funeral procession exited the onion-shaped church, blinding white in the afternoon sun.

"I feel sorry for those people," Alphonse said, folding his wings. "They look so sad!"

"Well," Alain replied, "they do believe in an afterlife; it's a cornerstone of the Christian religion."

"Do you suppose that the dead can be seen in the afterlife?"

"No; but some Christians believe that they can see *us*."

"So what do the dead do?"

"They look on and get in the way."

Simone Weil

"What are those buildings down there to the left?" Alphonse asked Alain as they flew toward the Seine.

"The Ecole Normale de Superieure. Along with the Sorbonne, it's one of the two great universities in Paris. My namesake, the philosopher who called himself Alain, taught there for many years. His star pupil was the religious thinker Simone Weil."

"Religious—she obviously wasn't an existentialist like Sartre!"

"Hardly—Sartre and Weil looked at things from very different perspectives. For me, her greatest pronouncement was—actually I think Sartre would've agreed—'Evil dwells in the heart of the criminal and is not felt there. It is felt in the heart of the man who is afflicted and innocent.'"

Having said this, Alain experienced a rush of emotion, feeling that so many of the Parisians walking the sidewalks below must unknowingly embody Simone Weil's terrible words; and, struggling to express his thoughts and knowing that he could not, he simply added, "Poor mankind."

They flew on in silence toward the river.

A man and a woman

Down the hill from Montmartre, Alphonse and Alain paused in their sojourn and flew in an open window. A man and a woman were talking quietly; unseen, and with nothing better to do, the butterflies decided to eavesdrop.

"My dear," the man said, "I have a terrible confession to make. I've taken a lover!"

"But I, too, have taken a lover!" the woman returned.

"Thus we've sinned against French Catholic custom."

". . . Thus we've sinned against French Catholic custom," the woman echoed, nodding slowly.

They bowed their heads.

"Well, monsieur," Alphonse said as they flew out the window to resume their travels, "there's another marriage on the rocks!"

"Who said they were married?"

The Pont Neuf

"I had a dream last night," Alphonse said, resting next to Alain on a railing of the Pont Neuf. "I dreamed I was an emperor fanning himself in a tea garden flooded with sunlight. But when I woke up, I didn't know whether I was a butterfly who dreamed he was an emperor, or an emperor dreaming he was a butterfly."

"Monsieur, you dreamed about that ancient Chinese parable of Chuang Tzu," replied Alain. "It questions the nature of reality."

". . . So I'm not dreaming now?"

"What does it matter?" Alain stretched his wings. "You're in Paris!"

And they flew on, high above the domes, spires, gardens and fountains dreaming in the Parisian sunlight—the only reality they would ever know.

The Bastille

Alphonse and Alain made their way down the Rue Sainte-Antoine, pausing before Number 232—the old location of the Bastille.

"Look, monsieur," Alphonse exclaimed excitedly, "there it was! The storming of the Bastille, as you know, was the jewel in the crown of the Revolution. It—"

"Don't be naïve," Alain shook his antennae. "By 1789 the Bastille only housed seven or eight grumpy old men who just wanted to be left alone."

"You mean—"

"I mean, *there* you have the true spirit of the French Revolution in a nutshell!"

Gargoyles

As they hovered near the façade of Notre Dame de Paris, looking upward Alphonse said in a frightened tone, "Monsieur, what are *those*?"

"Relax, mon ami," Alain said. "They're rainspouts in the shape of gargoyles—pagan statuary intended to ward off evil spirits."

"Pagan statuary—on the façade of a *Christian* cathedral?"

"Yes," Alphonse laughed. "Say what you will about Christians, they have a—what's a good word?—delicious way of hedging their bets."

Three kings

"Who are your three favorite French kings?" Alphonse inquired of Alain.
"At the top of the list, Louis the Fourteenth."
"Second?"
"Louis the Sixteenth."
"Third?"
"Charles de Gaulle."

The U.S. Embassy

Alphonse and Alain rested on a hedge in front of the United States Embassy.

"Look!" exclaimed Alain. "There goes the American Ambassador. He represents the land of the free, you know."

"As in 'free elections'?"

"As in 'free lunch.'"

Two petty bourgeois

Alphonse: "What's the difference between a German petty bourgeois and a French petty bourgeois?"
Alain: "The German language and the French language."

The tomb of Napoleon

Flying over Visconte's Dome des Invalides housing the tomb of Napoleon, Alain remarked to his companion,

"Did you know, monsieur, that Napoleon contemptuously dismissed the English as 'a nation of shopkeepers'?"

"And he was *French?*"

Near a fountain

Near a fountain in the Luxembourg Gardens, as their mothers sat on a park bench eating *pommes frites* dipped in mayonnaise from paper cones, two little boys peed on the cobblestones and giggled insanely.

"Not for nothing did Darwin call it the *descent* of man," Alain observed as he and Alphonse fluttered past.

Leonardo

Alphonse: "Did you know that the inimitable Leonardo, painter of 'The Last Supper' and 'The Mona Lisa,' died in France?"

Alain: "I can only presume that he decided France is a better place to die than Italy."

Alphonse: "Is that a good thing or a bad thing?"

Alain: "Depends on whether or not you're Italian."

The truest democracy

Flying over the *arrondisement* Marais on the Left Bank, Alphonse asked Alain,
"Monsieur, why don't the French like the Americans?"
"The Americans bailed them out of two world wars."
"That's a strange reason not to like someone."
"Not really," Alain replied. "One always resents one's benefactors."
"So how do the French feel about the Germans?"
"Obviously they dislike them too."
"And each other?"
Alain laughed.
"Oh, they despise each other every bit as much as they do Americans and Germans.
Not for nothing is France considered the truest democracy in Europe."

Herman Melville and Victor Hugo

Alphonse: "Did you know, monsieur, that at the Sorbonne literature professors spend an entire academic year on the first six chapters of Melville's *Moby-Dick*? Think of devoting all that time to an American writer!"

Alain: "Better that than the *Collected Works* of Victor Hugo."

At the zoo

As he and Alain cruised over the ape compound at the Paris zoo, Alphonse exclaimed, "Monsieur, look at those little boys imitating that monkey's behavior!"
"Try again."

Gerard de Nerval

As they made their way down the Boulevard Montparnasse, Alain remarked to Alphonse,

"The poet Gerard de Nerval used to walk his pet lobster on a pink leash down these sidewalks."

"Mais pourquoi?"

"I think he wanted to demonstrate that he was less bizarre than the Parisian man in the street."

Above Sainte-Chapelle

Soaring far above the exquisite cathedral of Sainte-Chapelle, on the Ile de la Cite, Alphonse complained,

"We're flying too high! Everything's a blur down there."

"'Why has man not a microscopic eye?'" quoted Alain. "'For this good reason: man is not a fly.'"

"But we're butterflies!"

"Oh, you'll go far, monsieur."

Pierre Elliot Trudeau

Alphonse and Alain cruised up and down Baron Haussmann's broad Boulevard Raspail, when Alain saw a procession of dignitaries enter a hotel.

"Who's that?" he inquired, indicating a tall, distinguished-looking personage.

"That's Pierre Elliot Trudeau, ex-prime minister of Canada," Alphonse replied. "He comes to Paris now and then in search of his roots. He once said, 'There's no place for the state in the bedrooms of the nation.'"

"And he's of *French* ancestry?"

The grave of Tristan Tzara

On another visit to the Montparnasse cemetery, Alphonse and Alain happened upon the grave of Tristan Tzara, just up the row from that of Charles Baudelaire.

"Who was Tzara?" asked Alphonse.

"He was a co-founder of Dada. Dada, to answer your next question, was an art movement which embraced the ridiculous and nonsensical—for example, the fact that butterflies have the ability to speak."

"Are you trying to insult me, monsieur?"

"I was referring to our *ability* to speak; I said nothing about what we have to say to each other."

The waiter

Alphonse and Alain hovered above the Rotonde, the famous and overrated out-door café in Montparnasse. As Peugeots and Citroens whizzed past a few feet away, a waiter served a carafe of *vin ordinaire* to a young American couple.

"It seems that the exhaust fumes affect his nose," Alain remarked.

"Oh, no, monsieur; France has strict new emissions laws—"

". . ."

The Boulevard de Sebastopol

Late one chilly afternoon on the Boulevard de Sebastopol, Alain and Alphonse rested on the lower branch of a plane tree. As the rays of the setting sun shone through the leaves, Alphonse opened his wings to the light.

"Oh, look, maman," exclaimed a little girl as she and her mother passed by, "a stained glass window!"

"Oui, cherie," replied the mother. "Butterflies, you know, are little bits of colored glass fallen from the dome of heaven."

"Did you hear *that*, monsieur?" Alphonse said, preening.

"A little *de trop*, my friend," Alain replied, watching the mother bundle up the little girl more warmly.

"Have you no illusions at all?"

Alain folded his wings. "Butterflies can't afford the luxury of illusions," he said, watching as mother and daughter disappeared down the Boulevard. "The higher orders, on the other hand. . . ."

Near the Avenue Anatole France

Bright yellow leaves floating down a stream of air, the butterflies approached the Avenue Anatole France. Alphonse asked,

"Monsieur, would you say that French higher education and American higher education correspond in any way?"

"In America," Alain replied, "the only thing as difficult as getting a doctorate in French universities is—"

"Getting a doctorate?"

"Flunking out of community college."

The second dumbest thing

Alphonse: "What's the dumbest thing the French government ever did?"
Alain: "*Bien sur*, monsieur, building the Maginot Line."
Alphonse: "The runner-up?"
Alain: "Awarding the Legion of Honor to Jerry Lewis."

Jean-Luc Godard

Alphonse: "Isn't it depressing that our lives are so short—a brief beginning, a middle, and an end—and nary a middle at that!"

Alain: "Yes. Where's Jean-Luc Godard when you need him?"

"Why Godard?"

"In 1966, a reporter from *Cahiers du Cinema* remarked, 'Surely, M. Godard, you agree that a film should have a beginning, middle and end.'"

"'Of course,' Godard replied, 'but not necessarily in that order.'"

The Rue Chevert

In a tight spiral down toward a sidewalk café on the Rue Chevert, Alphonse asked Alain,

"Where do you think we go when we die?"

"The bosom of Abraham; how the hell would I know, monsieur?"

"But if there *is* an afterlife—what do you suppose we'll miss the most on earth?"

"Autumn leaves," Alain said as they came to rest on a table and folded their wings. "Brilliant flags in the ranks of death!"

The lovers

As they flittered and fluttered for hours high over the boulevards and parks of the Left Bank, Alain said to Alphonse,

"Monsieur, think of the hundreds of pairs of lovers we've seen down there, walking through the Bois, the Luxembourg Gardens and along the Seine; billing and cooing at sidewalk tables; kissing—"

"Appalling, isn't it?" returned Alphonse. "Elbow to elbow like that, overhearing the banalities and sweet nothings whispered in the ears of strangers—'What are you thinking?' 'What are *you* thinking?' 'No, my dear, what are *you* thinking?' I admit to being a sentimentalist, but for pity's sake!"

"But don't you see? That's precisely why—or how—they fall in love!" Alain interjected.

"What're you talking about?"

"Let me put it this way. When the writer Guy de Maupassant had lunch at the Eiffel Tower every day without fail, he never missed a chance to bad-mouth the Tower in the most vociferous terms. When a waiter summoned the courage to ask him if he despised the Tower so why he came there, Maupassant replied, 'Because it's the only place in Paris where I don't have to look at the damned thing!' There you have your answer!"

McDonald's

Alphonse: "Monsieur, did you know that there are no fewer than 73 McDonald's fast food restaurants in Paris?"

Alain: "That's appalling! We're talking about tens of thousands of customers every day."

Alphonse: "Oh, well! At least we know where the Americans go."

Alain: "Who said anything about Americans?"

The Tuileries Gardens

Settling on a park bench in the Tuileries Gardens, Alphonse and Alain watched a group of small boys sailing paper boats in the fountain. A few yards away three young girls slurping cups of *glace au chocolate* sat with their mothers and looked on.

Suddenly a squabble broke out and one boy promptly sank the boat of another, who immediately retaliated; whereupon both boys burst into tears. Observing this, the three girls began giggling.

"Why are they laughing?" Alphonse asked.

"Actually, they're learning a valuable lesson," replied Alain, beating his wings. "They're starting to appreciate how different they are from boys, even at an early age."

"What about when they grow up?"

"When they grow up the difference between them will be this: When the boys say 'I love you' in the heat of passion, they'll regret it more; when the girls say 'I hate you' in the heat of passion, they'll regret it less."

The Place d'Italie

Skimming low over the ring of narrow streets leading to the Place d'Italie, Alphonse remarked,

"Parisians have always been partial to American blacks, haven't they—not only Josephine Baker back in the nineteen-twenties, but many others."

"True," agreed Alain. "And the blacks like it fine—a good arrangement, as long as they don't have to live next to them."

"But there's nothing wrong with black people."

"When I said 'them,' I was referring to the Parisians."

Les Halles

In the *arrondisement* of Les Halles, Alphonse and Alain saw a housewife lean out the window, shout, and shake both fists at her husband, who'd just emerged on the street. He shook his fists back at her, uttering several expletives, and stalked off.

When he reached the corner a few minutes later, she yelled,

"*Bonne chance*, Cheri!"

"See you tonight, Cherie!" returned the husband, waving.

"What's *that* all about?" Alphonse asked in astonishment.

"Communication."

The doctrine of 'No More'

Fluttering low over the Bourse, the French stock exchange, Alphonse wondered aloud what French and American political philosophies have in common.

"Contemporaneously," Alain answered, "just one thing: the presidential doctrine of 'No more.'"

"No more what?"

"In France, no more grandiose military figures from the recent past; in America, no more Southern governors."

In harmony with Mother Nature

"I keep hearing this phrase, 'in harmony with nature,' remarked Alphonse as they came to rest on a cigarette and magazine kiosk near the Blanche subway stop. "But what does it really mean?"

Alain thought a moment. Then:

"For men, it means an uneasy truce with Mother Nature. After centuries of abuse and neglect which began during the Industrial Revolution, environmentalists now wish to find ways to convenience her, so to say, in the hope that she won't inconvenience *them*—sort of like ex-spouses who agree to get along. For us butterflies, or what men unfathomably call the lower forms of life, harmony with Mother Nature means acceptance; we simply do what we're told. And that's truly why—never mind the pretty patterns on our wings—men find us beautiful."

A kiss at the University of Paris

Above one of the beautiful, sprawling campuses of the University of Paris, Alphonse caught a glimpse of a white-bearded professor kissing a student behind a tree.

"What's going on down there?"

"They're having an affair," Alain replied, "or they're about to."

"What attracts him to her?"

"Her body and her looks."

"And what attracts her to him?"

"His wisdom," Alain laughed, his antennae jiggling.

"That's not a fair bargain."

"No. And think of how disappointed they'll both be when they find that out."

The Sorbonne

One cloudy day in the quad of the Sorbonne, the butterflies observed a long-haired student standing precariously on a folding chair, haranguing his cohorts.

"Vive la France!" he shouted, "Vive la France!"

"My goodness, what's up with that?" Alphonse asked.

"He's keeping the spirit of the campus rebellions of 1968 alive," replied Alain.

"What spirit is that, monsieur?"

"Non-conformity."

The cinema

As they flew past a cinema featuring a retrospective of American westerns, Alain laughed, "Typical, monsieur! The French have always been wild for the American West. They fancy themselves as gunslingers shooting from the lip."

"Don't you mean 'hip'?" Alphonse asked.

"I don't say what I don't mean," Alain replied. "Another typical French trait, by the way; it explains why the French have always made terrible diplomats. The only exception to that rule I'm aware of was Louis VII, who intentionally kept two emissaries from the court of England's Henry II waiting for two weeks and then, when he finally summoned them, asked sweetly, "Fresh from England?"

"That doesn't sound very diplomatic to me."

"Louis was a king, you dunce; he didn't need to be a diplomat."

Buttes Chaumont

Fluttering their way through the narrow cobblestone streets of the arrondisement Buttes Chaumont, Alphonse asked Alain,

"Monsieur, what's the difference between a French bourgeois and an American bourgeois?"

"For a French bourgeois, time is money," Alain replied. "He's always thinking about his bank account. For an American bourgeois, money is time. He's always thinking about the leisure that his money can buy."

"You sound like Tocqueville."

"I do, don't I?" Alain laughed, pleasantly taken aback by Alphonse's acuity. "Leave it to a Frenchman to read the fine print on the American soul!"

"But wasn't it Benjamin Franklin who said, 'Time is money'?"

"Oh, Ben was a Frenchman at heart," Alain said. "Just ask the courtesans of Paris."

The old woman

As they banked toward the sun near Gae Aulenti's Musee d'Orsay, Alain and Alphonse spotted an old woman in rags tottering below them on the Rue de Lille.

"Alas, monsieur, ancient women are the invisible ones of Paris," Alphonse sadly remarked.

"Yes and no," Alain replied. "Baudelaire made them visible in his book of prose poems, *Paris Spleen*, published in 1859. He was the first French poet to express compassion for the poor, the very old, and the downtrodden."

"Would you mind quoting a few lines?"

"'A wizened little old woman felt gladdened and gay at the sight of the pretty baby that everyone was making such a fuss over, and that everyone sought to please; such a pretty little creature, as frail as the old woman herself, and toothless and hairless like her. She went up to him all nods and smiles. But the infant, terrified, struggled to get away from her caresses, filling the house with his howls.

'Then the old woman went back to her eternal solitude and wept alone, saying, 'Ah, for us miserable old females the age of pleasing is past. Even innocent babes cannot endure us, and we are like scarecrows to little children whom we long to love. . . .'"

Winter

Alain: "Monsieur, you *do* know that we won't be around to see the coming of winter."
Alphonse: "How sad."
Alain: "Oh, *I* don't know; they say that Parisian winters can be pretty unpleasant."
Alphonse: "I suppose we'd just stay at home with the wives."
Alain: "QED."

Versailles

On a two-day visit to Versailles, Alphonse and Alain flew past the apartments of Madame Maintenon, the notorious seventeenth-century courtesan.

"Tell me, monsieur," Alphonse said, glancing through the windows. "Would you rather be gone but not forgotten, or forgotten but not gone?"

"That depends."

"On what?"

"On how important the irregularities in your life are to you."

The Place de la Madeleine

Alphonse and Alain lighted on a table in an outdoor café in the Place de la Madeleine.

"Monsieur, the Germans and the French have been squabbling over the province of Alsace-Lorraine for centuries," Alphonse observed. "And yet French and Germans *both* live there. So what's the dispute about?"

"Which country least deserves it."

The Quai de Bourbon

Soaring over the Quai de Bourbon on the Ile Saint-Louis, Alphonse said to Alain,
"Monsieur, I've been pondering and pondering."
"Oh, dear!"
"Which phrase rings truer: 'deceptively deep serving dishes in Chinese restaurants,' or 'deceptively shallow serving dishes in Chinese restaurants'?"
". . . Only a modern French thinker would split hairs that way!" Alain waggled his antennae. "No wonder French philosophy after Derrida is a laughing stock."

The Unknown Soldier

The butterflies made their way toward the Arc de Triomphe, location of the tomb of France's Unknown Soldier. As they settled, Alphonse exclaimed,
"What a shame! If he could only have known that he would become the Unknown Soldier!"
". . ."

The Parc de Monceau

As they swooped over the rhododendron gardens of the lovely Parc de Monceau, Alphonse said,

"Look at the lovers kissing on that bench down there."

"Chances are they're both thinking of someone else."

"How do you know that?"

"It's the French way."

"But if all French lovers are thinking of someone else, then—"

"Exactly. It all equals out. That's why the French are the only people that set divorce above marriage, though they won't admit it."

The Grevin Wax Museum

As they awoke from a nap in the rose garden of the Grevin Wax Museum, Alphonse asked,
"Monsieur, how much should one tip a Parisian waiter?"
"It depends on how many times he insults you."
"Don't you mean, 'It depends on how *few* times'?"
"I don't say what I don't mean."

The Butterfly Effect

Riding a soft breeze over the busy Rue Fabert, Alphonse asked his companion, "Monsieur, what's the so-called 'Butterfly Effect'?"

Alain replied, "It's a key component of chaos theory. According to the Butterfly Effect, a storm in the Atlantic sends out permutations of wind for thousands of miles, causing other permutations, which in turn cause still others, gradually diminishing, until they come to Paris where, as they reach the end of their appointed journey, they gently ruffle our wings."

". . . Doesn't it work the other way around?"

"Not if you're a butterfly."

The Faubourg St. Germain

As the butterflies executed barrel rolls high over the upper-crust district Faubourg St. Germain, Alphonse asked Alain,

"Monsieur, which would you rather be—a soul in search of a body or a body in search of a soul?"

"A soul in search of a body."

"Mais pourquoi?"

"A body in search of a soul risks finding it."

Heaven

"Regardez!" Alphonse called as Alain dipped low over the Parc du Champs de Mars. "There's a guy with a butterfly net down there, sitting on the edge of that fountain!"

"Check this out."

Alain commenced to dance and twirl tantalizingly just out of reach of the butterfly hunter, who leapt to his feet and gave chase. Alain led him in circles around the fountain until, with Alphonse looking on, the hunter lost his balance and fell in the water, net and all.

"Beautiful!" exclaimed Alphonse. "You've just earned your wings in heaven, monsieur."

"And what makes you think *this* isn't heaven?" Alain panted, fluttering his wings while treading air.

Alphonse thought a moment.

"Because it all ends all too quickly, I suppose."

Alain said nothing; instead he flew on, leading Alphonse over fountains, benches, statues, and horse-chestnut trees in bloom, into the grieving beauty of a Parisian sunset.

The Rue Amelie

As they cruised over the Rue Amelie, Alphonse remarked to his companion,
"I understand that among the common folk in America it's considered a sin to be wealthy; and yet the common folk want to get rich. I don't get it!"
"Nor do they, monsieur; nor do they."

Alain quotes Wordsworth

Alain: "Do you remember when you were a caterpillar?"
Alphonse: "Oh, monsieur, how I wish I could!"
Alain: "Remember too: 'The child is father of the man.'"
Alphonse: "On second thought."

The Rue Barbousse

Following a handsome young couple walking hand-in-hand up the Rue Barbousse, Alphonse and Alain were content to watch and listen as they whispered endearments, exchanging pecks on the cheek; passersby smiled at them.

"You seem down in the mouth today," Alphonse remarked as the lovers strolled by a charcuterie.

"Oh, I was just thinking of something the Spanish philosopher Miguel de Unamuno said," Alain muttered. "'Love is the sole medicine against death, for love is death's brother.'"

"I don't understand what that means, monsieur."

"Think of a vaccine," Alain explained. "Then think of what the vaccine is made from."

"It's made from the virus it's designed to conquer."

"Voilá!"

"I still don't understand."

"Well," Alain said, still eyeing the lovers, "maybe we're not meant to." And he felt a rush of friendly affection for Alphonse. "Speaking of death," he went on as the couple exchanged another kiss, "we won't be around when those two cozy up together in a warm bed this winter. So let's wish them well!"

"Bonne chance, mes belles amis!" exclaimed Alphonse as the lovers disappeared around a corner.

Le President

Alphonse: "My English isn't that shabby, monsieur, but I don't know the meaning of the word 'irrelevant.'"

Alain: "Le President Jimmy Carter."

The Rue de Villiers

The butterflies settled for a few moments on a stoplight on the busiest corner of the Rue de Villiers, whereupon Alphonse gushed,

"O monsieur, don't you feel Francois Villon in your soul? 'Where are the snows of yesteryear?'"

"Melted."

The Avenue Jean Jaures

Taking a break on a lamppost on the Avenue Jean Jaures, the butterflies returned to the subject of French attitudes toward America.

"Of all things American," Alphonse inquired, "what is it that the French dislike the most?"

"The American Medical Association, bien sur," replied Alain, shaking dust off his wings.

"Why is that?"

"The AMA classifies alcoholism as a disease."

Near the Place Vendome

"Everything is holy or nothing is holy," pronounced Alain as the butterflies flew over side streets leading to the Place Vendome. "One or the other, monsieur; it's that simple!"

Alphonse had no reply. Still, even as they hovered over a courtyard, two small boys wearing brown shorts appeared and began kicking a soccer ball against an ancient brick wall. Briefly—for a moment or two—they seemed somehow to incarnate all the *intricacies* of the mystery of the world: Parisian sunlight glinting in their dirty blond hair; flashes of light and shadow as the ball bounced obediently back and forth; shrill cries of pleasure wafting up to the butterflies in the early morning wind.

L'Opera

The butterflies hovered over Charles Grenier's l'Opera, designed for Napoleon III and reputedly the supreme expression of Second Empire baroque in all of France.

Then they swooped low, fluttering past the American Express Office nearby.

Alphonse turned to Alain. "Monsieur, do you have any further ideas about the difference between Americans and the French?"

"Bien sur!" Alain replied. "According to a recent national poll assessing their knowledge of well-known historical figures, nearly half a million Americans believe that Joan of Arc was Noah's wife. Do the math."

Near the Musee Zadkine

The hard-to-find Musee Zadkine, located on 100 Bis Rue d'Assas near the Jardin du Luxembourg, is named after Ossip Zadkine, a Russian sculptor whose works are on display there. As the butterflies settled in for a snooze on the lowest branch of a plane tree next to the entrance, Alphonse folded his wings and asked Alain,

"Monsieur, there *are* things in this world that never change—n'est-ce pas?"

"Sh!" Alain hushed him, turning his attention to a young couple strolling past directly below them. The girl didn't look happy.

"Cherie," said the man, stabbing the air with a forefinger, "I promise you that I'll change!"

"There you go," said Alain.

The Rue Jolivet

Lighting on a blue mailbox across the street from a boulangerie on the Rue Jolivet, the butterflies were silent for a few moments. A mother and her little boy exited the boulangerie, the boy carrying a baguette almost as tall as he.

Alphonse asked,

"What do you do when you're depressed, monsieur?"

"I think of the color yellow," Alain replied, "our color!"

"And that cheers you up?"

"It makes me more depressed."

"Why?"

"'Beauty is momentary in the mind—'" Alain quoted, "'The fitful tracing of a portal; but in the flesh it is immortal.'" He shook his wings. "Keep that in mind, monsieur, when winter rolls around."

"But you said that we won't live to see winter."

"Exactly."

Across the street from La Closerie des Lilas

At a coffee bar across the street from La Closerie des Lilas—a century-old restaurant beloved of Parisians until Hemingway's *The Sun Also Rises* put it on the map for American tourists—Alphonse commented on a good-looking young couple standing a few feet away.

"Monsieur, how happy they look! All of the world's bright promise appears to lie before them!"

Just then the woman murmured,

"Jean-Claude, I need you."

"Whoops!" Alain unfolded his wings. "End of the affair! Let's be off."

The Rue Joseph Barra

Settling on a chair at a sidewalk café just off the narrow Rue Joseph Barra, Alphonse and Alain spotted two women quietly chatting over glasses of white wine.

"Do *not* marry Andre," one said to the other fervently, tapping the table with a bright red fingernail. "I'm quite confident that you'll follow my advice, Cherie."

"Look," Alain threw his voice, "a flying pig!"

The friend who'd spoken looked upward, then behind her.

"Monsieur, there's no such thing as a flying pig," Alphonse objected.

"No, but she believed me."

Number Twelve Place Vendome

Skimming over busy traffic and fluttering past the rooms of Number Twelve Place Vendome where Frederic Chopin died in 1849, Alphonse asked Alain,
"Monsieur, what, in your estimation, is the greatest impediment to human progress?"
"The advertising sign on the side of that autobus says it all," Alain replied.
"'New and improved,'" Alphonse read aloud as the autobus turned the corner.

The Avenue Jean Jaures II

Chilling once again on their favorite lamppost on the Avenue Jean Jaures, Alphonse asked Alain,

"If you could belong to another nationality, which would it be?"

"German."

"Surely you're joking, monsieur!"

"Not at all; being German would be all the incentive I'd need to travel and see the world."

The Rotonde

Fluttering above a table at the eternally busy Rotonde—across the street from the Dome and, next to the Dome, Paris's best-known outdoor café—Alphonse and Alain noticed three young men drinking glasses of vin ordinaire. All three wore knapsacks sporting the green, white, and red of the Italian flag.

"So what's the difference between Italian wine-drinkers and French wine-drinkers?" Alphonse inquired.

"The Italians drink wine to get drunk," Alain ventured.

"And the French?"

"The French also drink wine to get drunk, but they're connoisseurs, so it's OK."

The Boulevard des Batignolles

As they navigated their way up the noisy Boulevard des Batignolles, Alphonse remarked, "Monsieur, the American satirist Ambrose Bierce claimed that France's state religion is mayonnaise. Surely that's unfair!"

"*Very* unfair," agreed Alain. "Even the Bishop of Orleans knows that it's Bernaise sauce."

The Rue Champagne Premiere

As the butterflies approached the Rue Champagne Premiere, Alphonse asked Alain, "Monsieur, is there such a thing as true love?"

"Of course not, you idiot!" Alain barked. "Love is the child of illusion, as Miguel de Unamuno teaches us."

"Is that a good thing or a bad thing?"

"Oh, a good thing, sans doute! The illusory nature of love is precisely what allows its wounds to heal."

"So the wounds are themselves illusory?"

"No, no, monsieur. They're quite real."

"Voilá! I've caught you in a contradiction!"

". . . Do I contradict myself?" Alain smiled. "Very well then, I contradict myself!"

". . . Je ne comprends pas," Alphonse shook his antennae as they turned down the adjoining Passage d'Enfer in search of a place to rest.

"Regardez!" warned Alain. "You're about to crash into that window!"

"Goodness!" Alphonse exclaimed, backing off and hovering. "The glass is so clear I thought the window was open!"

"*Now* you're catching on."

The Boulevard Malesherbes

Sailing on a brisk morning wind up the Boulevard Malesherbes toward the Place du General Catroux, Alphonse and Alain talked about solitude.

"I'm not ashamed to say it, monsieur," Alphonse began, "I'm deathly afraid to be alone!"

"When you feel that way," counseled Alain, "always return to Baudelaire's prose poem, 'One O'Clock in the Morning.'"

Alain quoted:

'At last! I am alone! Nothing can be heard but the rumbling of a few belated and weary cabs. For a few hours at least silence will be ours, if not sleep. At last! The tyranny of the human face has disappeared, and now there will be no one but myself to make me suffer.'

"Of course it's true," Alain continued as they approached the Place, "that the loneliness of great cities—of Paris in particular—can be a terrible thing. Au fond, however, *fear* of solitude ought to qualify as a cardinal sin, if it isn't already!"

"Mais pourquoi?" Alphonse exclaimed, clearly astonished.

"Because, monsieur, it sorely tempts us to use other people as cushions against the pricks of reality."

"What 'reality' are you referring to?"

"Other people."

The Rue La Fayette

Gliding over a sidewalk café on the Rue La Fayette, Alphonse and Alain spotted two Parisians arguing vehemently as they waited for the traffic light to change. When the light turned, they crossed the street, one shaking his fists at the other, who then uttered a stream of expletives, stalking off in the other direction.

"The national motto of France is 'Liberte, Egalite, Fraternite,' is it not?" Alphonse inquired.

"Two out of three isn't bad."

The Rue 4 Septembre

They came to rest on a wrought-iron lamppost next to the subway stop on the Rue 4 Septembre, whereupon Alphonse asked Alain,

"Who was that French golfer who almost won the British Open a few years ago?"

"Jean Vandevelde," Alain folded his wings. "He cruised through the back nine on Sunday, arriving at the eighteenth hole with a six-shot lead. He got greedy, chose the wrong clubs and made some foolish shots, and blew up to a bogey six, forcing a playoff—which he promptly lost!"

"Why did he do that?"

"Fear of success," Alain ventured. "—A French national trait, by the way!"

"Do you have proof of that, monsieur?"

"Are you kidding me? What else was the Maginot Line good for?"

The Ecole Militaire

Located on Avenue de la Motte-Picquet, the Ecole Militaire—designed by Jacques-Ange Gabriel in 1759—is a superb example of French Neo-Classical architecture. It was here, on the last day of April, that Alphonse and Alain decided to pay a visit, fluttering back and forth over the parade grounds as hundreds of gray-uniformed cadets practiced formations.

"How young they look!" Alphonse exclaimed.

"Too young," Alain remarked, "to remember what happened in 1940, when the Germans marched down the Champs-Elysees to begin their four-year occupation of Paris. A few days later, they forced the French generals to sign a humiliating surrender document in a railroad car, which had been brought from the museum at Versailles to a nearby wood for that very purpose."

"Why bring that up now?" Alphonse inquired, still gazing down as the solemn-faced, red-cheeked cadets drilled back and forth.

"Back in 1918, when the Germans were pummeled by the AEF, French generals forced the 'Hun' to sign the humiliating Treaty of Versailles in—guess where?—that very same railroad car. This, in turn, was payback for the humiliation of losing the Franco-Prussian War to the Germans in 1871. Fast-forwarding now to 1944, when Hitler saw the handwriting on the wall, he ordered the railroad car blown up, to deprive the French of the satisfaction of rubbing the noses of the Nazis in a mortifying surrender yet again. So it goes."

"So the chain of revenge was broken at last."

"Yes and no."

"Anyway, monsieur, it seems to me that the French and the Germans are more alike than they'd like to admit."

"Oh, most assuredly! When it comes to war, and like all combatants, they are—shall we say—one big unhappy family. It makes perfect sense. Siblings squabble and fight with each other more than they do with the kids who live down the block."

"Is that the only reason why the French and Germans go to war?"

"No, no," Alain shook his antennae. "There's another, even more compelling reason."

"And what is that?"

"The women are watching."

The Boulevard de Magenta

The best way to experience a crowd in Paris is to make your way down one of Baron Haussmann's great 19th-century boulevards—Raspail, Montparnasse, de Magenta—and this is precisely what Alphonse and Alain elected to do on a bright Tuesday morning in late March. Dipping and swooping low over the throngs walking up and down the Boulevard de Magenta, Alain said,

"Charles Baudelaire was of two minds, or moods, concerning crowds. On the one hand they inspired horror—he referred to them as 'rabble, born for the whip,' and 'that wretched mortal multitude'—but on other occasions they thrilled him—filled him, I should say, with what he called the religious intoxication of great cities. Just look below!"

And they hovered, gazing at olive-skinned Pakistanis, brown-skinned Moroccans, African Berbers in flowing red-and-white striped robes, doe-eyed Indian women in saris, and pasty-faced Parisians, Americans, Canadians, and Brits. Far from dismissing them as rabble or as wretched, the friends swooped even lower, so that passersby could've reached out and touched them. Alain in particular experienced a fervent wish to enter the lives of these exotic strangers—no, to *become* them; and, as they approached the end of the long boulevard, both butterflies freely indulged in what Baudelaire also called a divine prostitution of the soul. . . .

"Let's talk about something else":
a quartet

Near Planet Sushi

"Let's talk about something else," she said as Alphonse and Alain settled on the back of a chair at an adjoining table. The girl and the man were seated at an outdoor café across the street from the trendy Planet Sushi on the Ile de France. It was a cold, bright, sunny day in early April.

"It's no use," the man replied, smiling wanly and sipping his white wine. "We always return—criminals to the scene of the crime!—to the sore subject of our spouses."

"Why is that?"

"We need them," he shrugged, putting down his glass. "They're why we're here."

"Very well," she said bitterly. "Here's to your Catherine and my Jean-Phillipe!"

They clinked glasses and drank.

"Monsieur—"

"Don't even ask," Alain interrupted as they fluttered off. "Let's just say that was perfectly illogical, which is to say it made perfect sense!"

The Rue Grenelle

At a coffee bar down the Rue Grenelle from the underrated Restaurant la Petite Chaise, Alphonse and Alain perched on the back of a green wicker chair and eavesdropped on the following:

"Let's talk about something else," a girl said.

"What, for instance?" asked her companion.

"Me, instead of *you*."

"Oh, very well. . . ."

"Another doomed affair, monsieur," Alphonse remarked to Alain as they opened their wings to the sun.

"Not at all: they have everything in the world in common."

Near the Restaurant Helene Darroze

Settling on the handlebars of a shiny new Harley parked across the street from the four-star Restaurant Helene Darroze, Alphonse and Alain caught the following words being exchanged by a passing couple.

"Let's talk about something else," the girl suggested.

"Fine! Agreed!" nodded the man. "Look at that petit chien on a red leash across the street; it looks just like its owner!"

"Now you're dodging the issue."

". . ."

"Just skip it," Alain said, rising into the air as Alphonse started to speak.

The Rue Boisonnade

On the sunny side of the Rue Boisonnade, a woman walking with her husband smacks her palm repeatedly with the back of a tightly balled fist.

"Once and for all," she says, "my mother is *not* nosey. She's simply interested!"

"Let's talk about something else."

"Remind me to skip *that* next family bash," Alain says to Alphonse as they point their antennae westward.

The Rue Reamur

High over the nearly deserted Rue Reamur just after sunrise, Alphonse and Alain struck up a conversation about Germany.

"What's the Germans' favorite saying?" Alain asked.

"'Man is a swine.'"

"They should know."

The Rue d'Assas

Following a beautiful girl in a green dress up the Rue d'Assas, Alphonse and Alain saw her take a white envelope from her handbag and slam it on the table of an outdoor café, where a handsome middle-aged man was sitting alone eating a croissant and drinking café au lait. Walking swiftly, high heels clicking, she turned the corner and disappeared, whereupon the man quickly opened the envelope and removed the message; the butterflies hovered and read over his shoulder.

"Etienne," she'd written, "You asked me to leave Albert for you. I did that. You asked me to quit my job and let you put me up in an apartment to be at your beck and call like a courtesan. I did that. Now you refuse to leave poor Emilie because of 'the kids.' Don't ever call me again, you bastard. God, I hate the French!"

"I wonder what her nationality is," Alphonse said as they flew on.

"French."

The Bibliotheque St. Genevieve

The butterflies swooped over the grounds of the Neo-Grec Bibliotheque St. Genevieve, where they spotted a student on a stone bench, reading.

"Peter Abelard began teaching here in 1135," Alain commented as they drew near, "the very year John of Salisbury became his student."

"What's that kid reading?"

Alain dipped lower. "*John Lennon's Philosophy of Life*," he answered.

"Wouldn't Abelard and Salisbury be spinning in their graves?"

"Actually, Abelard himself was a rock star of sorts; he composed and sang scores of songs, all of which are unfortunately lost to us. Heloise always said it was his singing, not his philosophy, which seduced her."

"So what's the difference between John Lennon and Peter Abelard?"

"Abelard had a mind."

Sartre's grave

Making one of several visits to the Cimitiere du Montparnasse, the butterflies paused over the grave of Jean-Paul Sartre, a few rows down from those of Baudelaire and Tristan Tzara.

"Born 21 June 1905," Alain read out loud, "Died 15 April 1980."

"What sort of person was Sartre?" Alphonse inquired, settling on the gravestone.

"He was a shit—the very word he used to describe himself—in his relationships with women," Alain replied. "Like poets, philosophers aren't necessarily Girl Scout guides, you know."

"So what good is philosophy?"

"Ah, monsieur, what would happen to humanity's funny bone without it?"

The Philarmonie de Paris

Entering the suburbs of La Villette, the butterflies cruised over Jean Nouvel's postmodern Philharmonie de Paris, site of symphony and rock concerts.
Alphonse gushed, "Ah, music—the universal language!"
"Wrong again," Alain waggled his antennae. "Music is the universal aphrodisiac."
"But young girls look up to rock stars as philosophers, not simply singers!"
"Yes, and they're half-right—maybe."

Near the Musee Rodin

Entering a charming neighborhood park near the Musee Rodin, Alphonse and Alain flew in lazy circles above a bench where sat a handsome young couple.

"Last night was heaven," she said, gazing at the backs of her hands. "So why are we so miserable?"

"Because 'we have to stop meeting like this,'" the man smiled, making quotation marks with his fingers.

She looked at her wedding ring.

"God, I hate the rules of the game," she murmured.

"No, darling; what you—and I—*really* hate is the game of the rules," he suggested.

"Oh, look at that beautiful yellow butterfly," she exclaimed, pointing at Alphonse, who bowed imperceptibly. "That's what I want to be in my next life—a beautiful butterfly." She brushed a strand of brown hair from her eyes. "Et tu?"

"A giant panda," he answered, folding his arms. "They live in almost total isolation in a mountain jungle, with nothing to do all day but chew on bamboo shoots. No dangerous liaisons for them! . . . I'm so sorry," he put his arm around her.

She said nothing, looking across the grass at three small boys kicking a soccer ball back and forth. Alphonse and Alain left the man and the woman there, enveloped in stony silence.

"Not a bit of that is necessary," Alain remarked as they exited the park, turning in the direction of the museum. "And yet it seems it is necessary. . . ."

"So aren't you glad you're not a person?" Alphonse asked.

"No."

The Quai Branly

Banking over the Quai Branly across the street from the Eiffel Tower, Alphonse gestured to a tourist walking 100 feet below them, wearing a maple leaf-adorned knapsack.

"Canadian," he said.

"Fifty-fifty chance he's *American*," Alain replied. "Americans like to display the Canadian maple leaf so that Parisians won't spit at them."

"But I always thought that good manners were in French genes."

Alain laughed and shook his antennae. "In truth, monsieur, it's what one might indelicately call 'to the bad manners born.'"

On the Rue de la Parcheminerie

Alphonse and Alain paused to look in the window of the Abbey Bookshop at 29, Rue de la Parcheminerie. After a few moments of gazing at the titles on display, Alphonse asked,

"Monsieur, what are 'self-help' books?"

"'Advice' books; half the time they tell people what they should know in the first place if they had half a brain; the rest of the time they tell people what they *already* know, but feel the need to validate by shelling out twenty euros."

Then, as they resumed their odyssey down Parcheminerie, Alain added, "But these books do provide a considerable measure of self-help."

"Why, of course," Alphonse replied. "After all, if readers are willing to pay twenty euros to feel that they've gotten help, what's wrong with that?"

"I wasn't referring to the readers."

The Rue des Petites Ecruries

As they came to a brief rest at a sidewalk café on the Rue des Petites Ecruries, Alain and Alphonse overheard the following conversation between two Parisian men sipping cafés au lait at the next table.

"Monsieur," said one, "check out that biker type over there eating soup for lunch. He belongs to that spanking new Harley parked at the curb."

"What about him?"

"He had his finger up my ass last Tuesday."

". . . Get out!"

"I swear it's true, monsieur."

The other put down his cup and shook his head.

"Please say you're putting me on."

"Sorry; I'm coming out, monsieur! I'm coming out! And you're the second one to know!"

"No, no—I refuse to believe it!"

Then his companion burst into laughter.

"All right, all right," he waved his hand. "Actually he's my doctor!"

"Do you suppose that's true?" Alphonse inquired, turning to Alain.

"Sans doute, monsieur," Alain replied, adding as they fluttered off, "Typical French humor! Sometimes I think the Germans are better off not having any at all."

The Rue de la Grande Armee

Half-encircling the Arc de Triomphe, the Rue de la Grande Armee was the route of choice for Alphonse and Alain on a particularly lovely early May morning.

"Did you know, monsieur," said Alain, "three-fourths of France's electricity is generated by nuclear power plants?"

"So why aren't the French concerned about reactor meltdowns like other countries—America, for instance?"

"Because the prevailing winds blow across the Channel, toward England."

The Restaurant des Mille Colonnes

Three blocks from the Cimitiere du Montparnasse, Alphonse and Alain spotted two lovers billing and cooing as they strolled past the excellent and economical working-class Restaurant des Mille Colonnes.

"Is there a difference, monsieur," Alphonse inquired, "between the ways in which American and French girls rebuff suitors?"

"By 'rebuff,' I presume you mean what American males charmingly call 'the sloppy-lipped kiss-off'?" Alain laughed. "There is indeed a difference! The American girl pats the suitor on the shoulder and gently says, 'I don't like you *that* way.' The French girl simply says, 'I don't like you,' and walks away."

"Which would you prefer?"

"*Anything* but the American girl's obligatory follow-up, 'we can always be friends.' No, monsieur! A clean break is better in the long run! Let her put the suitor out of his misery by uttering another charming Americanism, 'Time to back up the garbage truck, Baby; we're talking dump city!'"

The Rue du Faubourg St. Honore

Skimming the tops of parked cars and autobuses, the companions drew near to the Palais de l'Elysee on the Rue du Faubourg St. Honore, a traffic nightmare loud with horns and the occasional screeching of brakes. Alphonse was obliged to raise his voice as he asked,

"Is it really true, monsieur, that—as the American poet Whittier wrote—'For all sad words of tongue or pen, the saddest are these: "It might have been"'?"

"Hardly, monsieur; the saddest words of all are, 'This isn't real; it's a dream.' Or is it the reverse? I forget, not being a real butterfly."

"Now you're being clever."

"No; just sad."

St. Sulpice

Leading to St. Sulpice—one of the lesser-known and -visited architectural glories of Paris—is the Rue de Severes. It was up this broad and busy avenue that the butterflies made their way one crisp Friday April afternoon.

Alphonse said,

"Are you aware, monsieur, that tens of thousands of our cousins in North America migrate from Mexico to Canada, resting on the trunks and branches of eucalyptus trees in a coastal California town of trailer parks and junkyards called Pismo Beach?"

"I've heard of it," nodded Alain. He thought a moment, then exclaimed, "Amazing!"

"Amazing that our cousins migrate all that distance?"

"Amazing that they would've chosen a dump like Pismo."

Near the Place Vauban

At twilight of the last day in March, hovering outside a window of a six-story apartment house near the Place Vauban, the butterflies spotted a little boy in green-and black-striped pajamas kneeling in prayer by his bedside.

"It's a little early for bedtime, isn't it?" suggested Alphonse. "Maybe he was naughty and sent to bed without his supper." He turned to Alain. "Do you ever pray, monsieur?"

"No. It isn't that I don't want to; I don't know how."

"Forgive me, but prayer might help you with your depressions."

"I'm not one to disparage prayer," Alain went on as though Alphonse hadn't spoken. "I don't believe that the desire to pray is sheer wishful thinking, or a knee-jerk reflex, or a bubble of gas in the stomach. Prayer is a very mysterious thing."

"And look, monsieur, at the sun setting like a benediction over the city!"

". . . Let's not get drippy about it," Alain advised. "And keep in mind, monsieur, we pray, not because the sunsets of this world are beautiful, but because their beauty isn't enough."

"Let us sleep now. . . ."

The Rue de Vaugirard

The gorgeous Palais du Luxembourg is best approached by taking the Rue de Vaugirard, which is exactly what Alphonse and Alain did at high noon on a cloudy Thursday. Adjoining streets and outdoor cafés were packed at lunch hour, and the butterflies took their time making their way toward the Palais. They dipped and turned and swooped and, after executing a barrel roll, Alphonse gushed,

"Isn't it a wonderful thing to be free, monsieur?"

"Yes," Alain agreed, "as long as you keep in mind that 'freedom's just another word for nothing left to lose.'"

"Must you burst all my balloons?"

"We're French," Alain reminded his companion. "We can't afford to be sloppy thinkers."

"So what about contemporary philosophers like Jacques Derrida, Helene Cixous, Luce Irigaray, and the tag team of Gilles Deleuze and Felix Guattari?" Alphonse asked as the Palais came into view.

"Excellent point, monsieur; not only did they feel that they could easily afford sloppy thinking in their works; they shelled out vast sums of intellectual capital for the privilege!"

The grounds of the Palais du Luxembourg

As he and Alain fluttered lazily about the spacious, beautifully-kept grounds of the Palais du Luxembourg, Alphonse returned to the subject of contemporary French philosophy.

"Jacques Derrida, Helene Cixous, Luce Irigaray, Gilles Deleuze and Felix Guattari—weren't their, ah, esoteric prose styles highly admired in the eighties and nineties?"

"That was then, this is now," Alain huffed. "Then *and* now, monsieur, my blanket criticism of that too dead crew would be, 'Go ahead and keep your secrets!'"

Off the Pont du Carrousel

Settling on the back of a chair at an outdoor café just off the Pont du Carrousel, Alain and Alphonse eavesdropped as a man leaned close to the beautiful girl sitting next to him.

Gently cupping her chin in his hand, pinning her with his brown-eyed gaze like a butterfly in an album, he murmured,

"Do you remember that line from Shakespeare, Cherie? 'My love is infinite; the more I give, the more I have to give.' Today, this minute, this hour, always—those words are my gift to you!"

The girl smiled shyly and moved her chair closer to him.

"Isn't that beautiful?" Alphonse enthused, dancing directly above the couple.

Alain said nothing.

"What's the matter now?"

"He wrote her a blank check," Alain muttered, rising and banking sharply toward the sun. "In matters of the heart, monsieur, all blank checks are made of rubber."

The Intercontinental Paris le Grand Hotel

Located at 2, Rue Scribe, the four-and-a-half star Intercontinental Paris le Grand Hotel looked splendid in the late morning sun as Alphonse and Alain rested on the white flowers of a horse-chestnut tree. They'd spent the day so far talking about European history, or what Alain called "a shameful farrago of disasters ever since the Hundred Years' War." Wearying of the subject, Alphonse said,

"Monsieur, certainly you're aware of the famous saying, "'Those who forget the past are condemned to repeat it.'"

"Yes, of course; those are the words of the Spanish philosopher Santayana."

"But what of those who *remember* the past?"

"They're condemned to invent it."

Near the Victoria Palace Hotel

On a bright Sunday afternoon, cruising up the Rue Blaise Desgoffe toward the Victoria Palace Hotel, Alphonse and Alain banked westward and entered a small park, where en plein air painters wearing the obligatory floppy hats and white baggy pants were busy at work.

"If it weren't for the Impressionists," Alain smiled, "not one of these would've thought to come here today."

"They seem to be enjoying themselves."

"Of course; and why not? French art is dead, but this is better than nothing. What is it Oscar Wilde said? 'Bad art is better than no art at all.'"

"What were the great moderns like?"

"Renoir was kindly and reclusive; Toulouse-Lautrec, half-demented. . . .When I think of Van Gogh, I recall an anecdote told by the world's oldest woman, who died right here in Paris not too long ago. When she was twelve years old, living down south in Arles, she worked for her father who ran a paint store. Every now and then Vincent Van Gogh would come in and buy paints; she remembered him vividly as foul-smelling and quite disagreeable. Poor dear man."

"What about Matisse?"

"Matisse was gentle, playful, tough-minded and serious all at once; a man's man!"

"And Picasso?"

"Picasso was a beast."

"I can't help but wonder, monsieur," Alphonse went on as they settled in a beech tree, "what sort of person would it take to capture *today's* Paris on canvas—man or beast?"

"Both."

The Pont d'Lena

In mid-April, wisteria and lilacs explode in white and purple blossoms in gardens, parks, and window-boxes across Paris. Enjoying the views and scents of the flowers that passed fifty feet below them, Alphonse and Alain approached the muddy Seine, electing to settle on a park bench near the Pont d'Lena, built by Napoleon in 1806-1814 to commemorate a victory over the Prussians.

On the other end of the bench an elderly man, oblivious to the butterflies' presence, quietly perused a worn green leather-covered book.

"He's wearing a bowler!" Alain whispered. "What is this, the mauve decade?"

Then the man began reading out loud softly to himself in a voice that trembled a bit at the vowels. He'd chosen a poem, "Mr. Flood's Party," by the American Edwin Arlington Robinson, featuring a tipsy elderly New Englander, Eben Flood, returning home in the moonlight from Tilbury Town to his lonely farmhouse:

. . . As a mother lays her sleeping child
Down tenderly, fearing it may awake,
He set the jug down slowly at his feet
With trembling care, knowing that most things break;
And only when assured that on firm earth
It stood, as the uncertain lives of men
Assuredly did not, he paced away,
And with his hand extended paused again:

'Well, Mr. Flood, we have not met like this
In a long time; and many a change has come
To both of us, I fear, since last it was
We had a drop together. Welcome home!'
Convivially returning with himself,
Again he raised the jug up to the light;
And with an acquiescent quaver said:
'Well, Mr. Flood, if you insist, I might.'

"Well, monsieur," Alphonse interrupted, waggling his antennae impatiently, "shall we be off?"

"Let him finish!" Alain hissed.

The elderly man wet his forefinger, slowly turned a page, and continued:

'Only a very little, Mr. Flood—
For auld lang syne. No more, sir; that will do.'
So, for the time, apparently it did,
And Eben evidently thought so too;
For soon amid the silver loneliness
Of night he lifted up his voice and sang,
Secure, with only two moons listening,
Until the whole harmonious landscape rang—

'For auld lang syne.' The weary throat gave out,
The last word wavered, and the song was done.
He raised again the jug regretfully
And shook his head, and was again alone.
There was not much that was ahead of him,
And there was nothing in the town below—
Where strangers would have shut the many doors
That many friends had opened long ago.

Even as the man ended and closed his book, a pretty brown-haired girl in a purple low-cut sundress and open-toed high heels walked past and blew a kiss to him, whereupon, oddly expressionless, he bowed slightly, touching the brim of his hat. It seemed a ritual.

"How sad," Alphonse murmured. "She's patronizing him."

"I don't think so!" Alain replied. "French girls think nothing of cultivating relationships with older men—sometimes much older men. American girls, of course, usually won't give them the time of day."

At that moment the elderly man stood up, tottered, and tilted his head sideways toward the girl as she disappeared, enveloped in the shadow of a plane tree.

"What's he doing?" Alphonse asked.

"Checking out her ass, you imbecile; what do you think?"

They heard a faint "Bonjour!" and soon another elderly man appeared, walked stiffly up to the bench with the aid of a silver-topped cane, and sat down.

"Ca va bien?" The man on the bench crossed his legs, laying his book between them.

"Pardon?" The newcomer was hard of hearing; the other repeated the greeting.

"Ca va, merci."

The newcomer looked in the direction the girl had gone.

"She was very cheerful today, was she not?" he observed, putting his cane aside and coughing.

The man in the bowler nodded. He kept silent for a long moment as a young mother pushing a baby carriage strolled past.

Then: ". . . She always reminds me of Claudette, a girl I knew when I lived on the buckwheat farm near Vezelay, right on a bend of the Loire. Once, this girl went away down south with her grandmother—on vacation, I suppose. When she returned, she wore a new hat with blue polka dots; she'd also bought ribbons of different colors to decorate the hat, one for every day of the week. Her grandmother bought them for her at a millinery shop in Arles. . . ."

He paused, staring straight ahead at nothing. The story seemed to be over. Then both men craned their necks, their gaze followed by Alphonse and Alain; high above, a silvery A380 Airbus from Charles de Gaulle airport climbed almost imperceptibly, finally banking west, toward the Atlantic. Then the newcomer took out a red handkerchief and blew his nose loudly. The butterflies weren't certain that he'd heard anything but the gist of what his companion told him.

". . . When did you know this Claudette?" he inquired, blowing his nose twice more.

"When I was definitely alive."

The newcomer said nothing. The man in the bowler carefully placed the green leather book in an over-sized pocket of his ancient coat; then he commenced to study the backs of his hands, sprinkled with liver spots. His nails were immaculate.

Then he said,

"I killed her."

"She must have been a very pretty girl."

"Monsieur!" croaked Alphonse; but Alain had heard. He caught a passing breeze that swept him off toward the Seine: a bright yellow leaf, floating down a stream of air.

The Best Western Aida Opera Hotel

The butterflies came to rest on a cornice of the Best Western Aida Opera Hotel, on the corner of Rue Richer and Rue du Conservatoire.

"Shall we have a literary conversation, monsieur?" Alphonse suggested.

". . . Did you know that James Joyce and Marcel Proust once met each other at a dinner in—when was it?—1923?"

"What did they have to say?"

"Nothing."

"Nothing?"

"Nothing."

"That seems strange."

"Not really, monsieur. What would Proust's Marcel—or Baron de Charlus—have to say to Joyce's Leopold Bloom? What would Joyce's Gabriel Conroy have to say to Proust's Albertine?"

"I take your point."

The same

Still perched on a cornice of the Aida Opera Hotel, the butterflies returned to the subject of Jean-Paul Sartre.

"Did you know that Sartre turned down the Nobel Prize in 1964?" Alphonse inquired, folding his wings as an airport shuttle pulled up to the hotel entrance.

"Shortly after the Nobels were awarded that year," Alain replied, "Sartre attended a dinner for literary luminaries. Seated to his right was Patrick Kavanagh, the greatest Irish poet since the death of William Butler Yeats. Seated to Kavanagh's right was an acolyte of Sartre's.

"'You do know, Monsieur Kavanagh,' the acolyte sniffed, accidentally wiping his mouth with Kavanagh's napkin, 'M. Sartre refused the Prize.'"

Kavanagh thought a moment, finally turning to Sartre on his left.

"'Didn't need the money, eh, M. Sartre?' he said."

The Albert Premier Hotel

Within walking distance of both the Gare du Nord and the Gare de l'est, Paris' two busiest train stations, is the Albert Premier Hotel. Alphonse and Alain began making lazy pirouettes over its tennis courts one breezy May afternoon.

Returning to the street, they followed a young husband and wife pushing a baby carriage; Alphonse in particular was attracted to babies.

"In your view, monsieur," Alain inquired, "what's the skeleton key to a happy and successful marriage?"

Alphonse thought a moment.

"Why, honesty and openness, I suppose."

"Why did I know you were going to say that? So let me ask you this: What's the most common question that husbands and wives—and lovers for that matter—ask each other?"

Alphonse thought some more.

"'What are you thinking?'" he ventured.

"*Exactly*; now, do you *still* think that honesty and openness is the key?"

". . ."

The Ecole Normale de Superieure

Hovering one unseasonably warm afternoon over the grounds of the Ecole Normale de Superieure, Alphonse and Alain eavesdropped on two students chatting under a white-blossoming horse-chestnut tree. Both wore the obligatory black berets.

". . . I didn't major in literature," one informed the other, "because I don't like looking for hidden meanings."

Alain laughed and nudged Alphonse with his wing.

"Typical misconception," he scoffed, still looking down at the kids. "Writers don't put 'hidden meanings' into their works; quite the contrary, they—I mean the good ones—want readers to know precisely what they're up to. Simply because you can't find something doesn't mean that it's hidden from you."

"I don't understand."

"You would've made a superb critic, monsieur."

The Avenue Hoche

Crossing over the Avenue Hoche, a street lined with ugly apartment buildings, Alphonse and Alain spotted a grim-faced individual carrying a black briefcase making his way toward a subway stop. Something was clearly bothering him; but just as Alphonse was about to speculate, the man disappeared down the stairs. Alphonse turned to Alain.

"Forgive me, monsieur, but *you* seem less depressed this morning."

"Yes," replied Alain. "I think I've arrived at what Sartre called the far side of despair."

"How did you do that?"

"I stopped reading Sartre."

The Rue de la Paix

On the Rue de la Paix, the butterflies spotted yet another couple pushing a baby carriage. This time Alphonse and Alain descended, coming so close that the baby, a girl wearing a yellow sun bonnet, reached out for Alphonse, who danced away teasingly. The baby laughed.

"Bless her little heart!" Alphonse exclaimed as the parents paused to cross the street. "Just think; she'll still have her adolescence in front of her when we're long gone!"

"Oh, monsieur, there will be unhappy days when she'll wish for nothing else in the world but the ephemeral existence of a butterfly. *And* there will be days when she'll be very happy *not* to be a butterfly; so it goes. Life's rich pageant, as they say, balances everything out."

". . . Do you really believe that?"

"No."

The Rue de Fleuris

As the butterflies returned to the Left Bank after hitching a brief ride on an empty garbage scow riding high on the Seine, Alain asked,

"Who is your hero, monsieur?"

"Jean Moulin," answered Alphonse promptly, "the French resistance fighter who gave the Germans fits. He was finally captured by the Gestapo and tortured to death, but he never 'talked,' as they say in the cinema. A very brave man! Et tu?"

"I don't know his name," Alain replied. "Henri Charrier writes about him in his book *Papillon*. This man went to court the same time as Charrier, but for the much graver crime of murder. When it came time to be sentenced, the judge informed him that he was prepared to be lenient if he could show some remorse. 'So explain to *me*,' the judge said as the man stood before him, 'why did you kill your wife with an iron?'

"The defendant knew the score, and yet he couldn't suppress a grin. 'Because, your Honor,' he answered, shocking the court by bursting into laughter, 'she needed smoothing out.' The judge, needless to say, was outraged, sentencing him on the spot to Devil's Island. That strikes somehow me as heroic—throwing one's fate to the wind in the service of a single joke! Yes, yes, we're talking about two different sacrifices on two different altars; but, in the end, sacrifice is sacrifice is sacrifice—don't you agree?"

"Funny you should put it that way," Alphonse paused, treading air. "Do you know that we just flew past the old location of 27, Rue de Fleuris, where Gertrude Stein and Alice B. Toklas once lived?"

"Gertrude, too, was a hero of sorts."

"But she was unreadable."

"QED."

The Faubourg St. Germain

On a return trip to the Left Bank, the thirsty butterflies flew over the ritzy Faubourg St. Germain once more, landing on a birdbath in a charming little backyard garden blooming with lilacs. The water, which had been standing since the last rain of two weeks ago, was russet-colored.

"Take a sip," Alain urged mischievously. "You'll never have to prove your courage in any other way."

Alphonse moved to a flower bed and helped himself to a few droplets of dew from the night before.

Then, joining his companion fluttering from flower to flower, Alain began to sing:

"'We are poor little lambs
who have lost our way.
Baa! Baa! Baa!
We are little black sheep
Who have gone astray
Baa! Baa! Baa!

'Gentleman songsters off on a spree
Damned from here to eternity
God have mercy on such as we
Baa! Baa! Baa!'"

"Where did we hear that song?" Alphonse asked.

"Don't you remember? At the Ecole Normale; a group of American exchange students from Yale sang it to a small audience of French girls. Ah, les Americaines! They are superior to the French in every way, except one: They're too kind for their own good."

"The French make up for it."

"Yes!" Alain agreed. "That, and a penchant for getting bogged down in dirty wars like Algeria and Vietnam, is what forges the link between the two countries."

"And yet they don't like each other."

"They see each other in the mirror—keeping in mind that mirrors reverse as well as reflect. . . ."

The Boulevard Periphetique

Boulevard Periphetique meanders about the Left Bank in a vast, lazy circle, encompassing twenty square miles and paralleling Boulevards Lefebvre, Brune, and Jourdan. Alphonse and Alain flew above Periphetique, swooping low over slate roofs featuring innumerable dirty skylights and chimney pots, crossing to Lefebvre and coming to rest, exhausted, on an art nouveau lamppost.

"Tell me the truth, monsieur," Alphonse wheezed, folding his tired wings. "In our travels, do you think that we're fleeing from life?"

"Are you happy?"

"Yes."

"Then keep in mind what Kafka said: 'How is it possible to rejoice in the world except by fleeing to it?'"

Near the Rue de Tolbiac

The Rue d'Alesia bisects Avenue d'Italie, becoming the Rue de Tolbiac. Settling on a bench in a small, companionable park of plane trees and wisteria off Tolbiac, the butterflies caught a man and a woman in the middle of a conversation. After eavesdropping on a few words, Alain whispered excitedly to Alphonse,

"Check it out, monsieur: the anatomy of a seduction!"

The man said,

". . . I like your husband; I really do."

"Why don't you two go hunting for wildebeest in the Bois sometime?"

"Oh, Etienne has his good side," the man pursued the subject diplomatically, crossing his legs.

"That's the ticket," Alain whispered to Alphonse. "Never bad-mouth the husband; that puts the wife on the defensive. And, if you impugn the husband, you impugn her taste in men, which, in the end, reflects poorly on *you*. Praise the husband, on the other hand, and you keep her off balance. Now she's curious."

"Why did you ask to meet me today?" she asked.

"And now it *really* begins," Alain murmured as Alphonse strained to hear. "Pay attention, monsieur, as they ask each other questions, the answers to which they know perfectly well! That's the secret of mutual seduction."

"Why did *you* come?" he countered.

She fell silent; then repeated her question.

"Actually I didn't expect you to come at all," the man dodged the issue a second time.

"The lying bastard!" Alain said. "But he knows what he's doing."

Then, gently rubbing the bridge of her nose between thumb and forefinger, she asked,

"What's that line from *Casablanca*? Someone asks Humphrey Bogart, 'Why did you come to Casablanca?' He says, 'I came for the waters.' 'There are no waters in Casablanca.' And he says, 'I was misinformed.'"

"That's brutal, Margot."

"Match point!" Alain nudged Alphonse.

She looked across the park at a flock of pigeons searching for bread crumbs, gray heads jerking back and forth. A group of little boys in green and yellow soccer uniforms whizzed by, followed by their coaches carrying a netted bag of balls.

". . . Every day of the week," she muttered, "I throw my life away. Then I pick up the pieces the next morning and start all over again."

"Yes, yes, she's giving him an 'in,' Alain hissed as Alphonse began to speak. "But he'd be wise not to take it—yet."

Sure enough, the man said nothing.

Then, suddenly, she brought them out into the open.

". . . If we slept together," she said, looking up, "what would it prove? What would it accomplish?"

"Not a thing," he said, "which is precisely why we ought to do it."

"Good answer!" Alain nodded.

Suddenly angry, she stood up.

"You're too glib," she accused, shaking her finger at him. "And I'm a damned fool!" With that she stalked off, heels and silver and turquoise bracelets clicking. The man remained, staring straight ahead at nothing and smiling.

"What do you think about that?" said Alphonse, fluttering his wings, "He blew it after all!"

"No, no; she showed emotion," Alain shook his antennae as they rose into the air. "In these situations, any emotion is better than none. He has her now."

The Rue Nicolo

Drinking black coffee and eating brioches at a sidewalk café on the Rue Nicolo, two attractive women, one tall, the other quite short, were engaged in a meandering conversation; Alain and Alphonse hovered a few feet away.

". . . For once I used *him*, as a guy would a girl," the tall one was saying. "But of course he was drunk, and in the middle of the night he lost control of his bladder, peeing all over me. Then he had the gall to say it was my fault!"

"Some wet dream."

Alain laughed; Alphonse looked at him.

After a long silence, the tall woman said,

"But why don't I leave him? Why don't I just walk away? I really don't feel that I need him, you know."

"She sounds like the title of a self-help book," Alphonse grumbled. "*I Hate You, Please Don't Leave Me.*"

"Quiet."

"How is he in bed?" the short one asked. "When he's not plastered, that is."

"Fair to middling; I had to teach him, of course, so I suppose that reflects discredit on me. . . ."

They didn't say anything. The butterflies settled on the back of a chair a few feet away.

The short woman nibbled her brioche. "Do you know what Dr. Chamfort said to me the other day? 'Have you ever faked an orgasm?' Can you believe he asked me that?"

When her friend didn't reply, she twirled a bracelet around and around her wrist; then she held up two fingers on each hand to signify quotation marks.

"'My life is an empty place.'"

"Who said that?"

"*You* did—before you met Antoine!"

The other took a sip of coffee, watching Alphonse and Alain watch her.

"As if my life weren't complicated enough, I think I have a crush on *my* psychiatrist," she offered. "I told him what he already knows, that you could put my sense of self-worth in a thimble. Then he paraphrased Nietzsche: 'The woman who despises herself nevertheless esteems herself as a self-despiser.'"

"Whoa!" Alain whispered. "When shrinks start quoting Nietzsche to troubled women, it's time to make like a baby and head out."

But Alphonse was already hovering twenty feet above the café, frowning and waiting for his friend.

La passerelle Debilly

Crossing over the historic La passerelle Debilly footbridge, built for the Universal Exposition of 1900, the butterflies watched as a glass-covered tour boat passed under them, the guide speaking into a cordless microphone.

". . . Kafka was in Paris in 1911," Alain observed when the boat had gone. "If he'd stayed, you know, he might not have starved to death in Vienna. No," he corrected himself. "I'm wrong about that. What Kafka *really* needed was to heed his own advice: 'Whatever is to be entirely destroyed must first be held very firmly; if something crumbles, it crumbles, but resists destruction.'"

"He might've been referring to *us*," Alphonse remarked gloomily, watching the tour boat disappear around a bend of the Seine.

Alain waggled his antennae.

"Every now and then—more then than now, mind you—you *do* impress me, monsieur! Your turn to lead the way."

The Rue Tronchet

Flying at noontime 200 feet over honks and occasional backfires emanating from the busy Rue Tronchet, Alphonse and Alain returned to the subject of Kafka. Alain quoted,

"'Two tasks at the beginning of life: to keep reducing your circle, and to keep making sure you're not hiding somewhere outside it.'"

"Monsieur, which of those protocols do you think we follow—if any?"

"Both."

The Jardin du Forum des Halles

On a partly cloudy day, in the fountain-rich Jardin du Forum des Halles, the butter-flies hovered above a young couple engaged in solemn conversation.

The man said,

"So men have no rights these days."

"You had rights forever and a day," she said. "No, that's not true. You had your *way* forever and a day."

"What are you going to do?"

"What do you think I'm going to do? I've made an appointment with Dr. Lascaux."

"Marry me."

"I'm not in love with you."

"You're Catholic," he offered. "Doesn't that make a difference?"

"Apparently not. . . ."

They didn't say anything. Then, abruptly, she stood up and walked off. The man put his face in his hands.

"Poor guy," Alphonse murmured.

"I doubt it."

The man sat that way for ten minutes, slowly shaking his head back and forth. He sighed, stood up, blew his nose, put on his brown beret, and began walking in the direction of the Seine. Alain and Alphonse followed at a discreet distance. The sun came from behind a cloud, bathing the park in pale yellow light. Flying red and green kites, a group of children ran across the field, dodging a fountain.

The man approached another bench, where a pretty girl sat, thumbing through the March issue of *Cahiers du Cinema*. She looked up, shading her eyes from the sun.

"Do you mind if I sit down?" he asked.

The Paris Dauphine University

Tucked between the vast ring of Boulevard Peripherique, and Boulevard Flandrin, are the grounds of the Paris Dauphine University, one of thirteen descendants of the University of Paris, founded ca. 1160. Cruising over the attractive grounds of Dauphine, the butterflies spotted a class of fourteen or fifteen students sitting in a circle on the slope of a wisteria-rich glade. A professor walked back and forth, reading out loud from a floppy blue paperback. It was a creative writing class in poetry.

"What kind of verse do they produce these days, monsieur?" Alphonse wanted to know. "Is it on a par with Verlaine or Mallarme, or even Rene Char?"

"God, no!" Alain shook his antennae vigorously. "But it hardly matters. The young writers of today are taught badly by bad teachers. You can't blame them for—shall we say—shoring the fragments of their bad poetry against the runes of the past."

"Don't you mean, 'ruins'?"

"No."

The Place du Marechal de Lattre de Tassigne

On their way to the Place du Marechal de Lattre de Tassigne, the butterflies swooped low over a complex of soccer fields, where very young players were engaged in one-on-one drills, practicing feints, jinks, and head fakes.

"Look at that!" Alain exclaimed, landing on a goal post. "I never realized till just now how much soccer—how much all sport—relies on deception. Think of American baseball. The pitcher hides the ball in his glove so the batter won't see where he's gripping it; then he throws a change-up, hoping to fool the batter into thinking it's a fastball. Meanwhile, the second baseman sneaks behind the base runner, hoping that the pitcher will fool the runner into thinking that he, the pitcher, isn't paying attention. Then the pitcher spins around and voilá! The runner is tagged out!"

"What about basketball?"

"The very essence of basketball is deception! The guard brings the ball down court, stopping and taking a step or two backward at the top of the key, still dribbling and lulling the defender into thinking that he's going to set up a play. Once again, voilá! He speeds up, leaving the defender's lingerie on the court, as sportscasters like to say. It's called a rocker-fake; you rock your defender to sleep. . . ."

"Everywhere you look—" Alain interrupted himself, leaping into the air as a soccer ball whizzed past, missing the goal.

". . . Everywhere you look," he went on, "deception, deception, deception! You know, monsieur, there's something to that wearisome cliché, 'the game of life,' after all."

"Deception is everything?" Alphonse said; it was less a question than a conclusion. Then he invoked Kafka: 'Can you know anything that is not deception? Once deception was destroyed, you wouldn't be able to look, at the risk of being turned into a pillar of salt. . . .'"

"Look at *us*," Alain nodded, letting Alphonse's remark hang fire for a moment. "When we sip dew from yellow flowers, we're invisible to predators. And there are butterflies in the South American rain forests whose camouflage is beyond remarkable. Eye spots on the wings have evolved to 'imitate' drops of rain water on leaves. And when a vein appears to run 'under' the 'rain-drop,' it actually bends, like a capillary on a leaf in sunlight! No lizard is smart enough to figure out deception *that* subtle—or suave. . . ."

Alphonse thought for a few seconds.

"So deception is reality and reality is deception. Is that a good thing or a bad thing?"

"We'd damn well better hope it's a good thing," Alain said as a nine- or ten-year old player faked an opponent off his feet, kicking the soccer ball neatly into the goal.

On the Rue Duperre, Alain delivers a lecture on fashion

Hovering thirty feet over the Rue Deperre, the butterflies noticed how sloppily-dressed most of the young people passing below them were. Then they remembered their last visit to the Sorbonne, where some of the professors wore blue jeans and t-shirts. Even in Paris, it seemed, one had to look long and hard for a woman dressed to the nines, wearing dresses and high heels, and—except in the Bourse district—for a man wearing a suit and tie.

"This is nothing," Alain remarked as they came to rest on a magazine and tobacco kiosk. "In America recently, two national champion sports teams, one male, the other female, were invited by the president to a ceremony at the White House. Half the girls wore flip-flops, all the boys wore running shoes; the boys didn't even go to the trouble of tucking in their shirts!"

"So people these days wish to dress casually—what of it?"

"'Casually' is putting it charitably, but never mind," Alphonse gestured with his antennae. "What needs to be seen, monsieur, is that bad taste isn't the real issue, neither in America, nor in France, nor in other countries of the West. There's a *psychology* of fashion that was understood—more, appreciated, even embraced—as recently as the twenty years entre deux guerres. Think about women; they used to dress, as the cliché has it, not to please men but to please other women. But I'd go further—they used to dress to please *themselves*. The same is—excuse me, was—true of men. Put another way, the psychology I refer to is one of self-respect—which is, one might say, to self-esteem what love is to affection. Not taking the trouble to dress up transcends laziness; it reflects, or so I believe, a lack of respect for oneself, and therefore lack of respect for others.

". . . I guess what I'm suggesting," Alain concluded as they fluttered into the air once again, "is that people almost everywhere seem to have forgotten, not to think, but *how* to think about the psychology of fashion. And that tells me that the dumbing-down of culture goes hand-in-glove (as if anyone bothered to wear gloves any more!) with the dressing-down of culture."

The Ecole Normale de Superieure

They returned yet again to the campus of the Ecole Normale de Superieure, a favorite haunt. Hundreds of students streamed out of classrooms, slinging brightly-colored backpacks onto their shoulders, chatting and laughing.

"Monsieur," Alphonse asked, gazing down at the young people, "what, in your estimation, is the essence of this generation, born in the eighties?"

Alain replied,

"They're sweet kids—good kids, afraid of so many things. . . . Still, the answer to your question, I fear, is simple. If you recall Paul Eluard's terrible phrase, *'le dur desir de durer'* ('the difficult desire to endure'), change 'difficult' to 'easy,' and voilá! You have your answer."

The Rue Charles Sud

On the Rue Charles Sud in the heart of Pigalle, Alain and Alphonse came to rest on a green Citroen parked a few doors down from the seedy Cabaret Danse Club. Then, fluttering over to an *International Herald Tribune* newspaper rack, Alain called to Alphonse, who'd folded his wings,

"Look, monsieur, it says here that another renowned public figure in the United States has been caught with his hand in the cookie jar of marital infidelity. His wife hasn't simmered down, so he's arranged for a family vacation to repair his marriage."

"I imagine they'll have a lot to talk about."

"That'll be difficult, since he's not planning to go himself."

The Rue Kleber

As they swooped and twirled, inscribing fleurs-de-lys in a cloudless sky over the Rue Kleber, Alphonse commented,

"Monsieur, as the philosopher Alain, your namesake, said, 'To be totally brave you must lose all hope.' Is that really true?"

"I hope not."

The Cimitiere Pere Lachaise

No tour of Paris is complete without a visit to the Cimitiere Pere Lachaise, named in honor of Louis XIV's confessor; it's located on the exquisitely-named Rue de Repos. Luminaries buried at Lachaise include Chopin, Oscar Wilde, Delacroix, Balzac, Musset, Jim Morrison, and, most famously, Heloise and Abelard.

On a windy May afternoon threatening rain, the butterflies flew over the Gambetta metro stop and entered Pere Lachaise, taking their time as they fluttered from grave to grave.

Some tombstones were hideous, but most were lovely.

Settling on the grave of Jim Morrison, Alain pompously began,

"It's odd, monsieur, that an American should be buried here, because the difference between French and American cemeteries is as striking as it is instructive! American cemeteries are entropic and homogeneous, punched out of cookie-cutter patterns, so to say; graves in French cemeteries—throughout most of Europe, for that matter—are heterogeneous: individual works of art, so many of them. The former inspire horror of life and love of death, the latter horror of death and love of life. . . ."

The same

From Jim Morrison's grave the butterflies joined one of the free cemetery tours, then peeled off and fluttered a few rows over to the grave of Balzac.

Alain ventured,

"It seems that there are as many dead characters here at Pere Lachaise as there are in Balzac's novels!"

"Surely that's an awkward way of putting it, monsieur," Alphonse laughed. "You make it sound like the characters in Balzac's novels are 'dead.'"

"No, no; just most of them."

The same

Alphonse and Alain visited the grave of Oscar Wilde, who died a persecuted yet proud man in Paris in 1900.

Alphonse remarked,

"When Oscar visited New York, he told a customs officer, 'I have nothing to declare but my genius.' *Was* he, in fact, a genius?"

"I'd say so, yes," Alain nodded. "Keep in mind, though, that Oscar *also* said that he put his talent into his work and his genius into his life."

"How does one accomplish that?"

"By becoming a rebel and a martyr, how else? Actually, my very favorite saying of Oscar's is, 'We always kill what we love.'"

"And how do 'we kill what we love'?"

"By passing the buck of martyrdom to friends and lovers who get in the way by *embracing* our rebellion, therefore rendering it impotent."

The Rue Feydeau

The butterflies visited yet another small park, this one just off Rue Feydeau, named after the French master of farce who died in 1921. As they flew above neatly-kept plots of yellow roses, lilies, asters, rosemary, carnations, and irises—the latter known fondly as the "flower emblems of France"—Alphonse spotted a class of pre-schoolers linked in a line with one teacher in front, the other bringing up the rear. When they reached a fountain, the teachers brought out bite-sized pieces of green and white soft candy and began to distribute them; all the children immediately jumped up and down, squealing and holding out wiggling fingers.

After observing this for a few moments, Alphonse recalled,

"An American writer talks of 'the magnetic chain that binds humanity together.' Exactly what *is* that magnetic chain, monsieur?"

"Well, just look at *these* little ones," Alain laughed good-naturedly. "They all want a piece of that candy, not necessarily because it tastes good, but because *someone else* is being given one. God love them, if little Jacques or little Natalie had a running sore, they'd all insist on having a running sore! There's the answer to your question about the magnetic chain."

The Rue des Petites Champs

On the Rue des Petites Champs, the butterflies flew over the grounds of a private lycee, or French high school. Blue-uniformed boys and white-uniformed girls milled about on their way to and from class. After a few moments of cruising back and forth, Alain remarked sadly,

"French education seems to be in decent shape—relatively speaking; elsewhere in the world, however, things aren't so wonderful. There are countries that espouse educational philosophies devoted to homogeneity above all: no individuation, everybody must be the same—turning the same pages of the same textbooks, taking the same tests, ideally achieving the same scores; teachers, administrators, curriculum designers, and school boards—all marching lock-step, in solemn foolery. . . ."

"Yes," Alphonse agreed, still watching the kids below. "The educational policies of communist regimes like China, Cuba, and Venezuela are *most* depressing, are they not?"

"I was thinking principally of l'Amerique."

The Rue Villedo

As they took a break on an art nouveau lamppost on the Rue Villedo, Alphonse inquired,

"Monsieur, someone said, 'Men and women marry each other for what they are not, and leave each other because of what they are.' Isn't the reverse truer?"

"The correct answer—God help both man and wife!—is 'yes and no'," Alain replied. "*That* conundrum of conundrums explains why Nietzsche called marriage 'a long stupidity'!"

The Rue Notre-Dame-des-Champs

Fluttering down the Rue Notre-Dame-des-Champs, Alphonse and Alain came to rest on a fire hydrant a few houses away from the pavilion where Ernest Hemingway and his first wife Hadley lived in 1923.

Alain declared,

"Kafka intimates that every story should begin the same way, with the phrase, 'And then he went back to his job, as though nothing had happened.'"

"What was 'his' job?" Alphonse inquired.

"Waiting for something to happen—naturellement!"

The Rue Therese

The Rue Therese welcomed them with its cheerful green and yellow umbrellas shading outdoor cafés, politely bowing in the stiff afternoon breeze of a late March afternoon. Alphonse asked,

"Monsieur, which would you rather experience—a small passion or a great friendship?"

"But don't you see? You and I enjoy both, monsieur. In the first instance we have Paris. In the second—not to get drippy about it, mind you!—we have each other."

The Rue Cherubini

One cool afternoon, a dozen feet or so over the deliciously-named Rue Cherubini (dozens of schoolchildren were running and skipping on their way home as Alphonse and Alain dipped and twirled above them), Alphonse spotted a young couple walking slowly arm-in-arm, the bubbling stream of kids parting neatly around them.

He said,

"Monsieur, on the subject of fidelity, the brilliant young Sorbonne philosopher Andre Comte-Sponville says, 'Love me as long as you want to, my love, but do not forget *us*.' Strictly speaking," Alphonse went on, "*is* there an 'us' in a marriage? I mean— can there ever truly be an 'us?'"

"The 'us' is an illusion," Alain nodded, "or, more precisely, a *truce*. Infidelity, on the other hand—to turn what von Clauswitz says about diplomacy on its head—is a continuation of war by other means! But that, of course," he added, gazing down at the busy sidewalk, "is the furthest thing from *their* minds."

"Bien sur!" Alphonse agreed. "What need have children of such knowledge?"

"I wasn't thinking of the children."

The Parc de Belleville

Set like a jewel in a sterile urban setting, designed by architect Francois Debulois and "paysagiste" Paul Brichet, the twenty-year-old Parc de Belleville is a marvel of pure beauty. Here, before refreshing themselves at a fountain, Alphonse and Alain hovered for a few moments over a bench, where two elderly men talked and watched as pretty shop-girls glided by in twos and threes.

"May I speak frankly, monsieur?" one began, crossing his legs stiffly. "When I was a young squirrel on the streets of Passy, it seemed as if sex was everywhere—so plentiful that I took it for granted, as we all did, I suppose. I even became indifferent to it, like a gourmand who constantly fills his belly with truffles! These days, naturellement, it's the only thing I think about. . . ."

"I wonder what they see when they glance at us?"

"Nothing."

"Sometimes I hate them," the other grumbled and gestured with a bony hand as more girls passed, chattering and tossing their hair in the pale sunlight. "Then I wish them well—all in the same breath, so to say!"

Alphonse began to speak but Alain hushed him, quoting from Baudelaire,

Angel of beauty, do you wrinkles know?
Know you the fear of age, the torment vile
Of reading secret horror in the smile
Of eyes your eyes have loved since long ago?
Angel of beauty, do you wrinkles know?

Angel of happiness, and joy, and light,
Old David would have asked for youth afresh
From the pure touch of your enchanted flesh;
I but implore your prayers to aid my plight,
Angel of happiness, and joy, and light. . . .

The Place Edgar Quinet

As they fluttered in circles around a newspaper and tobacco kiosk on the Place Edgar Quinet off the Rue Delambre and a block from the Cimitiere du Montparnasse, Alphonse inquired of Alain,

"Monsieur, would you say that 'redemptive suffering' is an oxymoron?"

"For those redeemed by never having to suffer, yes!"

The Rue de la Banque

Looking down at the hordes of employees scurrying like ants up and down the Rue de la Banque—Paris's hub of national and international commerce—Alain remarked,

"You know, monsieur, at the end of the day it's not a bad life being *Lepidoptera*. Think about it: we're neither susceptible to flabby bladders, privy to the heartbreak of psoriasis, the public humiliation of septic system backup, or the embarrassment of male pattern baldness; we don't wait in long lines for flu shots or auto emissions tests; we needn't listen to dental hygienists prattle on about flossing. And we don't fix leaky faucets, sweep out garages, pay outrageous overdraft fees, or get calls from telemarketers at dinnertime. Acne doesn't ravage our schoolboy and schoolgirl complexions—"

"But we *do* die young."

"As I was saying. . . ."

Near the Gare St.-Lazare

With no particular itinerary in mind, the butterflies decided to take a tour of several neighboring subway stops. Beginning with Le Peletier, they continued on to Cadet, Poissoniere, Notre-Dame de Lorette, Grands Boulevards, Quartre Septembre, Bourse, Auber—and Liege, on the Rue d'Amsterdam near the Gare St.-Lazare.

Finally Alphonse landed on top of an ancient red Renault parked in an alley across the street from the Liege stop.

"This is boring me to tears," he said.

"Bored in Paris?" Alain smiled. "Still," he added thoughtfully, "Baudelaire himself called boredom the disease of modern life. . . ."

"It's just that today's travels were so monotonous."

"Ah, monsieur, never bad-mouth monotony out of hand! Remember what my second favorite French genius—no, she wasn't a poet, like Baudelaire—said about monotony."

"You mean Simone Weil."

"She said, 'Monotony is the most beautiful or the most atrocious thing. The most beautiful if it is a reflection of eternity: the most atrocious if it is the sign of an unvarying perpetuity. It is time surpassed or time sterilized. . . .'

"'The circle is the symbol of eternity which is beautiful, the swinging of a pendulum of monotony which is atrocious. . . .'"

The Rue Rivoli

The companions navigated the Rue Rivoli, turning left at the Place de la Concord. Then they flew past the Jeu de Paume and pointed their antennae toward the Orangerie.

Alphonse noticed a side-street cinema featuring a Stephen Spielberg retrospective; the current offering was 'Saving Private Ryan.'

"That film has the reputation for depicting war in the most realistic fashion possible," he observed.

"'Saving Private Ryan' is an overrated Roadrunner Cartoon—nothing more, nothing less," scoffed Alain. "If you want to 'experience' the horrors of war, go back and read *The Iliad.*

"I quote,

'Then his teeth flew out; from two sides,

Blood came to his eyes; the blood that from lips and nostrils

He was spilling, open-mouthed; death enveloped him

In its black cloud. . . .'

". . . And that, monsieur," Alain went on as they entered the grounds of the Orangerie, "is one of the *milder* descriptions of death in battle to be found in the *Iliad.* Why does Homer do it? Not for the sake of—what's the popular phrase these days?—pornographic violence: that's Steven Spielberg's game. No, such horrific depictions in Homer are, as Simone Weil said, a means to the end of dramatizing the eternal truth that war transforms men into *things.* . . ."

The Rue Rameau

The Rue Rameau meanders through the heart of the new "golden triangle" of Paris—minutes by foot from the Louvre, the Opera, the Palais Royal, the Gallerie Vivienne, and the shopping paradise of the Rue Ste Honore.

One sparkling May morning our companions landed on the ledge of an upper-floor apartment at 9, Rue Rameau, located in a renovated pre-Revolution building. On the sidewalk immediately below them, a strange tableau was unfolding: a turbaned, black-robed Iranian, cradling what appeared to be a school textbook in the crook of his arm, ranted and chanted, "DOWN WITH THE GREAT SATAN! DOWN WITH THE GREAT SATAN! DOWN WITH—"

"Goodness!" Alphonse exclaimed. "America just can't catch a break in this town!"

"America? He's talking about Bill Gates."

Alphonse and Alain

The morning air was nippy as Alphonse and Alain opened their yellow wings to the sun for the last time. They were perched on an empty table at an outdoor café two blocks from St. Denis, the splendid cathedral designed in the early twelfth century by Abbot Suger.

"My friend," said Alphonse, "how do you know that you exist?"

"Because I think, as Descartes said."

"And how do you know that you think?"

"Because I exist, as Sartre said."

Poof! Alain and Alphonse both vanished. And a black-caped student nursing his café au lait—witness to what had happened—was left behind to think on these things.

Fin

About the Author

In 2005 Steven Carter retired as Emeritus Professor of English after teaching in the university for thirty-eight years. The author of sixteen books published here and abroad, he served as Senior Fulbright Fellow at two Polish universities in 1991. He is the only two-time winner of Italy's coveted *Nuove Lettere* International Poetry and Literature Prize. In 2010 he won the Eric Hoffer Foundation's Montaigne Medal grand prize for his book of essays, *Devotions to the Text*. Carter and his wife Janice divide the year between Arizona and Montana.

The Complete Secrets Series

A Special Edition

By Ellie Jay

This book is an omnibus or boxset edition of previously published works.

If you have previously bought or read Secrets Of The Volkovs, Family Secrets or Secrets In The Flames, be advised that some of this book may be familiar to you.

However, this edition also contains new versions, updates, edits, and bonus content.

For everyone who supported me, an unknown indie

author, throughout my publishing and writing journey.

Especially those who took a chance on The Secrets Series

and fell in love with these tales of action, humour, and

heartbreak.

Acknowledgements

So much work has gone into this project.

Three novels, five short stories, six illustrations and countless cover designs (and redesigns) later, I feel it's time to thank everyone who made it possible.

The only possible starting point is with my family.

My mother, who is still ridiculously proud of the first scribbled 'book' I wrote in childhood, who finds me story competitions to enter and celebrates every single book I sell.

My father, who stole my author copies, read them all back-to-back and issued me with a list of corrections. And who still talks about them.

Not forgetting a whole host of relatives who have followed me on social media even though that means they have to put up with my bizarre rambling.

My brother, James, his girlfriend, Amy, my cousins, aunts, and uncles who have supported me are all so important in my life. James is responsible for funding a huge percentage of this project, out of the kindness of his heart.

Special thanks to my sister, Rosie, who, thanks to our childhood scribblings, was my first writer friend and critique partner. We were about nine years old, but it totally counts.

And to my cousin, Sarah, who was the first person ever to buy a copy of Family Secrets.

I'm also indebted to my grandmother, who I recently discovered has bought and read every single one of my books.

But you don't need to know my entire family tree. And there are so many other people who I must mention.

The one and only Dr. Mansur Hasib not only helped me create movie-quality audiobooks for Secrets of The Volkovs and Family Secrets, but he also takes the credit (or possibly blame, depending on your point of view) for encouraging me to be more sarcastic, chaotic, and unhinged.

He taught me about marketing, personal branding, and standing out in the overwhelming world of social media.

Patrick Smith is a loyal reader and reviewer of my work.

He has also earned the title 'Official Ellie Jay Fan Club President,' meaning that I do, at least, have one fan.

He deserves a mention for all his hard work in shouting about my books when even I don't feel like doing so.

There are so many other readers and reviewers who I could mention. But among them, E. R Sanchez of Fried Potato Press stands out for his stunning editorial reviews of the entire Series.

I cannot possibly credit *every* writer, reader, and reviewer I've met. But I'm extremely grateful to them all.

I also owe thanks to everyone who helped to inspire me when I was struggling to create bonus content for this edition. Mark Jonathan Runte was responsible for 'the Volkov Project' as he joked with me about the meaning of 'Volkov.' Mark can also take credit for numerous sales and reviews of my work, along with several ideas, snippets and moments of encouragement shared across direct messages on Twitter.

My father's flippant comments about Vladmir Putin take credit for 'Charity Work,' though it was heavily adapted to avoid getting me put on some kind of Russian hit list somewhere. If my own flippant remarks haven't already done that.

Last but not least, I've connected with some truly fabulous people in online communities.

Silvia Hartman, Neil Bush, Justine, and Romulus C. Kulik-Draco all take credit for inspiring, feeding back on and helping to create the cover for this book.

Romulus also deserves a shout-out for buying everything I've ever written, backing the crowdfunding campaign for this book, and texting me at all hours with his thoughts, reviews, and ideas.

My friends from the #LincsConnect networking tag and the resulting writing group deserve so much credit.

Particularly Rosanna McGlone, who prompted me attending my first ever writing group and connected me with these amazing people; Marie Sinadjan, for helping me branch out and sell books in-person as well as online; Philippa East and Sarah Ridding, for their amazing writing retreat (in collaboration with Flourish Wellbeing).

Thank you all for your continued love and support.

Foreword

I promise I'm nearly done talking at you. Soon, you can dive into the story and forget all about me.

But first, let me explain how The Secrets Series came to. Because it was never planned. It was entirely accidental.

I've been a writer in some sense all my life – scribbling stories on stapled together scraps of paper at five, writing (really bad) Star Wars Fanfiction at 12, getting semi-decent at Fanfiction writing later in my teens...

That's where it began. As my 'chapters' moved away from terribly spelt 200-word monstrosities, I picked up a few loyal readers.

By the time I was 18, I was drafting 40,000-word stories and fully proof-reading them first.

I know. Shocking.

With reviews on some of my work numbering thirty, I decided to have a go at writing something new. Original. And completely my own.

My attempts at this floundered at first. I had no plot in my mind, no characters ready to go and no clue where to begin.

So, I cheated.

I went back to an old story of mine, copy-pasted the first 500 words, and replaced everyone's name with 'placeholder'.

All of a sudden, with a ready-made page in front of me, I found I was able to write.

As I wrote, characters grew, gained their own names, and took shape. Places were borrowed from real life, on the basis that I'd worked on another project set in Russia recently.

And the story became unrecognisable, so far from that old fanfiction that it would be impossible to trace.

At least I hope so because that story was awful.

I finished the first draft of Family Secrets in October 2019. By this point, I was a student, taking a Creative Writing degree.

I was close enough to the world of writing to hear about sending your work off to publishers and literary agents.

Unfortunately, I wasn't close enough to realise that your first draft is always rubbish and you shouldn't send it to anyone.

So, I charged madly at every publisher or agent I could find.

I got a few surprising replies. A couple of offers.

My joy soon fell apart when these 'publishers' asked me for £2000… just to publish my book on Amazon.

I contacted my university tutors and asked if this was normal. Then I learnt what I know now. Aspiring writers – run if someone asks for money.

They're a vanity publisher and will rip you off.

Disheartened by these offers and the secret sting in their tails, I wasn't sure what to do next.

Fortunately, my family are weird, and we actually talk to one another.

So, a conversation between my grandfather and my father threw up the suggestion that I put my own work on Amazon, cutting out the middleman.

And, of course, clueless little me decided to sign up for Amazon's Kindle Direct Publishing service and hit 'publish' on the same day.

That's right, my first ever novel went out into the world without a single edit and under a cover I created using Amazon's own, limited, free assets.

Then I sat back and was surprised by the lack of sales for a few days before someone, I forget who, put the idea into my head that, if I just went on social media, I could sell copies.

At this point, I was days away from my 20h birthday and had never set foot on social media of any kind.

But I somehow found my way onto the platform formerly known as Twitter. There, I met the amazing people of the #WritingCommunity.

They gently guided me through editing, re-formatting and creating (several renditions of) covers. All while lifting me up and encouraging people to support me.

The new, improved Family Secrets did begin to sell. Not only that, but it garnered some lovely reviews.

Those fools only encouraged me.

I decided to expand on the story, writing both a sequel and a prequel. Because obviously, you start a series on Book 2.

And this decision came at the height of lockdown. Meaning I could draft these two novels in just three months.

The rest of the story isn't that interesting. A lot of editing, re-writing, publishing… And then, The Secrets Series was officially born.

Once I began marketing it as a whole series, I was blown away by the reaction.

And I knew I had to do more – for the characters, for myself, but most importantly, for all those people who took a chance on my pathetic first attempt to publish and fell in love with this series.

Welcome to the special edition.

Secrets of the Volkovs

By

Ellie Jay

Antonin
Ilya
Sasha
Vladimir
Katya
Nikolina
Dariya

Family

Nikolina Moroz shuffled her notes in one hand and the frying pan in the other. She was trying to cook up a hearty breakfast for her family, but her eyes were fixed rigidly on the paperwork in front of her.

Shaking his head despairingly from his seat at the nearby dining table was Alexander, her little brother.

"Sis, chill! I'm sure this case of yours will be fine, even if you tear your eyes away from your notes for a second!" He tried to reassure her, seeing that his older sister was incredibly stressed.

"I wish I had your confidence." Nikolina groaned in reply, still not looking up from her work.

"Well, you better lend her some fast, Sasha, or our breakfast's gonna set the house on fire!"

Another flippant voice chipped in as Ekaterina, the duo's younger sister ran into the room with a bag slung casually over her shoulder and plonked herself down on a chair beside her brother.

"Katya, enough! Now is no time to tease your sister!"

The scolding, fatherly tones of Mr. Ilya Moroz, their single father and a fearsome parent who often forgot to reserve his sharpest tones for the criminals he dealt with as the local chief of police, thundered out across the room.

He saw Katya's frozen expression and softened a bit. "I know, I know, you were only joking. But Lina's a little busy right now..." he pointed out.

Nikolina was still intently focused on her work.

"Lina, your work ethic has been wonderful since you started on this case, but you always do so well at work. I'm sure you know what you're doing without all this," he gestured at her paperwork, "and if you can at least put it down and put breakfast on the table, then we can get these two sorted out," he pointed at his other two children, "You know Katya can't afford to be late to college again."

He turned a sharp, emerald-eyed glare on his youngest and most troublesome child, before glancing over at his son.

"And Sasha... Well, what are you planning to get up to today, Sasha?" he paused, questioning the young man.

The response was an absent-minded shrug, followed by Sasha beginning to explain to his father, "no idea. Detective Honesko said he wouldn't need me this week..." he trailed off at this point, giving a little sigh.

This made Ilya sigh too and survey his children thoughtfully.

Nikolina, or Lina as she was affectionately known, was the eldest at twenty-eight. She was a pretty young woman, favouring her late mother in looks, as she bore Elena's long, blonde hair.

It was straight and fell down over her shoulders, though this morning it was wound up on her head in a tight bun.

She was also tall and slender, with a thin face and pointed features. Again, she took after her mother here.

Elena had always reminded him of an elf or pixie from a fairy story. He smiled fondly. Nikolina's resemblance to her mother always took him back to a happier time.

But she was not unlike him, either. She had deep-set emerald-green eyes as well, and she had definitely inherited certain important values of his.

Her strong, almost devoted work ethic put him very much in mind of himself, as did her sense of justice.

That, along with her three years of hard work at a local legal firm, told him that, despite her obvious stress, her first solo case as a lawyer would turn out just fine.

But right now, she seemed a little distracted by her family. Of course. In the nine years since her mother died, she had taken on the duty of looking after her younger siblings, to the point where it was a habit for her to make the family meals and take care of their home.

He was deeply grateful for that. It allowed him to keep working as hard as his job required and still know that everything was taken care of.

Still, now of all times, it wasn't right. He turned back to Sasha. "If you're not doing anything, then help Lina out!" he told him.

The younger man got up and took the frying pan from his sister, who immediately wandered away dreamily, still clutching her papers.

Sasha soon finished making breakfast and started dishing it up for everyone. As he did so, his father's thoughts turned to the middle child.

Alexander, better known to the family as Sasha, also favoured his mother. He had short, wavy blond hair and her wide, baby blue eyes. Though he had inherited his father's strong build.

The twenty-four-year-old was at a bit of a loose end at the moment. He was a recent criminology graduate but had quit the first job his father had lined up for him - In the police force, of course - because he had a unique way of doing things, by following his instincts, not necessarily the rulebook.

Often, Sasha was right in these cases. He had a great arrest rate in his time as a cop, and he was compassionate in his way of administering justice.

But he had felt he was putting his father in an awkward position. It looked bad if the chief's son could break the rules and still have a great record.

Ilya hadn't thought of it that way, but Sasha had made up his mind, so he had moved on. Out of a sense of duty to help his considerate son out, Ilya had found him a second job, helping out an old friend who ran a private detective's firm.

But apparently business was slack right now, and it was getting the young man down. Yet, Ilya felt sure that would be short-lived.

Sasha had his whole life ahead of him. He was well-qualified, with his father's sense of justice, his mother's compassion, and his own sharp instincts. Things could only get better.

Right now, the man in question was busy with breakfast. He placed a plate down in front of his father then handed one to his younger sister.

As Ekaterina took it, Sasha turned to watch Nikolina wander towards the stairs with her gaze still on the papers she was carrying.

"Sis? Aren't you going to eat?" He called after her in evident concern.

Ekaterina shook her head.

"She's not paying any attention, bro. Before long she's gonna walk into something…. It'll be the only way she'll look up." She thoughtfully commented on her older sister's activities before diving into her breakfast.

Ilya sighed again. Then, of course, there was Ekaterina. Katya was sixteen, the baby of the family.

She stood shorter than her siblings' by at least half a foot and had slightly darker blonde hair than the others' platinum tones, closer to her father's own locks. It bounced down her back in wild waves.

The wild hair and her sparkling green eyes reflected much of her nature. She was loud, flippant, and full of mischievous cheer.

He wasn't sure where she got that attitude from. His wife had been a bright soul, certainly. He often struggled to begrudge Katya the trouble she caused him because her smile put him in mind of Elena.

But Elena had never been so... over the top.

He despaired of Katya's endless energy, wondering how she would ever be persuaded to settle down and find herself a steady job.

Not that that seemed truly relevant right now, seeing as she had no idea what she wanted to do with her life.

She was currently enrolled on a writing course at a local community college, but her plans after that were vague, and she was more focused on having a good time with her friends than actually attending and passing the course.

Still, she was certainly a unique soul. He could only hope she would settle down a little.

It was here that Ilya's thoughts came to an abrupt end. Sasha was beginning to panic, chasing after his sister worriedly.

Ilya stood up and strode over, stopping him with a simple hand on the shoulder.

"You sit down and eat your breakfast. I'll go and talk to her. See if I can get her to re-join us... and I'll fetch Antonin down as well." He assured Sasha, who began to head back to his seat.

Antonin. He brought Ilya back to his family as he set off up the stairs, musing on the fifth, final and unofficial family member.

The young man had first entered his life as a colleague, eight years earlier. A trainee police officer with a fiery temper and stubborn attitude, who he suspected had just joined the force in search of an adventure.

Antonin had been a huge red flag to the serious, dedicated police chief.

So, he had appointed himself the man's mentor. That was seven years ago, and now, well, Antonin was still Antonin, of course.

But he had calmed down somewhat and gained a new respect for his job. Even if Ilya suspected that he still craved adventure more than anything else.

What was more important, though, was the fact that the two men had somehow become good friends, despite their differences.

They had begun to visit each other informally, away from the office. That was something Ilya rarely did, and it was also how Antonin met Nikolina.

Ilya wasn't sure he believed in love at first sight, but his student and his daughter clearly did.

They had met a few years ago and now Antonin had enough of his things in Nikolina's room that he might as well live there. He certainly slept over often enough.

With that in mind, he headed there in search of the young couple.

Meanwhile, Antonin was resting on his girlfriend's bed looking out of the window as the traffic crawled past.

Even this early on a late spring morning, the Moscow suburb was busy.

Watching the cars helped him think. He needed to think right now, as he was carefully considering his future.

He was unaware of Ilya's thoughts about him being an unofficial member of the family, but he certainly wanted to be a part of the Moroz family.

He loved their house, which had soon become his second home.

Estranged from his own family, his living options consisted of his own tiny apartment several miles away, which was an inconvenient, cramped place with no entertainment, or the Moroz house. The latter was much more appealing.

There was plenty of space and something was always happening. It was an easy trip into work every morning via Ilya's car, and most importantly, there were other people.

Nikolina was his favourite companion there, of course. He loved her to bits. It certainly helped that he had grown close to her father and was beginning to get to know her siblings too.

It was a start at least. One day... One day, they might feel like family.

In fact, he was considering making himself a proper part of their family very soon. That thought made his hand slide to his left pocket instinctively.

The ring box rested in it neatly. He had been planning this for a while. Today was the day.

A shadow fell over him, and he looked up expectantly. Nikolina stood in the doorway. His heart leapt when he saw her and he jumped up, but she wasn't paying attention.

Her gaze was still on her notes and her brow was furrowed with obvious stress.

He hesitated. Was now the right time? She was so wound up over her case that it might not go down well if he interrupted her, whatever the reason was.

While he was still considering what to do next, Ilya appeared behind Nikolina and broke the silence.

"Are you two coming down for breakfast or not?" He questioned.

"We'll be right there," Antonin nodded. He reached out and tugged the papers from Nikolina's hands, "there's time to work later, babe, let's go and eat," he encouraged.

"But..." she looked anxious, her eyes following her notes as he dumped them on the bed.

"The case will be fine," he tried to soothe her, pulling her into a hug and rubbing her back gently, "I know you don't believe me," he added, realising how empty his words sounded, "but can you at least eat something before you start worrying about work again? Otherwise, you'll scare me."

She leaned against him and allowed him to try to calm her down. He was right, it wasn't working, but she didn't want him to start worrying as well. So, she sighed and gave a small nod.

"Okay, fine..." She wasn't hungry, but maybe if she ate, her family and her boyfriend would all stop worrying about her.

"Great," Antonin smiled and pecked her forehead, a quick gesture of affection, "Now let's go."

Reassured now that he had got their attention, Ilya led the way as they trouped back downstairs to eat.

For Antonin, breakfast was the end of his peaceful morning full of hopeful thoughts for the future.

As soon as he had eaten, Ilya announced that it was time to leave, and he had dash off upstairs again to grab his bag.

On the way back out he blew a kiss to Nikolina, who was once again lost in work and barely seemed to notice.

Then, he hurried to the car, eager to catch up with Ilya who was already waiting in the vehicle with the engine running.

He threw his bag into the boot and jumped into the passenger seat hastily, fastening his safety belt. "Ready to go!" he called to Ilya.

These mornings…. They were great, but they were always a rush as well. It would be stressful, but hey, at least it was livelier than his boring old commute.

As the car pulled out of the drive, Ilya struck up a casual conversation.

"By the way, I have a surprise for you at work today," he revealed.

That struck Antonin as odd. Ilya usually took work very seriously. It wasn't the time or place that he would arrange a 'surprise'. Besides, he wasn't big on surprises.

"What are you up to?" Antonin questioned curiously.

"I'm not 'up to' anything. It's just that I've been thinking," Ilya started to explain himself, "it's about time you had your first assignment. Now, I think I've found a perfect case."

"You have? That's great!" Antonin couldn't hide his excitement.

It wasn't that he didn't like the everyday parts of his job, but he had been longing for a little more action away from the confines of the station, for a long time.

Ilya chuckled, the younger man's reaction confirming all his suspicions.

"I thought you might say that," he replied, "let's get to the station so that I can officially fill you in," he added.

"Of course, protocol." Antonin rolled his eyes. Now he was eager for the details but would have to wait.

Preparing

It wasn't until later at the debriefing in Ilya's office at the police station that Antonin learned the full, thrilling and slightly terrifying nature of this assignment.

"We're dealing with a complicated case here," Ilya began solemnly, hoping to get Antonin to look beyond the idea of an adventure and take this seriously, "there have been threats, disappearances and even a few deaths."

That revelation caught the younger man by surprise. Antonin had been expecting a bigger case than the usual, run-of-the-mill stuff, of course, but this wasn't something he had even considered.

"Do we have any leads at all? It's not going to be easy to sort this kind of thing out..." he mused aloud, at a loss for where to start.

Ilya nodded.

"The local department has some suspicions about a mafia operation, you'll have to talk to them to find out more," he explained.

"Huh?" Antonin frowned, confused. Why would he be dealing with a different department in this case?

"Is this not a local issue?" he questioned further, needing to know more.

"No, it's not. In fact, the case is in Yaroslavl. But Chief Sunnikov, a friend of mine who happens to run the department there, specifically asked for outside help. She didn't tell me why, but I assume she wants to be sure there's no conflict of interest or internal corruption." Ilya explained.

Once again, Antonin found himself feeling very confused. He was torn now as well. He had been craving a case of his own that held a little more action than the mundane daily part of his job.

This definitely ticked that box, but he was a little scared. And then there was the other problem that Ilya seemed to have forgotten about...

"Well, I'm flattered that you thought of me, but Yaroslavl is 173 miles away. How exactly am I supposed to get there?" He raised the topic.

But Ilya hadn't forgotten at all.

"I was just getting to the travel arrangements," he explained, "you can take a car, we've got some new ones coming in. And Chief Sunnikov says she's arranged somewhere for you to stay. When you get there, check in with her and she'll fill you in on the details."

"Right." Antonin nodded.

Well, at least that cleared that up. The only remaining question now was whether this was going to be a thrilling adventure to talk about for years to come or a terrifying near-death experience.

And there was only one way to find out, so he decided to be brave. "I'd better go and get a car, then. And pack some things."

Ilya got up. "I'll get a car ready for you." He agreed.

They made their way back outside and over to the garage that sat on the other side of the car park.

This was where they kept the cars that weren't being used. It was shut up at the moment, but Ilya had some keys on him and soon unlocked it, pulling open the doors.

"There we are, then, take your pick." He gestured to the rows of cars inside.

Antonin was insistently interested, stepping inside, and walking around the cars as he carefully inspected them.

"Hm... Well, I better go unmarked, if there's a chance that I'm heading into an organised crime group's headquarters. Don't want to spook them. Or be a target," he mused, moving along the line, "that just leaves the question, which of the unmarked ones is fastest?"

Ilya rolled his eyes. "Enough of that. Pretending to be a speed demon when you haven't driven in five years."

"Hey, I've just been saving my skills for the right opportunity. Besides, I might need to make a fast getaway. Or give chase, or..." Antonin began to protest.

"You watch too many movies," His boss commented, before grabbing some keys from a nearby shelf and tossing them to him.

"These are for that one," he pointed to the car Antonin was standing by, "it's pretty quick since you're looking for a new toy. And it'll get the job done as well. Just try to bring it back in one piece."

The other man caught the keys and rolled his eyes.

"Yeah, yeah, sure. I better take it home and get some stuff packed," he said, opening the car door.

"Just a minute, I'll get your other stuff from my car." Ilya reminded him. He'd forgotten about his bag, which contained all his usual work stuff and left it in the other man's car.

After a few moments, he came back and handed over the bag, which Antonin bunged carelessly into the front passenger seat of his new car, before sliding into the driver's seat.

"Right, time to go then. I'll let you know how it goes when it's all over." He told Ilya casually, putting a brave face on the whole situation.

Ilya nodded. "You do that. And bring yourself back in one piece, as well."

He told him, which Antonin guessed was as close to a fond farewell as he was going to get.

He pulled the door shut, strapped himself in and started the engine, cursing when his first attempt stalled.

His break from driving had taken more of a toll than he expected. But on his second attempt, he pulled away, waving half-dismissively and half as a goodbye to the laughing Ilya, who had found his mistake quite amusing.

Now where to? Antonin wondered as he pulled out of the police station car park. The best bet would probably be back to the Moroz family's home.

While he hadn't technically moved in, he had most of his possessions in Nikolina's room at the moment.

Besides, he would have to say goodbye to her.

That thought hit harder than he had expected. He didn't think about that earlier, but he would be going away from her for a long time.

Leaving her in her current, stressed mood while she waited for her case to start that afternoon...

He groaned. This wasn't going to be easy.

But it was soon a reality that he had to face up to, as before long he was pulling up outside the house again.

He left the car, pushed open the front door and wandered inside. He waved to Sasha as he passed the other man in the living room, then made his way upstairs to Nikolina's room.

She was still sitting on her bed, going through her notes when he found her. She didn't appear to have noticed his arrival, so he called out to her softly.

"Lina?"

Finally, she raised her head and looked at him, "Antonin? I thought you were at work!"

"I was..." he admitted, before hastily changing the subject, not wanting to begin the conversation on his bombshell news, "how's your prep going?"

"I'm just making sure, but I seem to have all my notes ready now." She told him.

But she wasn't going to be completely distracted, "why did you come home again?" she asked.

Well, now or never. "I... I came to get my things." He finally let it out.

She wrinkled her brow, confused. "Why?"

"I've got my first assignment." He told her, starting with the good news.

She smiled, "That's good! So, we've both got our first cases now?"

"Yep, both moving up in the world, babe." He agreed as casually as he could while picking up some of his bags.

Just the ones with the clothes and other essentials, he wouldn't need the rest, would he?

No, he could leave his guitar behind, and his music books. And his comics. And...

Then the penny seemed to drop.

"Do you have to go away for your assignment or something?" she asked, interrupting him as he pondered what to pack.

"Yeah..." he nodded reluctantly, "The assignment is in Yaroslavl..."

"What?!" That got her to discard her papers, at last, throwing them down on the bed and getting up.

"That's miles away!"

"I know, babe," he sighed, dropping his packing, and turning to her, "and I'm going to miss you while I'm gone... But I have to. They've got some serious trouble over there."

Nikolina looked torn.

"I am glad you're helping and taking your job so seriously... But I will really miss you too!" She ran over to hug him.

After a few moments of peace as they held one another, she finally questioned. "What kind of 'trouble' though? Will you be safe?"

"It's a mafia job," he told her. Upon seeing her concerned expression, he added, "but I'm sure I'll be in my element, finally getting some action and all."

His grin at the end of that statement must have convinced her and he thanked God that it had because otherwise, she might have noticed that he hadn't actually answered her question.

He wasn't sure of that himself, and he didn't want to lie to her.

"I'd better pack." He told her, moving away again reluctantly and starting to sort his things out.

It took a little while, but eventually, he had his essential belongings all sorted out and was ready to go.

Apart from one thing. The ring box, a tiny little thing, seemed to weigh heavily in his pocket, especially with Nikolina watching him forlornly as he prepared to go.

Leaving his bags on the floor, he pulled her into his arms again, kissing her. When they eventually broke apart, she sighed.

"I guess it is time for you to go now, then? Is this our goodbye kiss?"

"Almost," he admitted, "but before that happens, there's something I want to give you," he reached into his pocket.

"What is it?"

Taking out the ring, he smiled at her sweetly.

"It's just a promise. I want to be able to promise that, when I get back, we'll get married. Will you agree to that?" He asked as he opened the box.

She threw her arms around him again, "Of course!"

He laughed cautiously. "Lina, Lina! You're going to knock it on the floor in a minute, calm down!"

She let go and slipped the ring onto her hand instead, looking sheepish.

"Sorry, I got excited. But still... This is just about the best way to say goodbye if you have to go." She told him, cheering up a little.

"I know." He grinned, before pulling her into another kiss.

That was their final goodbye though, as time was marching on, so when they parted, he gathered his bags and headed back to his car, ready to start his mission at last.

The Mission Begins

All packed up and ready, Antonin sat in the car and stared out through the windscreen. He had a long journey ahead of him, and while it might be exciting, it was beginning to dawn on him that it would be very difficult as well.

Leaving his fiancée had already sobered him up after his initial excitement, and part of him suspected that was only going to be the tip of the iceberg as far as challenges were concerned.

But it was too late to turn back now.

Besides, there was only one way to find out what the mission held, challenge or adventure. He started up the car and put his foot down firmly, taking off into the distance.

He kept driving, making his way through the city, then onto the open roads leading from it.

He raced through villages, towns, and cities of all kinds without a glance, determined to get to Yaroslavl and get the mission underway.

It took three whole hours, but soon he was driving into the city. He slowed down as he entered, taking his time to look around.

Everything seemed quite normal. In fact, he had driven through several cities just like this on the way here.

There were clusters of houses, shops, a port with a large river... And yet there didn't seem to be anyone about.

He frowned. It was lunchtime on a Tuesday, he would have expected to see people on their lunch breaks, milling around and chatting, heading to the restaurants or shops.

There were very few people around, and they hurried from place to place, looking around suspiciously. Several glared at him as they saw him watching.

Either people in this city are *really* unfriendly, or the crime spree has had some kind of effect on the local atmosphere, he thought to himself as he drove down the main street.

But that was something he would have to investigate further after he had a little more information about what was going on around here.

Time to head to the local police station and find out what they knew so far.

He drove on, peering around for any sign that told him where to go.

Feeling lost was bizarre to him, he was used to living and working in a city he knew like the back of his hand. But this was all new.

However, after a while of aimless, confused driving around, Antonin arrived at the police station.

He pulled into the car park, stopped, and jumped out. Well, here he was. The mission was beginning in earnest now.

Wandering in, he made his way to the front desk and showed his badge, explaining who he was and why he was there. That was simple enough, and before long he was shown into an office to talk with the chief.

Chief Sunnikov was a tall, stately woman with slick, tied back grey hair.

She looked to be at least in her sixties, but she got up and moved to greet him with an easy kind of speed and energy that took him by surprise, shoving her files aside and stepping in front of her desk swiftly.

She took his hand and shook it heartily.

"Welcome to Yaroslavl, Officer Jelennski. I *am* sorry to drag you into this, but I suspect this case won't get solved without outside help, and Chief Moroz can always be relied on to support me. Since he recommended you, I'm sure you'll be a great asset."

He hadn't expected her to be quite so talkative and stood there, a little taken aback. Eventually, he rallied.

"Thank you, Ma'am... Um, well, I'll do my best." he said, though he was a little nervous now. She seemed to have exceedingly high expectations.

"What's the situation, though? I'm afraid we didn't get many details." He got to the main point of his visit: Finding out more about his case.

"Oh, yes, I forgot! I didn't want to share too much valuable information by mail in case it was intercepted. Sit down, and I'll fill you in!" She nodded, heading back to her own seat with him trailing behind her.

It took a while for her to find the relevant file, jiggling her paperwork around until she located it. Then she slid it over the desk to him.

"These are all the notes we have on the case, but I'll talk you through the important parts anyway..."

He sighed in relief. It may only be a surprisingly slim file, but he didn't want to get anything wrong on his first case.

Listening to her clear tones made him feel more confident that trying to decipher her handwriting did. A glance just showed squiggles. Lost, he sat back and let her take over.

"To start with, as I made clear in my earlier notes, there have been several incidents, most of them violent and all of them quite horrible. They all appear to be linked to one house."

She began her explanation, reaching forward and tapping the first page of the file.

The piece of paper had an address printed on it, above a few images of the house. It was an odd place.

The building was large, towering above those on the other side of it. It was made of dark stone and had a black door set in its centre. Dotted around were little windows, covered by black curtains.

None of this was particularly odd in itself, despite a rather dull colour scheme, but the images gave him a sense of foreboding.

"This is the place? Any idea what's going on there?" He asked.

She nodded.

"We suspect that the family who live there are running some kind of mafia business," she reiterated the suspicion Ilya had mentioned, "these people, the Volkov family, they have a reputation among the locals, but we can't get anything solid. People are too scared. They're definitely a strange bunch though. There are loads of them living there and they all keep to themselves."

Antonin considered this. It didn't look hopeful.

If no one was coming forward with solid evidence and the family avoided all interaction, how could they get to know the secrets behind the family's activities?

"Do you have any leads at all?" He questioned hopefully.

"There's one," the Chief revealed, "I think the ringleader is Vladimir Volkov. His daughter, Dariya, doesn't appear to like him very much. And she seems to be the weak link in their operations too. I've been wondering if she's an unwilling part of all this, but nothing's come of it yet. Try chasing it up. If she isn't on board with Vladimir's plans, there's a chance that she'll help us out. But it won't be easy to persuade her. We can't just storm in and demand she talks to us."

"So, what *do* we do?" Antonin pressed, sensing that she had some kind of plan.

"I think the best way to handle this is to have an undercover operative get close to her, then see what she knows," Sunnikov explained, "that's what I want you to do. That's why I asked for outside help. Someone from our force would be recognised."

Antonin nodded. That made sense, but there was one thing bothering him.

"How do I get close to her if they all keep to themselves?"

"Dariya is the only one who tends to go out. Occasionally, she goes to the Blue Mango Club, in the city centre. Go there this evening and look for her," she pulled out a picture of Dariya, "if you see her, try to get her attention. If you have to, seduce her." the Chief instructed.

"Right. The Club. Got it." Antonin nodded awkwardly, choosing to ignore the 'seduce her' comment for now. He wasn't going there!

"Anything else, Ma'am?" he asked.

She nodded. "Two things," she handed him another piece of paper, "here are the directions to your hotel. The expenses have been paid, so don't worry about that."

"Thanks. What else was there?"

"You might want to change in the men's room before you go. You're supposed to be undercover from now on and walking around in full uniform will probably attract attention." She pointed out.

"Right..."

That might explain the odd looks he had got earlier. He bid her goodbye on that note, wanting to change and get on with his case as soon as possible.

She watched him walk away, then tidied up her abandoned paperwork and crossed to the window, glancing out across the car park and into her city.

All she could do now was hope for the best.

He ran back to the car, grabbing his bag full of clothes and tossing the papers into the boot in its place.

He was rushing now, eager to get on with his case, and severely startled a maintenance man who was painting new lines on the parking bays.

The man jumped up, splashing paint on his car and shouting, but Antonin didn't have time for him, his mind full of his case.

"Sorry!" He yelled over his shoulder as he tore off into the station again.

He got a nod in return, but was already back inside, oblivious to it as he made his way down the corridors.

It was only then that he slowed down a little, in order to follow the Chief's advice. He didn't want to put his life on the line by blowing his cover before the mission even began.

So, he slipped into the men's room to change. Once he was suitably dressed in a more casual outfit of jeans and a blue t-shirt, he checked himself in the mirror.

The surprises of the day had already taken a toll on him. Though he was normally pale, he looked even more so now, and there were bags under his indigo-blue eyes.

Well, he hadn't slept properly for a couple of days, he had been considering his future too much.

It wasn't all to do with the mission, though he suspected that wouldn't help at all.

He ran his fingers through his chestnut-brown hair, following it down until the waves fell around his neck, and sighed.

Tiredness and stress were just what he needed on a mission where things might get physical.

Still, he supposed, despite his health, he was in pretty good shape. Standing at 6'2", he was a pretty big guy, with muscles to back him up.

He just hoped he wasn't going to need them. But that was something he would only find out later.

Right now, he had to go and check into the hotel. Maybe then he could try and get a little rest before he went to try to find this 'Dariya' girl.

Dariya

The club was dark and full of noise. It was very disorientating to Antonin as he stumbled inside. This wasn't his kind of thing and never had been, so he felt lost.

Once he adjusted to the light level, he tried to shut out the thumping music and the shouts of the more intoxicated revellers while he looked for his target.

He glanced down at the picture Chief Sunnikov had given him.

He was looking for a young woman with tan-coloured skin, shoulder-length black curls and piercing grey eyes. She had a distinctive scar along her left cheekbone as well, which he hoped would make her easier to spot.

Committing this information to memory, he slipped the picture into his pocket and scanned the room instead.

The first time he looked, his eyes passed right over her, and he didn't even notice. It was only on his second, puzzled look around the room that he noticed her. The girl was slouching against the wall in a corner.

She didn't look like she was there to party like everyone else was. For one thing, she was dressed in a plain black, oversized tracksuit. And she blended into her shadowy little corner easily.

She was just standing there, watching everyone else carefully.

Well, at least he had found her. He supposed that was progress. But now he had a harder task ahead of him: getting close to her without arousing any kind of suspicion.

He made his way over to her as casually as he could, even though he felt out of place here.

"Hi..." he tried to start a conversation.

She looked up at him with an expression of genuine confusion, as if she couldn't quite work out what he was.

He didn't realise he seemed *that* out of place, but apparently, he did. Perhaps he wasn't very good at this undercover business.

He was just pondering this and trying to decide whether or not he was going to get a response when she spoke.

"Do you want something?" She asked.

The comment wasn't as abrupt as he had expected it to be. She sounded quite polite, just at a loss for any reason why he was here, talking to her.

Why *was* he here? He thought hard for some sort of excuse and blushed when the only words that came to him were Sunnikov's embarrassing comments from earlier.

No, he reminded himself. That's not happening. Maybe just... Try to be her friend?

"I just wondered if you'd like to hang out for a bit." He asked her, again with a degree of forced casualness.

She gave him a doubting look, "Really? That's all?"

"Yeah." He nodded.

For a moment, he thought it would really that easy, that they would simply become friends and that that would give him inside access to all the Volkov family's hidden little secrets.

Because for a split second, there was a flicker of something like hope in her eyes.

Then it was gone, and she shook her head with a snort of disbelief.

"Yeah right! What are you really here for?"

Now she had him backed into a corner and he didn't know how to persuade her now. He sighed.

He seemed to be all out of options, so he took a deep breath and went for it.

"I just thought I'd buy the prettiest girl here a nice drink." He told her, trying to sound sincere, though talking in even a vaguely flirtatious manner to someone other than his girlfriend felt weird and awkward.

But Dariya nodded as though he had passed some kind of test or at least done what she had expected of him.

"Alright then, go for it. I'll have a margarita." She told him.

"And I'll have your phone number." He replied, trying to at least get something useful out of this interaction since it had been a dead-end so far.

But as soon as he turned up the flirting a bit, he felt sick. That was a stupid thing to say!

She laughed. "Forward, aren't you? Alright, if that's how you want to play it, you get my number when I get my drink." She retorted.

He rolled his eyes as he walked away to the bar. This girl seemed pretty demanding. He hadn't even got a 'thank you' yet.

Then again, her attitude and her tone of voice didn't seem to match up. It was the same with her dismissal of him at first.

She hadn't been rude, despite her sharp words. She seemed calm, even when what she was saying wasn't. It was almost like listening to a bad actor read from a script, speaking the words without their real emotions.

Perhaps that was it. It occurred to him that there might be more to Dariya Volkova than there seemed to be.

He certainly hoped so, anyway, since she was supposed to be their lead, and it didn't seem like she was helping him bust a crime ring right now.

Nevertheless, he grabbed her drink and made his way back over to her. She took the drink.

"Thanks." She said finally, sipping it.

"No problem." He nodded, then thought for something to say.

It was difficult. He wanted to blurt out questions about her family but had to act normally instead.

"So, what's your name?" He asked her.

She raised an eyebrow, looking surprised by his question, and a little disbelieving.

"You're not from round here, are you?" She asked after a few moments.

"No," he shook his head, "why, are you famous or something?"

"You could say that" she nodded, "My family practically runs this city."

Bingo, he grinned to himself. Finally, he was getting somewhere.

"Oh, how's that? Is your father the mayor or something?"

"Something." She responded with a smile that didn't reach her eyes.

For a second, he felt nervous, as though her mismatching words and tones, expressions, and feelings, were all some kind of warning that he should turn and run.

Perhaps she sensed his unease, because she stopped for a second, then gave him a more relaxed, genuine smile.

"It's actually refreshing to meet someone who *doesn't* know me. I'm Dariya, nice to meet you," she greeted him.

He smiled.

"It's nice to meet you too. I'm Antonin. I'm just here from Moscow on a business trip, so yeah, I don't know a lot about how things work around here," he told her as much of the truth as he could without giving himself away.

"Would you like to?" She asked suddenly, and again, it was jarring.

So very jarring that it threw him, and he had to question her.

"Would I like to what?"

"Would you like to learn how things work here? I can teach you, so you feel a little more comfortable while you're here. It must be very different, after all."

"Uh... Sure."

He gave a confused nod. It was a strange offer, but it helped his goal of getting more information, after all.

Dariya smiled in that odd, grating way again. "Great! You should come and meet my family!"

"Now who's forward?" He responded before he could help himself, a little stunned by the suddenness of that invitation, though theoretically, it was what he had wanted.

"That's not what I meant, silly! I just meant that if you want to know how things work in Yaroslavl, you need to meet them," she explained herself.

More information. So, the Volkov family really were the key to all this.

That meant, despite how odd Dariya's offer was and the fact that he felt as though it'd be walking into a trap, he really ought to go and get to know them.

"Alright then. When?" He asked.

He wasn't expecting her to down the rest of her drink and say, "now," before striding off towards the exit, leaving him running along behind her to try and keep up.

As he dashed through the crowded club, he could only wonder what to expect from meeting her notorious family so suddenly.

The Volkovs

The walk was surprisingly short, and soon Dariya stopped outside the house.

Antonin glanced up at it. It was the same as it had been in the picture, but somehow more real now that it was towering over him. He wasn't sure he wanted to go inside.

It was a little late to make that decision.

"Here we are!" Dariya turned to him with that same bright, false smile.

He wondered if he should call her out or question her about it, ask if she was okay. This didn't seem normal.

But they barely knew each other, she wouldn't open up to him, would she?

Besides, she was already shoving the door open. He reluctantly trailed after her, stepping inside.

The house was even weirder on the inside because suddenly, everything was different. It had been big, dark, and looming outside. Yet now, he had stepped into a narrow, white-washed, corridor.

He blinked and looked around. This place was definitely weird, but he couldn't exactly put his finger on why it felt that way.

So, he kept following Dariya, hoping she would lead him to some kind of answer.

She led him down the corridor and opened a small door at the end, which brought them out in a much larger, but equally featureless, white room.

This one was crowded, and Antonin couldn't help but stare as he took it all in.

There seemed to be loads of them, milling all around the room, chattering incessantly. But they all looked the same.

Not just vaguely related, but almost identical to one another, down to minute details like the scar they all bore on their left cheeks.

The effect was quite disconcerting. It was also very strange and made him curious as to exactly what was going on here, why they all looked like that and how the scar had come to mark them all like that.

There were so many questions, but he couldn't ask any of them in case they aroused their suspicions.

So, he simply stood silently behind Dariya and waited to see what would happen next.

Dariya cleared her throat, and her various relatives turned to look at her curiously.

She gave them a cheerful wave.

"Hey! I just thought I'd bring my new boyfriend to meet you all!" she trilled with a bright smile.

Antonin stared at her. "Boyfriend?! We jus-- Ouch!!"

He had been hissing a rebuke at her under his breath, feeling horrible at being called some random woman's boyfriend when he had a bride-to-be waiting for him at home, but Dariya's movements were swift, and her elbow was surprisingly sharp.

He fell silent, his ribs aching and wondered why she had suddenly attacked.

They had seemed to be getting along... Obviously she hadn't wanted him to speak up and make a scene in front of her family, but he hadn't meant to, which was why he had whispered to her.

It was probably best just to keep quiet and see what the Volkov family had in store for him.

They were watching him quite closely now and he shifted from foot to foot, feeling uncomfortable under the pressure of their staring eyes.

"Another one?" Someone spoke up at last. The voice was sharp and sarcastic. It seemed to be enjoying a nasty joke at their expense.

"Where did you find this one?" The questions were addressed to Dariya. Everyone stared at Antonin, but no one spoke to him.

They crowded around though, others joining in and asking more questions about him.

They were basic questions - His name, where he came from, how they met - But the scenario and their attitudes turned it into some kind of strange interrogation.

Dariya managed it well though, introducing him and talking quite calmly about their first meeting - Though she carefully made it sound as though it was more than five minutes ago.

She seemed quite used to handling her family. And he noticed as she elaborated about their 'relationship', quite good at lying to them.

He wondered why that was. Perhaps she was keeping secrets and therefore, really was the key to finding out all about the local crime spree.

Or perhaps she lied to help their illegal enterprises. It didn't seem like she was helping them now, but she was exceptionally good at lying, so perhaps she was deceiving him too.

Watching the conversation reminded him that he had to be on his toes about that kind of thing anyway and that he mustn't fall into the trap of trusting anyone here.

But it also made him surer than ever that he needed Dariya's help. There was definitely something very odd about this place and this family, and they were never going to cooperate with an outsider since they completely ignored him.

He couldn't trust her. But he couldn't do this without her.

He just wished he knew what she was up to.

She must have brought him here for a reason, but now she was spinning strange stories to her ever-stranger family members while he stood, quiet and ignored, trying to observe, and failing.

He couldn't understand any of what was going on here. Even their conversations were beyond him, despite the fact that they spoke perfectly normally and seemed to be talking about him. But the conversations were full of lies and little inflexions that made him question what was being said.

Perhaps they had slipped some form of code into their conversation to confuse him or talk about him to his face and get away with it.

It was the kind of conversation that seemed perfectly innocent but made him feel awkward and overly aware of every little comment.

He hadn't encountered that since high school, but they were much better at it and much more persistent.

It was starting to make him want to scream.

Very softly, a door shut behind him.

No one had heard it open, nor had they heard the front door. But as it shut, the conversation came to an abrupt halt.

Antonin followed the others as their gazes turned. He needed to know what had caused such a sudden change in them.

There was a man standing in the doorway. He was tall and well-built, his tan skin mostly covered by his dark suit.

He had a prominent scar on his cheek, and jet-black hair that was flecked with grey, with a beard to match.

His eyes were lighter grey than those of the others. They were so pale that he almost looked as though he had blind, milky eyes.

But he could see. The look on his face suggested he could see through souls.

Antonin recognised him instantly, from the pictures in the file. It was Vladimir Volkov.

The silence was finally broken as he stepped forward with a benevolent smile.

"I'm home, children. Who's our guest?" He added, his gaze wandering to Antonin.

It felt as though he was looking through him, but his grey eyes had settled on his face. They were slightly defocused, gazing left in a dreamy kind of way.

That was easily more uncomfortable than the hard stares and gossipy whispers that Antonin had been longing to escape from. Perhaps he should have been careful what he wished for.

Again, Dariya filled the breach quite calmly.

"This is Antonin, my new boyfriend," she explained, "Antonin, this is my father," she added, introducing them properly.

Damn, Antonin thought to himself.

He'd been hoping that Vladimir would be as rude as most of his relatives and ignore him, so he could get away without having to talk to the creepy older man.

Instead, he rather reluctantly shook Vladimir's outstretched hand and forced a smile.

"Nice to meet you," he lied.

"Yes, isn't it?" Vladimir answered cryptically, holding onto his hand for a little too long.

"Why did my lovely little Dariya decide to bring you here today? Are you planning to join our family sometime soon?" he asked him, still looking right through him.

Turning red, Antonin looked desperately to Dariya for help. She didn't look much more comfortable than he was with her father's sudden, blunt questions, but she rallied.

"We... We haven't had that conversation yet, Papa," she told him as carefully and tactfully as she could.

Vladimir looked genuinely stunned by that news, then, after a few moments of consideration, politely asked, "Would you like to? We can leave you two alone for a private chat if you want."

The two looked at one another a little helplessly. This was getting worse by the second. Then Antonin sighed.

The only way he could think of to make this experience less uncomfortable was to ask Dariya some questions he couldn't ask in front of everyone.

"Uh... Yes, I think that might be a good idea," he said finally, needing to get some answers whether it blew his cover or not.

Or at least to get five minutes away from the strange, staring Volkovs.

Planning

The door closed, leaving Antonin and Dariya alone.

He waited for the footsteps of the other Volkovs to fade away before he turned to her and demanded to know, "alright, *what the hell is going on?*"

Perhaps for someone supposed to be undercover, this question lacked a certain amount of tact, but he was at a loss for any other words to express his current feelings.

Dariya paused. She walked to the door and rested her head against it for a moment.

Then she ran her hands over her clothes, smoothing them out. Something fell to the floor. She trod on it.

All this out of the way, she finally began to speak.

"Okay, okay, I owe you an explanation," she admitted.

Now, her voice was different. The edge of cheer that made her seem as though she knew what she was doing was gone. She sounded nervous.

"Yeah, that would be great. I mean, things are strange enough here, without one drink being enough to make us boyfriend and girlfriend and that somehow giving your family a right to talk over my head!" he retorted, genuinely bewildered by everything that had just happened.

Dariya sighed.

"Look, I didn't want to put you in an awkward situation, but ultimately, I had a choice to make. And I admit I made the selfish choice. But I needed your help."

That wasn't what he had expected her to say. Why would she need some random stranger's help, assuming he hadn't already managed to blow his cover?

He didn't know how to respond to that, especially not without any context, so he waited patiently for her to explain herself.

Eventually, after glancing at the silent young man nervously, she started again:

"You see, my family are... Abnormal. I'm sure you've noticed that. But they're worse than that. My father only runs this place because everyone here's scared to death of him, me included. He's a monster, and he wants to make the rest of us monsters. As I said, no one here's ever going to oppose him or live long enough to do so effectively. So, I wait for a stranger to come here, let them know that it's not a good place to be, and try to convince them to get me away from here. That's why I 'date' a lot of people, 'cause my father only lets me bring people who might 'join the family' here. But you don't want to be a part of this family!"

She began to ramble now, her voice wavering as her distress became more and more apparent.

She had hidden it well beneath her brittle smile, but now she was on the verge of tears.

And, to Antonin's horror, he felt like celebrating this announcement, because it meant their intelligence was right.

Perhaps if he told her the truth, she would help him. Then, at the back of his mind, the tiny voice of doubt spoke up. Should he reveal his cover so soon? He didn't know that he could trust her… Though her emotion *did* seem genuine.

But if this was some kind of ploy, if they already knew he was here to take them down, then the stakes could be pretty high. They might trap him or kill him.

"Well, will you help me?" Dariya's pleading tones cut through his thoughts.

His brain whispered that he should proceed with caution, but his heart couldn't ignore her distress.

"I'll try to," he offered a compromise, not telling her the truth immediately, but offering help anyway, "but..." he hesitated again.

Should he tell her? If he was going to help her, he would have to, sooner or later, right? After all, she wanted him to take her away from the city, but he couldn't just yet, because of his job.

He ran the issue through his mind again, then began again.

"I'll help, but I have something to explain to you first," he revealed.

She nodded. "I'll listen if it'll get me out of here."

"It will. You see, that's kind of why I'm here in the first place. I'm a police officer," he confessed, "I want to stop your father, but I need your help getting some evidence against him."

"I know. Why did you think I asked you?" she replied calmly.

He stared. Seriously? His first ever undercover mission and he had been figured out by some random woman?

"For real?!"

He wished he could have thought of a better response, but shock got the better of him.

She nodded. "You spend enough time in this dump, and you soon figure out when someone doesn't fit in. So, I take it you are here to help?"

At least that explained why she had gone from treating him as a weirdo to being his new 'girlfriend,' he supposed.

Nodding, he explained, "I came to find you on purpose, hoping I could infiltrate your family and find out what's been going on here. We've known it's not right for a while..."

"You can say that again... It's actually a relief to tell someone how I really feel about them for once, instead of playing along," she said with a sigh.

Antonin nodded, relieved to start getting things off his chest now that he was over the shock of his swift discovery.

"It's definitely nice to drop all the acting. All that flirting and pretending to date was... Weird," he commented.

Dariya pouted. "I'm not that bad, am I?" she asked.

Despite their more serious conversation earlier, he couldn't help but chuckle at her expression. "No, no, that's not what I meant. I'm just not used to undercover work yet," he tried to explain.

She sighed. "When I figured out you were a police officer, I kind of hoped for someone with experience, not a rookie..."

Now it was his turn to be hurt.

"I'm not a rookie! I've dealt with lots of cases, I'm just used to being able to operate with others, not hide away. And I certainly didn't plan to have to cheat on my fiancée for this job!"

His words were full of anger, and her surprise was evident in her expression.

"I'm sorry, I didn't know that! I guess this is a very unusual case..." she admitted, before smiling, "It's cute that you're so worried about your fiancée, but we're only pretending," she tried to reassure him.

He calmed down a little. It was just the stress, the stress of working so hard, under these unusual conditions, and away from his beloved Nikolina.

"I'm sorry too, I'm just not used to pretending, undercover work is hard..." He sighed.

"Well, I guess so, since I caught you," she joked, before taking on a more serious tone, "but then, I'm barely used to not pretending to be something I'm not around here," she told him sympathetically.

"But if we have to get on with a case to stop Papa, then I'll do everything I can to help you out! In fact, I think I know where to start. We'll just have to plan it out carefully so that we don't get caught. If my father finds out, he'll try to kill you," she revealed, changing the subject suddenly.

"Yeah, we'll definitely need to think about how to avoid that at some point," Antonin agreed, repressing a shiver.

He didn't want her to see that he was scared, but Vladimir was definitely disconcerting.

He tried to focus on the positives, telling her, "I'm glad you've got an idea, I hope it'll work. So long as we can prove Vladimir's committing crimes here, we can finally lock him up."

Doubt clouded her features briefly, "and I won't get into any trouble?"

"Not if you help me," he assured her.

"Great!" She smiled, and it was finally a genuine smile.

"Then we can get to wo..." she paused partway through her sentence and shushed him suddenly, whispering, "they're coming back!"

Instantly, they both fell into silence and straightened up, doing their best to look innocent.

A moment later, Vladimir opened the door, and the family crowded back into the room, still staring at the 'couple'.

"Well?" Vladimir asked, "have you come to a decision yet?"

They exchanged glances awkwardly. What was it they had been supposed to discuss again? In the heat of the moment, it had all slipped their minds.

Dariya remembered first and hastily jumped to come up with an excuse.

"Not exactly, no! We thought it might be better if Antonin moved in for a bit, so we can all get to know one another better and bond as a family before he," she paused, turning slightly red, "...You know..." her voice faded to a mumble.

Despite that part, Antonin had to applaud her. She must have been dealing with her father's questioning for a long time to be this good at coming up with rapid-fire lies.

He wasn't entirely sure that was a good thing, though. He had been raised to believe any kind of lie was wrong, hence all this undercover work didn't sit well for him. But he understood there was a need here.

For Dariya, it must be a kind of survival instinct. And for him... Well, it would have to become one.

He tried to think of something comforting, and Nikolina came to mind. She always said that sometimes, lies were necessary. He hadn't believed her until now. Perhaps he never should have doubted her. When he got home, he'd tell her how right she was, while he held her in his arms.

"Antonin?!"

Dariya's voice nudged at him, and he looked around guiltily, embarrassed to be here, pretending to be her boyfriend, while he dreamed of another woman.

"Uhm... Yeah?" he questioned.

"I said, when do you want to move in?" she asked him.

'Never' was his first thought.

He didn't want to live with these frankly creepy people. But he had to think of his mission, and the sooner they could start to gather evidence, the better.

So, he said, "can we start moving in tomorrow morning?"

Vladimir chuckled.

"You're keen, aren't you? Alright, you can share Dariya's room. I'm sure she'll help you move in tomorrow. Then later in the week, once you've settled in, we can properly welcome you to the family..." he smiled, a warm, welcoming grin.

Antonin didn't fully understand that comment, but it made him want to run as far away as possible.

Instead, he nodded mutely and glanced at Dariya nervously, hoping her plan was something special so they could get this over with as quickly as possible.

The First Secret

The next day, Antonin woke up with a crick in his neck and groaned, sitting up.

"I told you that you should have taken the bed," Dariya told him, looking down at him with a concerned frown.

"It's fine." He shrugged, instantly regretting the movement.

Sleeping on her bedroom floor wasn't the best idea he had ever had, but Vladimir had been quite insistent that he stay the night but then hadn't given him his own room.

Since he was pretending to be Dariya's boyfriend, it had been assumed that he would stay with her. And, of course, her room only had the one bed.

He had felt it too mean to kick the young woman he was supposed to be helping out of her own bed, even if she had offered, so he had settled for the floor.

Unfortunately, it didn't seem as though this house was designed for comfort, even in the bedrooms.

Dariya's room was as plain, empty, and featureless as the rest of the house. There wasn't even a carpet to cushion him, only the wooden floor.

He had managed a few hours of sleep, but it was still barely getting light, and he knew he wouldn't get back to sleep now.

That left him at a loss for what to do now. It seemed early to get up - Especially in a house that wasn't his - and risk disturbing other people.

Speaking of which... He looked over at Dariya.

"How come you're awake? Did I disturb you?" he asked.

She shook her head. "Nah, I don't usually sleep very well anyway."

An idea occurred to him. "Anyone else likely to be up? Maybe we can look around for some evidence..."

She thought about this for a moment.

"I don't think so. The guards don't start work until later in the day, I'm pretty sure, and Papa isn't an early riser..." she explained, thinking aloud as she went through the routines of anyone who might get in the way.

"We should get away with it," she nodded, "c'mon!"

After her realisation, she wasted no time at all. Jumping out of bed in her nightgown, she didn't even get dressed before she ran off.

It was all Antonin could do to get up and follow her.

She hurried past rows of doors and downstairs.

They ran back through the living room where Antonin had first encountered the other Volkovs, and through some more similar rooms.

Eventually, Dariya reached a door and fiddled with it.

"Damn, it's locked. Hang on, I know he hides the key around here somewhere..." she muttered, looking around.

A few minutes later, she discovered the key embedded in a candlestick.

It was a decent hiding place, but Vladimir could have done with decorating a bit more if he wanted it to be convincing,

Antonin couldn't help thinking. In a house this bare, anything unnecessary like a candle stood out.

But that didn't matter, and he was probably overthinking, slipping into work-mode, and looking for clues already.

He tried to ignore that instinct and followed Dariya as she unlocked the door and slipped into a corridor.

It was much darker in this part of the house, which lacked any windows to let in natural light.

He was beginning to wonder if the candle was unnecessary after all when Dariya finally found the light switch and flicked it on.

They were in a long corridor that had a steep flight of steps at the other end. Dariya led the way determinedly, and he followed her, a little nervous.

"What exactly are we going to find down here?" he asked.

"My father's workshop," she told him.

He was still none the wiser. "Workshop? What does he do?" he questioned.

The girl sighed. "All kinds of... Unnatural things..."

"Unnatural?" Every explanation only raised more questions.

"It's... Hard to explain. Just wait, okay?" Dariya answered, clearly not wanting to continue this conversation.

Antonin still wanted to know what he was walking into, but she seemed uncomfortable with his line of questioning, so he let it go for the moment and continued down the corridor.

They reached the steps and descended.

The staircase was longer than he expected, but eventually, they reached the bottom, and it opened out into a large cavern under the house.

But, unlike the house above them, this was far from empty. He stared around him, shocked and confused by what he was seeing.

"I told you," Dariya said, "He does unnatural things. Calls himself a scientist, but most of what he does here is scheming. He pays or bullies real inventors into doing the important stuff," she commented, pulling a disgusted face.

"And... That's what all this is? *Inventions?* What *for?*" He demanded to know as he gawped, turning this way and that to get a better look.

The room if it could be called that, was huge, and it was bursting. Everywhere he looked there were tables strewn with odd bits of metal and strange devices.

Some were clearly weapons, gun-shaped but lit-up like Christmas trees, suggesting they were far from ordinary weapons. Others were unrecognisable.

Some were too big for the tables and were piled up around them, in parts or completed. In the middle of the room was a sheet-draped structure that stood taller than a grown man and hummed ominously.

Dariya shrugged.

"For power, I suppose. He's crazy. Thinks he's some kind of genius and that 'his' inventions will help him take control of the world," she revealed.

"And this city is his first step..." Antonin breathed.

Suddenly, the puzzle pieces fell into place. This wasn't just some crime ring, run for profit. This was... Practice. See if you can scare a city into doing what you want, then a country, then the world...

He shuddered. He had to stop this. But how exactly? There was a nasty little flaw in the idea of using this for evidence.

"But I'm not sure he's technically doing anything illegal..." he frowned, confused.

These things were bizarre, of course, and definitely wrong. But were they against the law? How could they be if the law didn't know what the hell they were?

But Dariya shook her head grimly.

"Just wait," she told him, "This is just the tip of the iceberg... He's got things hidden away down here that are *definitely* illegal."

"Right. We'd better look at them, then." Antonin nodded, trying to brace himself for... Well, more than he had been previously prepared for.

It's one thing going prepared for murder, but if you suddenly find out you're dealing with world domination plans, you have to adjust.

Any mind is capable of killing if pushed too far, but the kind of mind capable of planning world domination is... Special. You have to be prepared for *anything* at that point.

Dariya hesitated; her eyes fixed on the... Thing in the middle of the room.

"We should, but... First, I suppose I should be completely honest with you from the start." she began.

Antonin paused, looking over at her with sudden apprehension. What was this about? The kind of conversation that started like that was never good.

Had she tricked him after all, lured him down here to betray him? But if she meant to harm him, why would she reveal all this first?

Unless, of course, she didn't think he would escape. His eyes swivelled to the stairs. They weren't far away; he could run to them. But they were steep, and it was a long way up.

He shifted his weight, ready to make a break for it, just in case, then nodded.

"Alright, something's up. Hit me with it."

Dariya's Secret

Dariya walked across the room and yanked the sheet aside, revealing a large, almost rectangular machine.

It had a glass door, shut at the moment, which closed over a human-shaped compartment. Several tubes connected to it, all leading to the compartment.

She turned back to Antonin, shaking slightly.

"Do you know what this is?" she asked him.

His mind raced, but he couldn't think of an answer, so he shook his head.

"This is what brought me to life," she told him.

"Huh??"

He wrinkled his brow, too confused to articulate a better response, but nevertheless needing some kind of explanation.

What was she trying to say? It didn't make any sense...

Dariya sighed, seeing his confusion.

"Sorry, I get that this is weird, but what I'm trying to tell you is that this," she gestured to the machine, "is a cloning device. My father made it so that he could create... I don't know, pawns in his game. People to further his nasty little plans."

She pulled a face, shuddering.

Antonin surfaced slowly from his shock to try to make some sense of this.

"And he... Made you with this to achieve that?"

"Not just me, but all of us. The others are all my siblings, but I was the first, his test subject. He took his own DNA, and... Altered enough for me to be a different person. My gender and things like that. But not too much, because clearly, he thinks he's the best blueprint for the rest of us." She rolled her eyes at that point.

"That sounds insane, but I have to admit it makes some sense. I did wonder how you could all look so exactly alike. Even family don't share everything..."

"Ha!" Dariya's laugh was bitter and hard now.

"That's not even the tip of his insanity-iceberg! We all look *exactly* the same, right?" She raised her fingers to touch the scar on her cheek.

"This isn't genetic, this is another wonderful little idea of his. It's part of a loyalty test in our 'family training.'"

He stared at her, feeling sickened by the implication. "He did that to you...?"

"Worse, he made us do it to ourselves," she told him chillingly, "still, it's better than his latest plan." she shuddered.

He flinched at the look on her face. "I hardly dare ask, but what is his latest plan?"

"He wants another generation of our family, this time from slightly different DNA, that he can raise to be even more powerful. They'll be the test subjects for his first push outside of Yaroslavl. If anything goes wrong, these children will take the fall, and if not, he uses them to take over the world..." She saw his look of horror and matched it with her own disgusted look.

"But what I hate most about his plan is that he chose me. He wants me to be their template, their 'mother'. My siblings call it an honour. Perhaps it would be. I've always wanted children, but I don't want them to be weapons in this twisted game..."

The pain of what she was revealing cut her off, her voice shaking. She couldn't go on this way.

For the first time since they had met, Antonin began to feel some understanding towards Dariya. At first, she had just seemed like a closed-in girl, suppressing, or faking her emotions.

Then she had been... Odd, attaching herself to him too fast and lying to her family about their relationship. Then she had become an ally. Well, more like a tool. He had to admit he had just been using her to do his job.

But now he understood that her own father, a man who should have been there to help her, had messed her up inside.

She lied to survive, hid her emotions to keep him from knowing the truth and she didn't really have a life of her own.

It was a lot for someone to go through at such a young age. He knew from her file she was only twenty-two, six years younger than he was.

At her age, he had just been starting his own life and had been full of excitement. She had never felt that.

And that was just the beginning. Vladimir wasn't just destroying her life. He was using her to destroy other lives. Other lives that he had created just for that reason...

That was sick. But it wasn't just morally sick, it was more personal.

He didn't just want to help Dariya so that she would help him in return. He wanted her to be able to live a normal life.

And for that to be possible, he had to take Vladimir down. Not just because of the law and his job, but because this madness had to be stopped.

The sooner, the better.

"Let's get to the evidence now!" he urged her on.

She looked at him with a strange mix of confusion, hurt and anger. "Is that all you care about? Aren't you *listening?!*"

That unexpected attack stung, and he hastened to reassure her;

"That's not what I meant! Look, I'm sorry if it seemed like that... It's just... He's been messing with you long enough. I want to stop him as soon as possible. Obviously, I wanted that anyway, but I didn't know how far this went. As if killing people wasn't messed up enough, he's living their lives for them too!" He let out all his disgust at what she had told him in one rant.

As he spoke, he saw Dariya's scowl fade into a smile. "Ah, there it is, the sign that you actually care. I wasn't sure you would, you know, because my father... He always says the police would never care about people like us. That all they want is to lock us away, and we shouldn't trust them. But you didn't seem like that, so I took a chance... I've never told anyone before, you see... I guess that's why I'm so defensive. Sorry." She looked a little sheepish.

"Look, some people might just want to lock you up, but that's not why I'm here. I want to help. Anyway, your father's the real criminal here, so I'll focus on him. He's probably the one you shouldn't trust," he pointed out.

"But I get being defensive. It is a pretty big secret. That's why I didn't really know how to respond. But whatever you are, however, you came into being, it doesn't change that you're still you, your mind's still your own... That fact you're helping me proves that," he told her sincerely, reassured now that she had told him this.

It helped him feel that he could trust her. Otherwise, she wouldn't be saying this.

Her response was a surprise though. She threw her arms around him.

"Thank you!" Her words came out as a cry.

A few moments later, she pulled away, blushing.

"That was weird, I'm sorry. I just haven't really been accepted as anything but an extension of my father before," she told him gratefully.

"Not your fault," he shrugged it off, "sometimes, you feel more connected to other people than your real family." he mused, thinking of his life with the Moroz family over his own, distant parents. But that was different. Both families at least treated him as a human being.

Dariya nodded. "Strangers are more like family than *him.*" She didn't need to explain who *he* was.

"Not really surprising." Antonin shrugged. "After everything. He's got a nice little benevolent act though."

"Yeah, he's well-practised," she commented disdainfully. "After he took over, he made himself mayor. That's just his public relations act... But anyway, we should probably start looking for our evidence before he gets up. I don't particularly want to be here when he decides he wants to see me."

Evidence

As they had lost some time to Dariya's confession, the search for evidence became more urgent. It wouldn't be too long before Vladimir got up, and he might decide to check on his 'workshop'.

So, Dariya led the way through the chamber of inventions and to another door, almost hidden as it blended in with the wall.

"This is... You might want to brace yourself," She murmured nervously.

That, along with the disgusting smell that had become noticeable as he walked over to the door, was all the clues Antonin needed.

"He... He actually kept his victims' bodies down here?" He choked out over the smell.

He had expected murder, he just hadn't expected the killer to be this dumb.

"He wanted to use them for experiments. He's started some... It's pretty horrible," Dariya admitted.

Antonin sighed. "Well, I guess I have to look anyway..."

Dariya nodded and covered her mouth and nose, trying to block out the rotten stench before she pulled open the door.

Antonin pulled his shirt over his face a little, hoping it would block the smell enough for his eyes to stop watering while he examined the evidence in front of him.

There was a pile of bodies. More than he had been expecting. More than there had been disappearances here... They must have missed several of the cases.

The victims were all kinds of people. Their genders, races and ages didn't appear to enter into it.

No, Vladimir Volkov didn't target any one group, he simply went after anyone who was in his way. And kept their bodies, in various decaying states, piled up in his basement. There was even a knife still sticking out of one of the bodies.

How could this self-proclaimed genius have covered his tracks so badly? Was it sheer stupidity, or the arrogant belief that he would never be caught?

Which led him to another question... How had it been so hard for the local police to solve this case with glaring evidence like this?

When he heard that they had struggled so much, he had assumed that there was little evidence, or it would be difficult to locate. But it was just sat here, staring him in the face.

There was no way any self-respecting, genuine police officer would have missed this. There must be something bigger going on.

He made a mental note to talk to Chief Sunnikov when he got out of here. She would surely investigate her department for corrupt officers...

But what if Volkov's spy or spies acted faster than he possibly could?

He might be okay, she might not have told anyone about his undercover mission, but she had other key information on record, such as her suspicion of Dariya...

His new friend could be in grave danger already.

That just meant he had to work faster!

He had to document this and return to the station right now so that they had the evidence to storm the place en masse and arrest Vladimir. Confronting him alone would be stupid, but a raid couldn't fail.

There was only one slight problem. All his equipment was on his uniform belt, which, of course, he wasn't wearing while he was undercover.

He couldn't get started, he couldn't even dust that rather obvious knife for fingerprints...

"Damn!" He growled to himself.

"What?" Dariya questioned, suddenly nervous.

If there was a problem with this much evidence that was all so obvious, then there wasn't much chance of finding anything better. Were their hopes lost already?

"I need some stuff, but I left it at the hotel..." he admitted.

"Then go back and get it, quickly!" She urged.

"But then we'll have to find another opportunity to get back down here. How likely are we to get another chance?" Antonin asked uncertainly.

Dariya considered this, then shook her head.

"We won't, not today. He'll be down here as soon as he gets up. We'll have to get the stuff today and come back tomorrow."

Antonin looked at the pile of disturbing 'evidence'. Then thought of Sunnikov's words and his own suspicions.

No, if they had this huge case and it had taken them this long to get anywhere, then the Volkovs must have a pretty useful dirty cop somewhere in Yaroslavl.

Meaning he didn't know how long it would be until they were tipped off that the investigation was happening again.

"We might not have time to wait until tomorrow!" He groaned.

Dariya bit her lip and tried to think.

"Okay... So, what do you need?"

"I need fingerprint powder, a camera, my police notebook and... Screw it, just those essentials, that'll do if we don't have time." Antonin decided.

"Right, so if we can't risk leaving and having to wait until tomorrow, you stay here, and I'll go and get them." Dariya told him.

Antonin looked sceptical. "And if someone finds me?"

"They won't. I'll lock the door and take the key with me," she assured him.

So ... You'll lock me in the creepy basement full of rotting corpses and go and take my stuff? Antonin thought. *Great plan.*

But it wasn't as though he had a better one. Besides, if he couldn't trust her, who could he trust?

"Alright then. Here..." He dug a slip of paper out of his pocket with his hotel room's address on it.

"it should all be there. Just tell them you're visiting me and get in and out as fast as you can. The stuff should be with my uniform, so check the closet," he instructed her.

Dariya tucked the piece of paper into her pocket hastily.

"Got it!" She nodded. "Wish me luck."

"Good luck!" He replied sincerely.

She nodded and slipped away through the basement, disappearing up the stairs.

Antonin edged away from the bodies, found a workbench that was empty and sat down to wait, hoping Dariya could move with speed and get the tools to finish this grim job.

It was turning out to be a lot less of an adventure and more of a nightmare.

Footsteps faded away above him and were replaced with the sound of the door slamming shut, then the click of it locking behind Dariya.

Now all he could do was wait. And hope to God that there wasn't a spare key anywhere in this awful place so that he would at least know that the unlocking of the door meant she had made it back.

But until the door unlocked again, he would just have to sit and wonder if he had done the right thing by letting her shut him in here and leave.

The 'Moving In' Mission

Dariya shut the door behind her, turned the key in the lock, then slipped into her pocket carefully and checked her watch.

Damn, she really didn't have much time. Her knowledge of her father's routine indicated that he would already be up.

He'd go and have breakfast, and then... Then he would notice that something was wrong.

She was relying on his arrogance to do the rest. He would, she hoped, assume that no one could have possibly infiltrated his precious workshop without his knowledge and that the issue was, therefore, a stuck lock.

Which gave her and Antonin however long it took him to fix the lock. She knew he wouldn't do that himself.

He'd get Valeria, her expert lockpicker sister, to do it for him. And at this time in the morning, Valeria would be otherwise engaged in her usual round of fighting with Vladlena.

Both girls insisted this was only for practice, but really, they were at each other's throats every day.

Normally, Dariya despaired of the fact that none of her family members appeared to make any effort to get along, but today it served her purpose.

Because she calculated, it would take her father another five minutes to finish his breakfast, five to notice the lock and alert Valeria, and at least thirty for Valeria to stop fighting. Then properly about fifteen for her to get it open.

Which gave her and Antonin fifty-five minutes in total. Given that he had to document everything, that wasn't much time.

But it was the best chance they were likely to get, so she just had to be fast and hope her calculations were correct.

She hadn't gone into all this detail when revealing her plan to Antonin. He was clearly already worried about their tense situation.

She didn't want to cause him to panic. Granted, right now that left *her* doing all the panicking, as she tried to speed-walk along the corridor, wanting to get on with her mission, without running and drawing attention.

It shouldn't be too hard to get through the house without anyone becoming suspicious.

She wasn't likely to encounter anyone until she got back to the living room, and if they started asking questions, she would just tell them she was helping Antonin move in, as she had promised to, then go about her business as quickly as she could.

She nodded to herself as she reaffirmed this plan in her head, trying to use it to calm herself down. I'm okay, I've got a plan...

The door ahead of her opened suddenly and Vladimir stepped out of the living room and walked towards her.

The panic was back instantly. She had never felt so trapped by the sight of her own father before, but now she felt as though guilt was written all over her and there was no way to get away.

And, at the back of her panicking mind, the still-thinking part of her brain realised that his sudden arrival meant her calculations were wrong and they had a lot less time than she had first thought.

That only made the panic worse. She stared at her approaching father with silent horror, which she hoped wasn't as obvious as it felt right now.

"Morning, Dariya, Dear!" Her father beamed at her, apparently oblivious to her terror. "What are you doing out here at breakfast time?"

The question seemed innocent, and his smile was still bright, but his eyes were suddenly hard and suspicious.

Was she not supposed to be here? She glanced around out of the corners of her eyes, trying not to be too obvious as she searched desperately for an excuse.

The rows of doors around them stared back at her impassively.

One door, identical to all the others yet known to her, threw up an excuse, and she blurted it out hastily.

"Just... Just showing Antonin where the bathroom is!" It was a poor excuse, but it was the only one she had.

Vladimir raised an eyebrow, "Wouldn't the one upstairs be more convenient?" he questioned.

His voice was calm and cool. He wasn't accusing her of anything. But the doubt was there, underpinning all of his questions.

She hated it. It made her feel as though he knew something.

"...It was occupied!" she answered him hastily again, before moving on, "Anyway, I better go and get started on the moving!"

Again, there was a slightly surprised look from her father. "You're not waiting for him?"

"He asked me to get started without him. I know where he was staying and where all his stuff is, so I can handle it," she answered.

"I see." Vladimir nodded and walked on, passing her by calmly.

Inwardly, Dariya breathed a sigh of relief. There, no more questions. She had finally satisfied him enough for this interrogation to end.

She began to walk away from him, heading out.

He stopped and spoke up behind her.

"In that case, I'll come along and help you," he told her in a friendly tone.

She froze, thankful that he couldn't see her face right now because this time she knew she couldn't hide her horror.

It wasn't an offer, in spite of his light tone. He was monitoring her now, and she would have to be quick to slip anything past him.

As his footsteps started to come towards her again, she forced her face out of its frozen rictus and into a smile.

"Good idea, thank you!" she trilled as innocently as possible, while behind her smile, her mind raced for a way to accomplish her task without him noticing.

"No problem," he answered sweetly, catching up to her and walking along with her.

The father-daughter duo walked along in relative silence to the hotel. Dariya wandered along awkwardly, hoping Vladimir didn't start asking her more questions, but he was mercifully quiet.

It didn't take them long to reach the place, make their excuses at the desk and hurry up to Antonin's room before any further questions were asked.

"Right," Vladimir began as they stepped into the room, "where do we start?"

Dariya crossed to the wardrobe.

"Clothes should be the easiest thing to move, right? Let's get them out of the way and come back for anything bigger or more awkward," she suggested, needing to locate Antonin's uniform as he had instructed her.

And, she realised suddenly as Vladimir nodded and moved to help her, she had to find it before her father did.

He had some strong opinions about the police. Namely that they should all be killed. He had gone into quite graphic detail on that subject many, many times.

Glancing down, she saw an empty travel bag at the bottom of the wardrobe and grabbed it, ready to shove anything incriminating - In her father's warped opinion, anyway - out of sight. Now she just had to find it...

A flash of light glinting off something gold caught her eye, and she lunged forward, catching hold of the source and checking to confirm her suspicions.

Yes, the light had been shining off his police badge.

She glanced at her father. He was lingering by the door, waiting to see if she needed help.

Thank God he hadn't charged in to 'help' regardless. She thrust the uniform into the bag and piled other clothes on top hastily until she couldn't cram anymore in.

"Alright, first load done!" She told him cheerfully.

"Do you want to run back home with this lot while I stay here and get more ready?" She suggested, hoping that would allow her to hide anything else that was 'suspicious' before he was back.

But Vladimir seemed to have something on his mind. He was staring at the floor as though he was transfixed.

"Hm... No, I think it'll be better if you go back, Sweetheart. I can handle things here."

Dariya knew there was no point in arguing with him. Even if the argument was over something seemingly trivial like this, it never ended well.

He insisted on things going his way, all the time.

She just had to hope that Antonin had been right, and all of his police stuff was with his uniform, safely stashed in the bag.

At least she had time to get these to him, so he could get to work while Vladimir was out of the picture.

She gave her father a quick nod and hurried out before he could say anything else and ruin her plans all over again.

He seemed to have a knack for completely screwing all her plans up. It was as though he knew what she was thinking, though she hoped he didn't, otherwise her days were numbered.

Pushing that rather grim thought away, she scurried back to the house and ran to her room. Inside, she threw down the bag and delved into it.

Tugging the uniform from the bottom, she fiddled with all the compartments on his belt and his pockets, checking all the equipment he had asked for was there.

When she realised it was, she sighed in relief. Somehow, she had managed it even with her father breathing down her neck.

Now she just had to get the stuff to Antonin. She grabbed another, smaller bag, this time from her own wardrobe, thrust it in, and headed downstairs.

Unlocking the door, she hurried down, hoping Antonin was alright.

Her plan must have been hard on him, leaving him shut in that horrible place, but it had been the only way she could think of keeping one of them able to access the evidence and getting the things they needed.

As she reached the bottom of the stairs, she heard him sigh in relief.

"You're back, great!" He smiled, thankful to see her and know the plan had worked.

"Here's your uniform." Dariya pulled it out and thrust it at him. "Everything's here. Now I better go again..." She added, thinking of her father rummaging through Antonin's belongings.

"Thanks!" He beamed gratefully, knowing how much he needed the tools that she had smuggled to him. "But why do you have to go back?" He frowned.

She had said everything was there, after all.

Dariya sighed.

"Papa asked what I was doing. I said I was helping you move. He insisted on helping, so I guess we're putting all your stuff in my room for now..."

Antonin shrugged. "Okay, I guess, if it keeps him from getting suspicious."

"I hope it will." Dariya nodded.

 "Good luck with your work," she called to him as she began to depart again.

He smiled, waving to her as she left, before he turned to the evidence and got started.

Dariya arrived back at the hotel a little too late, otherwise, she might have found her father's behaviour odd and become more alert.

Vladimir crossed the room to the wardrobe, stooped and picked something shiny off the floor.

He glowered at it as he turned it over in his hands, then pocketed it. Then he turned away from the wardrobe and began to look through the drawers instead.

It was only when he heard Dariya's hand on the door handle that he slammed the drawer he was looking through shut and hurried back to the wardrobe, continuing where she had left off.

So, she didn't see anything and entered a perfectly normal scene. No warning signs of what was to come.

The Attack

Vladimir and Dariya continued to work in silence. Dariya didn't speak for nervousness. Her mind was currently full of worries about Antonin.

She could only hope that he was able to get his work done with speed, but without drawing any attention from her siblings.

And then she was worried about what might happen afterwards. It would be a bittersweet victory.

Her father would be taken from her and would no doubt be full of anger, swearing vengeance.

He may even try to mobilise the rest of the family to enact that vengeance. But at least her own fate would finally be in her own hands. She could choose to travel and go where they couldn't hurt her.

Perhaps she would follow Antonin. They had only known each other for such a short time, but he had shown her more love and support than anyone else, and so she was growing very close to him, thinking of him almost as a brother of sorts.

After all, he had taught her that one could choose who was 'family', and she needed a better family than her own.

Vladimir's silence was different. He was distracted, deep in thought. There was something horribly wrong... He had worked so hard to build this city into something great that would serve his every need.

And now, at the heart of it, there was a festering infection.

He had been... Working on getting rid of the city's rather persistent police department for a little while, but he had decided to take his time, while they could still serve a purpose.

After all, *some* of them could be persuaded to be useful.

This was different. An outsider had barged in on his territory and threatened to take all his hard work away.

Of course, he had known for a long time of the Chief's plan to get other people involved. At the time, this had not worried him.

He'd thought he would easily identify the person as soon as they set foot in Yaroslavl. They would never survive.

That, of course, was the point. Someone whom he could easily identify and take down would no doubt throw a spanner in the operation against him.

The death of a police officer, made to look like an accident, would confuse the authorities and mean more paperwork for them to go through. Meanwhile, he'd be left alone.

It had very nearly worked. On the way into the hotel, he noticed the white spatter on the back of a car parked outside and nodded to himself.

It had added up neatly with the tip-off he had received from his 'friend' in the police department.

But his spy was clearly a coward. Too weighed down with doing things quietly and subtly, never actually getting their own hands dirty… They could have easily just given him Antonin's identity.

Instead, they had played games with him, marking a car, sneaking around, trying to draw the process out so they could demand more money from him.

That was hardly the point though. He could deal with them later. Antonin was his most pressing concern.

The man had crept into his operation, hidden the signs away and, most disgustingly of all, seduced his poor, innocent daughter.

He ground his teeth in frustration as he glanced over at Dariya.

Yes, that was it. His child had been treasured, carefully raised... She would never betray him; despite the stupid rumours he had heard. Instead, she had *been* betrayed.

That only added to Antonin's list of crimes. The first was being an outsider, a Muscovite in *his* city, the second was being a *police officer.*

He felt the badge he had discovered earlier, still sitting in his pocket, and wished that metal could tear, for he longed to destroy it. Police officers were always the enemy, for they would never understand why he was special, above their petty laws.

But the third crime was most serious.

Antonin was interfering with his family, the one thing that he needed most to achieve his goal, the warriors that would one day be the jewel in his crown... That was tainting something sacred to him. It was unforgivable.

He was pleased that he had, at last, caught the intruder, and that he had been the one to discover the badge.

Dariya wouldn't have to face Antonin's betrayal just yet, and when the time came, he would be there to reassure her. He could reiterate his lessons about not trusting outsiders...

But for now, he had to take the horrible little man down.

He let his fury take over and stormed out of the hotel room, determined to find Antonin, and put an end to his treachery before it harmed the family.

Mystified and alarmed by her father's sudden anger, Dariya abandoned her task too and hurried after him.

Antonin was hurrying too, moving quickly as he took fingerprints from the weapons he found with the corpses.

The knife wasn't the only one, after all. One body had a syringe shoved into the throat; another still had an axe embedded in the back...

He took prints for them all, vaguely wondering how many weapons these people had and why they had been so dumb to leave them with the bodies.

Unless this was some kind of weird shrine to their murderous nature... But that puzzle wasn't why he was here.

With the fingerprints recorded, he took his camera out and snapped some pictures to show what he had found.

He made sure to take some notes in his book as well, loathed as he was to record all the gory details, it was sadly necessary.

He double-checked the records, then stepped away from the bodies.

Shutting the door behind him, he decided to leave things as he had found them just in case someone came looking before he could get the records to the police station and start further action.

That meant he had to leave nothing out of place... He was hesitant to approach the machine Dariya had revealed earlier - Something about Vladimir's 'inventions' chilled him, even though they weren't against the law, and so technically weren't his business - But he had to.

He pulled the sheet over it hastily and walked away, watching the thing warily in case it did something.

When nothing terrible happened, he gave a small sigh of relief. It was over, his dealings in this creepy old basement with these frankly disturbed people were finally over. He could walk away, leaving the local police to arrest Vladimir.

And he would have made good his promise to Dariya, restoring her freedom.

So, he could go home and make good his promise to Nikolina as well. He was really missing her.

But the thought that all this was soon to be over lifted his spirits as he headed up the stairs.

He hadn't heard Dariya lock the door upon her second exit since her father - The only person likely to go down to the basement - Was out of the way.

He was glad she had thought of that. He didn't want to delay making his report any longer.

He slipped out and hurried through the house, hoping to avoid a collision with any of the Volkovs.

He was in luck; the corridor ahead was empty. He hurried through it and into the living room, which was also deserted.

Not much further now, he assured himself as he grabbed the handle of the hall door, pushing it open.

At the same time, Vladimir shoved the front door open and ran down the narrow entrance hall, rushing directly at him.

Bewildered and alarmed, he tried to move to the side, but the older man tackled him, pushing him to the ground with a thump.

He groaned, shutting his eyes briefly on the impact.

When he opened them again, he glanced past Vladimir's eyes, which hovered before his, burning with a white-hot rage, and saw a stunned Dariya standing in the doorway, staring at them.

His view of her began to blur, and it was only then that he realised Vladimir's hand was tightening around his throat.

Rescue?

Struggling to claw Vladimir's fingers away from his skin, Antonin could hear the other man laughing.

"You really thought you could stop me? You're going to die, and your pathetic police friends won't find your body. They never found the others!" He mocked.

Even though he was gasping for breath, Antonin kept face by cursing at the other man. Inside though, he was shaken up and scared.

How had Vladimir found out about his job? Did whatever corrupt police officer that was helping him work that fast, or had Dariya betrayed him?

He didn't like either idea one little bit, but right now, his main priority was living long enough to find the truth, and that was becoming a challenge in itself.

He was feeling very light-headed now, and breathing was a struggle.

He tried to focus, his eyes still blurred and his hearing seeming distant...

He could hear the faint sound of running footsteps. Air rushed past him. Air. That would be great right now.

He tugged at the hand around his throat weakly and tried to breathe, gasping loudly.

He could hear Vladimir's mocking tone of voice, but he could no longer focus on the words. Somewhere, a long way off, a series of clatters rang out.

The part of his mind that was still able to think through the dizziness and pain wondered what was happening.

The hand around his throat briefly relaxed, indicating confusion from his opponent too. But it wasn't enough for him to free himself.

Vladimir wouldn't allow himself to be distracted for long. Antonin swore internally. He had had one tiny chance, and he had missed it.

Now the man's grip seemed tighter than ever, and he couldn't hold out any longer. The light was starting to fade, his blurry vision leaving him altogether now.

The last thing he remembered was another sound, distant in his ringing ears...

BANG!

Dariya waited a few minutes and then nervously pushed the door open a crack, peeking through.

The fog had cleared now, and she could see them. Both men were slumped on the floor, showing no apparent signs of life.

Just as she had planned.

She finally walked out into the room and approached them.

Vladimir had collapsed on top of Antonin, and she stooped over them, taking her father by his arms and, with considerable effort, heaving him off the other man.

His lack of complaints, as well as the lack of comment from Antonin, confirmed her hopes. She had rendered them both unconscious.

She could feel her father's pulse under her fingers, and Antonin's chest was rising and falling gently, so she was reassured that they had at least survived the process.

Now she just had to decide what to do with them, and quickly, before any of her siblings responded to the explosion sound.

It had unfortunately been necessary. She had been at a loss to help Antonin without attracting her father's attention... Then she had remembered one of his 'experiments' that he had boasted about a while ago.

He had created a grenade that would render anyone nearby unconscious.

As soon as she had remembered that she had fled to his workshop, hearing his smug words about his daughter being 'safe now' ringing out behind her as he continued to battle with Antonin.

It hadn't taken her long to find the grenades, but she had been nervous to use them. Her father vastly overestimated his own intelligence, when in actual fact his 'inventions' often went wrong.

But it wasn't like she had a choice. She had to act now or lose her only hope at freedom and her first real friend at once.

So, she had secreted herself in the next room and thrown the grenade. Hiding behind the door so that it wouldn't affect her too, she'd hoped for the best. To her surprise, it had worked.

For the next part of her plan, she eventually decided on dragging her father to his own precious basement and leaving him.

It was easier said than done. He was heavier than he looked. In the end, she hauled him as far as the door, shoved him through and locked it.

No doubt when he woke up, he'd find a spare key, let himself out and then rampage around looking for whoever was to blame, but she hoped he wouldn't realise what had actually happened.

So, she left him there and returned to Antonin. When she got there, one of her brothers was standing over him with a bemused look.

"What happened to him? There was a bang..." he said.

Dariya smiled to herself. They had heard, but thankfully, they had sent Dmitri to investigate.

Dmitri was her favourite brother, a kind soul. But he wasn't the brightest spark, leaving him vulnerable to the others bossing him around.

She had always wanted to teach him to stand up to them but had been too nervous herself. But for once, she was grateful for his willingness to believe what he was told.

"He fainted. The bang was him falling," she lied.

"Oh... I hope he's okay," Dmitri replied.

"He will be, Dima," she assured him.

Accepting this with a nod, her brother trotted off dutifully, probably back to whoever had sent him. She looked down at Antonin.

It was probably not a good idea for him to be here when her father woke up. But how were they going to get anywhere else in time?

She couldn't exactly move very quickly if she had to drag him with her... Her only chance was the car.

Fortunately, her father kept the car keys on the living room table and let them all use it for whatever tasks he had given them.

*Un*fortunately, she couldn't legally drive. She hated to break the law, feeling it made her no better than her father.

But right now, her friend's life was in danger. And it wasn't as though she was going far.

Reluctantly, she grabbed the car keys from the table and pocketed them, before dragging Antonin to the hallway.

She paused to gather her strength and pulled him to the front door.

Opening it cautiously, she looked around for anyone who might see.

Two of her father's hired guards watched the front of the house with an air of boredom.

They were simply a showing off tactic, paid to boost the old man's ego even further. They never did any real work. No one around here would ever dare attack the house.

Fortunately, they were the only people around. She supposed she should have anticipated that. The locals tended to avoid this area if they could, just in case. And the guards were either paid well enough or disinterested enough to turn a blind eye to just about *anything.*

She finally could finally stop worrying about how suspicious she undoubtedly looked as she dragged Antonin's slumbering body out of the house and to the car.

She opened the back door, lifted his feet onto the seats and shoved him inside. It wasn't the careful and dignified way she would like her friend to be handled, but she didn't have much choice. She couldn't lift his entire body at once.

It wasn't as secure as she would have liked either, but she didn't have time to worry about that.

She slammed the door, jumped into the driver's seat, and took off, driving as fast as she dared, which was about thirty miles per hour.

It was fortunate that the local police station wasn't far away.

Aftermath

Waking up shirtless in the back of a strange car gave Antonin quite a jolt. The last thing he could remember was fighting with Vladimir... He rubbed his throat tentatively. It still hurt.

He must have passed out as the other man choked him, but what had happened since then?

Someone appeared to have taken off the baggy hooded jacket he had been wearing as a shirt, which was bad news because he had, in order to get the evidence past the Volkovs, resorted to bundling his uniform up underneath it.

For once, he had been grateful for the fact that his mother's 'care packages' always consisted of ill-fitting clothes. And his own lack of care when dressing, of course.

But his plan had failed, and his missing uniform still carried all of his important equipment, and so wherever it was - Presumably with his stolen shirt - The evidence was there too.

The obvious answer was Vladimir.

He must have stolen it while he was unconscious! That thought shook him to his core, though, because it meant Dariya had definitely betrayed him.

Vladimir could have uncovered his secret by complete accident, but he wouldn't know about the evidence without her input...

He'd thought he could trust her after all they had done together, but now he wished he had never believed that.

Though... If she had betrayed him, her plan seemed like a strange one. Why reveal all her secrets first?

She could have lied to him, he supposed. She admitted to being a practised liar... But the inner workings of Dariya's mind were a puzzle he would have to figure out later.

Right now, he faced a much more important problem - Where the hell was he and how was he going to get out of here?

Clearly, he was in the back of someone's car... They were probably taking him somewhere where he wouldn't be found.

Though it could be useful to know where they took their victims, he didn't fancy hanging around to find out.

Especially since there were two options: Either he was assumed to be dead after Vladimir attacked him, and they had searched him for anything important, then intended to dispose of his 'body' with a little more ceremony than they had the others, or they knew he was alive and were keeping him for some other, doubtlessly sinister reason.

Neither being disposed of nor being their prisoner appealed to him. So, he sat up and tried the obvious route out first, fiddling with the door.

It was locked, but fortunately, unlocked from the inside with the push of a button.

Well, if he was being kidnapped, that was a rather stupid oversight, he thought to himself, still smug about his escape.

He opened the door and climbed out of the car, only to see someone bearing down on him from across the car park.

His attacker was apparently wearing his own hoodie.

Whoever this person was, they must be responsible for his current situation. It was probably one of the Volkovs.

That thought made him freeze up for a moment, but he jolted himself out of it hastily.

There was no time to panic, he just had to run before they could reach him. There was no time.

Upon seeing him, they had begun to run towards him and were now nearly on top of him.

"What are you doing, idiot?! Get back in the damn car!" Dariya's familiar voice was amplified now as she screamed at him, trying to grab him.

He pulled away from her. "What the hell?! Why would I listen to *you?!*" he flung his words back at her accusingly, still stung by her betrayal.

He heard her gasp of shock before she managed to stifle it.

She seemed genuinely surprised. Perhaps she hadn't expected him to figure it out so quickly.

Then she pulled herself together, responding in anger rather than letting him see her shock and hurt.

"Why listen to me? Maybe because I'm the only one in this whole city who bothered to try and save your sorry ass!"

He snorted derisively. Oh, she was convincing, but hadn't she convinced him once before? Not this time.

"Save me? How is letting your psycho father choke me half to death, then stealing half my stuff and locking me in your car 'saving' me?!"

Her response to that was quick and decisive.

She slapped him, *hard.*

He'd never expected a small young woman to hit so hard, but there was a lot of emotion behind the blow, and it rocked him, stunning him into silence, despite his own anger.

It seemed to stun her, too. For a moment, she stood staring at the red mark she had left on his cheek. Then she turned away, blushing at the awkwardness of the situation, but still seething too.

"Just... Just get in the car and we can talk about this privately..." she muttered.

Antonin looked at her in disbelief. Like he was going to just get back into her car!

Then he looked around and it began to dawn on him where they were. They had been yelling at one another, about extremely private issues, in the middle of a public car park.

Which, he noted, seeing the building in the background for the first time, appeared to be the car park to Yaroslavl's Police Station.

Why would Dariya have brought him here if she had been kidnapping him on her father's behalf?

The voice of doubt slipped into his mind. Maybe she was worth listening to after all.

Silent and red with embarrassment that he had only just thought of this, he slipped back into the car through the still-open back door and sat down quietly.

Dariya took a breath, composing herself again, then opened the front door and sat in the driver's seat. Once both the doors were shut and they had both taken a few minutes, she finally spoke.

"I'm sorry I hit you. But you hurt me, not believing me. I really was trying to help..." she tried to explain.

Antonin nodded mournfully. She seemed as though she was on the verge of tears, and he regretted not stopping to listen to her sooner.

But in the heat of the moment, he had let his thoughts guide him.

Often, that worked. His quick-thinking and ability to jump to conclusions based on evidence made him a good policeman, but every once in a while, it went wrong.

He had jumped to the *wrong* conclusion, and let his emotions take over from there.

"I'm sorry too. I should have listened. I just couldn't understand what had happened to get me from fighting your father at your house, to being locked in the back of a car..." he admitted.

It was Dariya's turn to nod her understanding and realise she hadn't considered the other side either.

"I guess that would seem suspicious. But I promise I didn't mean you any harm!" she clarified.

"I see that now," Antonin agreed, feeling ready to trust her again now that he had calmed down and heard her out, "but at the time... I was hurt at the idea that you *might* do that. I felt we were friends."

Dariya turned in her seat and smiled at him. He was taken aback to see tears shining in her eyes. The whole ordeal had clearly upset her.

"We *are* friends!" she insisted passionately.

"And so, you helped me somehow?" he asked, touched that she would do that, but still confused as to exactly what had happened.

She wiped her eyes.

"Sorry, this has just been... A lot to deal with," she commented, before trying again, "anyway, yeah, I helped you. I had to. Papa was going to kill you! Fortunately, I used one of his inventions against him. Knock-out grenades. Put you both to sleep and shut him out of the way, then brought you here," she revealed.

She paused, then looked down and realised she was still wearing his hoodie.

"Oh! Yeah, I also handed your evidence in. I had to. Now that Papa's onto you, we don't have much time. It took me a while to find it, and I also needed a disguise," she gestured to the hoodie, the hood of which practically covered her face.

"My father probably has some low-level officers snooping around for him. I can't be seen around here. Besides, thanks to him, I'm a 'suspicious person' to most police officers. Thankfully, once I got in and got to see her, the Chief was very understanding. I explained everything."

"Wow..." Antonin murmured.

He hadn't expected her to go up against her own father, even indirectly, to save his life, let alone take the huge risk of continuing his job while he was decommissioned.

"Thank you! I mean it, thanks to you, we might still be able to pull this off!"

Dariya's eyes shone with joy this time. "I know right! And I saved your ass on top of that!"

Just as they started to laugh, she remembered something and instantly sobered up.

"...Seriously though, I wasn't being weird when I told you to get in the car. You're gonna want to keep a low profile and hope this case is finished soon. Pretty sure my father's not going to give up after one attempt on your life."

Antonin sighed.

"I guess every silver lining comes with a cloud. We'll just have to hope Chief Sunnikov can handle it. I'll find somewhere to lay low in case I'm needed again. I'm only going back to Moscow when Vladimir's safely in prison." He added determinedly.

"You might be here a while then. I'll find somewhere for you to stay," Dariya told him.

He nodded thoughtfully. He'd need somewhere to hide if Vladimir was looking for him, but he couldn't abandon the case altogether, not now he had been through so much and come so close.

Hiding Out

Antonin spent most of the rest of that day sitting in the car while Dariya took over. She drove to the hotel and checked him out, then took him somewhere else.

He wasn't entirely sure where it was, she just drove down some side roads. Endless twists and turns eventually led them to a large grey building.

It looked a lot like an abandoned warehouse.

Dariya stopped the car.

"Wait here, I have to check something," she told him, before getting out.

Time seemed to pass very slowly, and he began to wonder what she was doing. Why would she have to check something?

If it wasn't safe already, then why had she brought him here?

He had expected 'somewhere to lay low' to be another hotel or something, but the more he thought about it, the less sense it made.

The local hotels would be the first places Vladimir would look for him. No one was likely to look for him here. Even he didn't really know where 'here' was, after all. So, it was the perfect hiding spot.

But he still hated it. He hated hiding, acting like a fugitive when he was the one in the right.

And he was still confused by the nature of this place and what Dariya was preparing. He had to accept it though; he had to sit tight and wait for her because the Volkovs really did run this city.

They would hunt him down.

The only other place to go was home. But this wasn't over. It wouldn't be over until arrests were made and the case had been through court.

He couldn't abandon it now, even if he *was* in danger. So, he had to go along with whatever Dariya's plan was and hope it worked out for the best.

She soon re-emerged and nodded to him.

"It's alright, I just wanted to make sure the power still works. It's been abandoned for a while and I didn't want to leave you without power at all," she explained.

He could understand that. If he was going to have to be here for a while, he didn't want to be stuck in the dark all the time.

"And it's connected?" he checked.

"Yeah." She nodded again. "All connected. Lights still work. I checked the water in the toilet too, so you have that. I'll bring some food and bedding over when I get a chance."

Well, it looked like he was going to be living with just the essentials for a while...

He tried not to mind too much. In his current position, it was good of her to find him somewhere to live and provide for him at all. Especially after their recent argument.

"Thanks." He smiled as graciously as he could, finally getting out of the car. "I guess I'll go in and get settled. I'll see you... Whenever you can come," he added, feeling a little sad to be saying goodbye to her.

It would probably be the longest that he had been separated from her for the mission, and he had grown quite close to her by now.

Certainly, she seemed to be his only friend around here. But of course, she couldn't stay. Her family would ask awkward questions...

She appeared to understand, giving him a sad smile. "I'll try not to be too long. Stay safe!"

He watched her get back into the car and drive away before he went inside. His new safehouse was indeed an abandoned warehouse and so was pretty bare.

But at least he knew he was safe here. He also had the luxury of space. He could easily walk around inside, which was better than he had expected.

In a hotel, he would have probably been holed up in a single room for however long. True, a room would have provided more comfort than this huge expanse of empty space.

There really was nothing in here besides the damp on the walls, the tiny side room where there was a toilet and a tiny sink that was inhabited by a whole civilisation of spiders.

He turned on the strip lights. They were glaring, but he had had quite enough of being shut up in the dark after investigating Vladimir's dingy basement.

After that, he had exhausted the things that he could do, so he sat on the cold, hard ground and waited for Dariya's return.

While he waited, he reflected on his recent experiences.

The week had started so well, with his first-ever solo assignment and his proposal to Nikolina. It had been so full of potential and hope for the future.

He had seen himself and Lina doing well in their jobs, getting promotions, settling down together, and having kids.

Perhaps that was boring and predictable, but he was beginning to see that the adventurous life wasn't as much fun as it seemed in films.

It was certainly a lot more stressful and a lot more painful. He had been expecting blazing guns and wild car chases, out of which he would emerge - A fearless hero - unscathed.

He hadn't expected to be afraid for his life, hiding away like this, with bruises around his throat and dangerous people on his trail.

He wished he could go back home and immerse him in 'boring' paperwork with Ilya.

Or listen to Ekaterina and Sasha squabble while he tried to eat his breakfast. But most of all, he wished he could be with Nikolina.

He wanted to find out how her case went, what she was up to, what plans she had for their wedding.

But he still felt he had to be conscientious and finish the case he had started. Besides, Dariya had helped him out so much and was banking on him to help her out too.

He owed it to her to stay until she was free from her father's grasp, then... Well, then she could make her own life for herself, and he would just stay in touch, like a good friend.

When it came down to it, he realised, people didn't do dangerous jobs to be movie-style superheroes.

He wasn't a superhero, nor were any of the other cops he knew. Ilya did this kind of thing to take care of his kids, he was out here doing it to help Dariya and so that he could go back and start his own family.

Ordinary people, like him and Ilya, did dangerous jobs because they wanted to look out for their friends and families.

He smiled to himself, cheering up a little. Perhaps that was a better motivation, after all. Don't try to save the world, just focus on the bits of it that are worth saving.

These thoughts kept him in good spirits, even though he was in a pretty bleak situation at the moment.

And Dariya helped, for she was good to her word and returned the next day with a small portable stove, some provisions that he could prepare on it and some bedding.

She also brought news.

"Things aren't going too badly at the moment. I've managed to convince my father that he passed out during the fight, and I moved him so you couldn't attack him again. He doesn't suspect me. I also told him I didn't know what happened to you... I thought about saying you died, but then he'd want to see your body," she explained.

"Well, at least he doesn't hate you now as well. Though I take it he's still looking for me?" he responded, taking the news as a mixed blessing.

Dariya wasn't in danger, but he wasn't off the hook yet.

"Oh, yeah. He's practically obsessed with it. He's got loads of people out hunting you down. But you'll be safe here," she tried to reassure him after breaking that bit of unwelcome news.

"And it shouldn't be too long until he gets arrested..." Antonin cheered himself up with that thought.

Dariya looked a little sceptical. "I don't know, we haven't seen any signs of activity yet..."

"It won't be instant or obvious," Antonin told her, "but don't worry. It's bound to happen now. It's been coming for a while; all they needed was evidence. There's no way he'll get away this time."

The Traitor

Antonin's days ticked by in relative peace, if not boredom. Nothing seemed to be happening, which became very frustrating.

He had been through a lot to get to the point where the police could take Vladimir Volkov down and now, they were wasting time.

Frustration gave way to suspicion as time passed.

He was beginning to think that either something had gone wrong when he had recorded the evidence and Dariya had turned in it, or Yaroslavl's corruption problem went a lot further than he had realised.

He couldn't really do anything right now though. He was effectively a wanted man.

Dariya had warned him that going outside was bound to get him killed. So, he was stuck with nothing to do but wait, his frustration and suspicion growing by the day.

Dariya wasn't finding things any easier. She might not be stuck in an abandoned warehouse, fearing for her life, but she was stuck at home, listening to her father rant.

Vladimir had deployed most of his children to hunt for Antonin across the city, but Dariya was kept at home to 'help' him with plans that he had.

So far, she hadn't discovered the nature of his plans because he had spent the time ranting and raving. She just tuned most of it out, but it didn't stop him.

Currently, she was sitting at the dining table, eating lunch, while her father paced up and down the room, spitting fire.

"How dare that slimy little maggot come here and interfere with our business?! He lied to you just to spy on us!" He growled.

"I know..." Dariya sighed.

Her sigh was mostly one of boredom. She had heard this far too many times.

Vladimir, in his emotional state, mistook it for sadness and shook his head.

"I am so sorry, my dear, how were you supposed to know? To think, he could have destroyed all of us, if I hadn't accompanied you and saved you!"

She rolled her eyes while he wasn't looking. He was just using this as extra fuel for his stories about how brilliant he was and how she should just stay around him, where she would be safe, forever.

 It would just be another excuse for him to control her life. She could already hear him starting up again, his rants a familiar backtrack for her thoughts.

Eventually, she couldn't tune him out anymore and decided it was time to interject.

That could be a risky business, knowing his temper, but at this point, all she wanted was to shut him up.

"Papa, really, it's not as though any harm's been done. I expect all he did was run away. He's probably long gone by now," she tried to pacify him.

It was too much to hope that he would buy it and leave Antonin in peace, but if she was calm and tried to be the voice of reason, she might get beyond the ranting and find out how much he knew.

She had already uncovered how he had found out about Antonin's job, but she wanted to know all the details, just in case there was anything that could help her friend or at least keep him out of danger.

"No harm? My dear, naïve little Dariya," she gritted her teeth at her father's dramatic, patronising tone, "that man could have toppled my whole brilliant organisation and ruined everything! And I know he's still in town... I *will* find him."

With every word, he made her hate him more. But already, she was learning more unsettling but vital information. He knew Antonin was still in town. How?

The best way to uncover more seemed to be to make him think he had to explain the twisted-up workings of his mind to her.

When he had thought she 'didn't understand', he had inadvertently let something useful slip.

So, she wrinkled her brow at him, feigning confusion.

"How would he have done that? Anyway, there's no way to be sure that he's still around... Surely, he'd go back to Moscow?"

Vladimir seemed angry at the reminder of how his whole precious operation could have been destroyed.

"He broke into my workshop! He could have done so much damage!" he cried out in fury. "And of course, he's still creeping around here! His car's still at the hotel!"

Dariya stopped. She didn't want to make her father any crosser and risk endangering herself. If he suspected her, he'd surely kill her.

Besides, she had learnt a disturbing amount. Vladimir definitely had someone more powerful than she had suspected working for him.

She hadn't even known Antonin *had* a car here, but Vladimir had it under observation.

And how could he know about Antonin accessing the workshop? They hadn't broken in; it had all been done very neatly. He couldn't possibly know.

Unless...

Her heart skipped a beat as the thought crept into her brain. There *was* a way for him to know. If he had seen the evidence.

She could only think of two possible chances for him to have seen it. He could have looked while he had been fighting Antonin, but he had been focused on killing the other man and hadn't stopped to think or to search him.

The only other way for him to know would be if one of his spies was the person who she had entrusted their vital evidence to.

The one person Antonin had had any dealings with while he was in Yaroslavl, other than her. The one person who would know all the details of this entire case.

The Chief of Police.

It was a horrible thought, but it made too much sense. If her father had the Police Chief on his payroll, it would explain why no local case against any member of her family had ever stuck.

The police department always dropped them due to 'lack of evidence' before they made it any further.

But its current implications were much, much more serious. Her heart had leapt into her mouth.

She *had* to go to Antonin and tell him about her suspicion right now. If she was working for Vladimir, then he was in more danger than they had realised.

Her father had access to more information than they realised. And he had someone in his organisation who could easily dispose of their precious evidence, waste all their arduous work and destroy Antonin's case.

Without a case to help him get rid of Vladimir, Antonin had nothing to potentially protect him from the wrath of the Volkov family.

Increasingly dark thoughts swirled in Dariya's stricken mind, and she knew she had to act now if she wanted to help her only friend survive.

"I see." She nodded to her father, just so he was placated with an answer of some kind before she hurried away.

"Anyway, I better go check how things are out in the city," she quickly came up with an excuse.

It wasn't a great one, but he often sent her to check on his territory, so it worked well enough.

"Yes, yes," Vladimir nodded, "you do that. I have to work on my plans. Now that he's violated my space, I'll need to move the workshop somewhere more secret... And make some kind of space to keep difficult customers like him, so they don't escape in future..."

He was muttering away to himself now, planning things out, so Dariya could take her chance and slipped away.

It only took her a few moments to reach Antonin's hideout, and she hurried inside. He only needed to glance up and see her grave expression to know something was very wrong.

He jumped up off the floor and hurried over to her.

"What? What is it?!" he demanded to know.

"My father knows more than he should. I think someone powerful is collaborating with him!" She got straight to the point.

He bit his lip, looking nervous. "How powerful?" he questioned.

"The Chief of Police..." she admitted to her suspicions.

Antonin lapsed into shocked silence as he considered Dariya's suggestion and its terrifying implications. They had given all their evidence to Sunnikov. She had been the one to bring him here…

So, surely, she couldn't be spying for Vladimir Volkov? He would have known more, and much sooner.

But then again, how *had* Vladimir found him out? Sunnikov had been the only person in Yaroslavl's police force who had known his true identity…

Dariya must be right! How hadn't he realised this before? He had been so stupid and reckless, in his desperation to solve the case.

He had forgotten about his own safety.

Now the case was bound to be compromised. Sunnikov would have all the information and evidence.

Every blasted file. She could destroy it all!

He visibly paled.

"You're serious? Th... I have to get out of here!" He looked around in a panic, checking for anything he might need to take with him.

"Get out of here? Why? You're still safe..."

"This isn't about me! She'll destroy the evidence! I have to go to someone higher up! If I go home, Ilya will help me, I'm sure," he explained.

"Ilya?"

"The Chief in Moscow. He sent me here at her request, but that was clearly some kind of trap, so she could get rid of any evidence against your father, then pass the blame to another department. But if I speak to him before she can, then he'll know how to stop her. I can't, obviously, she outranks me..." he reasoned.

"How are you going to get to Moscow before she can do anything? She's had the evidence for days now. You still have to travel one hundred and seventy-three miles without getting murdered by my crazy family!" Dariya seemed flustered by the idea.

Antonin looked determined. "We'll just have to get there as quickly as we can. It's not like I have a choice. I can't let her do this."

"We?" Dariya frowned, confused by his sudden use of the plural pronoun.

"Well, I can't leave you here! You'll be in danger. Doesn't she know that you helped me?" he insisted.

She shook her head, "I told her everything I had to, but I kept my disguise on, and I didn't tell her my name..."

"But she told me to target you because they suspected you would help me," he revealed, still concerned about her.

She shrugged. "They can't prove anything, and I know how to play my father by now. I'll get away with it. Besides, if we both vanish, it'll be more suspicious, and they'll definitely come after us. This way, they'll come after you and I'll try to distract and disrupt as much as I can."

He nodded. "I see..." he felt a little sad about that.

He had hoped he could help her out of her, away from her insane family, before everything got a whole lot worse. But he had to focus on his mission.

"Then I'll appreciate any help you can give me. Best to get ready to go now..." he replied, knowing that he would have to be ready to leave.

His only chance to save this case was to move faster than Sunnikov.

Escaping Yaroslavl

Antonin left when darkness fell that evening, hoping that the night would provide him with some cover so that he wouldn't be spotted.

Again, Dariya came to his assistance.

She waited until the search had stopped for the day and all of her siblings had returned home, then threw as much of Antonin's stuff as she could, as well as one or two other items she hoped would help him, into a big bag and slipped out of the house.

She had hoped using one of her own bags rather than his would avert suspicion, but she needn't have worried.

The others seemed distracted. They were 'making progress reports' to her father, which seemed to consist of arguing over who had got closest to finding Antonin.

Knowing them, this argument would keep them occupied until Vladimir got bored and told them to shut up.

He enjoyed watching his children squabble for his attention, so she probably had at least an hour.

She pulled a hood over her head as she left the house, trying to cover her face as much as she could.

She never knew where her father's spies were these days. He was expanding his powerbase, intimidating, or bribing people into reporting everything that happened in the city directly to him.

She had to be careful. So, she stuck to the shadows and walked quickly, heading down to the hotel where Antonin had briefly stayed.

The car was parked at the roadside outside. She stopped by it and glanced around.

No one seemed to be watching. She took his keys from her pocket and let herself into the vehicle, dumping the bag in the passenger seat.

Soon, she pulled up outside the warehouse-cum-hideout and honked the horn three times.

Antonin had been waiting for this. They had planned out his departure carefully, to try and minimise the danger.

After all, the entire mission depended on him making it back to Moscow, alive and on time. They were both pinning their hopes on this.

He hurried out of the building and met her at the driver's door, ready to swap places and leave.

She climbed out and pulled her hood down to face him, fighting tears. Here was her first real friend, a man more like a brother to her than any of her real brothers had ever been.

And she had to say goodbye and leave his fate in the hands of God because he had risked his life to help her.

She felt she should say something and searched for words that wouldn't make her cry.

"I... I got as much of your stuff as I could. Sorry if I missed anything."

She focused on the practicalities, the packing and preparing, because, as her father had always taught her, her emotions made her weak.

She had never considered him so stupid as she did now.

Antonin seemed upset too.

"You did everything you could," he told her, his voice wobbling slightly.

She got the impression he was talking about far more than the packing.

She nodded. "Right, I did. I added some stuff too. Things I think might help you if they come after you."

"And those are?"

He was curious now, welcoming a distraction from their goodbyes, as well as any help he could get.

"You have a few knock-out grenades, an x-ray gun that should show you if anyone's hiding nearby, waiting to hurt you, and a radio that's on the frequency we use, so you can hear your pursuers talking to one another. They're at the top of the bag. Please use them if you need them!" She explained, hoping he would take her help. It would at least give her a little more peace of mind.

Antonin nodded solemnly, recognising what she had done just to try and keep him safe. Stealing from her father to help him was a grave risk.

Being here with him was enough of a risk. But she hadn't hidden away from the danger.

He risked a small smile as he stooped to plant a chaste kiss on her cheek.

"Thank you. For everything. I'll stay safe, I promise."

This time, Dariya gave in and let her tears fall as she stepped aside to let him leave.

"Good luck then," was her final goodbye.

He got into the car and shut the door, winding the window down and calling to her, "I could say the same to you. Stay safe."

With that, he pulled away and slammed his foot to the floor, determined to be out of Yaroslavl before the Volkovs came looking for him again.

This was, after all, his one chance to make his escape, and so he finally got to use the 'getaway' car's potential power.

Dariya watched until the car disappeared around a bend at the end of the road, then dried her eyes, pulled her hood up again, and walked away.

She wanted to get home again before she was missed.

The journey was short and soon, she stepped back through the front door. The familiar sound of arguing already attacked her.

Her siblings were still fighting it out in the living room. Ignoring their raised voices, she headed for the stairs. Time alone, hidden in her bedroom, was what she needed right now.

But as she got her foot to the bottom step, she heard the house phone ringing loudly. She hesitated.

The only people who usually called the house were Vladimir's spies. At the moment, he was focusing his intelligence resources on hunting down Antonin.

That information alone told her she should wait and try to listen in, in case she could learn something about her friend's safety.

Quietly, she snuck off the staircase and to the door, standing behind it tensely as she strained to hear.

The first sound was her father's voice, raised over the ringtone.

"Shut up, everyone! This could be important!" Then the phone abruptly ceased its ringing as he snatched it up.

"Yes? Who is it?!"

There was silence now and Dariya silently cursed. Why couldn't he be using speakerphone or something? Of course, that would be too easy...

"I see." she heard him speak up again after a while, sounding grave.

A clicking sound followed, and she guessed that he had put the phone down. Well, that was short and to the point.

But then her father didn't waste time with small talk when it came to the important stuff. All he wanted was his information.

She was about to leave when she heard him speak again, this time in anger.

"You've all failed!" he yelled at his children, "that little rat has got away from us! His car is gone!"

How on Earth had someone noticed so quickly? She had been careful, she had checked, no one had watched her, she was sure of that...

He really *must* have agents everywhere, who had been checking up on the car regularly. In which case, she had been lucky *not* to have been seen.

It was frightening news for Antonin though. The sooner her father knew he had escaped from Yaroslavl, the sooner the chase would start.

"What are you fools staring at? Get out there and find him!" She heard her father roar.

It was already beginning.

Dmitri and The Chase

Perhaps he was paranoid, but Antonin kept glancing in his mirror to see if anyone was behind him for any length of time as he sped back to Moscow.

Most of the time, there wasn't anyone close to him. He wasn't too surprised by that. He was technically speeding, after all. But it was an emergency, he reasoned to himself.

No sooner had he thought that than he looked back and noticed a familiar car pulling into the gap behind him.

His blood ran cold. It was the Volkovs' car, the very same that Dariya had rescued him in. But he could already tell that it wasn't her driving.

He slammed his foot to the floor, pushing his car even harder, but his pursuer kept up with him determinedly.

Cursing, he tried to think. He had to get rid of them somehow because he still had over a hundred miles to go, and they were right on his tail.

Out of the corner of his eye, he saw movement in his mirror. Looking back, he spotted someone leaning out of the passenger's window of the chasing car. It was a man with a gun.

He was trying to aim it towards Antonin's back window.

Somehow, he doubted this was just an idle threat.

His heart was in his mouth now, but still, he waited.

He had thought of a plan now, but he had to wait until the right moment if he wanted to avoid the bullet. Swerving sharply across the road, he heard the gun fire behind him.

This time, he didn't dare look back, he simply prayed that he had timed his dodge correctly.

Someone shouted obscenities from behind him at about the same time as a stray bullet whizzed by. He had been lucky this time.

He knew, though, that it wouldn't be the last shot, and that dodging like that was a dangerous game to keep playing.

He was going to need another play if he was going to make it back to Moscow.

He thought of the presents Dariya had brought him. Would they help him at a time like this?

He knew there was someone behind him, he didn't need help figuring that out and he doubted they were bothering with radio communication at a time like this. That left the possibility of stunning them.

It was risky, on a public road. If it worked, it would cause a crash. But if it failed, he wasn't likely to survive.

Still steering with one hand, driving erratically now, he unzipped his bag and reached inside, groping in the dark to try and find a knock-out grenade without taking his eyes off the road ahead.

His hand grabbed onto something, and he pulled it out, taking a quick glance down to confirm his suspicions. He had the grenade ready.

He fumbled with the window, opening it just in time to hear another bullet whizz by. That sound made him feel giddy with excitement and nerves.

He was in the heart of a deadly situation now.

Would he last long enough to throw his grenade, the only weapon he had, his only hope of getting back to Moscow alive?

Dariya lay on her bed in silence, listening to her own depressing thoughts. She knew two of her siblings had taken the car and some weapons.

They had gone after Antonin.

Even if he had been going hell for leather, there was no way he would have got far enough before they had left.

They had his car's registration plate memorised and were horribly determined to hunt him down.

So, there would be a chase and eventually, there would be a fight.

It would be a fight to the death at this point because there was no room for discussion with killing machines, which was what most of her siblings had been raised to be.

And all she could do was lay and pray that Antonin would somehow come out on top, even though he was up against two heavily armed, half-crazed killers and he was one man, armed with nothing remotely deadly and too given to compassion for a ruthless showdown.

She knew what all this added up to: Her only friend would die. Her cruel blood relatives would kill the kindest family member she had ever had.

And, with no transportation and no allies, she had no way to save him.

Tears welled up in her eyes and she lay there numbly, making no effort to dry them. They poured over her cheeks as she began to weep.

She wept for Antonin first, then for his family.

In this, she included the fiancée he had spoken of, a woman who would have dreamt of a wedding, only to have it snatched from her.

She included herself too, someone who had become so close to him in such a short space of time but would never see him again now. There was no one else. He hadn't mentioned any real family.

Then she found she was crying more for herself because she had messed everything up. She had begged him, selfishly, to give her a better life.

True, he might have intervened because of his job, even if she hadn't been there, but what she should have done was stop him from doing that by scaring him away somehow.

She hadn't, though, because she hadn't been able to face being a prisoner in her father's city, forced to go along with his twisted regime, forever.

So, she had first betrayed her family, as her father would put it. This was apparently the worst of crimes.

Then she had lured a young man to his death. That was something she felt far worse about.

Even her attempt to help him had been wrong. She thought she was helping him when she turned over the evidence, but she had helped her father's spy instead.

And now her friend was gone. So was her chance to get out of here.

Now she was crying hard, practically sobbing. In her current state, she didn't fully realise that until Dmitri stuck his head around the door and stared at her.

"You okay there, Sis? I heard you crying..."

She tensed. This meant trouble. If her family noticed, they would start asking questions and wouldn't accept her answers unless they were suitably awkward for her.

After all, they had been raised not to believe in emotions and to treat everyone with suspicion.

Apart from Papa Dearest, who was clearly an angel.

She stopped herself there.

Why was she thinking like this? With most of her family members, cynicism and bitterness were normal and justified, but this was Dmitri, her cheerful, sweet little brother.

He somehow seemed to have resisted this lesson and remained innocent, just wanting to help his whole family.

The others looked down on him for that. But he didn't mind. He just trusted his family's judgement.

Through her sadness, an idea snuck. She sat up.

"Come in and shut the door."

Antonin took a deep breath and threw the grenade out of his window, hoping to at least get it close enough to the car behind to knock the shooter and their driver unconscious.

Hopefully, if their window was still open, it would be possible for the knock-out gas to be released into the car.

The grenade spun from his grip and into the road, landing with a crack. He cursed. It had missed the car. They'd probably not be affected now.

But, to his surprise and relief, the driver rode straight over the grenade and a piece of the metal casing snapped off, sinking into their tyre with a loud **BANG!**

The car veered off the road, out of control from the sudden loss of a tyre at such a high speed.

He stopped looking after that. It was enough that they were off his tail. He didn't want to hang about and see if they survived or not.

Instead, he urged his vehicle on. The rest of the journey, though long, seemed to speed by peacefully now that he was free from the attacks of the Volkovs.

Soon, he was driving past the Moscow signs, and he breathed out, sighing in relief. It was okay, he had made it home.

Everything might just be alright after all.

Big News

Antonin drove into the familiar car park at the Moscow police station, stopped the car and took a moment to relax. It was finally over.

Then he sprang into action again. The nightmare trip might be over, and he may be out of immediate danger, but the mission wasn't over yet. He had to find Ilya and expose Sunnikov.

Jumping out of the car, he hurried inside, barging past colleagues, ignoring them as they called out to him.

He felt a little bad, but he didn't have time for small talk yet. Later, he would catch up with everyone. Now, he needed Ilya's help.

He strode down the corridor to the Chief's office and shoved his way inside.

He wouldn't normally barge in on Ilya like this, but time wasn't on his side, and he had to expose Sunnikov before she could destroy his carefully gathered evidence.

Ilya looked up from his paperwork with a grim expression and gasped.

"Antonin! What are you doing here?!" He seemed confused.

That's right, Antonin remembered suddenly, his return wasn't 'official'. Ilya hadn't been expecting him.

But he didn't have time to notify him, and he certainly didn't have time to explain everything right now.

"I need your help!" he blurted out.

"What with?" Ilya's confusion was only growing worse as Antonin spoke.

The younger man pulled the door shut behind him. He couldn't be too careful. Then he finally began to explain how his trip had gone and why he needed Ilya's help.

His boss simply sat and listened, open-mouthed. He had expected a complicated case, but nothing like this.

What could he do? If everything Antonin was telling him was true, he would have to start a federal investigation...

The key was if it was true. He'd have to prove it if there was going to be that kind of investigation.

"That all sounds... Insane, frankly. But do you have any proof?"

"Of the part with the Volkovs, yes. Well, I did. I handed it over to Sunnikov and only realised she must be spying later. But I don't have any proof that she is..." Antonin sighed as he trailed off.

This was it, then. Even Ilya wouldn't believe him, or if he did, he couldn't do anything. They had lost, after all this. He had fought so hard just to be here, and it had all been for nothing.

Ilya paused for thought. There might not be much he could do, without proof, but he trusted Antonin's word on this.

Besides, the man was clearly distressed. *Something* was wrong.

Perhaps he could encourage an investigation without actually accusing her... The idea made him smile and he turned to Antonin to share the good news.

"Well, I can't accuse her of misconduct without evidence, but I can suggest a review of her department. After all, if she got us involved, she obviously doesn't trust her own team, so she should have opened a review anyway. But I'm guessing she wanted to shift blame, not draw attention to herself. I didn't suggest a review sooner because she was an old friend, but it might be necessary after all," he explained, considering the facts as he spoke.

Antonin still looked unconvinced. "Will that be quick enough? She could still get rid of the evidence..."

"The department's activities will be frozen under review and she'll be being watched. I doubt she'll be able to get rid of the evidence in those circumstances," Ilya told him calmly. "Which will mean that the reviewers will learn about the case, and it'll be suspicious if anything should happen afterwards."

"And you can definitely make this happen?" Antonin sought further reassurance, not wanting to fail at this crucial stage.

"Of course. You leave it to me," Ilya assured him with a great deal more confidence than he actually had.

He could tell Antonin wouldn't stop worrying unless he convinced him, but it wasn't up to him.

It depended on whether he could persuade the regulating bodies an investigation was necessary. And persuade them in time.

Dariya waited until Dmitri had followed her instructions and shut the door, leaving the two of them alone, then spoke to him.

"Can you keep a secret for me, Dima?"

"Sure." He shrugged, not seeing the importance of this.

She gave him a hard stare. She couldn't gamble with this if he wasn't going to take it seriously.

"I mean it. You can't tell *anyone.*"

"No one at all?" He checked.

"No one." She shook her head firmly.

He considered this in silence for a moment or two.

Dariya was a little bit surprised by that. She hadn't expected her happy-go-lucky little brother to give it much thought. Perhaps she had underestimated him.

That could be a good thing or a terrible thing, depending on his response. She waited, without much patience.

After a while, his answer came as he nodded slowly.

"Alright, I'll keep it a secret for you. What is it?"

"I'm worried about Antonin," she began to confide in him.

"After everything he did to you?" He wrinkled his brow in confusion, and she sighed. He had fallen for their father's lies.

He had told endless tales of Antonin being evil.

"He didn't do anything to me. He tried to help me!" She told him.

It might be a mistake to pour her heart out like this, but she wasn't sure she could keep quiet anymore. Hiding from her family all the time was becoming a strain. Besides, Dmitri was harmless.

She began to explain the truth about her and Antonin to him, backtracking to the start, when they had first met, and explaining everything.

He listened attentively and finally spoke up when she stopped.

"I see... So, you wanted to run away from home?" He sounded sad now and she felt a stab of guilt.

"Not home as much as Papa," she admitted.

He fell silent again, before finally muttering, "so I'm not the only one... I've always felt he was the reason why... Why the others bully me, you know."

She heard him sniffle and felt worse.

Dmitri always seemed so happy, but she had reduced him to sadness now. Or perhaps he had always been sad, secretly. He had just hidden behind smiles.

She put her arms around him.

"I know... I'm sorry I can't do anything."

"It's not your fault... It's always so hopeless here," he murmured as he rested against her.

"That's why I wanted to leave. But then I saw things differently. I thought Antonin could help... But now he's gone, and I can't do anything to protect him," she revealed her thoughts to him.

He looked up at her again and managed to smile through his tears. "Maybe he can help, if we find him again and protect him."

That was what she had hoped too. Maybe her plan would work.

"I'm not sure I can go... Papa would notice." she bit her lip, nervous and guilty.

Pushing him to go was cruel. It put him in terrible danger. But he wouldn't be noticed as much, so he was her only chance to get away with this.

He seemed to follow her thoughts, reading between the lines in a way that made her question his 'dumb' act again.

"But he wouldn't notice if I went. I can get a train to Moscow and try to find him before the others do."

"And you'll do that? Even though it's dangerous?" she asked him hopefully.

"It's not like I have anything better to do," he admitted, "This way, at least I can try and do some good!" He cheered up a bit.

She returned his smile, trying to cheer up herself, as she helped him get ready to go. No one noticed him slip away from the house. No one questioned it.

Antonin was also oblivious to the help Dariya was sending his way. He had found something far more important to do. And, for once in a while, it wasn't related to his case.

No, now he had been assured that he could leave that in Ilya's hands, he had something else on his mind.

Nikolina.

He grabbed his stuff from the car and hurried back to her house, letting himself in. It was quiet inside, there didn't seem to be anyone about downstairs, so he went up to her room to look for her.

Peering around the door, he spotted her, sat on the bed with her back to him. She appeared to be engrossed in writing.

Well, that was typical. She always was a bit of a workaholic.

He smiled fondly, then decided to let her know he was back. It was about time, after all. It had been too long since he had seen her.

"Lina?" he called to her.

She dropped her notebook and jumped up, whirling around to face him in one swift moment.

"Antonin!!" she ran over to him and threw her arms around him enthusiastically.

He caught her in his arms, laughing.

"Miss me that much?"

"Of course!"

"I missed you too, babe! But look, I'm back. Didn't I tell you I'd get back alright?" He was so relieved to be back and holding again that he couldn't help but gloat.

"You did. But that is not the point. The point is that you are home, safe and sound. Now we can start planning our wedding, right?" She suggested.

Antonin nodded.

"We definitely need to work on that. But let's catch up first, while I unpack," he suggested, finally, reluctantly pulling away from her and turning to the huge bag that he had dumped in the doorway.

"That is not the bag you left with." She pointed out.

"I know. I got into some trouble and a friend helped me out. It's her bag," he explained.

"That was good of her. What trouble were you in?" She pressed.

He sighed. She wasn't going to like the explanation, but equally, she wouldn't stop asking until she had heard it.

"It's a long story, Lina, I'll explain later, okay? I don't want to have to repeat it for everyone. Where *is* everyone, anyway? Quietest it's been here for ages..." He changed the subject.

"Oh, well, Papa is at work, of course, and so is Sasha. He got another case, so he is enjoying work again, thank goodness. I think Katya is at college, but with her, you never know," she explained.

He nodded. That made sense. Everything seemed normal here. And after the week he had had, that was a welcome relief.

"And what about your work? How did your case go?" He continued to question her as he opened his bag and began to pull out the devices Dariya had given him.

"I won!" She smiled.

"I have had a few cases since, as well. It is going pretty we- - What on Earth are those?!" she stopped in her tracks, staring at the things he was holding.

"Oh, that's great!" He smiled back at her, then followed her gaze to what he was holding.

Currently, it was one of the x-ray devices Dariya had given him.

"Oh, this is something my friend gave me to help on my mission," he explained, "Let me show you..." He pointed it at her, ignoring her startled expression as he pulled the trigger.

She was about to demand an explanation when he turned the display screen so they could both see.

"Then it shows an x-ray, se---" He cut himself off, having spotted something.

Nikolina was staring at the screen too. She turned to him in shock as she saw what he had seen. Then they were suddenly hugging again, tears of pure joy pouring down their cheeks.

This was turning out to be Antonin's best day for a while, though he really hadn't expected to learn he was going to be a father from one of Vladimir Volkov's weird toys.

Things at the Volkov house weren't quite so cheerful and they were certainly having a harder time forgetting about Antonin's mission.

The two Volkov agents who had failed to catch him had, after a long traipse at the side of the road, arguing all the way, returned home with nothing more to show for their mission than a few minor injuries.

As a result, a furious Vladimir had called another 'emergency meeting' to rant about 'the Antonin problem', as he called it.

Dariya was there, standing at the back reluctantly and hoping no one noticed Dmitri's absence.

She still had her fingers crossed that everything was going well for him. The return of her very annoyed and mildly injured siblings had been a relief, but what else was going on in his life right now?

It surely wouldn't be that simple to escape her obsessive, vengeful father...

Her father was talking.

"Right, since we didn't catch him while he was on the run, we'll need to track him down. Vadim? I asked you to do some research on him. Don't you let me down as well."

The young man in question shook his head nervously.

"No, I found some stuff! I got his phone number and an address. It's not his though. Apparently, he lives with his girlfriend."

Someone interrupted at this point, confused.

"I thought Dariya was his girlfriend?"

Vladimir took over again now, having found another reason to hate Antonin.

"Clearly, the slimy little rat was two-timing her! And this little 'girlfriend' was probably in on it... What do you know about her?!"

Dariya flinched. He had found another innocent person to drag into it. Now Antonin's fiancée was a target too.

Vadim started talking again.

"Her name's Nikolina Moroz. Apparently, she's the Moscow Police Chief's daughter..."

"Great, *another* damn cop! Put Moroz and his family on the hit list too, would you?"

This wasn't a request.

Dariya tuned out at this point, mostly due to panic. What could she do now? A whole family were in danger because of her! She had to find a way to warn them before anything happened.

She couldn't use Dmitri this time. He had already left. Besides, he was just protection, he wasn't meant to get directly involved with Antonin and his family.

That would be too risky. If he got discovered, their father wouldn't hesitate to cut him down as well.

But now her father was talking about sending some more killers to Moscow to take these people out and while they would be slowed down by train travel - Since the car had been the major casualty of Antonin's escape - They would find their targets unsuspecting and unarmed.

She had to do something. The only option was to contact Antonin directly.

She elbowed a sister aside and slipped through the crowd of siblings until she was standing behind Vadim, able to see the phone number scrawled on his notebook.

It was a long shot, of course. She didn't see any context, only a number. Which she would have to remember.

But she had to try, didn't she?

With that thought, she slipped through the crowd, heading determinedly to the phone.

It was time to take some direct action again before an innocent family were all murdered.

The Call And The Wedding

The phone ringing interrupted Antonin's attempt to catch up with his girlfriend. He sighed and reluctantly pulled away from her.

"I better answer that," he said.

Nikolina nodded, "I guess so."

She did her best to understand. He was busy.

But she had missed him so much, lying awake worrying about him at night. Now he was home, safe, and to top it all off, she had just learnt that she was carrying his baby.

Yet still, they couldn't spend any time together.

She tried not to mind too much though because work was important to her, and she knew his job was important to him too.

So, she sat there and waited for his attention to come back to her, putting her hand to her stomach as she waited.

The news had been sudden and hard to process, but of course, it was a good thing. They would finally have a family of their own...

While his girlfriend was deep in thought, Antonin picked up the phone and hesitated. He didn't know who was calling or what to say.

He didn't get a chance to speak as Dariya's voice piped up as soon as he answered, coming across quickly and panicked.

"It's me, Dariya. Sorry, I don't have time to explain how I got this number or time to talk. I just hope you're there and you got home safely. But you're in danger again, you, your girlfriend, and her whole family too. All of you need to get out of there! Go into hiding or something, change your names, whatever you need to do!"

For a moment, he was completely overwhelmed. Then he shook his head disbelievingly. No, they couldn't be in danger, not now.

All that was behind him. Ilya was tying up the loose ends of the case and then he and Nikolina would move on to live happily ever after.

After all, after such a delightful day, how could he believe otherwise?

"Dariya, calm down. I'm sure it's not that bad," he tried to assure her.

"Not that bad? Please, listen to me! They've found your address, and some people are coming to kill you, her, and anyone else they can find!" She practically yelled at him.

He froze up. Suddenly, it all seemed real again. He could picture the Volkovs bursting into the house with guns.

Nikolina's face rose up in his mind. He couldn't let them do this to her.

"I... I see. Thank you for letting me know. I have to do something, fast! My fiancée did nothing to them, I can't let them kill her and our child!"

He thought aloud as he tried to come up with a plan.

"She's pregnant?!" Dariya's surprise was evident.

"Yeah. We just found out," he told her.

"Damn... On any other occasion, I'd offer you my congratulations, but right now all I can say is keep your family safe. I've sent what help I can, but I don't know if it'll be enough."

"We'll have to see what we can do," Antonin agreed, "don't worry, I'll think of something," was his last reassurance before he hung up.

He had planning to do.

Well, his top priority was Nikolina. Not only was she the love of his life, but she was carrying his child. He had to protect her.

He also had to make good his promise to her. Yes, that should be the first thing, to marry her. Then if they killed him, he would at least die knowing he had fulfilled his promise. And she would be taken care of as a widow, allowing her to provide for their child.

But he probably didn't have much time to do this. The wedding plans would have to be dispensed with, and it would have to be done as quickly as possible instead.

On the other hand, that wouldn't be that difficult. Nikolina was on good terms with the local priest, and he would probably agree to do a ceremony. They'd just need a witness.

That meant involving someone else at short notice. Where was he going to find someone to drag in?

Ekaterina sauntered into the house casually and waved at him.

"Hey, you're back and you didn't die, nice going!"

"Thanks. What are you doing this afternoon?" He got straight to the point.

She gave him an odd look. "Why? You better not be trying to two-time my sister!"

He laughed. "No, no. I need someone to come to our wedding."

"That's *today?* Damn, you two move *fast.* Sure." She shrugged.

And that was why she was the perfect person to ask. She wouldn't ask awkward questions.

Nikolina, on the other hand, might be harder to persuade.

So, he settled for just sticking his head around the bedroom door and calling, "Hey, Lina, call that priest guy you know, will you? We're getting married this afternoon!" then running off before she could question it.

He had somehow managed to play that off a lot more casually than he had expected, given that he felt like screaming the whole time.

There were a few more things he had to plan for, of course, he had to make sure Ilya sent someone to handle the case and he wanted to leave something behind for his child in case something happened to him.

There was also the matter of Dariya and what would become of her if the case against her father failed.

He was worried about her, but he wasn't sure how to help her.

He would have to put together a to-do list of things to handle after the wedding.

 Get married, make sure everything and everyone important was taken care of... Then it would be fine to go on the run if he had to, without worrying that he was abandoning anyone.

That seemed like the best way to distract them and lure them away from his family, after all.

The other option was taking them with him and there was no safe way to do that. No, he would have to run for it.

And if going on the run wasn't enough to throw the Volkovs off the scent... At least he would die knowing he had done what he could to protect the family.

These thoughts were still running through his mind that afternoon when he met Katya and Nikolina at the church.

Somehow, despite the short notice and her obvious confusion, Nikolina had acquired herself a white dress. Katya had also dressed up.

Antonin hadn't bothered too much. His shirt was clean, and he had put a tie on, but he hadn't had time to acquire a full suit.

This would have to do.

Still avoiding his bride's questions, he made his way into the church and tried to hold back tears as he said his vows.

Putting into words what Nikolina meant to him somehow made the threat of losing her so much more real.

He heard Katya making 'eww' sounds in the background, the priest tutting at her and a camera clicking as the church's resident photographer for such occasions took a picture, but he wasn't thinking about any of that.

He just pulled his new wife into his arms and held on tight, knowing this might be the last time he held her.

Preparation

The night after the wedding, Antonin didn't sleep much.

This wasn't because he was enjoying his honeymoon, either.

Instead, he sat up in Ilya's living room, trying to take care of everything he needed to do. He didn't know how much time he had.

He wasn't sure where to start though. He had opened a notebook but couldn't think of a word to write. If he died, what might the ones he had left behind need to know?

There was only one person he could think of to ask for advice at a time like this.

He just hoped she would be able to answer, that she wasn't asleep or with someone she couldn't talk around.

He dialled the number Dariya had called him from before and waited as it rang.

"Hello?" Her voice spoke to him tentatively through the darkness.

"Can you talk?" he asked, double-checking before he told her anything important.

"Of course," she confirmed.

"Well... I need some advice. If... If anything should happen, what do my family need to know to stay safe?"

She didn't answer for a moment.

"I hope it doesn't come to this, but..." there was another moment of silence, and he tensed, wondering what she would say, "tell them about me and how to find me. I'll help them."

Antonin was confused now. "Won't coming to you put them *and* you in danger?"

"Perhaps it will, but I didn't help you as much as I could have done because I was afraid to stand up to my father. But now... He's pushing me too far. I'm going to raise a rebellion against him. Any loved one of yours who ever needs my help will find it, I promise you. And if I fail, I'll leave them a diary or something to explain everything," she told him, suddenly full of strength and fire.

Her words worried him a little. It was hard to picture sweet, kind Dariya leading an army. And it was bound to put her life on the line.

"Rebellion? What are you talking about?"

"He says it's time I had children again. And he's going to try some weird age acceleration on them, so they'll be 'useful' sooner. Well, if he's going to weaponize my children, I'll come right back at him and raise them to hate his guts. A whole new generation can easily overthrow him," she explained.

He could hear the bitterness in her tone. It made him nervous. It wasn't like the soft, kind Dariya he had known.

He was beginning to suspect that somewhere beneath that persona lurked a warrior.

Vladimir didn't know what he had got himself in for when he had screwed up his daughter.

"Well... I wish you luck with that. And you'll be there for my family if anything happens?" He steered the conversation back to his original point.

"Absolutely. But warn them: Don't trust my father. He'll try and trick them," she told him.

He nodded. "Thanks for the heads-up. I can give them a little more preparation now..."

Then he lingered. The conversation had reached its natural end but now neither of them wanted to go.

Eventually, she sighed. "It's late. I should go... I miss you."

"I miss you too. Stay safe," he replied.

She didn't answer, she didn't return that comment. She couldn't because she knew he wasn't going to be safe.

She hung up the phone and lay on her bed, not sleeping.

Antonin put his phone down and began to write carefully. The first thing he felt he had to do was to write something for his child.

If he died, he would never get to meet them.

They deserved to know why that was, but he knew if something happened to him, Nikolina would be too heartbroken to explain things properly, even if she figured them out for herself.

Which was why he hadn't told her about the danger he was in yet. She had worried enough last time when he had left for his mission.

He didn't want her to go back to worrying again as soon as he had got back. No, he would tell her another time.

But when it came to his child, he would feel guilty not addressing the issue personally.

Nikolina had had time with him, she had memories, and he hoped they would have more time together. His child had nothing, and if he couldn't return, they would never know the truth.

But if the diary was found... Then they would be in danger. He had to be careful here, in case, if the worst-case scenario occurred, he was dead and the Volkovs were in control.

Dariya had promised her help, though.

He didn't like to do this. It felt like he was incriminating her, but she would be the best person to guide his child through something difficult like this.

He wrote out a message with her address, just to be sure.

Now what? Nikolina... Would Nikolina get involved?

He had a feeling she would hide away.

That was her usual response to things that upset her. She never spoke of her mother's death, for example.

That was why he worried their child wouldn't get any support from her and would need Dariya's help.

Would she give the child the diary though? He hadn't thought of that problem and now, it bothered him.

He would have to find someone who would. Ekaterina, possibly.

She didn't know the truth, but she had helped him without question before, and unlike her other relatives, she wouldn't be intrigued enough to look inside, so she would probably be the safest person to entrust it to.

Still, though, it hurt him too much to consider not leaving Nikolina something to remember him by.

Perhaps he should leave her something special, and a little carefully hidden advice as well, just in case she took things differently than he expected. Just in case she decided to get revenge upon the Volkovs.

He knew how to do that. It would fulfil another promise.

When he had started dabbling in music, he had promised to write her a love song. Now, he could leave it for her and if he managed to get out of this situation alive, he would sing it for her one day.

If not, he would leave a secret message encoded in the music. He was sure he could do that if he thought about it.

It would be safe from prying eyes, and this way, even in her grief, she would be sure to keep it. A note, she would throw away, but not a gift.

He sat up the rest of the night, writing until he had got the perfect song to express his feelings, as well as acting Dariya's advice to warn her about Vladimir.

In the early hours of the morning, he scribbled another note and slipped it, with the diary, under Ekaterina's door.

He could only hope she would keep it to herself.

Now he was ready. He wouldn't be leaving any loose ends if anything happened to him now.

All he had to do was wait for the Volkovs to attack, so he could lure them away from his unsuspecting family.

The Volkovs Invade

The attack began a little while before dawn. Antonin had sat up, lying in wait. He didn't want to be unprepared.

Thankfully, everyone else was asleep, out of harm's way.

The house had been silent all night and it was beginning to get to him as he sat at the living room table tensely, but eventually, the silence was broken by the twinkling sound of shattering glass.

They had broken the kitchen window, he guessed, focusing on where the sound had come from.

He jumped up and ran to the kitchen, checking his pocket for knock-out grenades as he did so.

There were only two left. He had to be careful now. They were the only serious weapon he had on him. No doubt his attackers were much better equipped.

Even after that thought, he headed towards the danger because it was better to face them than let them sneak up on him, or worse, sneak up on his family.

He was just outside the kitchen door when he froze. He could hear them talking. Perhaps if he listened, they would say something that might give him an idea of their plan.

"Right, so we're looking for Jelennski... And there's some girl?" Someone checked in a rather confused voice.

"Yes!" A fed-up voice responded, "But we might as well just get rid of everyone here. There's some other copper here as well."

"So, where are they?" the first voice asked.

"They're not going to be awake right now, are they? Let's go upstairs..."

Antonin cursed internally. He hadn't heard anything useful and now they were heading this way. He'd have to engage them now to stop them getting to the stairs.

He stepped into the doorway.

"What the hell do you think you're doing?!" he demanded to know, hoping to stop them in their tracks.

The two men exchanged glances, then one of them hissed to the other.

"That's him, get him!"

The bigger man rushed at him, while the second moved his hand down to his belt as if to pull out a weapon.

Now Antonin didn't keep his curses in his head, swearing loudly as he turned and broke into a run, sprinting through the house.

He heard footsteps behind him and hoped they were both following him. Dangerous as that was, if one of them stayed behind then his plan had failed.

Then a gunshot rang through the night.

He ducked down, sliding beneath the living room table as the bullet whizzed over it.

Standing up on the other side, he saw it stuck in the wall at exactly the right height to have hit the back of his head. He was lucky he had fast reactions.

Running towards the door, he thought he heard someone move upstairs and prayed his pursuers hadn't heard anything as he grabbed the door handle and pulled it open, dashing out into the night.

It wasn't until he reached the corner of the street that he dared to glance back and saw them both running at him.

Now there wasn't just one gun pointing at him.

Well... Wasn't this what he had wanted?

He had got them away from the house and he was certainly getting an 'adventure' fleeing from them.

He just wished he had a proper weapon and that he had hung onto his getaway car.

But he hadn't, so he was just going to have to rely on fast running and dumb luck. Which didn't give him great chances against two angry, armed mobsters.

It was a pretty desperate situation, but he had to hope he was quicker and smarter than them. Otherwise, he was dead.

Nikolina lay completely still in her bed for a few minutes, trying to decide if she had heard anything or not. It could have been a dream...

But there was still something, some background sound she couldn't quite place running through the house.

Perhaps it was just someone moving about. Antonin hadn't come to bed yet, after all. She had wondered about that.

He hadn't seemed himself today. It had been a happy occasion, of course, but her usually bubbly husband had been distant.

It made her question if she had done something to upset him, somehow. But if that was the case, then why on Earth had he married her?

He had been quite insistent that, instead of planning a beautiful wedding with their friends and families, they get married that afternoon in a sudden, secret ceremony.

And she had gone along with it, despite her dislike of spontaneity, because their relationship was more important to her than one day being perfectly planned.

Then he seemed to be upset with her about something. She didn't understand any of this. Something wasn---

That time, there was *definitely* a noise. A sharp, sinister one, like a gun going off. It rang through the house.

She froze up.

What should she do? What was happening? Her husband...

Was in danger. It came to her suddenly. How had she not seen this before?

After everything he had told her about his mission, he had then started behaving strangely and now, something had happened to him.

Well, she wasn't going to lie here any longer and leave him like that! She jumped out of bed and ran.

She charged into her father's room first, because she wanted to save Antonin, but if someone down there had a weapon, her father was more likely to be able to defend against them than she was. Even when panicking, she had to be practical.

Ilya was, unfortunately, a very deep sleeper though and she charged into his room, only to have to shake him awake, uncomfortably conscious that while she was trying to rouse him, there was something else going on.

A door slammed.

"Papa, wake up!!" she screamed at him in frustration, feeling her fear mounting.

She needed his help *now!*

Ilya rolled over and squinted at her through half-open eyes.

"Wha'?"

"Something's happening! Antonin's gone and I heard a gun, and I don't know what's happening!!" she babbled.

And suddenly, he somehow seemed to be fully awake, pulling himself out of bed.

"Alright, sweetheart, calm down. I'll check it out." He opened his bedside drawer and pulled out a taser.

She took a breath and tried to compose herself.

"I... I'm going to come with you," she nodded after a moment.

He gave her a sharp look, which was slightly spoilt by the fact he was still in his pyjamas.

"Are you sure that's wise? I don't want you in danger."

"My *husband* is in danger," she pointed out, equally sharp.

He sighed. She was a little *too* like him sometimes.

"Very well, but stay behind me," he commanded.

She didn't argue. That was why she had wanted him there. Because she wanted to save Antonin, but she didn't feel that brave on her own.

He took the lead and headed downstairs, brandishing his taser in front of him. But everything was quiet now and no one was around.

"Well, darling, I think maybe--"

Ilya was about to cast doubt on whether she had heard anything, after all, when he saw something embedded in the wall.

A bullet.

He paled visibly and a concerned Nikolina followed his gaze. He heard her gasp and fought to reassure her, despite his own rising worry.

"Now, don't panic, dear. I'll... I'll call for back-up, and we'll find out what's going on here..."

Nikolina paused again, pulling herself together and thinking as quickly as she could. Her jaw set determinedly; she nodded to him.

"Right, you stay here and do that." She headed for the door.

"Where are you going?!" Ilya seemed startled that she would contemplate leaving in this kind of dangerous situation.

"To find my husband, of course," she answered coolly.

She knew it was dangerous; she knew it was foolish, but right now, all that mattered was that she was there for him when she needed him.

Even if it meant they would die together.

Fighting to The Death

Antonin kept running, though it was getting harder to breathe and he could hear his own heartbeat pounding through his head.

It wasn't like he had a choice. He couldn't stop or he'd die.

The trouble was he wasn't sure how much longer he could keep running. It was getting harder and harder to keep going and the Volkovs were gaining on him.

He looked around for a way to escape, desperately hunting for anything that would give him the upper hand.

But he had dragged them out onto the edge of the city again, trying to avoid putting anyone else in danger.

Here, there was nothing but sleepy suburban streets. No one else would suffer.

But he couldn't see how this would help *him.*

Well, maybe he had run far enough now. He had got them away from any innocent bystanders. That was good enough. Besides, he couldn't go much further.

He'd have to grab his grenades and take his chances. It might work, after all. And if not... Well, he wasn't afraid to die.

He had made sure he didn't have any unfinished business. He could take the hit without feeling, in his last moments, that he had left regrets.

Making peace with himself with that thought, he stopped running, ducking into an alleyway instead.

It was a dead-end, but it was cover enough to keep him safe while he tried to find his weapons.

Closing his eyes, he slipped a hand into one pocket and drew out a grenade. Pulling out the pin, he threw it around the corner. Then he lay back against the wall, waiting for his pulse to calm down and things to go quiet before he checked to see if it had worked.

He heard a clatter, something rolling and then a splash. Then some shouting:

"Hey, what happened? Where did he go?!"

"He's in the alleyway, idiot. Didn't you see that? He's trying to attack us with grenades. Stupid guy can't throw right, but he rolled one down the gutter. It's the drain now, so that might blow up his precious city!" Someone snorted.

Damn! Antonin cursed in his head. How had he forgotten that the gutter was there, and the drain was open?

Granted, it wouldn't blow up, it not being a proper grenade, but it meant he only had one weapon left and they knew where he was hiding.

He fumbled with the other one, trying to pull it out as their running footsteps hurtled towards him.

The two men skidded around the corner, and both raised the guns at the same time. He was cornered, but the grenade was still in his hand.

He watched them carefully, trying to gauge whether or not he would get away with moving.

The movement would be swift and brief, a second long - That was all it would take to throw the grenade.

But how quick were their reactions? Were they watching him as closely as he was watching them? Would he get away with it?

He didn't have a choice, so he pulled the pin back with one finger, under the cover of his sleeve. It was time to find out how lucky he was.

Ilya watched his daughter walk away with a growing sense of helplessness. He couldn't bring himself to stop her, though he knew she would be in danger if she followed him.

He wanted to protect her, but he couldn't stop her from being with her husband in his hour of need, could he?

Besides, there was something more important he could do for Antonin.

There was still the case against the Volkovs to attend to and he could take fingerprints from the broken window to prove that they were involved here.

More evidence. Not that it would be of much use if he didn't get rid of Sunnikov. But now he had greater grounds to do so. The case wasn't just in her area anymore. It was a federal matter.

He waited for his team to arrive and take the fingerprints, ignoring their questioning looks. He knew they were all curious about this.

Not just the fact that a crime had happened in his house, but where and how he lived in general.

He kept things at work very professional, but now they had the chance to snoop.

He let them. He had bigger priorities.

He had to push for that investigation now, even if it was ridiculously early in the morning. The situation had become urgent.

He grabbed the phone and made some calls to some powerful people. The responses were generally disgruntled, due to the time, but changed very quickly when he explained the gravity of the situation.

It seemed as though they were ready to listen, after all. Sunnikov's downfall may be beginning.

Nikolina stepped out into the cold dark morning and looked around carefully. Where would Antonin have gone if he was under attack?

She tried to think like him, and it came to her in a flash. Away from the city centre, into the suburbs. He wouldn't have wanted to put anyone in danger.

Was that what this had all been about?

Keeping other people safe while he was at risk? It was very typical of him and very noble, but she couldn't help but feel it was stupid.

He had put himself in danger. If he had just told her, she would have...

Done what?

She could have told her father, who probably already knew since he had known about the mission in the first place. And he would have done what he was already doing: the best he could do if he followed all the rules.

And right now, even with her own legalistic outlook, following the rules seemed stupid too. Someone was in danger!

She couldn't have done anything if he had told her. She wasn't sure she could do anything now.

But she decided as she set off determinedly towards the nearest suburbs, she was going anyway because she had to try.

After a few yards, she thought of Antonin again and broke into a run. The sooner she reached him, the better she would feel.

Even if she couldn't do anything, she'd be there to reassure him. If they had to, they could run away together, somewhere where these Volkov people would never find them.

She was running through the suburban streets when she saw something fly from an alleyway.

It whizzed over the wall on the opposite side of the road and vanished, out of sight. Still, that was unusual... She supposed she should investigate.

It might have something to do with Antonin's disappearance, after all.

Antonin stared in horror as his last remaining weapon whizzed over the heads of his attackers and flew across the street.

He heard them start sniggering.

"You really thought that would work?" One sneered at him disdainfully.

He didn't bother with a reply. There wasn't really any point.

"Well, it didn't, did it?" The man continued.

He rolled his eyes. Even when he had him cornered and was holding a gun, he was making stupid comments to try to goad him. What was the point?

He wouldn't play that game, anyway.

He wasn't wasting his precious time talking when he could look for a chance - Any last chance - To get away again.

His gaze fell on a stone in the alleyway... Okay, that was a long shot and probably a stupid idea, especially after the grenade tactic had proven he couldn't throw well enough to do this.

Did he have another choice?

He dodged to the side, bending down, and seizing the stone.

"Stop right there!" One of his attackers shouted at him. "I see you, plotting! You're not getting away this time. Now stay still, put your hands up!"

Cornered, Antonin dropped his new makeshift weapon. He couldn't see any way out of this.

True, they were going to shoot him anyway, he was fairly sure of that, but if he didn't provoke them, maybe another opportunity would come up...

That was how it worked in the movies, wasn't it? The hero would get a second chance. But this was real life. How likely was this to work out?

The investigation started that same day, much to Ilya's surprise. He had expected red tape and formal meetings.

But he supposed this seemed more serious now that someone of his rank had been attacked in his own home, by people connected to the case Sunnikov was supposed to have handled by now.

Meeting with the investigators in his office, he explained the situation from the beginning.

"One of my officers helped on the case and has assured me he's put together sufficient evidence. Now I have more and I'm really not sure why this case isn't closed yet..." He left that sentence dangling, waiting for an answer.

The answer came crackling through his phone, which was on speaker. Sunnikov hadn't been able to attend the meeting in person due to distance, but she was quite indignant.

"We're working on it!"

One of the inspectors looked sceptical, before questioning, "Why is it taking longer? With the evidence in place, the first stage of arrests should be starting..." he pointed out.

"Perhaps federal assistance is required?" Ilya suggested innocently.

"No!" Sunnikov's answer was sharp and sudden. She realised this and cleared her throat, regaining her composure.

"No, that's not necessary," she added, in a calmer tone.

Another investigator cut in.

"Nevertheless, this is now a federal matter. The case is clearly becoming too complicated for you to handle. You will transfer the case files to us."

Ilya heard Sunnikov's angry intake of breath.

Then there was a long silence, before she admitted, "I'm afraid I can't do that..."

"Why not?!"

Now the first inspector to speak did so again, instantly suspicious.

"There was a fire. We lost some files," she replied.

The excuse sounded well-rehearsed, but it fell flat.

"Hm... We'll have to open an investigation then."

Ilya smiled to himself. He had won. Well, nearly... The evidence had gone. Antonin had been right about that.

But while Sunnikov might have been faster than him, she wasn't going to get away with this.

He sighed softly as the inspectors left his office. It was a mixed victory.

He had put her in place, but she had helped the Volkovs get away with most of their crimes. And Antonin was still in danger... So was his daughter.

That thought prayed on his mind. But at least he had the new evidence from his house.

He might get rid of the two attackers from the Volkov ranks, at the very least.

His muddled-up thoughts were suddenly interrupted by Sunnikov, who still hadn't hung up.

"I thought I called on you to *help* me, Ilya, not make things difficult," she told him accusingly.

"Olya, you and I may be old friends, but I won't ignore corruption. I know you're on Volkov's payroll. You called me to shift the blame and now you're bitter that you failed," he answered her calmly, presenting the facts.

"That's slander, you know," she fired back, "You don't have any proof."

"And you have proof that there was a fire? Photos of the damage, records from the fire department to back you up, that kind of thing?" he suggested, suspecting she wouldn't have thought that far.

He remembered Olya Sunnikov as a clever woman, but one who thought too fast, never stopping to check that she had all her stories lined up.

He was hoping like hell that she hadn't changed.

There was a pause. He grinned. She hadn't. Her old failings were still standing in her way.

"Alright, I did it! Can you blame me for wanting just a little bit more money? The department is hardly well-funded, since we're not some huge, important city," She snapped back at him, sarcastic and annoyed.

"I had the perfect plan to get all the funding I needed. If I sacrificed some pawn and sold the information to Volkov, he'd pay me pretty well. Then I could extort him, and he'd keep paying me..." she was ranting about her plan now, but he had tuned out.

Eventually, he heard her whine:

"Ilya? Are you still there? You're not going to make trouble, are you? We're supposed to be friends..."

He shook his head. "Friends hold one another accountable. This conversation has been recorded. Goodbye, Olya."

He hung up the phone as she began to yell at him and sauntered after the investigators.

He had a feeling that they would want to talk to him some more.

Oblivious to her father's successes, Nikolina was still waiting in terror for her senses to come back.

Because she knew she had to be in that alleyway. But she didn't have the courage to go in there if she was risking seeing Antonin in a dangerous situation...

She shut her eyes and tried to convince herself to go.

It was only a few steps; she could do this. Then she would be with her husband again and if he was hurt or in danger, she could try her absolute best to help him.

Then she heard a horribly familiar sound.

The chilling bang that she had heard ring out in the house echoed through the street.

Still unable to move, not daring to open her eyes, she heard footsteps running away from the scene and prayed they were Antonin's, though the pessimistic voice in her head highly doubted that that was the case.

The End Of A Life

Time suddenly sped up again and Nikolina opened her eyes. Until that moment, everything seemed to have stood still from when she had heard the shot.

But life poured back into her world as the frozen chill of shock was replaced with panicked realisation.

She ran into the alleyway and dropped to her knees beside her bleeding husband, tears springing to her eyes.

"No, no... Antonin!!" she yelled out desperately, her voice coming out shaky and strained as she tried to speak to him, mostly just to work out if he could hear her or not.

There was an open wound in his chest, blood spilling out. He was as white as a ghost.

She squeezed her eyes shut again, not wanting to look, not wanting to believe it was real.

But it was. She had got there too late... Okay, so she couldn't have saved him, but she would rather die with him than see him like this.

He didn't manage to answer her, but stirred in her arms, making her jump. She felt for his wrist, checking for a pulse.

There was something there... Perhaps she hadn't been too late after all. She could still get help for him.

Except they were far away from the city hospital, he was barely alive, and she didn't have a phone on her.

The brief flicker of hope his movement had given her hope to fight with the sense of despair she had been feeling since she had first seen the bullet in the wall at home.

Things had got crazy, out of her control, but maybe she could finally do something.

Trying to pull herself together, she took deep breaths until the sobbing stopped then got to her feet and ran again, hurtling into the street and knocking on the nearest door as hard as she could.

It was still early, just getting light, and the man that opened the door was still in his pyjamas. He stood and stared at her in silence.

She could understand that. She must look pretty insane right now, with tear-stained cheeks and bedhead, dressed in her nightdress that was soaked with her husband's blood and stained with dirt from where she had fallen to the ground.

Now wasn't the best time to think about that though. She had to act *now.*

"Please, you have to call an ambulance, my husband's been shot!!" she blurted it out, her shaky voice threatening to betray her and make her start crying again.

"Someone's been shot?!"

That woke him up. He seemed incredulous now.

"Yes, in the alley... He's still alive but he needs help, quickly!" she tried to explain the situation and plead with him at the same time.

He nodded. "I'll be right back!" he ran inside, leaving her standing there.

She stood on his doorstep in the chilly morning air, waiting impatiently. A few moments later, a woman emerged. She gave her a sympathetic look.

"Now, love, I know you've had a bad shock, but I'm a nurse. You need to take me to your husband, okay? I'll do what I can to keep him stable until the ambulance gets here. My husband is on the phone now," she explained gently.

Normally, Nikolina took herself very seriously and would bristle at her patronising tone.

But right now, feeling as broken as she did, she took comfort in the other woman's calm, gentle demeanour.

Trying to relax, she mustered a nod and led her helper back into the alleyway.

She stood well back as the nurse approached Antonin.

After her initial moment with him after she found him, she was suddenly afraid to get close to him again, in case this time, her previous fear was true and there was no movement or pulse.

She couldn't do it, and she knew she couldn't. She wasn't ready to lose him. She wasn't ready to accept his death.

Perhaps it would have been easier if the memories of their wedding weren't still fresh in her mind, or if she wasn't pregnant with their child.

But it probably wouldn't.

Regardless of all that, she loved him too much to let go.

Yet cruel fate didn't give her a choice.

She remembered - Would always remember - Standing in the freezing morning air and feeling the numb emptiness of heartbreak creep over her as the woman stood up and turned to face her, pale as a sheet.

"He's dead," she said bluntly.

That was it. That was all she remembered. She didn't know how she got back home that morning.

She didn't know what she did that day. Her mind just kept going back to that one moment, replaying it repeatedly.

If it hadn't replayed so many times in her head, she probably wouldn't have believed it. How could this have happened?

Antonin was young and bright, with his whole life ahead of him. He was getting on well at work and had just started a family.

People like that didn't die. Death was something that happened to the old and the sick.

The whole thing seemed totally surreal to her. She didn't know how to process it. In the end, she came to a painful but necessary conclusion.

Her husband had been murdered. She was in danger. Their child was in danger.

She took everything Antonin had left and stuffed it back into his big travel bag that he had only just unpacked.

She packed a bag of her own as well. Everything was ready.

But, out of love and respect for her late husband, she waited until the day of the funeral. It was a small, quiet event.

They didn't want to attract any unwanted guests. Herself, her family, and Antonin's family - Who had flown back especially and still looked shell-shocked by the whole thing - Were the only attendees.

No one spoke to her.

Her family knew she had pretty much withdrawn from the world and seemed to be respecting her decision on that, whatever they thought about it.

They had the decency to let her grieve her way, though Katya kept shooting her odd looks. She did her best to ignore that.

Antonin's parents avoided her too.

They seemed awkward about the whole thing. Probably because he had lived with her because they were never around.

And now it was too late. Perhaps they were guilty. She would understand that.

Or perhaps it was the fact that they hadn't met her before, even though she and Antonin had been married.

Whatever the reason, she had no desire to go and break the ice. For one thing, she felt awkward about the situation too.

Besides, she felt watched.

She had felt that way ever since his death. Perhaps she was being paranoid, but if not, she didn't want to risk putting them in danger as well.

So, the funeral took place in relative silence. It being a small event, it was over pretty quickly anyway.

But she lingered at his graveside for a while afterwards, while her father walked across the graveyard, talking soberly to Antonin's parents about the legal case against his killers.

Her siblings stood around behind her awkwardly, waiting for her, but eventually, they drifted away too.

She stood there a moment longer, finding it hard to leave. She had never been good at goodbyes.

Then she turned and walked away, determined to leave all this behind her, forever. It was too painful a memory and too dangerous a life.

Dariya's World After Antonin

Following a little way behind the grieving family felt a little uncomfortable, as though she was stalking them, but Dariya didn't want to intrude.

This was their time of grief, the last thing they needed were strangers showing up, crashing the event.

Besides, her very face meant she wasn't welcome here. She couldn't blame anyone for that. But even so, she was here because she owed it to her best friend.

She had first heard about his death when her brothers came home gloating. She had listened impassively because to cry would be to draw attention to herself.

But she had slipped away while the others were celebrating and caught a train to Moscow. She felt she had to be there.

So, what if they noticed her absence? At a time like this, it hardly mattered, did it?

Besides, she could always come up with a cover story. Dmitri was sure to help her.

He had met her at the station, awkward in her presence because he thought she would blame him for not being able to protect Antonin.

But, as she had assured him, it wasn't his fault that the rest of their family thought it was okay to murder an innocent man.

Now, she and her brother walked silently between the gravestones, lingering behind the official mourners.

No one paid them any heed. Dressed all in black, they looked like they were meant to be here.

Yet, she kept her distance, not intruding. But she did glance over to Antonin's grave across the field, her eyes watering as she did. She felt Dmitri take her hand to comfort her and squeezed his hand gratefully as she shut her eyes and let the tears fall.

When she opened her eyes again, she wiped away the last of her tears with the back of her hand and tried to compose herself.

It was over. Her first friendship was over and so was her first real chance at escaping the life her father had made for her.

The part of her life when she had felt the most alive was over.

She blinked away fresh tears and took one last look over at Antonin's final resting place. Most of the other mourners had moved on now, but one woman lingered.

She guessed this was his lover. Seeing her there was almost as heart-breaking as their loss.

The poor woman had lost her husband and now she was left with an unborn child to raise and a massive target over her head.

She wondered if she ought to offer her help. She was in a tricky situation, after all, and she had promised Antonin that she would take care of his loved ones if she could.

But she faltered, her legs not wanting to move towards the other woman, and she realised she was scared, scared that she didn't fit in in this different world and scared that she wasn't welcome, that she was everything that the other would hate right now.

Not just because of her family, but because their lives were worlds apart.

It had been easy to talk to Antonin, to trust him and grow close to him, in her world, on her terms. This was different. She didn't belong here.

Besides, if she was needed, Antonin had left instructions to find her. She had done what she could, or at least what she dared.

She turned to Dmitri.

"We should leave..." she murmured softly.

He shrugged and walked off, pulling her with him. She realised it didn't matter to him. He was just there for her sake.

But it felt harder for her to walk away, knowing what she was leaving behind her.

On the long journey back to Yaroslavl, neither she nor Dmitri said much. Her brother didn't seem to want to disturb her, and she had a lot on her mind.

For one, she was reflecting on the past. Everything that had happened with Antonin had left her even more disgusted by her father's actions than before, but it had also taken an emotional toll on her.

She didn't feel like herself anymore and the constant act at home was getting harder to keep up with.

There was no question of leaving though. She would be looked for... Besides, she had an obligation.

The first of the next generation of the Volkovs were beginning to be created.

She wasn't their mother, not really, but they would know her as such, and she didn't feel as though she could leave them in that situation. Especially not with her father in the picture.

That led her back to her plan for rebellion and the future. She was sure that eventually, her children would be her father's downfall.

She certainly hoped so.

But perhaps now that he had left them with that final message, Antonin's family would play a part as well. She wondered vaguely if their children would ever meet and what they would be like...

She would do her best to guide them together into as strong a force for good as possible, but with her father giving her children 'added strengths' and the legacy of Antonin's death there to motivate his child.

She wasn't entirely sure they were going to need her help. Still, she would always be there if they did.

But she knew if things got out of hand much sooner, before the next generation was ready to take on Vladimir, then she would have to turn elsewhere for allies.

Of course, she had Dmitri, who had proved surprisingly loyal to her, despite their father's influence.

And perhaps Antonin's wife would seek her out.

She hadn't been strong enough to reach out to the other woman that day, but if she came seeking help or even just vengeance for her husband, Dariya vowed she would be there for her.

After all, neither of them had many other allies to lean on. Not now, in this world that suddenly seemed a little darker and a lot colder.

Overall, she had a lot to think about, but it didn't seem like she had enough time. Before she knew it, she was back in Yaroslavl.

She walked back to the house with an increasing feeling of dread. That shouldn't happen. She was going home. But home had never been a safe place for her. Now, it was steadily becoming a nightmare.

Walking in, she could already hear the sounds of another argument. She exchanged glances with Dmitri.

Tired, resigned glances. Neither of them wanted to deal with this again, but there wasn't a lot of choice.

They could run to their rooms and hide but it would be suspicious. Vladimir had already been asking awkward questions about where Dmitri had been, which was why Dariya had told him they would have to return as soon as the funeral was over. She had hoped their absence wouldn't be noticed but Vladimir noticed far too much.

So, they reluctantly slunk into the living room, trying to keep their heads down until the shouting subsided.

It didn't work. Vladimir spun around as soon as the door opened.

"Where have you two been? Didn't you hear?!" He was still shouting.

Dariya sighed.

"Hear what, Papa?" She asked dutifully.

"These two idiots!" He rounded on the killers.

Dariya didn't follow his gaze. Lately, she had found it hard to face her so-called brothers without wanting to hurt them.

"These two idiots," Vladimir repeated, "left fingerprints in that Moroz guy's house. Now, he's not clever enough to get them on killing anyone, but he can prove they broke in. And this time our cop support's gone..."

Dariya bit back a smile. Antonin's death hadn't been in vain.

He had got rid of one of her father's allies, narrowing it down a little more, making his life a little bit harder.

She hoped her brothers would at least go to jail for a bit, though she was quite sure her father would find another way to slither out of that.

It was something though. A small victory was enough when it was probably all she was going to get for a while.

There was a court case, and they did get convicted. Her father ranted about that for hours, even after he had got them bailed out.

That wasn't the point, he said. The point was that their reputation for getting away with everything had been tarnished.

She celebrated that privately. Maybe now, if he couldn't get away with as much, her father would slip up and get into trouble.

Then she could make her escape while he was out of the way.

But he was making changes, trying to ensure that that would never happen. He had already switched his workshop to another location.

Not even she knew where it was now or how to get in. He kept that secret closely guarded.

She had crept into his basement to check that he actually had moved it and wasn't just trying to throw them all off the scent.

But all he had underneath the house now was a set of grim little cells. Presumably, in case anyone got too close and needed disposing of in a non-lethal way. Or, knowing him, a slow way.

The other major change was that she was no longer his favourite.

She had to be a little more careful herself now as he began to favour the children.

Ah, yes, the children, they were another major change. The first new clones he had successfully created and carefully aged up were alive.

She had twin girls now, who were already around five because babies were 'of no use' apparently, but he could twist the minds of children.

She hated it, hated *him.* She couldn't bear to watch him with them, instead, she tried to spend her own time alone with them, undoing his lessons.

It wasn't easy, with him lurking around all the time, but she had to try, after all.

The only other thing she could do was make sure that, if anything happened to her or if she couldn't speak up, there was something to tell them the truth.

Suddenly, the diaries she had promised Antonin she would write seemed more urgent.

She didn't just need to commemorate the events of his case and his eventual death for his family if they ever sought the truth and she wasn't here to help them, but for her own family, so that one day, they would see through her father's lies.

The diaries were a deep, dangerous secret. If her father or anyone inclined to help him discovered them, her life would probably be over.

But they were necessary too, so she couldn't avoid the situation. She just grew better and better at hiding things away from her family and lying to them.

It wasn't right, it never had been. But she didn't have a choice. Her life was on the line. Other lives had already been lost.

Sometimes you just had to lie, even to your family, because if you didn't, the bloodshed would never end.

She didn't like thinking this way. It was grim and dark. But it was the way she had been raised. Do what you have to do to survive in a world where everyone is your enemy.

Her father had given her that advice in regard to helping him survive against the justice system, but now, it seemed to her, she had to survive against him instead.

Her family had become the true enemy, and she had to hide from them in plain sight.

At least until such a time as she and her allies were ready to tear down Vladimir Volkovs' dark little world of lies and secrets.

Nikolina's New Life

Nikolina left the night of the funeral. She left a note on the living room table, letting her family know she was safe but going into hiding.

She didn't want them to worry but didn't have the courage to say goodbye in person, nor the strength to go through the inevitable argument about whether or not she should go.

Then she grabbed her bags from her room and slipped out of the house. Wandering the dark streets alone made her think of the day Antonin had died again, but she fought off the feelings.

She had to stop dwelling on that and be practical if she was to avoid the same fate. The darkness would provide her with some cover if she was being watched.

Besides, she was leaving by train, and the late-night trains were less crowded. The passengers were less chatty too.

Whenever she used public transport, she found the strangers who thought sitting beside her and talking was a clever idea annoying.

She didn't have the energy to deal with them tonight.

When she reached the train station, she bought a ticket for somewhere she had never heard of before, on the basis that it was a long journey and was probably a long way out of the way.

She had no other plan beyond that, but she would figure out what to do next once she was out of harm's way.

She sat in the station waiting room by herself and reached into her bag. In the side pocket was an envelope.

The church had sent it to her after the wedding, with the pictures they had taken enclosed. She hadn't looked at them yet, wondering if it would be too hard.

But she supposed she would have to look at the pictures sometime. She reluctantly peeled open the envelope and took a couple of pictures out.

Staring at them, she felt tears spring to her eyes again. They could have been so happy.

Despite her confusion at why he had suddenly sprung the wedding on her, that day had been the happiest of her life.

Perhaps that had been the point. He had wanted to leave her with a beautiful memory.

But she wished he had told her the truth instead.

It seemed so stupid that he had wasted his last hours pandering to what he thought she wanted when they could have worked out some plan to save him.

Hurt by her own emotional thoughts, Nikolina pulled the pictures out of the envelope and ripped them into pieces, before chucking the tattered remains into the nearest bin.

What was the point in keeping something that was meant to be beautiful if all it did was make her cry?

She sat back down and took out the *other* envelope, the one Antonin had left.

She had found it with his things. It had been on top of the music books he had left in her room. It was addressed to her, so she supposed it was about time she read it.

Opening it up, she read it slowly and carefully, going back through it a couple of times to make sure she had understood it properly.

She had to check because she had never been very musical, but it seemed to be a love song.

She didn't know whether to smile or cry. He had been learning more music recently and had promised that when he got the hang of it, he would write a love song for her.

He'd said he would play it on his guitar and sing for her.

She had been looking forward to that, but then he became busier and busier at work and... Still somehow found time to finish it but never had a chance to sing it.

Fresh tears fell and this time, she didn't have it in her to destroy the cause of them.

She folded it up instead and opened one of Antonin's old music books, carefully slotting the sheet of music inside.

As she did so, she spotted something else on the floor and grabbed it, assuming it had fallen from the envelope too.

She couldn't bring herself to look at anything else that might make her cry, so she stuffed it into the book with the song.

Shutting the book, she shoved it back into her bag. That was enough memories and enough emotions.

She had to learn to compose herself perfectly from now on and give nothing away about her grief, lest her husband's murders use it against her.

The train soon arrived, and she left on it. The journey was long, and she fell asleep a few times on the train, but at the very end of the journey, she stepped out and looked around.

Well, she was somewhere new, ready to start a new life whether she wanted to or not. But now what?

She had to find somewhere to stay, to start with.

She had been prepared for that, though, and taken some money out of her bank account to make sure she could pay for decent accommodation.

It would have to be suitable for her and her future child to live comfortably, after all.

Then she wasn't sure what would come next. Finding a job here, probably. But she hadn't considered that before, so she had never officially left her other job.

Of course, there was no question of going back to it. Either her father would inform her boss of what she had done, or she would just stop turning up and eventually would be fired.

That was a shame, it had been a decent job, and she had just found her feet there.

Still, there would be other jobs, wouldn't there? It wasn't the end of the world, she told herself.

She would have to learn to put all the attachments of her old life behind her and move on without getting emotional.

She tried to convince herself it was for the best as she walked away from the station, off to start her new life.

It took her a few months to properly establish herself again.

She rented a small, one-bedroom flat in the outskirts of the town she had landed in and for a while, she just stayed there, out of the way, keeping herself to herself.

Then she had to address the employment issue, as money began to run low. It wasn't easy.

By that point, she was noticeably pregnant and that seemed to put off potential employers.

But she managed to find something, eventually.

It was a menial shelf-stacking job at the town's only supermarket, nothing like as challenging as her previous job. But it allowed her to keep paying rent and providing for herself, so she took it.

She was able to save some extra money, which she vowed she would use to provide for her child as well when the time came.

That was the only important thing right now. She didn't bother talking to her co-workers much, leaving them to gossip about her being 'stuck-up'.

She didn't care. She just wanted a quiet life in which she and her child would be safe, and the past would be left behind her.

So that was how she lived until one night, she went into labour. After several hours, she found herself holding her daughter and feeling overwhelmed.

There were too many emotions running around her head for her to process right now. She was happy, of course, to finally meet her baby.

But she was hurting too. Holding her and Antonin's baby in her arms, she looked down and couldn't help but think of him. It was a bittersweet moment.

There was also a hint of fear that was only growing stronger as she looked at her daughter.

This child was so tiny, so fragile... And she was already in grave danger. She had been born in danger and may never escape it. And she couldn't even protect herself.

Nikolina didn't know how she was going to protect this precious, helpless little life.

She was doing what she thought was best, but she was all on her own and had to look after not only herself but the baby as well.

The panic suddenly gripped her. What was she going to do? How could she do this? She couldn't! She couldn't do it alone!!

Out of the panic rose one calm, clear thought. *Then go home.*

She bit her lip. Could she go back home?

Her family would welcome her, and she knew that they would do everything they could to help her. But wouldn't she be putting them in danger too?

No, because they already *were* in danger, she reminded herself. They had been since the break-in, yet none of them had tried to run from it or hide away.

They faced it calmly. *Together.*

They said there was strength in numbers, after all. And then, if something did happen, her baby would have a family to look after her.

Here, she had nobody but Nikolina, who was rapidly getting less and less confident that she could do anything useful.

She was out of her depth here. She had to go home.

Hiding The Past

Nikolina left town as soon as she had recovered from the birth of Nadezhda, her young daughter.

She caught another train and went home. It felt strange repeating the journey again, this time holding Nadezhda in her arms and trying to soothe away the child's cries.

Not as weird as it seemed at the end of the journey, though, when she had to leave the train and trek back home.

It seemed surreal, standing outside her family home, and wondering how she would be received when she entered.

She knew they would welcome her home, of course. But how would she answer their questions?

She had disappeared for nine months and now she was showing up on their doorstep with a baby in her arms.

She had never even told her family members that she was pregnant. How was she going to handle this?

There were two options that came to mind: She could tell them the truth, with all its uncomfortable emotions.

That would be hard for her, and it might also put her daughter in danger. If she shared her true identity with anyone, it could leak out and back to the Volkovs.

Maybe she was being paranoid there, but she couldn't bear the idea of her baby being hurt.

That was why she hadn't put Antonin's name on her birth certificate. She hadn't mentioned him at all.

So, she wasn't being entirely truthful, but the second option would take that much further. She could actively lie about her daughter's life.

 If no one except her knew that Antonin was Nadezhda's father, then the danger would be... Not gone but minimised at least.

But how would she do that? She needed to get her story straight and tell everyone the same thing.

And it had to be plausible. But she had never had another partner besides Antonin, so how would she make this convincing?

... Adoption! She could tell people she had been away to adopt Nadezhda. That would make sense. She nodded to herself.

Alright, that would be the plan then. Time to put it into action.

She strode up to the door, trying to appear confident in spite of her nerves. Banging on the front door, she waited for a response.

Ilya answered. He opened the door calmly and then stared at her for a few moments.

"Nikolina? You're back!" He smiled and moved to hug her before noticing the baby in her arms.

"Umm..."

He didn't seem to know what to say. There was an awkward pause.

She tried to find the words to begin the lie.

"Well, yes, I am back. And awfully glad to be!" she added honestly, "But I suppose I ought to explain. I have adopted; this is Nadezhda."

She held up the baby.

Ilya looked down at his grandchild and smiled.

"Lovely, Lina, but do you think I'm stupid?" He was suddenly serious again.

That threw her. "What? Of course not!" She spluttered.

"Then don't lie to me. Adopted?" He saw her panicked face and sighed.

"It's fine, I understand. Come in and we can talk about it better."

Well, I'm clearly a terrible liar, Nikolina thought to herself as she followed him into the house.

At least he didn't seem mad about it. Maybe he would help her come up with a better plan for keeping her daughter safe.

She dragged her bags in as well and dumped them in the hall, before trailing after her father again.

Soon, she found herself sitting opposite him at the dinner table.

"Well, whatever you need to explain, go ahead," he told her, sitting back and waiting patiently, his expression impassive.

Nikolina nodded.

"Antonin and I found out we were having a baby the day that we got married. I thought I would wait to share the news when things were a little more settled and then when he died... I couldn't stay here. I felt as though I was in danger too and I was putting her in danger by staying. I don't trust those Volkov people to stay away... You haven't heard any more from them, have you?"

She trailed off from her explanation to question him suspiciously.

"No, not since I made sure those two who broke in went to jail... But I think you're right not to trust them." He nodded.

"What do you suggest I do about it then? Because I have tried so hard and all I have learnt is that I can't handle this alone!"

She felt close to panic again as she threw those words at him.

Ilya shook his head.

"I know. I don't think any of us can. That's why I've arranged police protection for us, just to be sure. I'll extend it to you and Nadya as well. Keeping her safe will have to be a priority. No doubt she'll be the number one target if they learn of her existence," he explained.

Nikolina nodded in agreement. "That is probably wise. Thank you." She smiled slightly, glad of his help.

"Is there anything else that we can do to keep her safe?" she asked, still anxious.

"Hm..." he considered the question carefully.

"Well, we should probably continue your plan and lie about her identity. The truth can be extremely dangerous. No one else should know, not even Sasha and Katya."

He sounded very grave, and she nodded, understanding.

"I know. But obviously, I am a rotten liar, how are we going to get them to believe all this?"

"I'll back you up, of course," he assured her.

And so, with her father's help, Nikolina settled back into her old life.

Ilya helped her with everything.

He gave her back her old room until she found somewhere else to live, he helped her get her former job back and helped out with childcare when he could.

And, as promised, he helped explain her return and her new child to her siblings. Somehow, he made them accept it.

He even tried to convince them that she had never been truly in love with Antonin, and that his death had put them all in danger because he had betrayed them while he was away on his mission.

Henceforth, the Moroz siblings stopped speaking of him. They stopped visiting his grave. They began to forget him.

Nikolina never did, of course, but she pretended to. Though she wasn't entirely sure that her siblings believed the united act of herself and her father.

Well, Sasha seemed to take it in his stride. But Katya, certainly, was behaving oddly towards her.

But she ignored the brewing tension between herself and her sister, hoping it would come to nothing.

She was only glad to be back with her family, all safe and sound.

She was grateful to her father for arranging protection for them. A part of her was still living in fear.

But life did move on and with it, hope for a better future trickled into her life.

Mostly it came through changes. She got her old job back and worked hard for a promotion. She saved up her money and got a home for herself and Nadezhda.

Living in her old room with a new baby and all the things she needed to care for her was getting hard.

She wouldn't have swapped it for another life though, even when it was painful to deal with the similarities between her deceased husband and her growing daughter.

She still struggled to handle the grief of losing Antonin in any other way than shutting away her emotions completely, but Nadezhda helped her to feel better and to have hope.

She kept an emotional distance between her and her daughter, not wanting to get too close, only to lose her, but she already felt a deep attachment to the child and every day with her made her hopeful.

This little girl who seemed so carefree and so joyous might be tiny and helpless now, but who knew what she could grow up to achieve?

Sometimes, when her daughter laughed - Which she seemed to do a lot - It felt like she could do anything, change anyone's heart for the better and even change the entire world.

She was being silly; she knew she was.

It was the sentimental stupidity of a loving mother.

There was nothing in it. But she needed thoughts like that to help her push away her other feelings and get through the day without breaking down into tears.

So, she would always speculate on the hopeful future, rather than the grim past.

That dark time, though it was not that long ago, was too much for her.

She had to shut it out almost entirely to cope with it. And to keep safe. If she mentioned it to anyone, even in passing, she could be putting herself and her whole family in danger.

Especially Nadezhda.

So, she hid away the memories.

She kept Antonin's old belongings blended in with hers around the house, so they wouldn't draw attention like they might if she suddenly got a skip and threw them all away,

But his old things were the only reminders of the dark past - Besides her daughter's resemblance to him - That she kept around.

She hoped that she had done enough to make the Volkovs forget about her and her family. And to make herself forget about the most painful part of her life.

She should have done.

She had run, hidden, and lied. She had got help and protection around her.

So that hopefully, her daughter would never have to suffer like this. She would never even have to know about it.

End of Book 1

Family Secrets

By

Ellie Jay

Sasha
Vladimir
Vasily
Katya
Nikolina
Nadezhda
Sof
Diana

The Discovery

The discovery was a complete accident, of course.

Nadezhda never set out to make an enemy of the woman she believed to be her adoptive mother.

She would never have suspected that anything was odd in her family. Her adoptive mother, Nikolina, was...Kind to her, in the sense that always ensured that her basic needs were fulfilled.

True, they weren't close, she had never called Nikolina 'Mama', they rarely hugged or kissed, but her mother had adopted her as a baby and cared for her patiently ever since.

She was vaguely aware that this couldn't have been easy. Nikolina was a busy woman, working as a lawyer in the bustling centre of Moscow, the city they lived on the edges of.

And as for her...Nadezhda had to concede she hadn't been the perfect child.

 Half the time, she was a reserved girl, shy, even, leaving her mother worrying that she didn't have many friends.

Then there was her stubborn side and her hot temper. They rarely surfaced, but sometimes...Well, she could remember fighting a war that lasted months with her mother over whether or not she could get piano lessons.

Overall, though, they had managed.

Her mother had told her she had never fallen in love with someone she could start a family with, but had always wanted a child, so she had chosen her.

That always made her feel happier on those days when Nikolina worked late and she was at home, lonely. She had been *chosen.*

It got her through the rough parts, like the little niggling doubts whenever she saw other kids with their more affectionate parents and the moments when she wanted to find her real parents or know more about her true heritage but was denied every time she asked.

Mostly, though, her life with Nikolina, and in general, was normal. Ordinary. Dull.

She went to school, got average grades, didn't dislike or like anyone or anything there strongly, then went home and waited for her mother to arrive.

On the evening of a long spring day, Nikolina was still out, so Nadezhda was sitting by herself at home.

Bored, she got up to look for something to do. Perhaps there was a book around here that she hadn't read yet or something...

She strolled over to her mother's bookshelf and leant against it as she scanned over the spines of the volumes there, looking for anything of interest.

Her weight against the shelf made it wobble, and a pile of old, discarded hardbacks that had been shoved on top of it, out of sight, crashed down.

She jumped back, dodging the flying books, then dropped to her knees to scoop them up.

To her surprise, they were music books. Was her mother interested in music?

She didn't think so, given the row they had had over the piano. Curiously, she opened one, gasping as she revealed something very unexpected...

Tucked inside the cover was a photo of a young man and woman, newlyweds by the look of it.

Nadezhda froze.

The woman in the picture was familiar. She had long platinum blonde hair, wound up in a bun, emerald eyes, and beige skin. She knew those features too - *it was her mother!*

Even though the idea of Nikolina in a wedding dress was totally unfamiliar, it *was* her.

The photo was old, worn and faded. And the woman was younger, not to mention smiling more than Nadezhda had ever seen her stern-faced, sharp-eyed mother do, but it was undoubtedly the same woman.

That was surprising enough, but then her gaze was pulled to the man.

He had the same light brown hair, blue eyes, and pale skin that she was so used to seeing when she looked in the mirror!

Blinking in surprise as the realisation hit her, she looked at the picture again.

Her *parents*. They were her parents. She had birth parents... Of course, she *knew* she did, but knowing anything about them was a strange concept.

She had daydreamed about what they might be like, naturally.

But that was childish, dreaming that the father she had never known was a hugely powerful man, or that her real mother was a gorgeous and rich movie star...

There was never any earnest consideration of her real birth parents, nor was there any discussion of them. Now, she was staring at them.

That was enough to try to get her swimming head around, without trying to process the idea that her 'adoptive' mother was her *real* mother. And had *lied* to her...

In the background of the photo, as her confused brain searched it in hope of finding some sort of clarity, she spotted another familiar person, similar to Nikolina, with long blonde waves flowing around her shoulders and sparkling green eyes.

Her Aunt Ekaterina, she realised.

Well, Nikolina will admit nothing, even if I confront her with the picture, she mused. Maybe Aunty Katya will tell me the truth?

She hoped so. In her childhood, she had got the affection her mother hadn't been able to give from her doting Aunt.

Katya was Nikolina's energetic little sister. She loved children. According to Nikolina, this was because she practically was one.

The two sisters had an odd kind of relationship. Ekaterina seemed fond of her sister, yet Nadezhda got the impression her mother didn't return the feelings... She used to, and when she had been young, Katya had often visited.

But then the visits had stopped, and the two sisters had stopped talking.

But Ekaterina was considered the 'fun' one of the family. Nadezhda loved her company.

She had a key to her nearby home, using it to pop in when those afternoons home alone got too boring.

Ekaterina ran her own business online, so she was almost always at home and usually flexible enough with her work to pay attention to Nadezhda.

So, the young girl made her way over there and found her Aunt sitting peering at her computer screen.

"Oh, Nadya! Hey, it's good to see you again," she called out affectionately as her niece, who had let herself in, entered.

It was only having greeted her cheerfully that she seemed to remember that this wasn't normal.

Her smile, sparked by seeing her niece, faded abruptly.

"What's up?" she asked, sounding concerned.

Was something wrong? On a normal day, Nadezhda would be at home. And the girl did look a bit shaken.

But she didn't overreact, wanting to let Nadezhda explain herself.

Which she soon began to, hesitantly at first, since she wasn't sure how Katya would react.

"I was hoping you could explain something to me, Aunty Katya," she decided to play it safe, at least to begin with.

"What is it you need explaining, and I'll do my best to help you."

As Katya assured Nadezhda of that, she rotated her seat 180 degrees to face her niece.

Nadezhda instantly seized this opportunity and pressed the picture into Ekaterina's hand, not finding any fitting words with which to accompany such a presentation.

The older woman held it as though it was somehow fragile, staring down at it nervously.

"How did you find this?" she asked nervously, wondering if Nikolina knew.

Had she told her at last? That seemed unlikely and would have no doubt lead to trouble...

Perhaps there had been a row at her sister's house.

The inevitable row that had been brewing for years. She had tried to tell Nikolina that Nadezhda would find out one day...

"I just stumbled on it." Nadezhda brushed past that bit, not wanting to explain that it had been among her mother's things.

Katya might think she had been prying. Besides, that was far from the most critical issue here.

"Anyway, can you explain? I want to know why she'd hide this. Why would she lie to me?"

After a small pause that seemed like an eternity, Ekaterina spoke.

"I don't understand it myself, but she said she was afraid." she explained.

"Of what, being a good mother?" Nadezhda questioned sharply, bitterness creeping into her voice.

"No!" Katya's rejection of her comment was sudden and almost scolding.

This, from her laidback Aunt, stung. Katya saw Nadezhda's expression and softened again.

"No. She was afraid for *you*," she revealed.

The room fell completely silent. Even Nadezhda's heart seemed to skip a beat.

She hadn't thought her mother cared for her very much, let alone wanted to *protect* her from... From *what?!*

The anger flooded back. What could be so terrible that you had to lie to *your child* to keep them 'safe'?

What did they need to be 'safe' from, when they already lived in a boring little suburb anyway?

"Huh!" she snorted, tossing her head. "What the hell do I need protecting from?!"

Ekaterina gave her a stern look, unusual for her, and suddenly looked a lot like Nikolina.

"More than you might think. But I can't tell you unless you *promise* not to blab to anyone else," she insisted.

The girl wavered. She was angry, but only because she wanted the truth. Was this her chance to get it?

"I don't think anyone else cares, but fine, I won't. Now tell me!" she responded after a moment's hesitation, curiosity beating anger in the long term.

"Right," Ekaterina nodded. "So, there's four of us who know about the wedding, me, you, the priest and Lina." She began.

Nadezhda nodded. 'Lina' was her mother's much-hated nickname. Her Aunt used it whenever she could. Then her brow wrinkled as confusion hit.

"Hang on, what about the groom?"

"You mean your father?" Katya pointed out.

She nodded; her mouth dry all of a sudden. That wasn't a word she'd ever said before, at least not about herself and her family.

Now, she suddenly felt that she couldn't. The concept was too alien to her.

"He was killed within days of the wedding. That's why Nikolina never told you the truth. She didn't want you to be in danger as well. She didn't tell anyone about you being her real child, even your Uncle Sasha thinks you're adopted, and you know how close they are."

Now her Aunt had turned away again and was speaking in a monotone voice, hitting her with facts now and trying to conceal her own feelings on the matter.

Another time, she might have questioned that and demanded to know all of Katya's hidden thoughts.

But there was a bigger issue. *Murder.* Her blood ran cold. Her father had been murdered, and she was in danger. *Why?*

"He was *killed?* What happened?!" she demanded to know.

There was another long silence. Then Ekaterina reached into her drawer and took out a slim leather-bound book.

"I don't know. Maybe this says something more helpful," she told her, handing it over.

Nadezhda took it shakily. "What is it?"

"Your father's diary. I don't know a lot about the situation, I didn't even know him that well, but he sort of roped me into being at the wedding, I was the only witness...And afterwards, he gave me this to give to his child. I don't know how he knew your mother was pregnant. And I certainly don't understand how he knew he was going to die. But he wanted you to know about it." Ekaterina revealed.

"Why did he give this to you? Why not my mother?"

Nadezhda only spoke two of the questions that jumped into her head. Her mind was reeling.

Ekaterina shrugged. "I don't know. Maybe the answers are in the diary?"

"Well, I..." Nadezhda looked down at the book in her trembling hands, hesitating.

What now? There must be more to the story than Ekaterina had revealed, in this little diary her father, a figure who was growing increasingly mysterious by the minute, had left behind for her.

It was her only connection now. And knowing it existed, she couldn't go back, walk away, and ignore what she had discovered.

"I'll find out what I can. I'll do whatever it takes," she vowed, looking back to her Aunt, visibly shaken but determined now, her mind made up.

"Thanks for helping," she added with as much of a smile as she could muster in her shocked state, before heading out.

Stepping out onto the street, she barely felt the freezing evening air hitting her face.

It had been mid-afternoon, just after school, when she had rushed over to her Aunt's. She had planned it to be a short visit.

She'd get the facts she needed and rush home before her mother finished work.

The conversation had taken far longer, but it didn't matter. Suddenly all sense of urgency had vanished.

She simply sank onto a low wall nearby and, with trembling hands, opened the diary.

The first page read:

To my child:

I'm sorry I was never around. And I'm sorry if you and your Mama had to live with the legacy of my work if you lived in fear all these years.

I would have loved to be there for you, but if I can't, then I can leave this for you. I've found someone to keep it, so that it won't be near you all the time, putting you in greater danger.

The moment you start wanting answers about me, you will be given this.

I didn't have long to write this, so there was no time for the full explanation. You need to find Dariya Volkova.

She's a friend of mine who knows everything, even more than your Mama could tell you.

Find her and trust her, she's promised to help you. In the meantime, trust no one. Here is what you need:

Underneath, there was an address.

Nadezhda stared at them for a little while, tracing her hand over the line of text thoughtfully, then flicked through a few more pages. That appeared to be all that was written in the whole diary.

Well...That's a waste of paper, she thought idly, before her brain kicked back in. Seriously, at a time like *this?* She snapped at herself.

I have so much to do. Let's find this 'Dariya' woman and see what she knows. But first...First I need to go home.

I need to speak to *Mama,* She thought, with a hint of sarcasm betraying her newfound bitterness towards Nikolina.

Besides, all my things are at home...She thought as she stood up and started her walk back.

She had intended to go home sooner before her mother would have left work, but now she was late.

Somehow it didn't matter to her anymore.

For the first time in her entire sixteen-year long life, she was yearning to see the woman who had deceived her for years: *her own mother.*

"Nadya? Is that you?" Nikolina's voice called from the older woman's bedroom as she let herself into her mother's apartment.

Stupid question, I'm the only other one with a key, Nadezhda thought crossly.

"Yes, *Mama.*" she replied, intentionally breaking Nikolina's lifelong rule.

She had been brought up to call her Nikolina, like everyone else. Despite their relationship, they had never been a close mother-daughter pair.

Her mother stepped out into the doorway.

"Do not call me that! I am not your real mother!" she almost shouted, looking flustered and upset, in spite of her permanent formal tone.

"Don't lie to me!" the words snapped out of Nadezhda's mouth as she thrust the photograph at her mother accusingly.

The older woman slipped her pale, trembling hands under the picture, staring at it.

"But this is... I got rid of these!"

Nikolina's usual perfect mask of emotionless-ness vanished, and she suddenly seemed very flustered.

Her daughter narrowed her eyes at her angrily.

"You lied to me!" she shouted.

The mother rolled her eyes dramatically.

"Calm down Nadya, I only wanted to protect you from our mistakes. Where have you had this attitude from?" she questioned her as her calmness returned.

"Aunty Katya told me everything!" Nadezhda snapped, not being entirely truthful as her anger got the better of her.

"You just hid everything from me! How the hell did that *'protect' me*?!" she yelled.

Then she stopped, taking a deep breath, before walking across the room and started gathering some of her things, never looking at her mother.

She grabbed hold of some of the music books. That was where she had found the picture... Maybe it was helpful in some other way.

"I'm leaving." She told Nikolina coolly as she picked them up.

"No! Do not be stupid! Where will you go? To *Ekaterina,* no doubt?!" Nikolina glowered to her daughter, spitting her sister's name bitterly.

She had told her too much and taken her daughter away.

"No. I'll find someone to help me," Nadezhda replied shortly, not wanting to reveal anything else.

She pushed past her mother and hurried to the door.

Behind her, Nikolina snorted.

"Help you with *what,* exactly?" she asked sharply.

"Finding out what you never told me. And the information Katya won't tell me." Nadezhda answered in a blunt, cold tone of voice.

Then she turned away, her father's diary and her other belongings in her grip, pushed open the door and strode out into the world determinedly.

Nikolina stared after her, dazed, wondering what would happen now.

The Journey Begins

Nadezhda kept her head held high and strode out confidently until she was just out of sight of her mother's apartment.

Then she sank onto a bench at the side of the street and, internally so as not to seriously disturb passers-by, screamed.

She had just walked out of the only home she had ever known and had no idea what she was doing.

Well, she reminded herself, she was going to find Dariya.

But hunting out an unknown woman with a sixteen-year-old address and sheer desperation wasn't really a plan she felt confident about.

Even if she could track the woman down, could she be sure, simply based on her dead father's assurance, that Dariya would help her?

Questions and problems swirled around in her mind, but she pushed them back and stood up again. *She had to try.* She didn't have anything else left now.

And a part of her was still desperate to know the full truth behind her hidden family history.

The address in the diary was in Yaroslavl, though. Yaroslavl was 173 miles away. In all the meagre belongings she had had time to gather, there was no money at all.

Reaching Dariya's address, if it was even correct, was, therefore, the first problem she needed to tackle.

Normally, she would turn to family for help. But Ekaterina didn't drive, she wasn't going back to talk to Nikolina *ever* again, and the one other option was her Uncle Alexander.

Uncle Sasha, as she affectionately knew him, was the calmer, more dependable one of the family, in between Nikolina's sharpness and Katya's boundless energy.

He was always there for her when he could be when she was upset, or ill and needed picking up from school.

And he just about kept his sisters together when things got tense.

So of course, the one person she could rely on to listen to her without judgement, then bundle her into his car and take her where she needed to go... Wasn't here.

The only unreliable thing about the rock of their family was that his job as a private investigator took him all over the world.

So, he was working God only knew where. He usually tried to make it back now and then to see Nikolina, to whom he was very close, but they hadn't seen him in a while...

So, she was *really* on her own.

Though for a few moments it terrified her, Nadezhda tried again to push down her feelings and think. Perhaps she could hitchhike or something?

There was bound to be a way to get there for free.

Someone might give her a ride if she found the main road pointing in the right direction.

It wasn't likely that she would find one person going the full 173 miles in one go who would take her... Actually, it seemed nearly impossible.

But she could travel in stages, hitching rides with various people until she got somewhere close to her destination.

A plan forming in her mind, she started to walk.

It wasn't far, by simply cutting through the city square, she reached a fairly main road which, if followed far enough, would connect to a few other towns and cities that were a fair way from here.

It was a busy road, going quite a long way in a westerly direction.

She was about sixty per cent sure that that was the way she needed to travel and tried to convince herself the rest of the way to committing as she stood at the side of the road.

When she had finally made herself believe that this *must* be the right way to go, she raised her hand and started trying to flag down one out of the thousands of cars that whizzed by.

If Nikolina had been aware of her daughter's current activities, it would have only added to the surge of panic that was attacking her now.

It was overwhelming. Nadezhda had *gone*. Just walked away because of a stupid photograph!

And what would happen now? Her daughter could be in all kinds of danger. And she could do nothing, because Nadya wouldn't understand.

It would be just like Ekaterina all over again. She hadn't understood or listened either...

On the other hand, her sister had somehow realised that this was going to happen. She had spent Nadya's whole life trying to tell her.

And they had quarrelled over it because her little sister had no right to get involved.

But... Doubt crept into her mind. Perhaps, even with her limited understanding of what had truly happened, Ekaterina had a point.

She had hidden too much from her daughter. True, she had done it to protect her, but...

Katya had tried to tell her she had let Antonin's death scare her too much. At the time, which had been a horrible thing to say.

Of course, it had scared her, her husband was murdered in cold blood by people she could only describe as evil.

Yet, sixteen years later, it still dominated her life and her mindset. And she had neglected her daughter because she was dwelling on his death.

Tears began to roll down her cheeks as she thought this over. She had made a terrible mistake, forcing her only child away from her and into the arms of grave danger.

Now, what could she do?

Nadezhda stood by the edge of the road, still waiting. It seemed as though the road was endlessly long and always busy, the traffic kept on coming, yet it also somehow just kept moving along without stopping.

Rain began to fall, turning to sleet as day turned to evening.

 By the time it was dark, snow was falling hard, big flakes swirling all around her as the freezing wind blew.

She was vaguely aware that she was shivering, but mostly, she was numb.

Only physically, though. Inside, the self-hating anger and the fear of what would happen now that she had fought so hard to repress were pushing their way to the surface of her mind again.

 Now the view was bleak, her thoughts were as well.

What have I done?! There's no way I'm going to get all the way to Yaroslavl by myself! Like it will help that much if I do!

All this because some idiot lied to me and because of that stupid, stupid photo!

This was why she had always hated her hot temper and her stubborn side; she reminded herself.

It always got the better of her whenever they surfaced, and she ended up in a stupid situation like this!

A car pulled up just as the tears started pouring out.

 The window wound down and she looked up, her face blue from the cold and streaked with tears.

The man behind the wheel was staring at her critically, as though he was trying to work out what she was.

Snapping out of her melancholy thoughts, she took the opportunity to do the same to him.

He was...Odd, in a way she couldn't put her finger on. Something deep in his steely grey eyes, she thought, something there was staring straight through her soul.

Other than that, he seemed like a normal man, even a handsome one.

He was young, probably only three or four years older than she was, with lightly tanned skin and jet-black hair. There was a scar running along his left cheekbone and...

And for some reason, he was driving along in the middle of a snowy night in a rusty old car but a brand-new suit. Yeah, he's definitely strange, she thought to herself.

"Well? If you've seen everything you wanted to, are you getting in or not?" he demanded to know, still watching her as he waited for a response.

Could she trust him? He was very odd, but then, right now, she probably seemed positively *insane.*

Besides, after the exhaustingly eventful day and the promises she had made to herself, she didn't seem to have many options.

"Where are you heading to?" she asked, one hand on the door handle.

"Yaroslavl." he stated it simply enough, but the word made her heart soar.

Exactly what she needed, had waited for all this time, and was nearly giving up on, had just arrived.

"I'm coming!" she told him as she yanked open the door and jumped into the passenger seat without another thought.

A ticket out of the cold was good enough, a journey that just happened to take her directly to Yaroslavl was like a dream come true.

Ramming her bundle of belongings through the gap in the seats into the back, she settled into the car and pulled on her seatbelt.

"Let's go then," she encouraged.

Her newly found driver gave her a puzzled frown. "We *are* going. The car's moving," he pointed out.

And *technically,* it was. Just very, very slowly.

"It *does* go faster, right?" she questioned.

The journey ahead of them was long enough with a top speed of five miles per hour. But in response, he simply looked over at her and smirked.

While shoving his foot down to the floor.

When she had finished screaming and his laughter died down, Nadezhda sighed heavily.

Of course, the only person going all the way she needed to go and was willing to help her out was an absolute madman.

Well, this was going to be *fun,* travelling across the country with a lunatic behind the wheel.

"Now that I've answered your question, you need to answer some of mine," he demanded suddenly, his voice interrupting her thoughts.

"What the Hell are you doing, trying to get a lift in this weather?" he went on before she had even had the chance to process his first remark.

She lapsed into silence, hurriedly trying to think this through.

His questioning surprised her and now, she wanted to make sure she had an answer that didn't sound too crazy or give away too much. In the end, she settled for the vague:

"Family emergency."

"Ah...Well, we're in the same boat there then." He nodded in reply.

I doubt it's exactly the same, she thought privately, but she didn't say anything too personal about her difficult situation, instead deciding it might be safest to settle for feigning some polite interest.

Most of all, she wanted to sleep, but when she was in a seemingly eccentric stranger's car wasn't the best time.

So, she merely asked, "How so?"

"I'm trying to get home for my mother's funeral," he explained.

"I'm sorry to hear that," she said politely.

He shrugged, "Not your fault," then, seeming to want to return the small talk, "What about you?"

Ah, damn it, she thought to herself. She should have been more careful and kept away from this line of questioning.

Now, she would have to find a way around the details.

"A... Friend of my fathers' needs some help," she tried to explain without saying too much.

This seemed to puzzle him. "Why isn't your father going with you, then?"

"He passed away...Anyway, it's all been rather sudden," she muttered, getting more flustered as the interrogation went on.

Silence took over for a few more moments.

He seemed to be thinking about her reply.

She just wished she knew what he made of it, whether he believed her, whether she had already said too much or if she ought to trust him at least a little bit more...

She sighed, needing to distract herself, and reached into the back of the car to grab one of the music books.

It would be a better use of her time to stop worrying and start searching for anything else of use to her, in case... Well, just in case.

She didn't want to consider what exactly it was 'in case' of.

So, she flipped open the book, ignoring the odd glances and icy silence from the driver. There was a label on the cover.

'Property of Antonin Jelennski'. *Who was he?* She wondered, running her fingers over the name on the label before she turned a page.

There was a sheet of music on it, nothing out of the ordinary.

Then, tucked inside the book, was another piece of paper. The music was copied out again, with some additions, and lyrics scrawled nearby.

Signed at the bottom, it read 'To Lina,'.

And suddenly, she felt odd, as though she was trespassing on something. It was in her father's handwriting; she recognised it from the diary.

This must be her father's book, and something he had left behind for her mother, 'Lina'.

It was a love song from her father to her mother... That was weird.

Why had her mother hidden it away? For the same reason that she had hidden the photo, she guessed. But why? *What was she so afraid of?*

Panic slowly began to subside. Nikolina was still worried and upset, of course, but she managed to calm herself down somewhat. Her daughter couldn't be that hard to trace.

Despite her earlier comments, she suspected she had gone back to her Aunt, who had helped her.

So, with great reluctance, she picked up the phone and dialled her sister's number.

The phone rang for a while, then she heard Katya's familiar voice.

"Hey!" she greeted.

And now for the hard part... Swallowing her pride after all these years. Nikolina hesitated, then began tentatively.

"Hello. It's... It's Lina," she told her.

"Lina? Is everything okay?"

Katya could hear the discomfort in her sister's voice and instantly began to worry.

After her discussion with Nadya, she couldn't help but wonder what on Earth had happened when the teenager had returned home.

"Nadya's gone, if that is what you're asking." Nikolina got straight to the point.

Katya gave a deep sigh. She had wanted to help the girl, not drive her way.

But now it looked as though that was what she had done, and she had given her sister another reason to dislike her, on top of all that.

"I'm sorry! I just wanted to help her!" She rushed to justify her actions.

"No, it is not your fault. You tried to warn me. I... I apologise for not listening. I thought I was doing what was best for her," Nikolina answered sadly.

This came as a surprise to Katya. Her stubborn older sister didn't usually admit she was wrong, much less *apologise.*

Normally, she might gloat over this, but she sensed now was a bad time.

Instead, she took this as progress towards setting aside their differences and extended an offer she hoped would help with that.

"I guess we've got some catching up to do. Wanna come over and talk about it?"

"That... That would be great, yes. Thank you," her slightly stunned sister agreed.

At some point while she had been musing about her confusing family history, Nadezhda realised as she opened her eyes, she must have fallen asleep. It wasn't a surprise, given the circumstances.

She had had a long, trying day. Her emotions had been in turmoil and her body frozen and weary by the time she had crawled into the strangers' car.

No wonder she had slept for so long.

And it really must have been a long time, for now, the midday sun was high in the sky, and she didn't recognise the road they were on, or even the area surrounding it.

Her book was laying in her lap, shut. She looked around her in confusion.

"'Morning, sleepy head. Or should I say afternoon?" The mocking voice of her mysterious companion cut through these early musings as she straightened up in her seat, blinking and looking around.

He was smirking at her from the driving seat, still, the same as he had been the night before.

Well, it hadn't all been a freakish dream, after all.

"Ughh...I don't know. Morning. Afternoon. Whatever," she managed to mutter at him, rubbing her eyes to drive out the sleep.

He chuckled at her. "Lovely. I guess you were really tired, huh?"

"You weren't this chatty last night..." the girl grumbled, "but something like that, I guess."

"Well, last night wasn't exactly nice, was it? Whereas today, the sun's shining, we're on the open road..." he gestured around them, taking both of his hands off the steering wheel to do so and making her shriek again.

The only response this gained was more laughter as he took the wheel again.

At least that sudden surprise had helped wake her up a little, she thought with a shrug.

As she looked around, she decided that things did seem a little better. She wasn't out on her own in the world anymore. She was surviving without Nikolina, the liar on whom she had depended for so long.

Perking up a bit at the newfound self-confidence these thoughts gave her, she managed a smile.

"I guess you're right," she agreed.

"Of course, I'm right," he retorted, "Now, why not get to know one another better? We've still got a long way to go, after all, and I don't like sharing a car with someone for 173 miles without even knowing their name."

She wrinkled her nose, confused. "You do that a lot?"

"No, but I'm trying it now, and I don't like it," was the answer.

Now, it was her turn to laugh. "Fine, you win. I'm Nadezhda," she introduced herself.

"Vasily," he stated simply by way of returning the introduction.

That little introduction out of the way, she relaxed a little.

After all, she had told the truth about something - albeit something as small as her name - to a stranger and the world hadn't crashed down around her.

She had just been paranoid because she was out in the world without her family for the first time, so she reassured herself.

There was nothing to worry about, though. The distance between herself and her home was growing, and she was coping just fine...

Her mother and her aunt weren't exactly coping as well, but they were certainly trying to work some important things out.

They sat around Katya's coffee table and talked for what seemed like ages.

Nikolina revealed things to her sister that she had never told her before, about what happened in the weeks and days leading up to her husband's sudden, violent death.

It was shocking for the younger woman to learn exactly what her sister had been through.

Of course, she had known something terrible must have happened to change Lina's life so dramatically. She had never doubted that. But she hadn't known what...

Dread suddenly filled her.

"And Nadezhda's gone to 'find out what happened!'' she gasped, frightened for her niece.

Nikolina paled.

"That was where she was going?! I thought she was just looking for some space to calm down... She's in danger!"

"Sasha!" Katya yelled out, her mind racing for a solution. "Sasha's a detective, he'll find her!"

"Of course," Nikolina jumped up and ran to the phone, "of course Sasha will help us!"

She dialled her brother's number and listened, disheartened, as his phone rang and rang.

Now, what could they do?

There was nothing to do, except sit and wait for Sasha to call back, or Nadezhda to return. If neither of them happened...

That was the deepest fear of the waiting Moroz sisters.

Yaroslavl

Once the ice was broken, the journey seemed to get much easier. The hours and the road zipped by, and they made small talk.

Then it progressed to bigger talk. Not talk about Nadezhda's quest, of course, she was still too hesitant to let that much of the truth slip to a relatively new acquaintance.

But they did get to know more about one another. He told her he was seventeen, leading her to divulge her age as well.

He admitted to her that he had been away from home on the pretence of doing some work, but really had just wanted some peace from his family in which to enjoy his hobbies, particularly practising his drumming.

She could understand that and told him about the times she would stay at 'after-school club' to secretly play on the piano in the school hall.

After all, it had stood disused most of the time and she had always wanted a keyboard of her own, but her mother had refused. That had been as close as she could get.

It seemed like a long time ago now though. In a time when she had been a normal kid, with no idea about her families' dark secrets. She didn't tell him that.

She didn't seem to need to.

When they stopped for lunch, having found a small town with an open café, he sat across the table from her, waiting for the food he had insisted on paying for after she had uncomfortably confessed to not having any money, smiled strangely, and asked:

"So, what are you running away from?"

For a moment, there was dead silence. Well, no, there wasn't.

The faint music still played on the old radio, the hundreds of conversations went on and the doorbell chimed every now and again as people came and went.

But that was all in the background. Nadezhda didn't process it. Her mind was racing. What should she say? Should she *lie?* Admit it? What now?

Her mouth was ahead of her brain and jumped in, answering the questions for her.

"How did you know I was?" she heard herself ask.

He laughed. It was a humourless laugh.

"Oh, come on, look at yourself! You've got nothing, no money and barely any belongings. And you were hitch-hiking insane conditions. As for your 'story', you made it up in a hurry. There is no family friend, is there...?" he prompted.

The girl was still reeling. She didn't know what to do or say now. Was he annoyed with her?

Now, he seemed to read her mind, or more likely her stunned, terrified face.

"Don't worry, I don't mind. I'm just curious."

"Well, fine." She came out of her shock at last and started to speak. She was briefly interrupted by a server placing their sandwiches and drinks in front of them, but resumed when said server had left.

"Fine, I'm running away from my mother. She lied to me my whole life. But you're wrong, there *is* a family friend. I'm going to someone I know will help me. Who just happens to be a long way from my mother at the same time."

This was as close to the truth as she wanted to get. She didn't want to reveal more about her mother's 'lies'.

And she didn't *know* that Dariya would help her, she was just desperately hoping she would.

He shrugged. "Fine, fine. I just wanted to know."

That slightly uncomfortable conversation out of the way, they finished their lunch and once it was paid for, headed back to the car.

The rest of the journey was mercifully short and soon, they were driving along the main road into Yaroslavl.

Presently, they pulled up outside a large house, with a black painted door and thick, dark curtains drawn over the windows.

Nadezhda looked at it curiously. It was...odd, in a way she couldn't quite place.

Vasily cleared his throat awkwardly.

"Well...This is - *was* - my mother's house..." There was a pause. "Will you be able to find your family friend okay from here?" He double-checked.

"I think so." Nadezhda nodded.

"Just let me check her address." She reached into her small bundle of belongings and pulled out her father's diary, the most important treasure she needed on her quest.

Opening it up, she held it close to her chest, clutching at it like a child guarding some stolen sweets, wanting to keep her family secrets to herself.

This mildly amused Vasily but was proved warranted, as he somehow managed to peek around her slight shoulders and read some of what was written there.

In truth, he only saw two brief words, but they made him gasp.

This recaptured Nadezhda's attention.

"What?" she questioned, looking up with a slight scowl, irritated by the newfound knowledge that he had been spying on her as she read.

"Dariya Volkova!" he gasped again. "That was my mother's name," he added as her reproachful stare seemed to silently question him.

This new revelation took time for her to process. The strange coincidence of her having met the son of the very woman she had been desperately seeking...

And the cruel twist of fate - That the only person who might know about her father and the mystery around his death was now dead herself.

Selfish as it might seem, tears sprang to her eyes. Not for the dead woman and the family she had left behind, but tears of sheer frustration that she had come so far to fail.

What would *she* do *now?*

But to the grieving son, her tears were touching.

"Our families must have been close..." he mused, "Though I have to say I don't know you. But, if you were planning to stay with my mother, then I can't leave you with nowhere else to go. Stay a while anyway," he offered.

Her head snapped up and she rubbed away her tears, surprised by the offer.

She *didn't* have anywhere else to go, but she had nothing much to stay for now, either. Dariya couldn't help her.

Yet... She couldn't go back home, could she? After everything that had been said and done, she didn't feel like she *had* a home left to go to.

She have to start over, whether she could find anything out about her father or not. And he was the only person she had *any* connection to right now...

Nevertheless, she worried that she might be intruding on his life by staying.

"Won't your family be grieving?" she asked tentatively.

"Oh, we are, but if you or your family are close to my mother, she - and our family - would welcome you at the funeral," he assured her.

"You're sure?" she checked again, concerned to intrude.

"Of course. I wouldn't offer otherwise," he pointed out.

"Then thank you! I don't have any other option." Nadezhda finally accepted, drying her eyes properly, though it was on the sleeve of her shirt.

Vasily smiled his strange little smile again. It was meaningful, but she was damned if she could work out what the meaning there *was*.

"You're welcome. Just one more thing..." he began.

She nodded and he went on.

"I didn't want to press you while you were in shock, but I'm confused. If our families are close as you say, I should have heard about you. What's your full name, please?"

There was another pause. Nadezhda didn't know if she ought to tell him. Would he have heard about her mysterious family history from his mother?

But after he had taken her in, even during a tough time for him, it was only fair to answer him that one question.

Besides, a part of her hoped he had heard something, because right now, there was no one else who would tell her.

"I'm Nadezhda Moroz," she answered after a few moments.

She thought she saw him pale slightly.

But maybe it was simply the light as he wordlessly opened the car door. Either way, he ignored her answer as he silently motioned for her to follow him into the house...

The House And The Deal

Entering the house, Nadezhda was immediately hit by the stark contrast between the hall she was now standing in and the house's exterior.

From the outside, the building was closed up, dark and tall, standing forebodingly over the street, its black door like that to some kind of dungeon and the drawn curtains making the windows into unseeing eyes...

It looked like a horror house outside, black, odd, and deeply uncomfortable just to see, although it wasn't in a way she could describe.

But the interior was like a hospital. They were standing in a whitewashed hallway with a white tiled floor, silent, empty, and sterile.

Perhaps it wasn't that different after all. It still seemed weird, and it definitely wasn't a 'home'. She didn't want to stay here. But she didn't have any other options right now.

"Are you coming?"

Vasily was somehow already at the other end of the hall, his hand on the handle of a tall white door.

Nadezhda had been hesitating in the entrance for a while. She sighed and nodded, following him to the door.

He turned the handle and pushed the door open. The room beyond was bare and white too. Whitewashed walls, a carpet like fresh snow and no furniture.

But this room was buzzing with noise and people.

The crowd, she guessed, had to be Vasily's family. They all looked like him, anyway. Almost uncannily like him.

What were they, clones? She caught a glimpse of one man's face from the side and could have sworn he even had the same scar.

And of course, everyone was in black.

Except her, she realised, nervous that she stuck out like a sore thumb now.

Vasily silently stepped inside and slunk to the side of the room as though he thought so too and was trying not to be noticed.

She followed near behind him, but it didn't work.

"Vaska!" Someone called out to him.

He turned around with a grimace of a fake smile on his face and reluctantly hugged a woman who had shouted out to him.

Nadezhda looked the woman up and down as he did, for some reason automatically suspicious towards her.

She was a petite young girl in a black cocktail dress, with the same tan skin and dark hair as him. Now the scar was definitely noticeable as well.

Maybe she's his twin sister or something, maybe the scar's from some genetic condition...

She mused, trying to reason past the uncanny resemblance that made her uncomfortable, before reassuring herself with the thought that he didn't seem overly fond of her.

"I heard you were out of town, I'm glad you could make it back."

The woman smiled before her gaze fell on Nadezhda, half-hiding behind Vasily.

She looked her up and down too, returning her suspicion with narrowed eyes.

"Didn't know you had a plus one," she quipped.

"Who's this?" That comment was said in a much less jokey, colder tone.

Vasily glanced over at her as if he was still trying to make his mind up about that as well, "Uhm..." he paused, unsure. The girl was tapping her foot impatiently.

An excuse, made up on the spot, rushed to his lips.

"She's my girlfriend," he blurted out.

"Really? Didn't know you had one, but I guess it makes sense you'd bring her along." She seemed to buy it, turning to Nadezhda again.

"Don't break my little brother's heart."

Nadezhda turned red at that idea with all its implications, and Vasily seemed to be flushed too.

"Di, please, you don't need to be like that!" he hissed to her, before switching the topic back to 'safe' small talk, "anyway, Nadya, this is Diana, my sister. Di, this is Nadezhda," he introduced them.

Nadezhda managed a strained smile, nervous in the face of Diana's barely masked dislike for her but trying to be nice to Vasily's family.

He was letting her stay in their time of grief, after all.

Lacking any similar motive to be friendly, Diana shrugged and walked away without another word.

"Well, that could have gone better..."Nadezhda muttered to Vasily.

He laughed. "Don't worry about Di, she just takes a while to warm up to new people," he explained.

His companion didn't seem convinced, raising an eyebrow at him doubtfully. "Are you sure? I don't want to intrude if your family don't want me to be here."

"They'll be fine, Nadya, trust me," he told her calmly.

She wondered why he thought she should, in the situation, seeing as they hardly knew one another.

But he had helped her when he didn't need to, so she was willing to do that. So long as he could answer one question that was on her mind...

"Why did you lie to them about me then? We're not..." she blushed slightly as she thought about that excuse that he'd given to Diana.

Why would he say that? What did they have to hide from his family? She wanted answers.

But she wasn't prepared for the answer.

He grabbed her arm and pulled her out the crowded room into a small kitchen, then whispered to her:

"Because I know who you are. And it won't go well if they find out."

Her mind and heart were both racing as she stood in shock, then just about managed to hiss. "What are you talking about?"

"Long story," he said dismissively, "And not one to discuss here. But just...Stick with me, okay? I'm trying to protect you," he added firmly.

Nadezhda tried to process this. Well, she didn't exactly have anywhere else to go.

And... Was it possible that Vasily really did know something about her? Or her father? If so, well, he was the best lead she had now...

"Fine," she replied at length, "I'll stay, but when we get a chance to talk safely, you need to tell me everything."

"Deal." he took her hand in his and shook it.

She wasn't quite sure why, as he did so, she took so much notice of how cold and smooth his skin felt against hers, and how easily his large hand enclosed her slight one.

This little adventure had become very strange, and as he had been her sole ally throughout it, she reasoned that it was only natural for some emotional confusion to creep into her life now, and for him to be at its epicentre.

Once she had convinced herself of that, it was easy to dismiss her thoughts and simply shake his hand in return before pulling free of his grasp.

Relieved, she hurriedly encouraged him to leave before the weirdness she had felt could sneak up on her again.

"Shouldn't we get back in there before anyone realises that we're missing?" she suggested, gesturing into the other room.

Instantly, his serious demeanour was back.

"We should," he nodded gravely, "and let's not talk about this to anyone else."

As they wandered quietly into the main room again, Nadezhda found herself wondering about that comment, and indeed, about Vasily's whole attitude.

From the way he had been acting, she was beginning to suspect the secretive history of her family was shrouded in some unimaginable darkness...

The Family And The Funeral

The rest of Nadezhda's first day in the Volkov family's home passed without event.

Vasily refused to shed any more light on what he knew about her father with his family around, so all she was able to do was follow him, the only person around that she knew, and try to avoid conversation with any of his relatives.

Finally, she had had enough - well, more than enough - of this and was tired.

 She muttered to him, "If you're still sure there's room for me to stay here and everyone will be okay with it...I'd like to go to bed now. Today's been..."

"Long?" he supplied when she failed to finish her explanation, trailing off.

"No problem. You're welcome in my room."

At the suggestion of sharing his room, the pale young girl coloured considerably. Her mind and her heart were both racing as she automatically rushed to an assumption...

"What?!" Was the only response she managed at first.

"People will expect it. They think we're together." He sounded cool and calm as he explained himself.

And who's to blame for that? Who put that little idea into everyone's minds?

 Her questioning thoughts were sarcastic as she gave him a hard stare, dealing with her own flustered confusion by getting annoyed.

"So where are you planning to sleep? Because we are not sharing a bed!" She snapped firmly, putting her foot down about that.

True, it was the first direction her mind had rushed in, but she was just... emotional at the moment, she told herself.

They were just helping one another out in a totally platonic way, no matter what else went through her head sometimes, and it would stay that way.

She wasn't here to get entangled with anyone. She was here to find out the truth about her family.

Despite having sternly reminded herself of that, she was still blushing horribly, and Vasily noted that she looked like a tomato right now.

He chuckled to himself but took pity on her anyway and finally answered:

"On the floor. You take the bed."

"I... Oh," she stammered softly, still trying, and failing to regain her self-control and dignity.

"Thank you..." she managed to reply.

"No problem," he smiled, "I'll show you up."

Gesturing for her to follow him, he walked out to the hall they had entered through, opening another door to a flight of stairs.

She trailed after him, glad of some silence in which to cool off from her embarrassment at their misunderstanding.

They walked on for what seemed like a long, long time. The stairs were short enough, but there were a lot of corridors and a lot of shut doors in the house.

Well, it was a big house, she supposed it wasn't unusual for there to be so many rooms - yet she couldn't help but wonder what all these rooms could possibly be used for in a family home...

She didn't dwell on it, though, and they eventually reached Vasily's room. He let her in, and she looked around.

Again, it was weirdly unhomely, with glaringly whitewashed walls and a plain white carpet.

There was a single bed in the room and nothing else, no personal touch or belongings that told her anything about him. It might have been a hotel room.

Nevertheless, she was tired, and it was a relief just to see the bed. Soon, she lay down and fell fast asleep.

When she woke up, there was no one else in the room. She wondered how long she had been asleep if Vasily had already woken up.

But there wasn't a clock in the room, and she didn't have a watch on, so in the end, she just got up and wandered out.

Standing in the corridor, Nadezhda pondered where she was likely to find Vasily. Well, probably downstairs with his family.

But...Should she join them right now, and have to face his annoying sister and the rest of his odd relatives?

Or...Perhaps she could explore up here a little bit, just to see more of the rooms she was so curious about last night.

For a moment, she entertained the idea out of idle curiosity, but then her moral ideals kicked in.

No, she mustn't. If she would just compromise her morality so easily, then wouldn't she just be like the woman who had instilled those same morals in her, then betrayed her. She didn't want to be a hypocrite like her mother.

With that in mind, she retraced the steps Vasily had led her on last night.

But as she reached the top of the stairs, the door at their foot opened, and a good portion of the Volkov family started to spill through it.

Vasily appeared and managed to raise his voice above the other clamours of conversation going on in the crowd.

"Nadya, good to see you're up! We're just going to get ready for the funeral..."

There was a pause, silence descending. Then he looked up to her with a warm smile that didn't reach his eyes.

"You'll join us, won't you?"

Nadezhda considered that. Well, it would seem heartless not to, after coming all this way to see Dariya.

And even more so if she was pretending to be Vasily's girlfriend. Anyway, sitting around in the house by herself would do nothing but tempt her into looking around...

But there was one minor problem.

"I'd love to, but...I don't have any mourning clothes with me," she admitted.

 That was true, she didn't have any clothes with her but those that she was wearing, a white blouse and light blue knee-length skirt, with her signature blue and white striped headband, an old gift from Katya, perched on top of her brown locks.

She had been dressed this way since she left her mother's place, and her clothes were damp from the blizzard, crumpled from sleeping in the car and generally worse for wear.

Clearly not presentable clothes for a funeral.

"Well, why did you come without them?" she heard Diana's sharp tones from below.

Vasily tutted at her. "Now, now, Di. We left in a hurry. But Di, since you're determined to get involved, why don't you help out and lend Nadya something?" he suggested.

There was just a hint of smugness about him as he rebuked her that made Nadezhda think that, despite his defence of his sister before, he enjoyed getting one over her in this small way.

He doesn't like her, she reminded herself. *Good.*

But, even with that satisfying her, she'd really rather not share a wardrobe with someone who couldn't be bothered to hide her contempt for her.

Diana, on the other hand, may have scowled slightly about it, but didn't seem to want to upset her brother, as she gave a grudging, "sure," before stomping up the stairs.

When she drew level with Nadezhda, she gestured for her to follow her, without a word but with a nasty glare.

Nadezhda sighed and trailed after the girl. Presently, they entered another bedroom.

It was as plain as Vasily's but had the addition of a large wardrobe against one wall. Diana strode over to it and yanked it open.

She pulled out a black dress and tossed it, hanger, and all, at her brother's 'girlfriend' silently.

Nadezhda barely caught it.

"Thanks..." she found the good grace to mutter, albeit not very politely.

"Where can I change?" she added, not wanting to do so in front of Diana.

The other reluctantly left her alone in the room long enough to pull the dress on.

It was tight on Nadezhda, for though she was slight, Diana was even tinier. She wasn't fond of the shortness of the skirt and the strapless, halter-neck style, either.

But she supposed she would bear it for however long the funeral was. For Vasily. And for Dariya, of course.

She kept her headband on though, in an attempt to still feel like herself now that she was totally out of place and away from anything familiar to her.

When she was dressed, she left Diana's room as fast as she could, returning to the main room of the house and waiting for everyone to be ready in awkward silence.

Vasily appeared a few minutes later, having wasted time with some mystery, seeing as he was simply wearing another black suit, identical to the one he had been wearing before.

He grinned at the sight of her, though.

"Nice dress," he told her, "getting along alright with my lovely sister?" he added teasingly.

"Not wonderfully, but whatever," she answered with a shrug.

"At least I'm dressed up and ready to go now."

He nodded. "You are. And maybe after that's...All over," he faltered a little at that point, "I'll be able to tell you more about you and your family."

Her heart thumped hard at the suggestion of getting the answers she had come here for in the first place.

But that had to wait. Vasily's family members started to trickle in again, in various formal outfits, and it was soon time to leave.

The parties made their way to different cars. Vasily put his hand on Nadezhda's arm and guided her to his. Diana trudged after them with a scowl.

The group got into the car, with Nadezhda sitting in the front at Vasily's side as she had on her journey here. Diana got into the back, grumbling.

"What's all this crap doing back here?" she snapped, pushing some stuff off the seats.

"Oh, I'm sorry, that's mine..." Nadezhda answered, looking over her shoulder into a death glare.

She reached back and grabbed some of it, making a token effort to fix the 'problem' by pulling it out of the way.

A piece of paper came away in her hand, so she shoved it hastily into the folds of her dress and turned away from Diana's glare.

She never got a proper reply though, as the other woman simply sat down, kicking at something under her seat.

When Diana looked down, she saw that it was a book that had fallen open on a page. The page bore her mother's name and address.

To the young woman, this was just what she needed. She had suspected her brother of lying to her, simply from his demeanour when he had introduced her to the 'girlfriend' she despised so much.

She knew him well and couldn't bring herself to believe he really cared for this annoying stranger.

 Besides, they were always acting oddly, whispering away together, and sneaking off. She was sure, absolutely sure, that something was going on. It wasn't just about her personal dislike for the girl at all.

Now, she had some proof. Maybe. It looked like Nadezhda had sought out her mother's funeral for some other reason...

The idea of a stranger barging into her family home at a time like this for some unknown reason, bewitching her brother to her cause and spreading lies made Diana form a plan on the spot.

Briefly making sure Nadezhda had looked away, she snatched the book from the floor, shut it and jammed it into a clutch it was nearly the same size as.

This was *evidence.* Evidence that needed examining later, in privacy, as well as in much greater detail.

She needed to find out who this woman was that her brother would lie to the family for, and what she had wanted with her late mother...

Oblivious to this plot against her, Nadezhda sat in the front of the car impatiently. After a busy few days, this quiet journey seemed odd.

At first, she peered around at the view from the window, but that was mostly snow and rows upon rows of houses. Nothing to hold her interest.

She tried studying Vasily's face as he drove, but she began to feel uncomfortable, watching him. Her hands were sweating, her face was flushed, and her brain was full of stupid thoughts.

So, she distracted herself by looking at the other passenger of the car. Not directly, of course, all that would give her was a crick in the neck and some venomous glares.

But in the centre mirror, she could make out Diana's face.

She hadn't paid much attention to the other girl's looks before, due to their mutual dislike of one another, but she had to admit Diana was pretty.

She had a short, sleek pixie cut of jet-black hair, the same tan skin as her brother, and a matching scar too.

Perhaps her odd feelings for Vasily were why she found Diana pretty, but it also added a disconcerting feeling to looking at her. So Nadezhda studied her for some unique features.

Her eyes, she realised, were a darker grey and slanted slightly.

She had a thinner face too, which, the girl recalled, gave her quite a sharp look when she was annoyed, as she normally was when they saw one another.

"Nadya!" Vasily was jogging her arm.

She jumped out of her thoughts a little guiltily and, realising they had arrived at the church, left the car silently. The others got out too, and they walked in silence into the building.

There was a coffin already placed inside. Flowers were arranged on top, around a photo.

Continuing on her earlier vein of thought in the hopes of feeling less awkward as the odd one out, the only person not a member of the family, Nadezhda studied the photo.

That's their mother? She thought. Well, it's easy to see where the looks come from.

And it was. Dariya Volkova had had the same tan skin as her children, the same light grey eyes as Vasily, although they were a lot softer in her photo, and the same jet-black hair, falling in soft waves to her shoulders.

She even had the same curved scar on her cheek. That was starting to freak Nadezhda out, the way they all had that mark.

But she shrugged to herself, now wasn't the time or place for that.

Perhaps later, after the funeral, when she held Vasily to his promise, they would end up sharing the freaky stories of their families.

She kept that thought to herself, merely blushing slightly as she took a seat by Vasily's side.

She sat patiently throughout the whole funeral service, as various almost identical family members stood up, said a few words, and sat down again. She shed no tears. Well, she had never really known Dariya.

But when they were in the graveyard, she wept. She wept knowing that one of the last people to truly know her father and his story had gone to her grave.

Her display of grief seemed to touch Vasily, and she wept more knowing that it was for selfish reasons, not for his departed mother, that she was crying.

Eventually, though, the tears stopped, and they bundled into the car again, driving to a pub that had been booked for the wake.

Then there was the wake itself, a deeply strange event...

Mostly because that was when Nadezhda met Vladimir Volkov. She had been vaguely aware of him throughout the funeral.

He had sat at the front of the church and stood by the very edge of Dariya's grave, throwing earth and roses in, but never said a word. He hadn't been at the house beforehand.

And, in the sea of black, he wore a long, white jacket. He looked like a doctor who had got lost. Albeit a retired doctor, from his grey hair and beard.

Diana had veered off to talk to him as soon as she had seen him, and a few moments later, she brought him back over to where Vasily and Nadezhda were hiding in a corner.

Vasily jumped when he noticed the old man.

"Oh! Grandpa...Good to see you," he told him.

Vladimir smiled.

"Good to see you too, Vaska and... Diana says you brought your girlfriend to meet us," he added thoughtfully, his eyes falling on Nadezhda, who blushed at the attention.

She still wasn't used to being referred to as Vasily's 'girlfriend'. It made her blush every time. Though she couldn't honestly say she minded.

Vasily looked over at her and blushed slightly too.

"Yes, this is Nadya."

He introduced her with a gesture towards her and a smile. His grandfather smiled too, reaching out his hand.

For a second, the girl didn't process that, then she put her hand in his to shake hands. He didn't shake her hand but clasped it in his, making her just a tiny bit uncomfortable.

"Lovely...Are you planning to join our family yet?" he asked, his eyes fixed on her left cheek.

That was odd, she thought, it was like a baby that couldn't quite focus on her eyes. Yet his gaze seemed intently focused.

His questioning made them both blush again. "W... We're not quite ready for that," Vasily managed to answer.

"I see..." the old man shrugged. "Well, maybe one day," he said, smiling absentmindedly as he released her hand again.

A few moments later, he wandered off to talk to someone else, taking Diana with him.

Vasily turned to Nadezhda apologetically.

"Sorry about Grandpa, he's a bit...Odd," he told her, "Anyway, now everyone's distracted and the actual, you know... the funeral."

He always faltered a little talking about his mother having passed, she noted, but that was understandable.

"Now that's over, why don't we find somewhere private and talk about what you wanted to talk about," he suggested in a whisper.

Nadezhda's heart jumped into her throat as she nodded. This was it. She was finally going to find out the truth about her father.

Hopefully. If he had heard the full truth from Dariya. If not, the secret she had travelled so far to uncover was already buried with the late woman...

Questions

While the various family members at the wake were chatting, arguing, or drinking, Vasily and Nadezhda crept out of the room.

Leaving the pub, they hunted for a private spot, but in the end, they settled on returning to Vasily's rusty little car, where they seemed to be spending an awful amount of time at the moment and driving around and around while they talked.

As soon as the engine had started, Nadezhda attacked Vasily with questions.

"So, what is it you know about me? What's the big secret? Does this have something to do with my father?" she demanded to know, everything pouring out in a rush.

He was tense, very tense. She could easily see that, but she was too desperate to pay any attention right now.

She needed to know, and he wasn't even the last resort, he was somewhere after that.

"What makes you think it's about your father?" he asked quite sharply as they drove at about 15 miles an hour down the road, ignoring the honking behind them.

"Because he's the only part of my life I don't know about!" she answered, equally sharply as the stress spilt over.

"And I have to find out. You have to know!" she added, desperation evident in her voice.

Vasily shrugged. "Why would I know?"

She almost growled but repressed it to an inaudible mutter. She always muttered when she was angry.

But after a few minutes, that subsided, and she managed to speak to him again.

"No one else seems to. But my father left me that book, with this address. He said to find your mother, she's supposed to be the only one who knows the whole truth, and she's not here. But you know something."

When all that was out, she took a deep breath. This whole thing was a lot to explain. It was just a lot.

Now Vasily sighed.

"Well, I know. Or at least, I think I do. As I said, it's a long story. Are you sure you want to hear it?" he replied, some of his stress fading now that she had explained her side of things.

"I have to hear it," she insisted, determined to know the truth even if it hurt her.

Despite her determination, she was clearly nervous, twirling one strand of her light brown hair repetitively as she waited for his reply.

"Fine, then."

He shrugged again, then opened his mouth to continue to talk.

BANG!

A car slammed into them from behind, cutting off Vasily's attempt to explain and sending them both shooting forward amid a mix of yells around them.

The shock and the confused situation washed over them, taking over.

They didn't manage to keep talking to one another as they were swept up in it, and before they truly knew what had happened, they were both at the hospital, being checked over.

There was a police officer in the room as well. When Nadezhda sat herself up, now that the doctor had determined that she was okay, the officer looked over at her.

"Ma'am, if you're sure you're okay, we have some questions for you about how this happened," he told her.

"That's... That's fine." She nodded, still a little disoriented and unsure of the situation.

She looked around the room as she got up to leave with him.

She could only see Vasily and other staff members there, there wasn't any sign of a patient who might be the driver. Shrugging it off, she walked out anyway.

On her way out, she passed Diana in the doorway. The two women exchanged scowls for a moment, then passed. Diana made her way over to her brother's bedside.

She didn't waste time with pleasantries or bother asking if he was okay after the accident, but said to him, "I see your 'girlfriend' is still hanging around."

Vasily looked quite baffled by that remark. "Of course she is," he replied.

"We need to talk about her," His sister added, folding her arms across her chest firmly as she spoke.

He opened his mouth to ask why, but Diana, smug in her discoveries, butted in without letting him.

"Did you know she's...From Antonin?" she questioned, a small pause and change of tone in words as she remembered that there was still hospital staff in the room.

She seemed to be using some sort of code to allude to Nadezhda's origins.

Of course, she was. It wasn't something they could openly discuss, but the Volkov family remembered Antonin Jelennski all too well.

And the names of those who had associated with him, including his girlfriend.

Nadezhda's parents' identities were enough to make her their number one enemy.

And, while Diana didn't know both her parents' identities, with a little research, she had been able to tie the writing in Nadezhda's precious little book to Antonin.

Any connection to him was enough to pinpoint Nadezhda as 'trouble'.

Her brother understood all this and paled visibly.

He had known, of course, he had. He knew, or at least he thought that he knew, her full story, but admitting that to his sister would have brought about the very scenario he had hoped to protect Nadezhda from.

"I... I didn't, no," he lied, badly, "What makes you say that anyway?" he asked, wondering how on Earth she had found out.

"You're a rotten liar, Brother Dear," she accused in a sarcastically sweet tone, "She has a book from you know who. With Mama's address in." she pointed out, suddenly serious again.

"Now why are you with her?"

"Sis, please, I'm just-" he started to talk, trying to piece together an argument as he spoke, but getting cut off again.

His sister didn't appear to be in a mood to listen to him right now.

"Whatever. Just know that if you're not planning to do what's best for the family, I will have to hand her over to

Grandpa," she told him, as though she was revealing her trump card in this little sibling argument.

His eyes widened. "You can't do that!" he snapped at her.

Her smirk said it all. She could, she would, and she was planning to.

He sighed.

"You know what? Fine, you give me some time to get out of here and talk to her, and I'll find a way to bring her to you. That's what you think is 'best', right?!" he sounded pretty bitter now.

"Yes." she answered simply, before holding out her hand.

"So, do we have a deal?" she demanded to know.

He glared daggers at her as they shook on it.

While they had been talking, Nadezhda had finished a pretty trivial questioning session with the police officer, having discovered that the other driver had fled the scene and that they were looking for information.

But she hadn't known anything about the other driver, anyway, seeing as they had been hit from behind.

So, she was wandering back into the room as Diana walked out, oblivious to the whispers that had taken place behind her back.

Betrayed

When Nadezhda made her way back to Vasily's bedside, he greeted her with as much of a smile as he could manage in his current state of nervousness.

It looked more like a grimace than a smile, and instantly prompted her to question:

"Are you okay?"

"Uh...Yeah, it's nothing," he answered, hesitating.

He was torn now, between his duty to his family, his urge to help and protect Nadezhda as he had promised to, and his fear of what Diana might be planning to do if she didn't get her own way.

Either way, he needed to talk to Nadezhda somewhere more private than this.

Whether it was to help her or to betray her as his sister had urged, he was yet to decide, but she was key to whatever would unfold next.

"So ..." he paused, wondering how to start this conversation.

She filled the gaps for him, something still weighing heavily on her mind.

"You never did get to tell me that 'story'," she pointed out.

He watched her as she spoke. She was so unlike any other woman he had ever met. Not that that was saying too much, he usually ended up only socialising with his family.

They didn't leave him much choice...His thoughts slipped off on a bitter tangent.

He reigned them back in hastily. There had been girls when he was travelling. And none of them had had the light that was shining in Nadezhda's bright blue eyes right now.

Perhaps it was because of her unusual background, her determination to find it...Perhaps he was attracted to her because she was leading him into something dangerous here.

It didn't matter why. He had been slowly realising he had become attracted to her for a while now.

In fact, despite his initial reluctance to pick her up when he saw her at the roadside, he had been growing more and more attached to her ever since she had slept in his car that night, and he had watched over her...

But he hadn't planned to address his changing feelings for her until he had been forced into this position, where he might have to betray her without ever exploring what might have developed from his desire...

The young man suddenly snapped back into reality as he became aware that she was waiting for him to speak.

He renewed his smile, trying to give her a flash of a carefree personality that he didn't really possess. He wanted to put her at her ease, after all.

"I didn't, did I? Well, I'll be ready to leave after a quick check with the doctor. Then...Why don't you and I get some lunch somewhere and talk it over?" he suggested.

Nadezhda paused. She had found Vasily intriguing, despite his strangeness, from the point of their first meeting, even when he had been grumpy with her about giving her a ride.

And the more they had got to know one another, slowly becoming companions, maybe even friends, the more she had begun to find his eccentricity a little charming.

After all, he seemed to grow nicer to her, however strange his behaviour was, and use his oddness to help her.

If it wasn't for his even odder family putting her off, and her own single-minded focus on her mission to find her father's story, maybe something more would have happened already.

With them pretending to be boyfriend and girlfriend, it was a wonder such a situation hadn't arisen already.

But now, when he was actually asking her out and making an effort to be charming, it felt wrong. His smile was brittle and his eyes dull.

She was still a little worried about him. But this could bring about the reveal she had been waiting for from the start.

And if he would speak to the doctor before leaving, she would know he was okay, wouldn't she?

Talking herself into it, Nadezhda nodded. "Alright, lunch it is," she agreed.

That was his cue to summon a doctor, calling one over as he passed by. The man didn't look too pleased to be interrupted like that but nevertheless agreed that it would be fine for them to leave.

With that, Vasily took Nadezhda by the hand and whisked the blushing young woman out of the hospital.

They were halfway down the street by the time she managed to think to ask:

"Why are you holding my hand?"

"What?" he asked absent-mindedly as he scanned the shops at the side of the street for a suitable restaurant.

"We don't have to pretend to be dating right now," she pointed out, not entirely sure she minded but curious about why he was doing this.

Unless he had some kind of feelings for her... She didn't dwell on that thought for long, not wanting to entertain it without being sure.

"Maybe I want to," he answered with a shrug, making her blush even more, wondering if and how he really meant that.

Again, she didn't get an opportunity to finish thinking about that, as she was rather unceremoniously dragged into a small café with a cry of "C'mon!" From her companion, who seemed rather enthusiastic about this idea.

When they were inside, she sat down at a table with him and asked, "Well?" Curious about his enthusiasm.

Perhaps he was finally preparing to tell her the full truth, just as she had hoped all this time.

He took a deep breath. This was it.

"Well, all the time we've spent together has led us to become quite close, and I really do think you're unique and beautiful. So, it would be nice if we were actually together, not just pretending, right?" he tried to explain his reasoning to her.

This came as a surprise. She had expected something else entirely and turned red at this. But after a few more moments of consideration, she managed a nod and began to reply.

"It would. But I was actually asking about the 'long story'. You know, with my father?" she prompted, cursing herself for being so vague, even though she was glowing from his compliments and him finally asking her to be his girlfriend.

Vasily flushed. "Oh ... I'm sorry. But you did agree with me, right?" he had to check, excited by the idea that he hadn't just been shot down.

After a nod, he calmed down and started anew, explaining.

"Well, you see, my family is...Kind of special. Grandpa organises us to achieve wonderful things. And one of those things was a cloning machine that allowed for some alterations...Mama was his first clone; we were copied from her. He knew he needed more people to reach his full capabilities. He's something of a genius, you know."

She sat, looking stunned at this information. It made sense though. They did all look scarily alike.

It just made her wonder what this 'genius' wanted from the world... And where she fitted in.

"How is this about my father?" she asked.

"He was... I think he started out as one of my mother's boyfriends," he revealed, "but Grandpa didn't approve. She told him too much, depended on someone outside of the family, and eventually, it was discovered that he was spying on us. He was a policeman, spying on us for his superior officer. And two-timing my mother with said officers' daughter..." he added with a scowl.

Now her mind was really reeling. She had known that her grandfather was a police officer, of course, though she had never met him, his children talked about him as though he was a great hero.

So, was that how her mother and father had met? Had her grandfather been involved in all this as well?

How little she had known about her family... Now she was only just learning that they had been involved in something very dangerous...

"And why-?" she cut herself off as his face paled.

He grabbed her wrist urgently and pulled her to her feet. But it was too late.

As he dragged her towards the door, hoping they could make their escape, it was thrown open by Diana.

Behind her, two other members of the family waited. These two were obviously the bouncers or something, both huge, muscular figures, looming over the sneering girl.

"Good boy, Vaska, you lured her into a nice little trap here," Diana smirked. She gestured at the two brutes behind her.

"Take her," she commanded.

Vasily stood there, staring down at his sister angrily. He had wanted to keep Nadezhda to himself for a while.

Talking to her had been fascinating, to the point where he had wanted to choose her over his family. But he couldn't, not noticeably. He had to go along with his sister's plan.

For now, at least. So, he stood back passively as his family members closed in on Nadezhda.

Nadezhda glared at her new 'boyfriend'. He had *betrayed* her.

For some reason, his family hated hers, some reason she might never know now that he had thrown her to the wolves.

She screamed at them and lashed out, only succeeding in kicking Diana's shin before she was picked up by one of the men.

He thrust his hand around her throat and squeezed until the struggling stopped and her world turned black.

Discoveries In The Cells

The light slowly started to creep back into Nadezhda's world as her eyes flickered open.

Blinking, she started to get her bearings and then jolted upright in a panicked frenzy as her memories assaulted her mind. What had happened?

They had grabbed her! She vaguely remembered struggling. But Vasily had just stood there, staring.

He must have betrayed her, his supposed girlfriend, for his crazy sister.

'Take her', Diana had said, so they must have done. And now she was...

Where?! For the first time, she took in her new surroundings, her bright blue eyes swivelling around madly as she tried to make sense of it all. Where was this place?

The room was too dark for her to make much out, but that didn't matter, because there was nothing to see anyway.

She was sitting on a narrow wooden bench in a small, bleak room, bare of anything else.

In front of her was a big wooden door. She got up tentatively, surprised at how much her body ached. What had they done to her?

With no idea and no way of finding out, she merely sighed softly and made her way over to the door anyway.

Trying to open in, it was obvious she was wasting her time.

She took another look around. High up on the left-hand wall, she could just make out a small, barred window.

But she wouldn't be able to use that for anything. Another frustrated sigh escaped her.

"Is somebody there?" A voice from the darkness called out to her.

"Uh...Yes? Where are you? Who's there?" She tried and failed not to sound too nervous.

It was very strange to hear someone speak from the shadows of what she could only assume was her prison. At least, that was what this place looked like...

"Nadya?!" A second, shocked-sounding voice cut in.

This one was familiar to her, but out of place here. Jumping up onto the bench, she peered through the bars curiously.

This was a wasted effort; it was too dark to make anything on the other side out.

Even so, she thought the identity of the second voice was clear, even though she didn't understand why or how she'd be hearing it here, of all places.

"Uncle Sasha?" she questioned, amazed.

Could her Uncle's latest 'job' have led him here? Had he not been home for a while because he had been locked up by the creepy Volkov family?

"Yeah, it's me... What are you doing here?"

"I was wondering the same thing."

The first voice entered the discussion again.

"Ooh, family reunion, how sweet! Can we hurry this up, please? I need to concentrate on the final stages of my plan."

Nadezhda blinked in confusion and was about to question the other presence on the far side of the window and what the 'plan' referred to, but Sasha spoke up again before she could.

"So, what are you doing here?" he still sounded very shocked as he started to explain some of the latest parts of their family drama.

Great, she thought to herself, this was going to be hard work.

Well, she supposed she had to start at the beginning and hope it didn't confuse him too much.

"I... I found some things of my mother's and she-"

Here, the girl paused abruptly, wondering how to tell him. He was so close to Nikolina, he might not believe her. But she had to explain and now she was passed a point of no return.

"She lied to me. I'm not adopted." She dropped the bombshell.

"What?" he gasped.

"Isn't it usually the other way around?" the mystery voice questioned in a jokey tone.

Rolling her eyes, Nadezhda ignored that comment.

"It's weird, I know, but it's true. I went to Aunty Katya, and she knew. She gave me a diary from my father. I came here to find out more information about him."

She cut a long story short and revealed her journey so far, "But err... I guess you can tell that didn't work out well," she added sheepishly.

She was starting to see why her mother had argued that the truth was dangerous. Now she was trapped God alone knew where...

But she didn't mention that right now. Just the abridged story would be a lot for her unsuspecting Uncle to process.

It was. Even though she couldn't see what was going on in the other cell, she heard him gasp and could picture his face, knowing his surprised expression all too well.

"Well...I don't know why Nikolina would keep something like this a secret! I can't believe she never told me..."

He trailed off, processing this sudden and unexpected news, before having to put aside his personal feelings about his sister's secret to find out more.

"I can only imagine how you must have felt. Just tell me one thing, how big was the argument after you found out?"

She blushed in the darkness at the fact that he intuitively knew they would have quarrelled.

Perhaps he knew them too way or perhaps their personalities were both just a little too fiery for their own good...

"It was pretty bad. Then I walked out..." she admitted.

"Oh dear..." she heard Sasha mutter.

She flushed more but was soon distracted from her embarrassment by the unknown voice that seemed to be sharing her Uncle's cell.

"Alright, that was painful to listen to...But if you're all caught up, I have some better news."

"What?" the relatives questioned in unison.

"My escape plan is ready. We're getting out of here."

"Huh?" Nadezhda wrinkled her brow in confusion, a visual effect lost on the other half of the conversation due to the wall between them.

Sasha started to explain. "Oh, Sof here's been working on a way out of here since we got caught," he explained.

That reminded the other that she hadn't yet heard his side of the story. "Caught?" she inquired.

"Oh yeah..." he seemed to only just remember not explaining to her earlier.

"We were investigating Sof's cousin's murder, and I guess we pushed our luck a little," he finally revealed, "We've been stuck in here ever since. It must have been at least a month now..."

"I thought you were just too busy with work to come home!" she exclaimed, astounded that her Uncle had been captured for a month or so without her even realising.

She knew his job as a private investigator often kept him busy for a long time, but she was sure she would have known.

It was something of a shock to learn so suddenly that the world could be sinister and cruel, that a loved one could disappear, and no one would even realise.

She pushed away her miserable thoughts and tried to focus. This 'Sof' must be his latest client... And had their cousin been murdered by the Volkovs?

It had become obvious that they were trouble, but she hadn't expected this.

"Did ... Did the Volkovs kill Sof's cousin?" she asked tentatively.

"We think so, but we haven't reviewed all our evidence yet so..." Sasha trailed off, and Sof cut in sharply.

"Bullcrap! Everyone knows they did. Everyone in this stupid region knows they're liars, murderers, and psychos!" Their voice spat.

"That's why we gotta get out of here and take them down!" They added enthusiastically.

"How are we going to do that?" Nadezhda asked.

The response from the next cell was a few loud crashes, Sasha gasping and Sof swearing. Then some more crashes.

Then, with a horrible rumbling sound, the wall dividing the two cells fell in.

Escape

Pushing aside some rubble, Nadezhda squinted in the dark to see what had happened. A figure scowled at her.

"Hey, I was nearly there. Just... got some of my measurements wrong, that's all. They were only estimates." Sof defended herself.

Nadezhda looked past the girl to a crude wooden mechanism, presumably carved up out of the cell's bench, seeing as that was missing and the wood looked the same. It was rather crushed now.

Presumably it had been supposed to take out the door, not the wall...

Then her gaze turned back to Sof.

Through the darkness, she could just about make out that the other girl was about her height - five feet three inches, if she remembered correctly from the last time she had checked - but had a curvier figure and shorter, chin-length hair of a strawberry blonde colour.

She was curious about her Uncle's mysterious client and her weird device to escape.

"You made that?" she asked.

"Of course I did," Sof replied.

"But we do have a plan B." She added smugly.

"You have a plan B." Sasha cut in, obviously going for plausible deniability if this plan failed as well.

Nadezhda couldn't help but laugh at his tone, but she was mostly just relieved that he seemed to be okay.

He appeared to sense that and responded only with a brief hug. This close, she could tell they had been trapped here for a while, he smelt like he hadn't washed for a while and was quite dishevelled.

She thought she could see a bruise on his face too and bristled with silent, protective indignation at the idea that they had hurt him.

"Again, can we cut out the family reunion until we're out of here?" Sof interrupted.

They parted, and turned to her, waiting for some information about 'Plan B.' She gave them a big grin and pulled out a knife.

"We're going to get one of the guards and hold them up at knifepoint," she revealed.

Nadezhda looked shocked.

"First of all, how did they not take that thing off you?! And secondly, what guards? When do they come around? And are you sure we can overpower them?" She started to interrogate the other woman.

"You ask a hell of a lot of questions," Sof noted, sounding rather amused by that, "but if you must know, they didn't check my boots, yes, they have guards, and I've learnt their schedule so don't worry about that... and I'm pretty sure we'll manage" Her eyes glinted at this point, and Nadezhda looked nervously at Sasha.

He looked nervous too. They both suspected Sof had another plan up her sleeve.

She did and soon revealed it, gesturing to the pile of rubble.

"You two grab a couple of those iron bars, I've got my knife, I'm sure we can take at least one of them down," she told them.

Nadezhda looked over at the rubble. The crumbled wall did indeed contain three iron bars, remnants of the barred window between the two cells.

She hesitantly picked one up.

Sasha's eyes widened. "I can't be involved in this, you know, my legal career..." he began.

Sof rolled her eyes. "Listen, if you're stuck here for the rest of your life, you won't have a career. This is the only way any of us are getting out of here," she snapped.

It had to be conceded that she was right. Neither of the Morozs were used to violence, but this was a whole new world to them, a world of chaos and violence where this was necessary.

Sasha silently grasped a bar as well, as reluctant, and nervous as Nadezhda. Then the three prisoners settled in to wait for a victim.

It felt like an awfully long wait, but a few minutes later, there was a commotion outside.

"The inside wall must be breaking down; we need to secure the area!" Someone shouted.

Sof swore. She had hoped no one would see the pile of rubble from the outside and that when a guard had been foolish enough to unlock the door, they could attack.

"Prepare for trouble," she muttered to her group, clutching her knife menacingly.

There was the sound of running footsteps in the corridor outside and then someone opened the door.

As soon as the key turned in the lock, Sof sprang into action, jumping up and holding a knife to the throat of the man who swung the door open.

He was at least six foot tall, muscular, and brandishing his key like it was a weapon.

She flinched and prayed that the others could be trusted to back her up. The other guards in the corridor could be seen over his shoulder. It was teeming with them.

"Oi, give that here!" he growled and grabbed her arm, trying to yank the knife from her grip.

She kicked him in the shin as hard as she could, making him yell and bend over to clutch his leg.

Nadezhda struck hard with the iron bar, her arms shaking as she swung it into his ribs with as much force as she could muster.

She wasn't normally inclined to violence, but she was afraid now and knew this was the only option they had for escape.

The guard in the cell crumpled in a groaning heap on the floor, but his loud exclamations had already alerted others.

Nadezhda straightened up and doubled the grip on her weapon, surprised at herself and what she had just done.

This whole search for her father had led her into things she had never thought were possible... whether that was good or bad, she had yet to decide.

And it was an issue best left until another time, given the current situation.

Sof stepped into the doorway, raising her knife.

"You two better be ready," she announced, "It looks like we're fighting our way out of here."

As she spoke, another guard ran at her.

She raised the knife and jabbed it towards his head, which he hadn't had the common sense to protect, and he stumbled away, blood running down his temple.

Somewhere in the corridor, he fell over with a faint thump.

She pressed on, moving forward, and the others followed somewhat more nervously, still clutching their makeshift weapons inexpertly.

A guard grabbed at Sasha, missing as the private detective ducked and came back up with an iron bar, swinging it into the man's jaw with a horrible cracking sound.

"I can't believe I'm doing this!" he moaned as he ran away from the wounded man, glancing back occasionally, shocked at his own actions.

"Me neither, but we need to," Nadezhda called back to him as she jabbed an angry guard in his groin regions and hurried down the hallway after Sof.

The other woman beamed.

"You're catching on," she retorted, before grabbing a guard who was in a cell doorway by the shoulder and tugging her back, pushing her knife up against her throat.

"Let everyone out and get out of here. Your allies aren't going to be much more help anymore," she hissed.

It wasn't until she was part of the crowd of bemused ex-prisoners surging up the steps that Nadezhda realised a few things.

Firstly, the frightening extent of the Volkovs' crimes was truly apparent now, and she had never even suspected this was possible before.

There must be hundreds of people here, all of whom these psychos had locked up!

Secondly, it dawned on her that they had been in some sort of complex underneath the house... she hadn't even known it was down here, but there was a set of stairs at the end of a corridor, and they stumbled up these, straight into the main house.

Thankfully, as they raced into the living room and out through the front door, it was empty apart from the fearful guard who had avoided injury by only co-operating with Sof's demands.

And to think, when she was with Vasily, she hadn't even suspected any of this! They must work hard to fool people, hiding their crimes behind their smiles...

Dazed with shock, she dropped her hastily seized weapon, not wanting to walk along the street waving an iron bar, and followed Sof, who seemed to be the crowd's new leader by general agreement, to wherever she was taking them.

Like the other freed prisoners, she wasn't sure where that was, but she was curious to know what the cunning Sof's plan for dealing with these crazy people was...

After all, they had to do something about them now that they had broken out, didn't they? This couldn't go on, or they would more or less be at war with the Volkovs.

And Sof, who had set all this in motion and always seemed to have a plan, clearly hated the Volkovs with a passion.

If she was leading the newly formed mob of rescued prisoners, it would be one hell of a war...

New Plans

Sof led her mob of escapees to a small house on the outskirts of the city, leading them inside.

They hardly all fitted into the living room, but they crowded inside anyway, all watching her expectantly.

They were of all kinds of genders, ages, and walks of life.

They were also varying degrees of dishevelled and injured, indicating that each one had a different story of how they had come to be imprisoned by the Volkovs and how long they had been there.

Some were confused, blinking, and squinting at the world they had been freed into, others were wild-eyed, seeking revenge.

All of them watched Sof, all wanting something, answers, revenge, whatever...

They just needed someone to lead them, to tell them how to respond to the Volkovs' reign of evil, and she had brought them here, so she must be their new leader.

Nadezhda stood at the back of the crowd with her Uncle. He seemed nervous, unsure of what was going to happen.

She didn't know either, but she was curious to find out what Sof had planned.

To be seen by the whole crowd, the other young woman had climbed up on the table, and now Nadezhda could see her clearly.

She had a soft tan, strawberry blonde waves, and bright blue eyes. She was wearing torn jeans and an old t-shirt, with some mud and a few bruises on one arm.

Yet no one cared right now about what she looked like, or who she was, or anything but what would happen now, what she could lead them to...

Slightly in awe but still confused by this rescuer, Nadezhda looked on, hoping there was some brilliant plan that would bring about justice.

Perhaps that was a naive hope, but she thought it was needed to satisfy them all. Herself included.

What these people had done in the dark, in a normal, unassuming city, had to be stopped... and not stopped quite in the way people here were suggesting amongst themselves.

Violence couldn't be answered with more violence, no matter how much she understood the desire for vengeance.

She had to admit that her mother - no matter how much she resented her and disagreed with how she had brought her up - had sheltered her from things like this.

Perhaps she really *had* just wanted to keep her safe, she thought with a twinge of guilt.

But now that she knew about all the world's little dark secrets, she wanted something to be done about them.

It was times like these that she admired Sasha for his job, helping people find justice, even at great personal risk.

She also couldn't help but admire Sof, though the other woman seemed to have a less legalistic and more personal, violent take on 'justice' and what the Volkov family deserved, she had still helped out many who were in danger, selflessly freeing them when she could have focused on getting herself out.

She hadn't abandoned anyone, even strangers, and that counted for something in Nadezhda's books, because it showed that, in spite of her hatred, her goal wasn't just revenge.

It was change.

Finally, Sof cleared her throat and started to speak.

"People!"

That was all she needed to say for everyone's attention to be on her, even more intensely than before.

Nadezhda was amazed that she didn't even appear nervous as she started to speak.

"I know we all have different plans and goals to think about right now, but we need to focus. Focus on taking down the Volkovs!" This point got a cheer.

"And to do that effectively, we need one plan..."

People started to clamour now, starting to suggest their own plans. Sasha cut in, calling out over the crowd.

"I think we should go to the police. With the witnesses here and the evidence we were trying to gather, they'll surely have to do something."

Someone snorted. "Don't know where you're from, Mister, but the police around here know what's going on and they don't give a toss!"

Nadezhda looked over at her Uncle in confusion.

"How can they not care?" she blinked.

"Corruption, perhaps," he shrugged, "But still, I've always worked with the law enforcement before and I'm sure I can get the point across."

There were a few more derisive comments from the crowd at that point, but Sof re-joined the conversation, determined not to lose control now when their united goal was so important and yet could be so easily lost to arguments like this.

"Then you go to them. You know what you're doing," she pointed out, "the rest of us will work on other plans. Firstly, I want to gather more support. There must be people they haven't got to yet who still understand how awful they are," she commented thoughtfully.

This suggestion seemed to calm things down a little, though there were still mutterings about taking more violent action against the Volkovs...

Nadezhda tried to shut out the worst of it and volunteered to accompany her Uncle to the local police station.

Perhaps that way, they could finally have that family reunion Sof had continuously interrupted in the name of getting their escape plan sorted.

There was a lot they still needed to discuss, and it would be easiest to do so away from the unruly crowd of 'allies' they seemed to have acquired through Sof's escape plan.

So, a few moments later, the two relatives set off determinedly on their walk, although Nadezhda seemed quite uncomfortable, because she was still wearing the tight dress she had borrowed from Diana for the funeral.

There hadn't been a good opportunity to change.

And there probably wouldn't be for a while, if they were now getting involved in planning action with Sof and her new Anti-Volkov group...

These thoughts were interrupted as Sasha looked over at her curiously.

"Well, I guess we have a bit more time now. What's the full story?" he asked after a few minutes.

She sighed, having been aware this point would come, but still not sure how she was going to handle it and explain everything.

It had seemed crazy to her, and she had lived through it. To anyone else, it would simply sound insane and unbelievable.

She started talking anyway, backtracking to the beginning.

"I found a photo, from my mother's wedding," she told him, "And I wanted to know the truth because she never told me she was married. She always said she was never in love at all..."

"I didn't know she was married either..." he put in, frowning in confusion.

Nadezhda continued anyway. If he was confused now, there was a lot more to tell him and it would only get worse, so she ploughed on.

"I knew she wouldn't tell me, but Katya was in the picture... So, I went to her. She told me that only she, the priest, and my parents ever knew about the marriage. Because they were afraid. And then, days after the wedding, my father was murdered. Before he died, he left me a book with Dariya Volkova's address and told me to find her," she revealed.

Sasha had stopped walking and was staring at her. It took a second for her to process that and stop as well, looking back at him.

"What on Earth...?" was all he managed to say.

"I don't understand it either. I went home and confronted Mama, but nothing came of it, so I left. I came to find

Dariya. But I met her son, who told me she was dead, but that he would help me, and we developed a connection."

She blushed, hesitating at the thought of that 'connection' and its nature. It had taken quite the turn before...

Here, she began to talk again, bitterness welling up in her voice at the memories of the betrayal that had followed.

"...I even borrowed this wretched dress to go to his mother's funeral, but he betrayed me! Then they locked me up." She finished her story.

Taking another look at her poor, shook-up Uncle, she added, "I know it sounds insane, but I promise, it's true. And I still don't know what happened to my father..." she trailed off.

"God..." Sasha replied weakly.

"All this in our family and I never even knew..." he gasped, before managing to pull himself together.

This shouldn't get to him so much, his job meant he had dealt with all sorts of things. He started walking again, trying to focus.

When she thought he had recovered a little, she dared to ask.

"What about you? How did you get here?" As she looked over at him curiously, taking everything in.

It had been a long time since she had last seen him, though he hadn't changed much.

His platinum hair was a little longer, his normally slightly tanned skin was paler after his time shut up inside, and one of his eyes was ringed in bruises...

That made her frown with worry. Nevertheless, she kept quiet and let him speak.

"Sof hired me to help her prove that the Volkovs murdered her cousin. We nearly had the evidence we needed, but we had to go in disguise and poke around in their house, and they caught us. Sof nearly murdered one of them..." he added, sounding alarmed all over again.

"But they caught us in the end, and our evidence portfolio got left behind somewhere..." he sighed. "I just hope we have enough proof without it."

"And how did you get that black eye?" she put in, suddenly sounding stern.

Though she had never been close to her mother, she was fiercely protective of most of her family, and since Sasha and Nikolina were so close, he had always been around, so she had grown up to be very attached to him.

He laughed softly.

"What?" she asked, confused.

How could the bruise on his face possibly amuse him?

"Nothing, you just remind me of Lina when you talk like that," he told her.

 When she scowled, he added, "sorry, I know you two aren't on good terms right now, but she hasn't always been the way she was with you. When we were young... When Mama died, she took care of all of us brilliantly. I guess she's just protective sometimes. Then she just went away for a while and then came back, with you as a baby. She said she had adopted you. She had changed though; she grew more withdrawn and hardened... I guess that was what losing your father did to her."

He realised, looking away with tears in his eyes as it finally dawned on him that his dear sister had suffered so much in silence.

Nadezhda felt miserable and guilty too.

She hadn't ever considered that there was more to her mother than a grumpy old woman who had deceived her, she hadn't thought about what she might have been through...

She had been an ignorant child, and she flushed as she remembered how she had screamed in Nikolina's face, accusing her of all kinds of hateful things.

But seeing her Uncle's sadness and wanting to take his mind off it, as well as to escape from her own unpleasant memories, she hastily changed the subject.

"You didn't answer my question."

He smiled, rolling his baby blue eyes at her in a good-natured manner.

"The guards were a bit rough," he admitted.

She shook her head, muttering, "Psychos."

"Psychos we're about to take down," he reassured her.

She looked up as he stopped walking. Here they were, standing outside the police station. She smiled and stepped inside, with her Uncle following close behind.

For a little while, they had to sit and wait to talk to someone, but soon a police officer appeared.

"Can I help you?" he asked haughtily.

Sasha nodded. "We're here to report a possible mafia operation in the area," he soberly admitted.

The officer frowned.

"That's a very serious accusation, we better examine the evidence," he sat down with them and watched Sasha expectantly.

He sagged, struggling to think of what they could prove right now.

"We have several witnesses." He managed.

"Come back when you can prove what you're saying. Otherwise, there's nothing we can do and you're wasting our time," the other man snapped, getting up and walking away.

Sasha got up with a deep sigh and Nadezhda followed him.

They traipsed back to Sof's house in gloomy silence. It had seemed like an exaggeration when people had said this would happen, but it truly had.

Either things were quite different here, or they had been naive to believe justice was the way forward...

When they arrived back at the house, Sof was waiting for them outside.

"No luck?" she questioned as she saw their faces.

"No," Sasha sighed.

"I think what we need is that evidence we lost, that would really prove it and then they would have to take notice...”

He sounded disappointed that they didn't have the evidence, but Sof looked surprisingly cheerful about that news.

"That's not really a problem, is it?” She shrugged.

He looked baffled. "Isn't it? We left it behind and it could prove everything!"

Sof's dangerous 'I have a plan' look was back.

"But we can break into their house and get it back again!” she announced with a grin.

Sasha groaned.

"You have to stop dragging me into illegal stuff...I'll go and do...Whatever it is the others are meant to be doing."

"Finding extra support," Sof reminded him, "but I'm not going alone."

"I'll come with you," Nadezhda offered, wanting to help out somehow.

Her Uncle looked at her like she had completely lost her mind, but Sof looked at her gratefully.

"Then let's go and make our plans,” she suggested.

"I'll go and get Nikolina and Ekaterina to help out." Sasha put in.

Now it was his niece's turn to assume he was mad.

"They'll help if they know you need them," he assured her.

There was still doubt in her eyes as he headed to his car, which had sat abandoned in Sof's drive for a few months, to drive home and enlist his sisters.

But right now, as they planned a raid on the mafia family's home and base of operations, they needed any support they could get.

The Moroz Family

Sasha had plenty of time to think on his long drive back from Yaroslavl to Moscow.

But by the time he arrived, he still hadn't thought of anything to say that would get his sisters on good terms again, let alone what would get Nadezhda and Nikolina to make up after their argument.

He knew both his sisters could be persuaded to help out with the complicated Volkov case, but it would be hard enough to deal with, without everyone at each other's throats.

It was time to bring the family back together. But knowing how headstrong they all were, that wasn't going to be a fun task.

Ekaterina and Nikolina were total opposites.

They hadn't been, but since the sudden switch in their oldest sister's personality - which he only now knew to be due to the death of Nikolina's husband - they had fallen out. He didn't even know why...

But now he knew about Nikolina's secret, it was time to find out.

And, though he was closer to Nikolina, he pulled up at Katya's house first. She was more likely to be understanding about everything that had happened lately and what he wanted to achieve.

She might help if he spoke to her in the right way. He wanted to get her on his side from the start, before approaching the more temperamental sister.

Wandering up to her door, he knocked and waited. A few moments later, a familiar cheerful blonde pulled open the door and beamed at him.

"Sasha, long time, no see, Bro! Come in." She beckoned him inside with a grin.

A slightly shaky grin, because she was both delighted to finally see one of her two missing relatives and terrified to have to tell him about Nadezhda.

Within a few minutes, he was sat at her kitchen table, enjoying his first decent cup of coffee for a long time.

Opposite him, his sister's warm, welcoming smile failed to mask the concern in her light green eyes.

"So ... To what do I owe the pleasure of your visit? 'Cause looking at you right now, I'm not expecting it to be good news," she commented, looking him up and down uncertainly.

He laughed slightly. One of the many things that annoyed Nikolina about their younger sister was her total lack of tact.

"I guess I've had a rough time lately. Listen, I need your help, and this is going to sound crazy, but...It's Nadya," he revealed the news.

Instantly, the woman sighed.

"She went off to 'get more info', right? And something happened to her?"

Great, just the news she had been dreading. But how had Sasha wound up involved? How, without talking to her or her sister, had he found out about Nadya?

 And he couldn't have spoken to Nikolina, because while they had been waiting for news, the sisters had had a pact to tell one another everything, as soon as they heard anything.

But the only way to find out was to listen to Sasha.

"Yes. How much do you know about this?" he asked tentatively.

Katya tried to start at the start. "Well, she's not adopte-"

He stopped her.

"She told me all that, Katyusha, we met up accidentally and caught up," he explained, "I mean what do you know about what Lina wanted to protect her from?"

"She didn't want to tell me." Ekaterina began. "For years and years, she didn't. She just told me it would be dangerous for all of us to get involved."

"But you found out eventually, didn't you?" he pressed, reading between the lines.

She nodded.

"After Nadya left, she called me. She was terribly upset, and she said she got things wrong. You know she would never admit that normally, but that's how upset all this had made her," she explained.

"So, we realised we had a lot to discuss, and we met up to talk it over. And to see if we could find Nadya and save her, of course..."

There was a pause here, so Sasha decided to jump in and fill the gaps.

"You two are talking again? That's great."

She smiled, a brief, small smile.

"Yeah, yeah, I guess it is... anyway, she told me about Antonin. You know, Papa's colleague who she was dating? Apparently, that 'mission' he went was spying on a mafia family by dating one of their members. Said they were doing some crazy stuff... Cloning, kidnapping, practically running a city... I guess they found out, and they killed him."

Her smile had disappeared by the time she had finished admitting all her sister had told her.

Sasha looked grim too.

"I didn't know all that. Did Papa know?" he asked curiously.

She gave a small nod. "Took that secret to his grave for her."

"And why didn't she tell me?" he demanded to know, suddenly realising that, besides his niece, he was the only one not to know.

"Because she knew you would want to investigate his death... And she was scared. She thought you would be killed. She thought Papa would be killed. She even thought they would kill the baby for a while!"

The sheer urgency in Katya's voice was enough to convey the terror their sister had lived in, turning Sasha white.

"Wow...Well, I, I guess I understand that. I wouldn't put it past those crazies," was the only response he managed to muster.

"You've met them?" His sister didn't miss anything, aghast at what his reply had revealed.

"It was an accident, trust me," Sasha assured her, "I was working on a case and ended up involved with them. I got captured, and they had taken Nadya captive too, that's how I found all this out," he admitted.

Again, there was a lull in conversation while Ekaterina processed all the new information.

Sasha was quietly understanding, he had been in her position recently and was getting used to that whole madness.

Then Katya seemed to recall something.

"So where does you needing my help come into this?" she asked.

Sasha looked directly into her eyes and smiled.

"Because we're finally taking them down. There's a whole group of us waiting. Nadya's on a mission to get us extra evidence, then they'll be gone."

His sister's face broke into a grin.

"About damn time! I'm in!" Then she stumbled slightly.

"Lina's going to be against this though, isn't she?"

"That's what I need your help with. Persuading her. I came here to try to get you on better terms then start, but seeing as you're talking again, you can help me persuade her." Sasha explained his plan to her.

"Well, I guess we gotta try, right?" Katya gave him an optimistic little smile, getting up.

"I'm going to see her."

Delighted that this difficult seeming task had proved so easy, he grinned.

"You mean we are, right?"

"Nah, you stay here. It's about time you took a shower and had a rest," she pointed out, sympathetic but still tactless. He smiled his thanks to her, nonetheless.

While her brother was enjoying the simple comforts a warm shower could provide after a few months locked up, the youngest Moroz sister set off to her oldest sibling's nearby apartment.

Once Nikolina answered the door, she stepped inside, not bothering with small talk.

"Sasha knows." she announced.

Her sister instantly knew what their brother must know. She had only ever kept one secret from him.

"How?" she asked sharply.

"He met up with Nadya," Katya revealed.

Nikolina sighed deeply.

"So, he knows everything?"

When there was a little nod from Ekaterina, she continued, "let me guess, he wants to take on the Volkov family? I wish he wouldn't insist on getting into danger like this! And Nadezhda too!"

She was starting to rant now, so Katya had to jump in again.

"Relax, Sis, it'll be okay this time! Sasha said that they've found evidence and hundreds of supporters..."

Nikolina stopped, turning to stare at her little sister with wide green eyes.

"You... mean there is hope? Hope that we could do this without being endangered?" she asked hesitantly, her world picture shattered in the best conceivable way.

"I think so." The ever optimistic one of the family put in.

There was a dangerous glint in Nikolina's eyes at this point.

"Then let's get to Sasha and head over there now. They're going to regret messing with us."

Allies

While her relatives were busy planning and eventually driving back again, Nadezhda was with Sof. The two girls had their own plans to make.

They were still hoping to be able to sneak into the Volkov family's house and steal the evidence.

However, they had quickly become side-tracked from their planning. It had been entirely accidental, but curiosity about her newfound ally had got the better of Nadezhda.

Of course, she knew Sof was involved because of her cousin, but that was all the information she had.

So, she had interrupted their planning meeting by looking over at the other girl and finally working up the courage to question her.

Though she was normally rather reserved in social situations, this time, curiosity got the better of her.

"If you don't mind my asking..." she began, aware that what she was doing was unusual for her and she was possibly about to ask some sensitive questions.

Sof looked up at the other woman. "What do you want to ask?"

"What happened, how did you and your cousin get mixed up with these people?" she asked.

There was a pause and a deep sigh from the other woman. Nadezhda watched her, nervous that she had upset her, yet expectant and impatient to hear what her reply might be.

Sof shoved aside the notebook she was using for planning and turned to face her.

"Long story, but to cut it short: My cousin was a lot older than me, and when we lost the rest of our family in a fire, he took care of me. He was one of the best engineers I've ever known, and he taught me some things. That's where I get that hobby from," she explained, gesturing to some strange devices that decorated free space in her home.

"But then he moved here for work. Those Volkov people hired him for something. Then when he said what they were doing was wrong, that he couldn't work for them anymore, and that he would tell the police, they murdered him..."

She didn't sound angry now, just cold, as though she had grown used to this reality, but that it had caused her some numbness, stealing away her usually bright personality.

Nadezhda shivered. She had known she would regret asking questions.

Yet she was down that rabbit hole, and for some reason, she pressed on.

"What were they doing?" she asked.

A part of her wondered if it was connected to these 'genius' cloning experiments and other sinister knowledge the family had - if Vasily was to be believed.

"He didn't tell me." Sof answered with a shrug.

"Nothing worth his life, I'm sure. But at least we can make them pay," she added, brightening up again at the idea of revenge.

Nadezhda wasn't sure if that was good or bad.

Of course, she had been raised to know that random acts of revenge were wrong, but Volkovs did need stopping. They had hurt too many people.

And she couldn't help but admire Sof's confidence and determination to stand against them.

She was determined too, to get to the bottom of all this and to help her family get out of this whole mess, but she wasn't anywhere close to confident.

Their movement was just beginning and depended on this one precarious mission...

Interrupting her increasingly worried thoughts, Sof retaliated with the interrogating.

"What about you? Sasha never mentioned your family having some sort of grudge against the Volkovs... unless it came up during your family reunion. I wasn't listening."

Nadezhda laughed a little at the woman's bluntly honest comments, before replying.

"My father was involved with them for a while, but he was spying for the police, apparently. They murdered him."

"So, we're both in this because of dead relatives, huh? There's something odd to have in common." Sof quipped casually, before continuing with the quiz.

"Were you and your father really close then?"

She shook her head.

"No, in fact, I never met him. He was killed four days after marrying my mother. But she hid it from me, and I found out. I was so angry I came looking for them," she revealed a rather abridged version of how she had wound up in this position.

"Huh, crazy things happen..." Sof processed this out loud, "or maybe they just killed a lot of people. Either way, I don't blame you for coming looking for them. But I'm guessing that didn't go well," she added, recalling the circumstances in which they had met.

Nadezhda sighed. She hadn't been planning on unloading all her emotional baggage and the whole journey from her old, ordinary life to this chaos.

But she supposed she had started this getting to know you game, and besides, Sof seemed trustworthy enough.

"Well, it did at first. I was angry with my mother, not them. Their address just happened to be the only thing connected to my father that I had. I didn't know they killed him. I found them, and one of them told me he would help me. But I was double-crossed, funnily enough. But before that, Vasily told me enough for me to guess that they had my father killed."

She had never actively realised that before, until Sof had been talking about her cousin's death, and she had replayed her conversation with Vasily about how they didn't 'approve' of her father. That and her knowledge, imparted to her by Katya, of his death...

It was so obvious now but so enraging. She tensed, biting back the rant she wanted to unleash.

No wonder her mother hadn't wanted her to know... They were murderers, on top of everything else they had done! And her father was another victim!

So why had he told her Dariya would help her...? Why would he send her into the den of his murderers?

A tiny voice in the back of her mind reminded her of that suddenly and treacherously.

The added frustration of not knowing only added to her anger, leaving her with a sudden, intense, burning fury deep inside her.

Sof was staring at her, knowing she was clearly annoyed.

"Wow...This is more messed up than I realised, and I knew they were awful people," she murmured.

"Don't worry, we're taking them down." she added, even more determined, her jaw set.

"I certainly hope so." Nadezhda met her gaze, with a similar look in her eyes.

They started to turn their attention back to their planning work, but the ding of Sof's doorbell was the third interruption.

Assuming it was most likely one of their allies reporting back, Sof hopped up and hurried to the door.

Sasha had arrived on the doorstep, his sisters behind him.

"I found some more allies," he announced with a smile. "Can we see Nadezhda?"

Sof grinned at them and then turned, shouting her newfound friend's name until the other girl appeared. Nadezhda's face instantly lit up when she saw her relatives.

She hadn't been convinced that they would all agree to come. Especially not her mother. And all she had been through had started to change her perspective on Nikolina...

She elbowed Sof out of her way at the same time as Nikolina pushed Sasha aside.

Throwing her arms around her mother for the first time in years, she clung to her and murmured:

"I'm sorry. I'm sorry I yelled at you. I know you only wanted what was best..."

But things had changed for Nikolina too. Sasha and Ekaterina had brought her new information.

There was hope for change she had never thought was possible. Change that would take down the Volkovs.

Now, she saw that her fear may have blinded her when it came to the right way to treat her husband's death and her daughter.

Her daughter, who had wanted to help and who had been brave enough to make all this possible. She wrapped her arms around her daughter, blinking back tears.

"Shush... I am proud of you. You are doing what I thought I could not..."

Nadezhda managed to straighten up, pulling away to look into her mother's eyes. Her own eyes were filled with matching tears.

"You can now. Thanks for coming to help us." She smiled through her emotional state.

"Aww, that's adorable. But I'm just here to destroy these nasty little people." Katya commented from behind them, motivated by the idea that she could put an end to the horrible people who had hurt her family so badly.

Mother and daughter rolled their eyes in sync, but as Sof got up and tugged Sasha to his feet as well, she grinned.

"I like this lady. Let's get our plan sorted and ruin these scumbags!" She cheered enthusiastically.

So, the group headed off to plan out the beginning of the attack on the Volkovs.

Planning and Catching Up

Gathered back around Sof's small dining table, making the place feel rather crowded, the Moroz family and Sof were finally working on a plan.

Sof, thankfully, appeared to know a fair amount about the house.

She even knew when it was likely to be left empty and promised Nadezhda that getting in and avoiding capture would be absolutely no problem at about 9 am the next morning.

Nikolina briefly objected to the idea of her daughter going straight into the Volkov family's den, only to be overruled by everyone, with varying levels of reassurance, from Sasha and Nadezhda, or dismissal, from Katya and Sof.

After that interruption, they proceeded to concoct the idea of Nadezhda and Sof sneaking into the deserted building through a back alley that Sof knew about from when she used to creep in to visit her cousin at work.

Once inside, the girls had to locate a file of evidence Sasha had left behind.

There was some debate between Sasha and Sof as to where exactly it had been left, but eventually, it was recalled that they had been caught in the belly of the beast itself - Vladimir's private quarters within the house.

So, they would have to get into that room, with or without a key, to complete their vital mission.

With this goal in mind, Sof began, rather unnervingly, sharpening her knife at the table, planning to use it on the door if it was locked and they couldn't find a key.

It could well be a necessary precaution, so objections that may have otherwise been made to this behaviour were kept silent.

Then the conversation turned to other evidence they might be able to find and use to help their cause while they were in the house.

"I swear there were security cameras in there too when we were in cells. If we could only get some of the footage of what goes on in that place..." Sasha began to point out.

"Well, if we can find the cameras and whatever database they're connected to, that might be possible." Sof looked thoughtful as she spoke.

"We would be able to prove that they were doing some pretty terrible things. But wouldn't our... escape tactics be considered illegal too?" She put in.

A baffled and very concerned Nikolina exchanged a glance with Katya. It seemed their brother had left out certain highlights of his story.

The escape had been brushed over, with none of the violence mentioned.

"What happened then? What tactics were used for this escape?" The oldest Moroz sister demanded to know.

Sasha looked rather uncomfortable.

"We had to fight our way out," he admitted, "But I'm pretty sure I could make a court believe that was self-defence if it came down to it. After all, they did a lot more to us before that."

He added that part quickly, eager to change the subject before his sisters could start demanding details of the fight. He was fairly sure Nikolina wouldn't approve.

And Katya would enjoy that story far too much. She would be bound to drag it back up when she was drunk at family reunions...

"Of course they have. But so long as we won't get into trouble for it, then we'll make sure we get that footage." Sof responded with a nod.

"How are we going to do that?" Nadezhda asked, sounding a little worried.

She wasn't entirely sure how they were going to pull off any of what they had planned, to be honest.

"We'll deal with that when we get there." Sof replied with a shrug, more bothered about smashing the Volkovs' crime ring than their own safety.

"Now, anything else we might need to remember when we're there?"

"To be very careful?" Nikolina responded.

Both girls rolled their eyes at that remark, but Nadezhda nevertheless nodded to try and reassure her concerned mother.

They were technically reconciling, after all. Though she had a feeling that would take time to happen. Their personalities seemed to naturally clash.

Katya had some more trivial-seeming advice that actually turned out to be rather useful.

"More practical clothing? No offence, Nadya, but that dress isn't exactly what I'd personally choose to go on a crime-fighting vigilante mission in."

It sounded like an off-hand quip, but Nadezhda gave a more sincere nod this time.

"Good point. I've been stuck in this thing for ages, and it doesn't even fit me properly," she agreed, tugging irritably at the hated outfit.

"It is not what you were wearing when you left," Nikolina observed, raising an eyebrow curiously.

At what point in all of this madness had her daughter had time to get changed? And where had she had acquired other clothes from anyway?

"I know, I had to borrow it, I'll fill you in later."

She answered, not particularly wanting to delve into the details of Dariya's funeral, Diana and all the other shenanigans she had been through with the Volkovs before Vasily had betrayed her right now.

Things were tense enough at the moment, with this life-or-death mission, their one chance to stop the Volkovs legally, looming over them.

They didn't need past events on their minds as well as the terrifying potential future if things didn't work out.

Her mother gave a small nod, seeming to just about accept this reasoning, or at least her daughter's reply.

There was probably a lot they needed to fill one another in on later anyway, all things considered.

Sof jumped into the gap in the conversation before they took it upon themselves to do it now.

She was getting more than fed up with family reunions at this point.

"C'mon, I'll find you some better clothes, then we ought to get some sleep before tomorrow's ordeal begins," she suggested, getting up from the table and beckoning for Nadezhda to follow her.

The two girls wandered up to Sof's room and raided her wardrobe for some reasonably practical clothes.

It wasn't too tasking, as most of her outfits consisted of jeans and t-shirts. They hung loosely around Nadezhda's slim frame, but they were more comfortable than Diana's tight dress had been, so they would do.

And as she changed, a piece of paper fluttered down from Diana's dress.

Nadezhda had forgotten about the one item she had managed to rescue from her belongings when Diana had got her hands on them.

She grabbed at it and unfolded it curiously. Music notes, it must have dropped from one of the books...

She shrugged it off and focused on ensuring her outfit was practical for their next quest, making sure she could run in it, in case they had to get away quickly.

After that, Sof retired to her bedroom, and Nadezhda headed back downstairs.

She, and many others in their group, had been making do with Sof's living room floor as a bed recently, settled down in the living room.

But on her way back, she passed a piano she hadn't noticed Sof owned before. Hesitating, she looked over at it, then at the paper she was carrying.

Well, why not? It had been a while since she had had a go at playing some music, and it might take a weight off her mind.

She set the sheet down on the piano top and read through it as she got ready. Then she froze... The notes were arranged carefully. They were telling her something...

Don't trust Vladimir... Get to Dariya. Dariya's diaries have all the information if she doesn't.

She put the music together and gasped. Her father! He had found another way to leave her messages that hadn't been in the diary.

She hadn't even expected him to leave her one message, let alone more, and she had nearly missed it...

Her mother had missed it! The messages must have been left for her mother, since they had been in with the songs that he had written for her, but Nikolina had never been very musical, so it had slipped by her.

But, right now, Nadezhda reminded herself, that wasn't the point.

The point was that she had to get those books back, in case there were more messages left behind. And apparently, find some diaries Dariya had written...

Unsure why, she nevertheless noted it, then ran downstairs to the makeshift beds of the group. No one slept much that night, though.

Firstly, she had to spill the news, sparking another family reunion and story sharing session, with Nikolina finally admitting the full truth about her husband and his tragic fate to her daughter.

And, of course, Nadezhda taking the time to fill in her relatives on everything from her time with the Volkovs up until that very moment, all that had happened since she left her mother's house.

They were still talking over the surprising events of their family's saga when the sun began to rise on the day that would reveal whether it had all been worth it or not...

The Hunt

Later that morning, when Sof was finally awake again, the two young women made their way over to the Volkov house, walking normally along the street until they started to get close.

Then Sof gripped her accomplice's arm and inched nearer to the wall, pressing herself against it.

Thankfully, the street was deserted, both of the guards to catch them and passers-by to deem them insane.

Once they had discovered this, they crept along the wall and slipped into a small alleyway.

Nadezhda looked around nervously, taking in the stacks of rubbish they were now among, from the broken glass bottles on the floor to the large dumpsters against the wall.

"Are you sure this is a good way in?" she asked in a whisper.

"Trust me, it'll take us almost directly to where we need to be," Sof assured her, before dropping her arm and taking a run-up.

To Nadezhda's slightly horrified surprise, she leapt onto the top of one of the industrial dumpsters.

It was now that Nadezhda realised what she was up to. Above her, there was a small balcony. With a door leading into the house...

Seeing her eyes fall on the door, Sof nodded.

"See? Easy way in. That door's never locked, and that room is directly below Vladimir's room. Easy-Peasy," she announced smugly, before beckoning to her ally.

"C'mon then," she urged.

"I don't know if I can get up there..." The other girl faltered as she looked up at the jump she would have to make.

Sof held out her hand to her. "'Course you can, just grab on!" she encouraged.

Nadezhda hesitantly reached up and grabbed her hand, letting her yank her up onto the dumpster, struggling to get a foothold on its sloping lid, an uncomfortably sticky surface.

"Let's just get this over with..." she muttered with a sigh, gripping the balcony's bars, and hauling herself up it, swinging her legs over the barrier and stepping on.

Sof swiftly followed her lead, joining her and then approaching the door to the inside. She gave it a shove, making it swing in soundlessly.

Inside, there was another generic bedroom, much like the one Nadezhda blushed to recall briefly sharing with Vasily. They hurried through it, hunting for a staircase.

On their way around the maze of corridors, Sof nudged Nadezhda in the ribs, pointing something out.

"Look, cameras everywhere! We need to find out how to get that footage..."

"Shouldn't there be a computer somewhere?" The other woman commented as she followed her gaze.

"Or some kind of screen and security system they're all linked to?"

She was more or less guessing now, unsure how such things were supposed to work.

"Yeah, but I guess we'll have to look for that once we've found this evidence..." Sof conceded, turning their attention back to getting to Vladimir's room.

That, in itself, wasn't a challenging task. They soon found a flight of stairs and hurried up it.

After that, it was simply a case of finding their way back to the side of the house they had entered on and counting the rows of doors until they located the right room.

Nadezhda tried the door. Unsurprisingly, it was locked shut.

This prompted Sof to draw her knife and try to force the door open, jamming the blade between the wood and its frame, then into the lock when that failed.

It wouldn't budge. Nadezhda finally stepped in to stop her frustrated friend.

"I don't think that's going to work...We need to look for a key or something."

Sighing, Sof withdrew her weapon and nodded.

"Fine, let's see what we can find," she agreed.

And so, the hunt began. They roamed all around the house, searching for keys, pulling open drawers, and raiding cupboards. They had no luck.

Finally, an idea occurred to Sof, whose ideas were usually troublesome. Nadezhda recognised the glint in her eyes when she saw it and asked, "What?" In a mildly alarmed tone.

"You know those bars and things we had when we were getting out? I bet those things would open up the doors," she suggested.

"Probably," Nadezhda admitted, "but where are we going to get those without encountering the guards again?" she added.

Sof pointed something out.

"I know their schedule, remember? They'll all be out, no guards, I promise. Besides which, right now, their dungeons are wrecked anyway. They can't keep anyone there, and so they don't need to guard them."

"Good point." Nadezhda nodded.

"Well, let's go and see if we can find any lying around," she suggested.

They located the door in the hallway that led down the steps into the cells.

There was still plenty of rubble on the floor, and thankfully, among it, was just the kind of bar they were looking for.

Sof seized it with a dangerously wide grin.

"Here's our 'key'," she announced, "Let's get that stupid door open!"

With that, she raced off, Nadezhda trailing behind her.

When they arrived back at the room, Sof busted the door open with remarkable ease, simply swinging the bar a few times and cracking the wood.

They stepped over the splintered door and looked around.

Nadezhda was a little overwhelmed as she examined the luxurious bedroom, also trying to peek into the attached rooms at the same time.

In comparison to the other rooms that she had seen here, it was amazing to see a whole apartment, with its own kitchen, an office and more attached to the room.

But Sof's eyes were scanning the quarters in a business-like manner.

"Well, either those idiots have removed the file and put it somewhere else, or it's just not here at all. because I know where Sasha left it and it's not there now..." she revealed.

Nadezhda groaned under her breath before asking, "What are we going to do then?"

"We'll just have to search this whole place thoroughly," Sof announced determinedly, not wanting to waste the effort of having broken in or to give up just yet.

Nadezhda wandered into Vladimir's office and started to rummage through his drawers, making a terrible mess in the process, slinging old paperwork over her shoulders in frustration as her hunting turned up nothing.

From the bedroom, there was the sound of Sof shoving everything, furniture included aside as she searched too.

Things seemed fruitless though, and Nadezhda looked up with a deep sigh, pausing in her search.

It was then that she realised she was stood in front of the office window, and that in the street outside, a familiar rusted car had just pulled up.

She gave an audible gasp and ran into the ransacked bedroom. Sof, who was trying, ineffectively, to drag the bed out of her way, looked up, nonplussed at the sudden interruption.

"What?" she asked as she struggled to get her breath back.

"They're here!" Nadezhda revealed.

Sof cursed loudly.

"We'll have to hide or something... Quickly, in here!" She grabbed Nadezhda and pulled her into the wardrobe, letting the doors slam behind them.

Nadezhda lay against the back wall, trying to calm down her wild heartbeat. As she did, her free hand closed around something.

There was what felt like another door handle behind them.

Without thinking, she twisted it. The girls tumbled back through the darkness as the sound of footsteps outside drew nearer.

Finding The Evidence

Panicking, Nadezhda screamed as she fell, sinking back into the dark and finally hitting something hard.

She struggled to pull herself upright in the darkness. Then something occurred to her. Would that have happened to her companion as well?

Sof's hand had been wrenched from hers on the way down...

"Sof?" she called out hesitantly.

There was a thump beside her as the other woman fell down too.

"Ow! Damn it, what did you do?" A grumpy Sof demanded to know from beside her.

"There was some kind of handle, and I turned it..." she admitted.

"Huh, a handle inside a wardrobe? ...Then this must be some kind of secret lair of theirs." The other guessed.

If that was true, Sof mused, then what else might be back here...?

"C'mon, let's find a light and see what you've found," she brightened up at that idea, getting to her feet.

There was enough room for her to stand here, and they had fallen onto a solid concrete floor here. It was still black though.

She groped around for a light and eventually found some kind of switch.

 Hoping it was actually a light switch and at the risk of it causing more trouble, she flicked it. A strange blue light flooded the area.

It seemed they were in a whole new corridor, not revealed by their earlier attempts to look around the house. Nadezhda got to her feet now too, looking around in awe.

"What is this place?" she questioned, baffled by it.

"Let's find out." Sof took a step further.

Nadezhda hesitantly followed her. They wandered down a long, poorly lit corridor, then, as it widened into a chamber, found themselves in some kind of laboratory.

It was as bleak and bare as the concrete corridor but simply packed with odd machines.

On one side of the room, the wall was taken up by a huge glass tank of some sort, with wires hanging down both sides and a shelf of vials suspended above it. Inside, liquids sizzled.

Both women stared.

But something entirely different had come to Nadezhda's mind when she saw it. Vasily had talked about cloning...

"I think this is their cloning machine..." she revealed thoughtfully.

It certainly looked crazy enough to fit that weird concept, and it was big enough for a person.

She shuddered at that thought. It was creepy as well...

"Oh, yeah... this old thing." Sof walked over to the machine, intrigued.

"I remember this,"

"You've seen it before?" Nadezhda questioned.

"I mean, Vasily told me they were clones when he was 'helping' me, but I didn't know this was behind it. What do you know about it?"

"My cousin helped them 'modify' it a while ago. They hired him to before he knew anything about them. He loved the idea because he thought he could do something good with it. Y'know, make it so it could be used to help people who needed rare types of blood donations or organ transplant matches..." She explained, looking wistful.

"He was really thoughtful...But then he found that wasn't what they would use it for. They got him to add something that would create mutations in their DNA, which gave them... Well, effectively superpowers." Sof revealed.

"What? They have some kind of superpowers?!" Nadezhda gasped.

"I know, it's a horrible idea, right? I thought he destroyed the part that would do that when he realised how they would use it, but..."

She gestured to a part of the machine. "I remember seeing him making it, and it's right here."

"They have superpowers?" her incredulous friend repeated.

"They might not, yet. He added it, then I guess he objected, and the fighting started, and he was killed. But it wasn't that long ago, and there aren't any of them young enough to have the powers yet..." Sof reasoned.

But Nadezhda wouldn't be soothed.

"Well, we have to stop them before they get them! They're already controlling this entire place, imagine what they could do with superpowers!" She pointed out, grabbing a spanner from a nearby workbench.

"I'm smashing this machine!"

Sof grabbed her arm.

"NO!" she yelled.

"The evidence! We need to get the evidence... then we can get this taken away from them and used for good instead!" she told her.

Nadezhda looked at her friend and was surprised to see tears in her eyes. She lowered the spanner.

"Thank you... I have to try to honour my cousin's true vision for his work," the other girl murmured.

Nadezhda placed the spanner back where she had found it and, embarrassed by the emotional situation, decided it was a good time to change the subject.

"Let's see what else down here, shall we? Hopefully, some camera footage of this crazy stuff..." she suggested.

Sof nodded, so they pressed on, walking out through the lab and on down the corridor.

Eventually, they came to a stretch where there were several doors on either side of them. Nadezhda gave one of them an experimental push.

It opened up to show a room full of filing cabinets. An idea occurred to her, and she rushed inside, starting to pull open various cabinets.

"What are you doing?" Sof wrinkled her nose in confusion as she questioned her. "This lot's just old documents."

"The file we need might be here." Nadezhda argued, pulling some more papers out.

"What does it look like again?"

Sof didn't answer but hurried in to join her in her search.

Unfortunately, though, they couldn't find anything useful among the documents. So, they opened up the next door.

This time they both stared for a few moments. Inside, there was a huge computer, all wired up.

On its screen, split up across the house, there were hundreds of images from different rooms and the cameras in them.

"We found the footage we can use..." Nadezhda breathed, excited by this potential breakthrough but in awe of the huge system at the same time.

But Sof had spotted something else. Lying on the desk near the computers was a black folder, with a label stuck to it, reading 'evidence' in Sasha's handwriting.

"We found the file too," she pointed out.

This was *perfect!* Somehow everything they needed was in one room.

Nadezhda snapped out of her shock and sprang forward. As Sof followed her, she shoved the folder into her arms and pounced on the computer.

"How do we get the exact videos we need? And get them off this thing?" she questioned, not entirely sure what to do but determined to do it if it would help their case.

Her accomplice grabbed her arm though.

"We'll come back for the footage. It's important, but this is more important! We have to get this file out of here now!" Sof urged, clutching the folder.

"How are we going to do that? They're out there!" Nadezhda pointed out.

But Sof gestured to the screen in front of them. There were no signs of life in the building.

"They must have left without realising what was going on. Which means we need to get this out before they come back and do realise," she argued.

"Then we can get the police on our side, and they can do some work for once and come back for the videos!"

Nadezhda saw her point and also saw from her expression that there was no point in arguing anyway.

She got up and followed Sof back out through the maze of corridors, until they returned to the entrance, steps up above them leading to the wardrobe, and therefore the exit.

"I don't get how this place can exist..." she murmured, looking up at it.

"Eh, with enough skill, people can build all kinds of hideaways," Sof replied.

"But never mind that, let's get out of here," she added as she walked up the steps.

Shoving open the door, she stepped out, Nadezhda close behind her.

"I'm afraid that won't be happening, ladies."

A voice cut in from somewhere in the apparently empty bedroom.

A Crucial Choice

Upon hearing the mysterious voice, both women froze. Sof was the first to move again, swinging around wildly with the knife she brought with her clutched in her hand.

She only wished she had hung out the iron bar she had used to get in earlier, it would make a better weapon.

Regardless of that, she was angry enough to take on whoever was here, shouting out:

"Show yourself and try to stop us then, you coward!"

Nadezhda jumped back into life again at that, startled by the other's words.

"Or we could just leave before they bother to?" she suggested in an urgent whisper, confused by her friend's actions.

Sof had been the one who had rushed her into leaving in the first place, but now she seemed enraged, wanting to stand and fight whoever was taunting them.

There was a soft chuckle from said teaser, and the reply, "well, if you insist," to Sof's remark.

With that, Vladimir stepped out of the shadows to the side of the wardrobe, leaning on a walking stick and smiling at them.

He looked like an innocent, benevolent old man, who couldn't mean any harm.

They weren't fooled. Sof was still brandishing her knife, pointing it towards him threateningly.

Nadezhda stood tensely, her eyes in the evidence folder in the grip of Sof's other arm.

They had to keep it safe, and he clearly meant to stop them from doing so. And from ever leaving the house again. Or at least from leaving it alive...

His steely grey eyes fell on her and for a second, she felt as though he was looking straight through her, his bright smile never fading.

"Ah, Vasily's charming girlfriend... He will be pleased. He was most upset when you ran off, you know," he told her, his tone laced with more condescension than she could stand and just a hint of anger at the same time.

"Maybe he should have thought about that before he got some of your thugs to throw me in prison!" she snapped at him.

He rolled his eyes at her, then looked away dismissively, without bothering to reply.

Instead, he turned his attention to Sof, who still looked like she wanted to stab him.

Honestly, Nadezhda was a little surprised she had refrained from doing so up until now.

Vladimir seemed to want to tempt her.

"And speaking of your little breakout, here's the instigator..." he looked her up and down.

"I shouldn't be surprised to find you at the centre of yet more trouble. Always trashing my house, aren't you? And it's really rather ungrateful, considering how my family left you alive and let you stay in our cells, free of charge..."

At this point, Sof got fed up and jabbed her weapon towards him again in a ferocious movement.

"Quit it with the stupid evil villain speech you probably spent years dreaming about getting a chance to make! Let's just cut to the part where you try to stop us leaving and I get to stab you in your dumb, wrinkly face!" She yelled at him.

This got more laughter.

"If you really wanted to do it, why don't you? Because you're too busy trying to be a do-gooder, right?" He snorted.

"Cute. But if you want to get to the fun part... Then fine."

He stepped between them and the battered down door.

Then, pausing to drop the walking stick Nadezhda had been fairly sure he didn't need and proving her right, he straightened up, reached into his pocket, and pulled out a gun.

Both girls visibly paled at the sight of the weapon. There was a click as he cocked it. A million thoughts raced through Nadezhda's head at once.

They had come so close; how could they possibly fail now? The cameras hadn't shown anyone there...

She had just reconciled with her mother, and she would never see her, or any of her family for that matter, ever again.

And they might not even know what had happened to her.

Neither would the hundreds of others they had helped to escape from the Volkovs, who their evidence could have helped if they had managed to escape...

They had failed.

Sof's growl beside her snapped her out of that state. Her friend let out a noise like a wild animal that had been cornered and hurled the knife from her hand towards Vladimir.

It sank into his arm, making him shout out in pain, curse her, and swing the gun wildly as he tried to keep hold of it.

He fired a shot, but with his hand shaking erratically, he missed, shattering his own bedroom window instead.

Finally, he had to give up, dropping the gun and grabbing at his bleeding arm.

"You'll *pay* for that..." he hissed at Sof.

She was about to respond when the sound of running footsteps stopped her in her tracks.

Nadezhda sprang into life.

"Leave him, let's go!" she urged, grabbing Sof's arm as the other woman stood, frozen, staring at the old man.

Her friend stirred slowly, coming back to life, and running with her to the window.

But Vasily was the faster runner and burst into the room as they drew near to their escape.

"Grandpa, I heard shouting, and the shot..." His gaze fell on Vladimir's bloodied arm, which was cut, the red stain making a sharp contrast against his white coat.

"Never mind about me!" His grandfather snapped, annoyed and impatient.

He wasn't prepared to fail, there were too many people over the years who would want to bring charges against him if those girls got away and went to the police.

It would only take one case to destroy everything he had built...That couldn't happen.

"Stop them!" he yelled.

Prompted by his shouting, his grandson seized the fallen gun and aimed it at the two figures by the window.

"Stop right there!" he demanded.

The girls, aware of the weapon trained on them, had no choice but to freeze, seconds from escape. *Again.*

Sof gave a sigh of frustration and turned around only so that she could scan the room for another potential weapon with which to get away again.

But Nadezhda wasted no time swinging around when she heard the new attacker's voice.

There he was... Her boyfriend, or ex-boyfriend.

They hadn't officially broken up, after all.

But given that they had officially got together seconds before he cruelly betrayed her and got her into this situation in the first place, not to mention how he had destroyed her trust and was now pointing a deadly weapon at her, it was safe to say they were *over.*

She couldn't love him now, after all. She hadn't expected it to be so hard to see him again, like this, though.

Oh, how she wished his true nature was reflected on his face, so she didn't have to still blush when she saw him, even when she was fairly sure he meant to kill her.

He lowered the gun slightly, gasping, "Nadya!" when he saw her.

Behind them, his grandfather gave a despairing sigh.

"For goodness' sake, get over her and end them, they're intruders!" He urged him on.

"I'm not going to kill her, she's my girlfriend!" The younger man argued back, seeming appalled by the very suggestion.

Part of Nadezhda was glad to hear that, but she told herself it was simply because his tone, defensive of her, might offer them a way out of here alive.

Sof was less amused.

"You didn't tell me you dated him!" She sounded quite disgusted.

"That was before he double-crossed me, remember?"

Nadezhda got defensive, blushing as she replied to that comment, but nevertheless gave Vasily a pointed look.

"We all make mistakes, Nadya, I tried to do what was best for my family. And sure, it didn't go right but... this time, we can start over. You could join us and be great." He smiled at her sweetly.

Suddenly, she felt as though his obnoxious side and the fact he couldn't be trusted were written all over his face after all.

She wanted to punch him, hard. But he was holding a gun.

In those circumstances, she settled for:

"You're kidding me, right?"

"Of course not!" he insisted.

"I'm not trying to deceive you. I'm simply making you an offer. You can stick with your snappish, troublemaking little 'friend' and you can die together, or you can save yourself, stay here and join our family... As my bride."

His eyes shone as he spoke, full of passion.

"I love you, Nadya, I will save you, I promise..." he vowed.

Nadezhda looked up, her eyes locked on his, her heart beating fast.

She knew, deep down, that he didn't love her.

They hadn't had enough time to get to know one another that well, and besides, someone who loved another wouldn't betray them so easily...

But his offer was a chance. They needed a chance to survive if any of this was going to be worth all the risks that they had taken...

But first, there was one crucial question she had to ask, before she could be sure it was a chance they could afford to take.

"What about Sof?" she murmured, her voice little more than a whisper as she wondered about her friend's fate.

Vasily shrugged.

"Does it matter? I'll get rid of her, or you can do it yourself if you want. But then, the most important thing is that we'll live happily ever after together!" He beamed at her.

"Whatever happens, it better happen soon!" The old man hissed from behind them, clutching his arm to stop the blood flow.

Nadezhda glanced from him to his grandson. Such a loving family, clearly...

She mused before the rest of Vasily's words sank in, distracting her again. So, whatever she did, her new friend would die.

She stared at the gun numbly and vaguely hoped that she was a good enough actor to mask the horrible way hearing that made her feel.

She was fairly sure she wasn't though. How could someone hide their heart sinking into their stomach and making it churn sickeningly?

She didn't look visibly sick though, just as though she was deliberating over the choice.

Sof moved to grab her arm and Vasily took a step closer, the gun pointing to Sof's head.

"No moving. Now, Nadya, my dear, who do you choose? That or me?"

His question made her instinctively turn her gaze to Sof. She stood there, framed by the open window...

Inspiration struck and Nadezhda carefully but quickly darted her arm out, aware she had to move fast to avoid the terrible possibility of Vasily shooting her for moving.

Her hand found its target, grabbing Sof's shoulder and shoving her backwards.

There was a brief look of anger, fear, and disbelief in the other girl's eyes before her friend and the vital evidence plunged out of the shattered window.

Shaking slightly, a pale Nadezhda turned back to Vasily.

"You're right. She doesn't matter anymore. I'll stay with you," she told him, fighting to keep all emotion out of her voice.

The Aftermath

Sof let out a shriek as she began to fall, shocked and frightened, quite sure that this was going to her end...

Then common sense kicked in, uprooting a memory from her mind, and pushing it through her fear to the front of her brain.

This was near where they had come in... there should be a balcony below her somewhere. As if on cue, she landed on something hard.

It was a sudden jolt, and her back ached, but the fall, unlike the one from the window to the ground below, wasn't far enough for her to be seriously hurt or killed.

She got up, keeping her groans silent as she glared up at the broken window above her. They didn't need to know she had survived.

But... Did Nadya know? Had she been helping her escape, or out to kill her?

She couldn't tell. Resigned to the fact that she may never know if she had been betrayed or not, she grabbed the fallen evidence folder from beside her, thanking her lucky stars that she had managed to keep hold of it and that it hadn't fallen open, losing their hard-earned evidence.

Now she just had to get out of here with it. Easier said than done, she concluded as she took a glance over the balcony's railings, into the alleyway.

Below, broken glass from the window coated the dumpsters. There was also a waiting figure, standing guard. She made out the shape of a gun in their hand and her heart plummeted.

If they were guarding an alleyway, they would be guarding everywhere... Every way out, anyway.

Her mind raced to think of one they might have missed, but the one she thought was least likely to be guarded - the one that had never, ever been guarded that she had known of - was the one below her.

In that case, there was nothing for it but to hope that it was just the one guard there and that she could sneak past.

She had no weapon to threaten them with this time, and they were armed...But she couldn't stay here.

Sof gritted her teeth and leapt over the edge. She landed heavily on the lid of the dumpster with a thump.

Now she was right behind the guard, and the woman was looking about her wildly, clearly having heard the noise.

It took all Sof's self-control not to curse everything that could have possibly got her into this situation.

Her heart was pounding now. Any moment now, she would be seen, she was sure...

Something occurred to her. It sounded crazy, even in her own head, but once again, she was faced with one chance not to get shot.

Tiptoeing around to the edge, she dropped into the corner where the guard wouldn't be able to see past the dumpster.

Hiding in the shadows, she knew she would be seen and attacked the moment she emerged. But from here, she could reach to flip the lid open...

Shoving the evidence folder between her arm and her body to secure it, she freed her hands to lift the lid, hoping it wouldn't make a sound.

Thankfully, it didn't. Jumping up, Sof managed to dive inside. The lid slammed above her. Now she was certain the guard must have looked around.

Her heart in her mouth and her mind arguing with itself as to whether or not this was a terrible idea that was bound to fail, she threw herself with all her might against the wall near where the guard had stood.

The thing was on wheels, after all. It rocked slightly, making her fear it would simply tip up and spill her back out into the jaws of the enemy, but then, with a shuddering movement that knocked her down but still made her want to cheer, it rolled forward a little.

"What the hell?" She heard the armed woman outside question as it rolled towards her.

Spurred on, she hurled herself into the wall again, pushing it forward. That was all it took.

The rest of the alley sloped downwards just enough to set the dumpster rolling. There was a scream and a thump as it hit the guard.

For one dreadful moment, it slowed, the impact almost stopping it, but with a little push, it moved on again, bumping slightly as the woman was run over.

Sof decided that probably meant she was safe and pushed open the lid, glad of the fresh-ish blast of town air that assailed her nostrils after even a few minutes inside the stinking dumpster.

She was a little bruised from bashing against it and fairly sure the smell of rotten fruit and other waste was never going to come out of her clothes, but glad to be alive and safe with the evidence.

The dumpster had rolled down to where the alleyway joined the street and stopped.

Some passers-by gave it - and her - odd looks, so she hopped out and hurried home before the guard managed to pick herself up and start a chase.

When she arrived at her house, hurried up the driveway and pulled open the door, she darted inside only to be met by a crowd. There were a lot of questions.

Sasha rushed to her first.

"Is that the evidence?" he asked, eyes wide with expectant hope as he pointed to the file under her arm.

She answered with a nod that gained a cheer, handing it to him so he could take it to the police.

His sisters emerged from the crowd now too, both together, but muttering and arguing among themselves.

"Where's Nadya?!" Nikolina demanded, breaking away from Katya at the same time as her sister inquired oh-so-politely as to what the smell was.

It was not an easy story to relay. Adrenaline had got Sof home but looking back brought out emotions she hadn't expected.

She had to bite back tears as she admitted Nadezhda had stayed behind, pushing her from the window. In her mind, she fought to convince herself it had all been a plan. It didn't work.

The friendship they had only just begun to form made her worry for Nadezhda; the betrayal made her angry with her.

Her emotions battled inside her as she tried to explain things.

Nikolina's response was equally emotional.

"You left my daughter with them? Oh, my lord... I should have known this was a bad idea... She will be hurt..." she was genuinely horrified.

Katya seemed more trusting.

"She'll pull through, I'm sure. Anyway, Sasha's going to get us the help we need to take them out and save her," she pointed out, sure her niece was only with the Volkovs unwillingly, but trusting her brother to help.

She wasn't dignified with a reply.

The group settled into a deep silence, filled with conflicting emotional wounds that it now rested on Sasha and Nadezhda to heal, both in different ways.

But both as fast as they could, now that they had the threat of the Volkovs' ability to mutate hanging over them, without ever knowing when it might begin.

Or how long they had to stop them before a wave of mutated criminals swept over the city...

New Priorities

Sasha's efforts to help started with a trip to the police station.

He expected to be met with doubt again, but he had the all-important evidence folder tucked neatly under one arm and an incredibly determined demeanour.

He strode into the police station and instantly looked for someone to talk to. He was soon approached by a young police officer.

She strode towards him firmly, almost intimidatingly, but she still seemed a little more friendly and open than the person with whom he had spoken previously.

She was definitely prettier, he couldn't help but notice, taking in her long, sleek, deep brown hair, tawny skin, and chocolate eyes.

But that wasn't where he should be focusing right now, and he shook his head, scolding himself.

He needed to keep his guard up since they were still unsure of how seriously this would be taken.

From what he had seen before, things were clearly unusual here. The evidence should help, but...

"Hello, how can I help you?" The police officer asked him with a smile.

He wordlessly passed her the folder and, catching a puzzled expression passing over her face, revealed:

"I'm a private investigator; this is evidence I've found of a gang operating in this area."

He spoke a little stiffly, still untrusting of the local police department.

The woman looked at him, then very cautiously flipped the folder open to take a peek inside.

The first document her gaze fell on, though he couldn't remember what it was, must have been enough to convince her he wasn't mad or trying to trick her.

She turned serious at that point.

"I see. Thank you for bringing this to our attention, I will make sure it is all reviewed. Will you leave a number so you can help with our investigation?"

He relaxed, smiling now out of relief that he seemed to be getting somewhere, at long last.

"Of course," he agreed, filling out a form with his contact details before making his way back to Sof's house, which had quickly become the Anti-Volkov group's designated headquarters.

Meanwhile, his niece was doing her bit, as best she could in her current situation.

And in her case, it had to start with a great amount of effort to keep her patience.

Because, while she was pleased with herself for concocting a plan to stay alive, it had suddenly landed her with a lot to deal with.

To start with, she wasn't sure if Sof was dead or alive, whether the evidence was safe or not, and if any of the Volkovs suspected that she was scheming against them even now.

But by far the worst thing she was having to deal with was Vasily.

Since her return to him, he had been uncomfortably attentive. She wasn't sure why, he hadn't seemed that way when they had begun to get to know one another, and he had betrayed her, after all.

But that didn't stop him becoming painfully clingy and wanting to spend all his time with her.

She had hoped she would have had time to look for the diaries her father's message had mentioned, or at least grab the video footage she and Sof had discovered... But no, he was with her every waking hour.

She hated it.

Despite still - she had to confess, if only in the privacy of her own mind - finding him physically attractive, after everything, she hated time with him and was repulsed by his personality.

He was a liar, a traitor, a fake. Yet, she couldn't find any way to avoid him, so she was enduring his company, rather uncomfortably.

Her own attraction to him made her uncomfortable too. She wished he didn't make her feel that way when he looked at her...

He spent most of their time together talking about their wedding plans. It was all being planned by his family, out of tradition.

And because he didn't seem to want her to leave the house, insisting it was a 'dangerous time' for their 'family', after his sister Diana had been found with quite a lot of injuries and, deliriously he assumed, claimed she had been crushed by a dumpster.

It was being very hastily planned too; she was surprised and a little nervous to learn. She had been hoping to hatch an escape plan before the date rolled around, but they already had a dress and a guest list...

She was starting to worry that she may have to go through with the wedding, and his constant conversation about it did nothing to reassure her.

Today, however, she was enjoying one rare moment in which they were talking about something else. Something that actually interested her.

They had been sitting on the floor in his room when he had brought it up, picking up on something she had hoped she was hiding well.

"Are you still upset with me about us capturing you?" he asked, staring directly at her in a new, disconcerting way he had developed since they were reunited.

Internally, she cursed. If he could tell that... She just hoped she was a better actor when it came to her other secrets, all her hatred for him and her Anti-Volkov planning.

She had to keep the plans hidden from him, or they were all in grave danger.

But even so, she didn't deny it. It may have been safer to pretend she had forgiven him.

But the curious part of her was too eager to hear what he might have to say about the whole incident.

"Why wouldn't I be?" she asked snappily.

He smirked. "Because you agreed to marry me?" he suggested, watching her blush at that comment and assuming that, even in her anger, she must love him.

In actual fact, Nadezhda was hoping that he was joking and didn't wonder why she had agreed, because she didn't have an excuse for doing that.

It had just been her best way of staying alive at the time.

Luckily for her, he didn't question it, merely sobered up to continue:

"Seriously though, Nadya, you shouldn't be angry with me, it wasn't my idea."

Under the intense heat of her glare, he added a hasty, "I promise! It was Diana and Grandpa, they found... I think Diana took something of yours that told her who you were."

He started to try to explain, piecing the events they had been through together as he went along.

"And she came to me when we were in the hospital. She told me that if I didn't lure you to her, she would tell Grandpa, and he would probably kill us both."

There was a flicker in her eyes. So, he hadn't truly betrayed her...? But then she scolded herself, of course, he had, he was just trying to get around her.

Besides, this didn't change what he was and what his family did... If he was a part of that, then how could he be someone she could love?

She stayed cold, as cold as she could in the light of such unexpected information.

"So that's why you asked me out? And you took me to the cafe? You didn't even want to tell me the truth about my father?"

She fired her questions at him to try to remain angry.

"Of course not! I did that for me. I left Diana, agreeing to her deal but not sure I could do it, and I saw you. That's when I knew I couldn't. I told you the truth that day, I would have said more, but I... I guess she doesn't trust me, just like I shouldn't have trusted her. She followed us there. Don't you remember when I got up and tried to get you to leave? I saw her, I was just too late."

He sounded weirdly sincere, still staring at her, but with tears in his eyes.

What was worse was that his passionate explanation made sense to her, and it made her hopelessly confused.

Who *was* he? A man who genuinely loved her one moment, and a terrible criminal who had pointed a gun at her the next...

She held strong, he didn't have an explanation for that, did he?! The inner angry voice urged her on, while her face remained stoic, though her gaze had softened a little after his new information.

He saw that, seeing some change, but knowing she was unconvinced.

"What would it take for you to trust me?" he asked her tenderly. "Do you want to know the rest of the truth?"

Nadezhda paused. Hadn't her mother already given her the long-awaited truth?

But... she was never quite certain who to trust, since that fateful day when she had found the picture, found out about her family secrets...

What if there was more? Something else only Dariya had known; something else that now only her family knew?

Why else would her father have told her to come here? Of all the horrible places, after everything it had led to.

There had to be something more. A lump in her throat held back any answer, but she gave a silent nod instead.

That was all it took. Vasily turned and hauled something out from under his bed. It was a box, which he pushed towards her.

She hesitated, then flipped open the torn open tabs to reveal a pile of leather-bound books.

"What are these?" she asked him uncertainly.

"My mother's diaries. They start around about the time she met your father. I found them in Grandpa's lair a while ago and dragged them out. I wanted to see what she had to say. I think you should too," he replied.

She ran her hand over the cover of the top book, hesitating to open it and see what it might hold yet deeply convinced that this was somehow particularly important. Her father had mentioned these books!

They were bound to be important. Perhaps here, she would find the full story.

The story Dariya hadn't been around to tell her, that Vasily had refused to tell her, and the story that had started all of this... Her father's story.

She looked up with an expression of surprisingly genuine gratitude on her face. Whatever he was, he was trying to help her. That had to count for something.

"Thank you," she murmured.

Vasily gave her a silent smile and watched as she picked up the first diary tentatively and opened it up.

She read with devoted attention, determined not to miss any of the information she was expecting to find.

There were details of Dariya and her father meeting, of him revealing his true identity and motives to her, then, to Nadezhda's surprise, her attempts to help him take her own father down.

She hadn't known Dariya had been working with him. That must be why he sent her here, but she scanned the page for information only Dariya would have known...

There wasn't anything.

She sighed and picked up the next book, determined now that she would sit here and spend her days reading them.

Until she found *something, anything, everything* there was to know about her family that had been hidden from her for all these years.

Dariya, Vasily, And A Desperate Dash

Antonin Jelennski had worked up a lot of courage to admit to Dariya Volkova that he wasn't interested in her as more than a friend but was investigating her family.

It had come as a grave shock for him to learn that she had figured him out but wanted his help.

She had been feeling trapped and used by her father, whose actions disgusted her, for a long time, and hoped they could take him down.

They had come dangerously close too. She had worked to help him secretly, and he had actively challenged her family.

But he had had to flee, with a car full of all the messed up 'experiments' he had stolen from Vladimir's lair when his cover was blown.

Dariya had feigned her innocence with a heavy heart and a mind full of fear.

She was scared for herself, worried that her own involvement would be exposed, and worried for her friend.

Over their time pretending to be lovers, they had bonded deeply, and he had told her about his own life back at home, he had told her about the girl he was in love with, whom he had promised to return to.

Now she had to worry for the young couple's safety, praying he had more sense than to actually go back and put her in danger as well.

But he had, and she had heard of his death. It was recorded in her neat handwriting and seeing it, though Dariya mentioned it quite formally, was somehow real and moving to Nadezhda.

Now she was beginning to wish she could have met this woman, who seemed to have had a unique friendship, formed out of a desperate desire to do the right thing that they had both shared, with her unknown father, and who had had such compassion for her whole family, without ever meeting them.

But she hadn't, she only had the diaries left behind, and they didn't reveal much else.

Except, Nadezhda realised, a small clue - one she had very nearly missed - into how her father had known about her.

The night before he had died, he had been sifting through the evidence in the hope of preparing a case against Vladimir.

During their catch-up session, her mother had revealed that much. Now Dariya's diaries told her that some of the 'evidence' he had taken with him had x-ray powers.

It was all starting to add up, and it amazed her. In some ways, it scared her to learn that Vasily hadn't lied, that it seemed Vladimir was some genius engineer and schemer.

The idea that Vasily hadn't lied meant she had to face a reality in which he might not be evil...

But in other ways, she was filled with renewed determination.

Her father and Dariya had started this quest to bring down the evil in the Volkov family, and now she was going to finish it.

Well, if Sof had escaped, if her allies were doing their part... Then she might have nearly finished it already!

She risked a grin at that thought and, after being immersed in reading, was abruptly reminded of Vasily's presence in the room.

"What did you find?!" he asked, excited that she seemed to be enjoying the added information he had provided.

She looked up, realising he had been watching her all this time.

"I just... I had no idea your mother was working with my father; it sounds like they were really close." She gave him half her thoughts.

"Like us," he grinned. "It even started with fake dating."

Well, that much was true, but she blushed and didn't bother to think up a reply. She was still unsure about him.

He was involved in something sinister, but he was still trying to help her survive in this world of chaos.

She changed the subject, backtracking to the topic that had started all this. Her father.

"That's not how you made things sound. When we talked about my father, you said he betrayed your family," she pointed out.

"In a way, he did. Look, the law enforcement are no friends to people like us, they don't understand what we're trying to achieve. Sure, technically it's 'illegal', but that's all they think about, they don't think outside the box and see how it would be better for people." He told her.

She scowled and was tempted to demand to know how it would be better, but he wasn't finished just yet.

"My mother was wrong to get him involved. But it was just poor execution, but a 'bad' idea, exactly. Grandpa might be... Special but he is growing old and stupid."

Now she was too surprised to attack his previous points.

"You... You want him gone too?"

That was what it seemed like he was implying, but he had previously made it sound like the old man was an amazing person who would be best for the universe if he was left to do whatever he wanted.

It didn't make sense to her anymore. Besides what she had heard of Dariya, it seemed like this whole family was absolutely mental.

Vasily nodded.

"Don't get me wrong, he's clever, but his time is over. I think if you and I finish what our parents started and get rid of him, we can really make our family great. You're special, I saw that straight away, and I've learnt from the best...”

He smiled at this, taking her hand, and caressing the ring he had bought for their engagement.

"Our partnership will be brilliant."

The young woman avoided his gaze, blushing.

Well, she wanted to finish what their parents had put in motion too, but not necessarily as his wife.

And certainly not as his partner-in-crime. She had no intention of running a mafia family with anyone.

However, the possibility that he could be useful in gathering more evidence to take down Vladimir, just in case...

In case the first evidence hadn't made it back to her allies, it occurred to her.

She forced a smile, hoping she didn't look or sound too suspicious.

"It will. But how will we get rid of your Grandpa?"

Vasily nodded.

"I've made a plan. We'll start a family.”

When he saw her blush and the flicker of anger in her eyes, he hastily added:

"Not like that! Do you remember I told you we're clones? Well, he has a cloning machine, and I had something added to it. We can make some special little children of our own and they will help us destroy him," he told her with a little smirk on his face, clearly sure he held the trump card.

The cloning machine... Everything Sof had told her about the modifications came rushing back. So, was this his plan?

To use children as weapons?! Her stomach churned. But this time he didn't seem to notice her distress, thankfully.

"Plus, I have access to his precious lair at the moment. Come on, I'll show you everything!" He urged, still too smug about his plan to notice the stunned look on her face.

Nadezhda recalled the lair. The video footage leapt to the front of her mind. It would be a perfect opportunity for evidence gathering, at last!

She jumped up and into action, still with her hand in his, pulling him to his feet too.

"Let's go!"

He hurried along with her, equally enthusiastic.

It would be easier this time he explained on the way because Vladimir was still in recovery for his injury and during his absence, had trusted him with access to everything in there.

It didn't take long for them to slip into Vladimir's quarters and Vasily opened the wardrobe.

They stepped in and opened the lair.

As they walked through the corridors and chambers full of contraptions, Nadezhda tried to think up a plan to get into the video room without seeming suspicious and escape with the evidence so that she could deliver it to her allies, without his knowledge.

She knew he wouldn't approve and thought he might try to hurt her if he knew she wasn't planning to help him after all.

In the end, to her embarrassment, the only thing that came to mind was to try to seduce him as a distraction.

So, as they neared the video room, she steered him gently but surely towards a door on the other side of the corridor.

Pulling it open, she suggested brightly, "let's look in here!"

It was a fairly bare room but featured a workbench, which she led him towards.

"There's nothing in here," he commented, sounding puzzled.

She smirked at him and pushed him onto the workbench.

"There's us... If all this is going to be ours, let's make some memories here," she suggested, hating herself for talking like this.

She had thought that her attraction to him would make flirting with him at least a little easier, but it sickened her somewhat.

He seemed pretty enthusiastic though, his hands seeking her waist and latching on.

"Good idea," he purred, craning his neck up to kiss her as she stood in his arms. Unable to go through with it, she pulled back hastily.

"Just... Just let's shut the door!" she suggested as he gave her a confused look.

It seemed to be enough to pacify him, so she took the opportunity and hurried to the door. And right out before he could say a word.

She slammed the door and leant on it as she heard him start to call out to her.

Searching wildly, she found a box and dragged it over to block the door shut, before darting across the hall to the video room.

It was just as she remembered it.

So, she took a seat at the desk and started to sort through the footage for useful parts.

It was taking forever, and she started to worry that her trapped 'lover' might make his escape and realise what she was up to before anything useful came up.

Then it dawned on her as she looked up, past the screen, how stupid she had been.

She didn't need to do this. There was a stack of discs behind the computer that were all neatly dated.

They were pretty big, and she only needed to grab four to cover the time since the prison breakout.

That would be enough, she was sure. For want of a better place to hide them, she shoved them under her - well, Sof's - thankfully baggy shirt.

Then broke into a run to find the exit and get the hell out of there.

Moving Forward

Nadezhda charged out of the house, ignoring odd looks from anyone around, and ran down the street, the stolen video discs pushing against her body uncomfortably but nevertheless being completely disregarded.

Just like everything else except her urge to get out of there with the videos and find her family.

She hurtled down the street almost instinctively, not having to fight to remember the way to Sof's house, her feet sure of themselves.

Before she had fully registered what she was doing, she skidded to a stop outside the familiar house.

There was a police car sitting in the drive.

She felt her heart leap, then sink again. There were two reasons that came to mind as to why it might be there.

Either her allies had succeeded in getting the local police to help them and were well on their way to proving a case against the Volkov family...

Or Sof had died, and her death was being investigated.

Well, she told herself, there's only one way to find out...

She tentatively approached the door and knocked, waiting in trepidation for a response.

Inside, things were pretty busy.

The police had followed through quite quickly on the evidence Sasha had handed to them, and now an officer was sat at the table with him, filling them in on a plan for raiding the Volkov's headquarters in a few days to take the technology they had been illegally making and arrest them.

It was also clear that the group would have to be heavily involved in the trial, as the main witnesses to many of the crimes.

The knock on the door made Nikolina jump. She had been sitting nearby watching Sasha discuss the case but in surly silence.

Ever since she had been separated from her daughter again, she had retreated back into the gloom.

However, whenever there was a visitor, she would snap out of it and investigate in case it had anything to do with Nadezhda.

So, she was quickly on her feet and hurried to the door, beating Sof there.

She yanked it open to reveal her out of breath, red-faced daughter. Nadezhda threw herself into her mother's arms, losing all her self-control.

Right now, she was just glad to be safe, to be 'home' with her loved ones and had to let it out.

In the same moment, the older woman wrapped arms around her daughter, starting to cry, overwhelmed at seeing her safe.

Then she pulled away with a little frown.

"Are you okay?" she asked, looking confused, glancing up and down the girl.

"I am now..." Nadezhda finally managed to get her breath and speak, before noting her mother's expression. "Why? What's up?"

"You feel... Different," Nikolina told her.

It dawned on her what her mother meant. When she hugged her, the discs would have been pressed between them.

She laughed it off and then pulled them from under her shirt.

"I got these," she revealed, presenting them to her still baffled mother. "They're footage from the security cameras in that place. So, evidence," she explained.

It was at that moment that Sof bounded over unexpectedly from where she had been watching, just behind Nikolina. She hugged Nadezhda too.

"I knew it, I knew you had a plan, and you came through!" she grinned as she did so.

Nadezhda was a little surprised and overwhelmed at the hug, as well as her friend's faith in her.

They hadn't spent much time together, and yet she had never known another friend who would believe in her and forgive her for something that could have killed her.

She remembered the look in Sof's eyes as she had first fallen and hugged her back tightly, upset with what she had done, but so, so glad that Sof had come to terms with it somehow and forgave her.

"I'm so happy it worked out..." she murmured in response.

Nikolina looked at the two girls and nodded.

"I am just glad that all this seems to be coming to a close. Nadya, you're back safely, I was worried that you were with those awful people forever, and as for the rest of us, we have nearly got this case sorted out, so we should finish our work."

She stopped, then held up the discs.

"These should go to that police lady..." she commented, before wandering off to hand them over.

Sof disentangled herself from Nadezhda and leant over to shut the door behind her. After the sudden surprise of her arrival, it had been abandoned, wide open.

Once it was shut, she turned back to her friend.

"Let's catch up," she suggested, glad to see her again.

She hadn't realised how much she had missed her until she had suddenly been standing there again, which was part of the reason why she had been so quick to forgive.

That, and the fact that she was reassured now that it had all been a plan. Of course, Nadya had never meant to harm her...

For her part, after spending her day trying to piece together the past, work around Vasily and escape without knowing what kind of situation she was charging headlong into, Nadezhda was only too glad of an offer to sit and do nothing more stressful than chatting to Sof.

"Good idea." She nodded gratefully, following the other girl as she led her way to her room, a quiet place to sit down.

"So, how did you get away from them? You didn't actually marry that moron, did you?!" Sof demanded to know as soon as they had settled down.

"Of course not! Though for a horrible little moment I thought I might have to before I had fully finished my planning. It was so hard to get a moment to myself, or even to leave the house there..." She shuddered as she recalled that.

It hadn't seemed quite so controlling when Vasily had been there with her, trying to help her, but looking back, she realised how trapped she had been.

Then she brushed it off before she could start to dwell on her weird, awkward but useful relationship with Vasily...

She still had Sof's questions to fully answer.

"I got out though. Because he tried to get me to help him against his Grandpa, and so he took me into the lair again. Then I trapped him there, and I got the videos..." she explained.

"Thank God for that! They'll be so much help with the police. They're already planning raids on the house, but more evidence will be great," Sof commented.

"And I must admit... I didn't realise how much help that evidence would be. The police around here aren't usually much good, but after your Uncle gave them that... It's been so much easier," she revealed.

Her time with Vasily still preyed on Nadezhda's mind, and she couldn't be optimistic just yet, even with such good news.

"That's great, but I... I have to tell you something. You know the cloning machine? It's Vasily... he wants to use it to make an army of mutant clones and lead them, first against his Grandfather, then against... against the rest of the world, I suppose..." she admitted, still feeling sick as she recalled his horrible plan.

The one he had wanted her to be a part of...

"Oh God... we better hope these raids happen fast..." Sof groaned, paling.

If the police didn't act fast, their movement could be facing an army of violent mutants coming to wipe them out.

"They will, now we have the evidence that we need."

Nadezhda tried her best to encourage her friend, though the same fear was swirling around her mind as well.

Sof did perk up a little, though, smiling.

"Yeah, and our allies are all more enthusiastic now! We've come a long way and gained a lot of confidence... Mostly thanks to you and your family. You've all been great!" She grinned, too cheered by her friend's return and their impending success to be kept down for long, even by dreadful news.

Another image flickered through Nadezhda's mind, a more positive one, from her past with Sof.

"And so were you. Wasn't it you who organised and motivated them all in the first place?"

The other girl looked a little shy about that. "I guess so," she admitted.

"Come on, it's true," her friend insisted.

There was a gentle knock on the door at this point, then, after a pause not quite long enough for them to respond in, Ekaterina's head popped around the edge of it.

"Hey kids, having fun?"

She grinned, taking some pride in the fact that this comment appeared to absolutely mortify her niece, turning the girl's face into a tomato.

"We're fine..." Nadezhda managed to respond, wondering what the older woman wanted but also wishing she would leave.

Or at least stop making deliberately silly comments...

"Yeah, we're having fun," Sof replied, playing it off coolly, "what's up?"

Katya's smile became a little more sincere and less teasing now.

"Well, sorry to interrupt, but we're going to have a proper talk about everyone's roles in this and our day in court now. I thought you'd want to be there," she revealed the reason behind her presence.

The two young women looked at each other, then back to her, and nodded.

Getting up, they headed off to see what all their efforts were going to bring in the next step, the legal proceedings...

The First Arrest

While Nadezhda had been running off to find out what had happened to her allies and deliver her newly snaffled evidence, Vasily had been venting his frustration on the door that had held him in.

Well, he hadn't intended to, but after he had waited for some time, it had occurred to him that she shouldn't have had to leave the room to shut the door, and, puzzled, he had got up to find and question her.

It was only then that he realised the door wouldn't budge and, unable to understand why, he had hammered on it in sheer frustration until - never that strong in the first place and only held shut with a box - it failed to hold up in the face of his assaults and flew open, sending him flying out onto the other side.

After he had picked himself up from the floor of the corridor where he had landed, he looked around for his fiancée.

That was when his eyes fell on the video room opposite and he grinned to himself.

Perfect, this way he could find Nadya without having to spend tiresome hours without her, trying to find her.

Wandering across the hall, he sat down at the computer, oblivious to the missing discs behind it, and started to search through the footage for any vague flash that looked like his wife-to-be.

The first to catch his eye was blurry footage of her running down the house's entrance hall and out of the front door.

Confusion and anger set in at about the same time and mixed together, swirling around his mind.

Why had she run out like that and left him? She had just abandoned him, after all the help he had offered her, everything they had discussed and planned out together?!

How could he have let her just run out like that after days of making sure she didn't leave his side apart from when it was absolutely necessary?

He found himself completely unable to answer any of his own questions, and yet he knew exactly how he could get answers.

He had to find her, bring her home and make her explain herself. Springing to his feet, he hastily abandoned the lair he had been trusted to guard during his grandfather's recovery and hurtled off in pursuit.

The fact that he had no idea where she had gone after she had left his family's house was quite forgotten about until he was out of the door and had skidded to a sudden halt in the middle of the street, looking around him in irritated puzzlement.

Then he could have sworn he caught a vague glimpse of her up ahead and raced off in that direction.

She seemed in a state, so much so that she didn't notice his approach, so he dropped back, slowing down enough to stay behind her without losing track of her.

Yes, he wanted to find out what was going on right now, but this process would surely lead to some idea of what she was up to, and he would never have to engage in anything as crude as questioning her.

Now he was strolling briskly but casually along, keeping the girl in his sights, and he found he was enjoying himself.

He got the privilege of watching the woman who fascinated him without her knowing.

He had noticed that whenever she noticed him staring at her, she would try to avoid his gaze. Now she wasn't hiding anything from him, too caught up in some pure emotional state.

And even her panic was fascinating, even more so than her normal state, because he was seeking answers and explanations about it.

But generally, she was simply fascinating to watch.

From the moment he had first seen her, standing in the snow, he had known she must have secrets, that she was complicated. No one else would be in that situation.

And he had, albeit quite reluctantly at first, had to give in to his curiosity.

His family hated secrets; they shared everything together. So, when he met someone with so much to hide, he had needed to know more.

That was why he had helped her, and that was why he wanted to watch her all the time, to stay with her, and to follow her right now.

Perhaps he had become a little obsessed with her, perhaps what he was doing bordered on stalking.

He considered this but didn't care. She had become a part of him now, and his feelings for her - curiosity, love, obsession - Whatever they might be, were not something he was willing to give up on.

Not even for his family. In fact, though his mother's desire to get rid of her father had begun to inspire him, and his own deeds had shaped his vision for the family, he thought that she could bring something unique to it.

That was why he had included her in his secrets, why he had confessed it all to her.

And how had she responded? By leaving. By running away from him.

He growled quietly to himself and sped up. She had halted now and turned, walking up the drive to a house.

This was odd, he noted, sure she wasn't from this area and didn't know anyone here, but he would find out was going on anyway.

He had made up his mind about that and nothing was going to hold him back.

So, he followed her still, approaching the house. A few minutes passed and he could hear a clamour of voices from inside.

The door slammed just as he stepped onto the pathway up to the door.

None of this stopped him. He strode up the path and banged heavily on the door.

Inside, the meeting had just begun.

There was some frustrated sighing and muttering when a knock at the door interrupted this long-awaited discussion of the justice system finally closing in on the Volkov family.

But eventually, Sof got up and went to the door. Upon opening it to see him, she scowled.

He recognised her as one of the main troublemakers for him and his family, as well as one who should be dead, and his eyes narrowed.

But he had more important things on his mind.

He pushed her roughly aside and barged his way inside, calling out, "Nadya!" as he ran into the living room where the group were sitting.

Nadezhda's eyes widened when she spotted him.

"Vasily? What are you doing here?" she questioned aloud, confused.

"I came to find you and take you back home," he told her with a sweet smile, considering it best to save the interrogation until she was definitely on his side.

There was clearly something going on here.

The girl bit her lip and looked around. If he had just followed her here, he probably wasn't armed.

There was a police officer nearby and they had the strength of numbers.

Given that she didn't like the idea of abandoning the movement again to pretend to take his side until they were ready to end things, now seemed like a suitable time to admit the truth.

"I'm not coming. I'm staying here." she confessed.

"What? Why? Who even are these people? Some little troublemaker who you tried to get rid of and somehow came back, a goddamn *officer*..."

He sneered here, his family's age-old prejudices coming out.

But Nadezhda cut him off before he could continue with his jeers.

"They are my friends and family!" she snapped at him.

"Better people than you and yours. I want to stay. And I want you to leave."

It was true, every time he seemed to do this to her, help her, then go right back to making her hate the sight of him, and right now she despised his very presence.

She wasn't alone. An angry Sof charged back into her own living room having been pushed about.

She glared at him, wishing looks could kill but not wanting to commit an assault in front of the police officer.

"You heard her, get out of my house," she growled at him.

"This is between me and Nadya!" he responded sharply, before reaching out and trying to grab his 'bride-to-be's' arm.

She jumped away from him and Sof came a little closer to injuring the man.

And Nikolina, Sasha and Katya rose as one, Nikolina forcing herself between her daughter and the angry young man, flanked by her siblings.

"And she has made her decision, so leave my daughter alone," she ordered him.

Then Vasily swung at her, his frustration, and his desperation to get to Nadezhda, get answers from her and take her back with him, getting the better of him.

He meant to strike her mother, but the blow missed, falling to the side, and catching Sasha in the side of the head.

The older man stumbled slightly, glowered at him, and considered retaliating.

His angry sisters were both just about to, but another voice broke the silence.

"Sir, you're trespassing on private property, and you just assaulted a man, I'm going to have to arrest you," The young policewoman was on her feet, red in the face with annoyance and the heat of the tense moment.

She saw him turn his angry glare on her and approached him, drawing a taser.

"I'm Officer Sobachkina and you're under arrest for trespassing and assault," she informed him, brandishing the weapon as she saw him contemplating another swing, this time aimed at her.

She continued to go through the necessary information and procedures as she took out her handcuffs, managing to wrestle him into them without being hit, though he began to protest, loudly and offensively, at this point.

They watched her pull him out of the building to her car, his protests ringing their ears, all slightly dazed.

One of them had been arrested. It had really begun.

Happiness Restored

Once it did begin, it was over remarkably swiftly.

The following morning, at dawn, armed police raided the Volkov family's headquarters, ramming down the door to the house and hauling people out.

It was loud and messy, but within a few hours, it was done.

They could breathe more easily knowing that Vasily's insane plan about mutants wasn't being enacted, and Vladimir couldn't be planning some kind of revenge on them either.

So, of course, at Sof's house, there was a buzz of excitement going around as people whispered the things that they had heard about the raids to one another and made wild guesses about the legal procedures that would follow.

Nadezhda watched the gossiping and general celebration from the side-lines. She was still distracted.

A lot had happened to her since that fatal day when, angry that she hadn't known the whole truth of her own life story, she had let her emotions take over and stormed out of her mother's apartment, the only home she had ever known.

Looking back, she wasn't sure she would still do that, but that was in the light of the truth.

At the time, she hadn't understood what could possibly justify having someone believe they were an orphan - albeit one fortunate enough to be adopted - for their whole life, when they weren't.

Besides, her relationship with her mother had been a purely functional one. Her mother had fed her, clothed her, and housed her, but she had never been a mother to her.

 She had never called her Mama, hugged her, or confided in her in times of need. She had been lacking, she realised in a sudden, jolting thought that almost shocked her, in affection.

She never had many friends, and it was only when Sasha came around or Katya babysat that she felt love.

Perhaps that was why she had, upon learning she had had another parent out there, she had been so desperate for some, any, connection with her father.

 Something that would reassure her that a parent had loved her when her mother didn't seem to.

The diary he had left started that, so she had charged headlong into danger over it.

Her eyes were drawn over to her family, a small group celebrating together.

Nikolina, who had been, for the majority of her daughter's life, so cold and withdrawn, was smiling as she hugged her siblings.

The young girl smiled softly.

In a way, her goal had been achieved, she had found parental love. Because she finally understood her mother.

In an incredibly sad way, knowing that her coldness had been her way of hiding because she was afraid.

Afraid of the very real danger of the Volkov family, which was why she had hidden all traces of her former life with her husband away, and afraid of loving when she could lose a loved one so easily.

At least Nadezhda could be grateful for one thing, whatever way the court case went, this whole ordeal had brought her family together.

It had brought back together Ekaterina and Nikolina, two sisters divided by a shared secret and the pressure to keep it, and it had brought her and her mother together for the first time, to understand one another properly, and meet in the middle of their own strong opinions.

From then on, they had become close. Now the whole Moroz family had fought together, and if it came down to it, then they would die together.

But thankfully, it looked like that wouldn't be necessary. The worst seemed to have passed.

Nikolina looked up over her younger sister's shoulder as she happily embraced her, looking forward to putting the Volkov family, who had destroyed her happiness and haunted her for years, in prison and truly in her past.

Behind Ekaterina, her gaze fell on the catalyst that had made this possible, in bringing her forward, out of her self-imposed solitude and back to finish the fight, her daughter.

She smiled, a little tearfully, emotional at that very thought. Behind her sister's back, she beckoned for Nadezhda to join the rest of the family in their time of happiness.

But the girl shook her head with a small smile and slipped out of the room before she could be questioned about it.

Because she might understand all her little family secrets and hidden issues now, but there was one thing that still completely confused her.

Vasily.

She still wasn't sure about, well, anything to do with him.

There had been moments, right at the start, when he had been a great friend, a lot of help and someone she had started to fall for.

Then he had seemed to betray her, and she had hated him passionately for treating her that way.

Yet, he hadn't betrayed her, and he had helped her again... But for his own reasons, selfish reasons.

He had used her, he had held a gun to her head, he had followed her and acted so possessive of her that he had tried to hit her mother and had hit her uncle.

It was one big mess. What the hell was he playing at? She wanted answers. Answers to everything.

And, after all this messing around, some closure, one way or another, on their 'relationship'.

So, she slipped out of Sof's house while the partying was in full swing and, on her way down the path, bumped into Officer Sobachkina coming back the other way.

She was a little surprised to see the police officer, and curious too.

"Oh, hello, Officer. Any updates?" she asked her straight away, guessing that must be why she was here.

The woman laughed at her eagerness. "No, not yet I'm afraid. I'm just Maria at the moment."

Catching her look of puzzlement, she added an explanation, "I'm off duty. But apparently, there's some celebrating going on and Sasha invited me over," she told her.

This was another surprise for Nadezhda. As far as she had been aware, any involvement with the police and the Anti-Volkov group had been purely professional.

In fact, most of them hadn't even known the woman's name, even her surname, until Vasily's arrest.

So, this thing with her uncle inviting her around... She briefly wondered how serious it was, but realised it probably wasn't a suitable time to ask that.

"Well, that's nice," she said instead.

"Hey, do you know if Vasily is allowed visitors?" she added, her mind turning back to her original point.

Maria looked at her sympathetically. "They are, but you're not still caught up with him, are you? Trust me, guys like that aren't worth it," she told her.

Nadezhda blushed at that comment. "Well... We had something for a while. He helped me. Kind of," she tried to explain their weird, complicated relationship to the other woman.

"Help you help him, or actually help *you?*"

The question was fired back quickly, interrogation-style, and there was nowhere to hide from it.

The girl turned red as she thought about their 'past' together.

It was true, Vasily's kindness in giving her his mother's diaries had turned out to be a tactic to get her on his side against his grandfather. Had that been his goal all along?

She thought of his proposal, an emotional seeming statement about happily ever after, and the offers of their future together that had followed it.

But it was a future in crime, and a proposal made at gunpoint that dismissed her friends, her morals, and the life she had started to build...

"I guess he wasn't trying to help me...” she realised, upset to know she had been so naïve, so easily manipulated, not once but twice, yet smiling in relief as she realised something; she had found the 'answers' she had searched for.

The closure to follow was in her own mind. She wanted nothing more to do with him apart from to get justice against him.

"There you go then." Maria smiled.

"You're better off without him,” she added emphatically, "now let's go before the party's over.”

She opened the door to Sof's house, a grateful and relieved Nadezhda following her back into the house to join the celebrations.

Little Things

The next day, the partying that had followed the initial joyous victory was over. There were more serious issues to focus on, such as the legal preparations.

Because eventually, there would be a trial, and they would have to be ready to make sure the Volkov family didn't find some way to wriggle away from justice.

Maria stayed around to offer advice, and Sasha used his legal experience to plan things out as well, sifting through the evidence and figuring out how best to use it against the Volkov family.

Ultimately though, this was when Nikolina became especially involved.

As a lawyer herself, she was prepared to prosecute the mafia family personally if she had to and spent a lot of time making sure she knew what to say about their crimes.

She had to work on what to get some of the others to say too, since Sof's idea of a good legal defence was, "they're clearly trouble, and morons to boot."

While they were busy with this important work, Nadezhda mostly kept out of their way, apart from giving her own statement on what she had learnt and witnessed to Maria.

She didn't feel like she had a lot else to contribute.

There was something on her mind to do with the recent raids though.

It seemed small and trivial when she considered it, but she couldn't help but wonder about it.

What had happened to the things she had brought with her? Diana had taken her father's diary if Vasily was to be believed.

The rest of the meagre luggage she had run away with had been abandoned in Vasily's car if she recalled correctly.

Then there were Dariya's journals. But she guessed those weren't truly hers.

It was a shame; they were the main connection with her father that she had found. And that was the main reason she had set out from her home in the first place, after all...

She sighed and stirred the tea she had just made herself idly. Katya looked at her across Sof's kitchen table.

"What's up?" she asked, "Are you getting bored too? Personally, I want all this prepping and paperwork the others are mad about out of the way so we can get that evil lot behind bars!" she admitted, revealing her own impatience.

"No... Well, maybe a little bit." Nadezhda had to confess.

"But mostly I'm just wondering about the stuff I left behind at their house...What do you think happened to it?"

Katya blinked in confusion. "You left stuff there?" she questioned.

"I did," she nodded, "I didn't mean to, but I kind of left in a hurry, and so I didn't bring the diary out, or a picture I brought, or anything," she explained.

"It's all still there?" Katya double-checked.

Nadezhda nodded again. "Unfortunately, yeah. And then there were the gifts Vasily gave me..." she sounded wistful now.

Her Aunt simply responded with a snort of disapproval though. "Why do you want stuff from him? He seemed like an idiot to me!"

"Oh, he is," the younger woman concluded, having eventually managed to see through him.

"But he did give me his mother's journals. And she helped my father back when he was here... They have his whole story in them. My father even left a message in one of his old music books about them. Then I went and left those, and the music books as well...” she revealed, sighing as she realised how much information about her father she had lost when she left the Volkov house.

Katya was silent for a while, considering this.

She could absolutely understand why that would be something her niece would like to keep, but she wasn't sure how to go about getting it for her.

After a few moments, something occurred to her and she stood up, leaving Nadezhda with the cryptic reassurance.

"I'll see what I can do about that."

The girl sat there in confusion for a little while, wondering what her Aunt had meant and exactly what she might be planning to do.

These musings were disturbed by Sof, who wandered into the room, sat down beside her, and stared into space.

After a while, Sof sighed, in a strange, slightly wistful but a little sad sounding way.

Nadezhda looked over at her curiously. They both seemed to be in the same boat.

They had fought hard to reach this point but had no legal experience and therefore were on the outside of the preparation for the momentous court case.

Having to hand over to the others meant that they finally had time to think over all the other tiny details that had slipped through the cracks during their busiest moments.

At least, she guessed that that was the kind of thing the other girl was dwelling on as well, but she wanted a little more specific knowledge.

"What's on your mind?" she asked gently.

"If you don't mind telling me, that is," she added politely, remembering that this was a little different to her own experience with Katya.

They were family, Sof was merely a friend of hers. And in the grand scheme of things, they hadn't known one another very long.

But Sof brushed that idea off immediately.

"Nadya, I risked my life with you and trusted you to push me out of a damn window, why would I be annoyed by you asking a question?" she demanded to know.

Nadezhda gave a sheepish little laugh.

"Well, if you look at it that way, I guess you have a point," she admitted, "So, come on, what's up?"

At this point, Katya reappeared, looking mildly smug about something, then took in the scene, with the two girls getting cosy around the kitchen table, laughing, and having a chat.

She grinned and made her way over.

"Still on with the girl talk, hey, Nadya? Mind if I join?" she asked as she pulled up a seat nearby again.

"What did you go for in the first place?" Nadezhda interrogated, partly joking around, exaggerating her desire for her Aunt's company a little, partly curious as to why Katya had vanished after her confession.

"Never you mind," the older woman retorted secretively.

"Now what's the goss?" she asked, back to her usual grinning self.

Nadezhda felt a little awkward then, not sure if Sof would want to talk to her in front of her Aunt like this. She hesitated.

Sof jumped in herself.

"It's not gossip, pretty serious actually, but if you still wanna listen, you're welcome to stick around," she explained.

Neither woman moved, except as Nadezhda visibly relaxed, relieved that her Aunt hadn't put Sof off talking to her.

So, Sof began to speak.

"You see, all this is what I've been working towards ever since Sergei was killed. Justice. And now it's right around the corner and I don't know what else I'm gonna do with my life. I mean, I was a kid when I started this... I've got nothing but the house and the money he left me to pay for it and other basics. No qualifications, no other family. Where do I go from here?" she questioned, seriously confused, and clearly upset.

Silence fell over the little kitchen.

Though Sof had told them it was 'pretty serious', neither of the other women had expected it to be this heavy. Nadezhda sat there, her mind racing.

What did she know about her new friend's life that she might be able to offer as a solution, or at very least, use to cheer Sof up?

Not that much, she had to admit. Just that she was lively, energetic, a good leader...

But she was only recalling the qualities that drew her to Sof, not anything helpful, she realised, blushing a little bit as she caught herself.

Correcting the error, she thought harder. An idea sprung into her mind.

"You could go into engineering! You're great at that, right? And you love it. Plus, you don't need too many pre-existing qualifications to get into a vocational trading school, and with your cousin's reputation, maybe people he knew can help...”

She started to babble, excited that she could offer Sof help. After all they had been through, it felt like the least she could do.

Sof's face lit up.

"That would be amazing if I could,” she admitted, pleased by the idea, "but I'd have to find a school to apply for or look through his things for contacts... I'll get on to that!”

She grinned, getting up and hurrying off to do so. At least it would give her something to do while they waited for the legal proceedings to be sorted out...

As she was leaving, Katya called out, "If you need any more help, we're right here!"

When she had left, the older woman smiled.

"Sweet girl, nice that you could help her," she commented.

"Of course, she's my friend," Nadezhda replied.

"Well, there you go, finally got something good out of all this," her Aunt laughed.

"We got justice too. Or at least, hopefully, we will..." the young woman added, thinking ahead to the whole point they had worked towards.

The Trial Begins

Getting to that all-important point, the trial, was more frustrating than Nadezhda had expected it to be.

Mostly because time seemed to pass slowly while they waited for that date to roll around.

The time they filled with parts of their lives that would have been important, had they not been waiting on something this crucial.

As it was, Sof's applications to countless engineering schools across the country, Sasha's budding relationship with Maria, and all the missed family time with Nikolina and Ekaterina seemed trivial to Nadezhda, as though it was simply a distraction from what they should be doing:

Bringing justice to the Volkovs. That was always their main goal, and it was what all their minds were still secretly focusing on.

Eventually, though, the court date came up and, accompanied by her family, Sof, and other friends from the Anti-Volkov group, she made her way over to the court building.

They walked in silence, all too bound up in nervous thoughts and what-ifs to make conversation.

What would today bring? Either a great victory or a terrible injustice that could have dangerous implications for all of their futures...

And only time would tell. Time, and the decision made by the court. It all depended on that precious decision now.

They arrived early and crowded into a small waiting room with a stale scent and horribly tense atmosphere.

Nikolina paced the room, reading all her preparations out loud. Time, clearly never on their side, ticked by slowly again.

After what seemed like an eternity, a court official emerged through some double doors and called their names.

There was a scramble to get through the doors, with Nikolina clinging to her paperwork and muttering under her breath as she barged her way to the front.

Nadezhda was quite surprised, never having seen her mother in enough of a state to act that way, but could understand, still tense herself.

She hurried inside too, the others filing in close behind her.

She glanced around the courtroom as she entered, noting the serious-looking group in suits gathered together, whispering.

She guessed they were court officials and lawyers, discussing the case. The jurors were already sat in their place, silent and severe looking.

Her eyes turned to the judge's seat, but it was empty right now.

The group quietly sat where the official directed them to and returned to yet more frustrating waiting around.

They stood and sat again in the same stiff, awkward silence as the judge entered.

Finally, the quiet of the courtroom was ruptured by some distant shouts of protest.

Then the doors flew open and banged shut again, the source of the protesting made obvious as a team of prison officers dragged Vladimir, Vasily and Diana, the main members of the Volkov gang, into the room.

Diana was attempting to kick one of the prison officers in the shins and failing, while Vladimir was threatening them and demanding to know if they knew he was and how they dared to do this to him.

Eventually, after some loud insistence from the judge, Diana's fighting stopped.

Vladimir continued with his irritated shouts, even when faced with being charged with contempt of court.

Nadezhda felt a little frightened by this display, yet there was a spark of hope in her. If he was going to add charges to his list, it would make their job even easier.

Then, at last, the trial was beginning. It seemed surreal and dream-like to watch as their evidence and her mother's painstakingly prepared legal arguments were presented to the judge.

They had numerous witness statements to make, with Sasha and Sof offering accounts of their original imprisonment, though Sof's had been considerably toned down by Nikolina beforehand.

Nadezhda made her own statement, explaining how she had been taken by Diana and two of their thugs, painfully aware of Diana glowering at her from across the room while she did so.

And, of course, Vasily's awkward staring. It grew worse as she went on to detail the incidents in the house when he had pulled a gun on her and Sof.

He and Sof began to speak angrily at the same time, with Sof calling out that they 'could have been killed' as Vasily protested that he 'would never do something like that to the woman he loved.'

They were both hushed into disgruntled silence by the judge, who then had his clerk play through more of the footage Nadezhda recalled stealing as evidence.

It clearly showed the incident with the gun, a strange moment to relive again with an outsider's view.

That whole incident took a long time to address.

To Nadezhda's distress, the court spent time discussing whether her and Sof's own violent actions were self-defence against the Volkov's and whether the pursuit of the evidence was a good enough reason to excuse their technically unlawful access to the house.

She fidgeted nervously, worried that now she had put herself and her friend on trial.

Beside her, Sof tensed too, struggling to hold in her own disapproval of this line of questioning.

She wanted to shout out protests and point out that of course it was self-defence, it was stupid to suggest that violently disarming a gun-wielding psycho mob boss was assault!

But Nikolina's advice on behaving in court ran through her head, as well as the judge's earlier argument with Vladimir, so she kept quiet. With extreme reluctance.

Both girls soon breathed audible sighs of relief, though, when the judge finally decided that, given the circumstances, they were innocent.

In that particular case, Vasily and Vladimir were both facing potential charges of assault, unlawfully detaining the girls and threatening behaviour.

But with the wealth of other evidence to be considered, the trial was far from over.

There was Diana's taking of Nadezhda's journal, which was both a theft and a more severe problem as she had deliberately used it to endanger her.

There was Diana's role in Nadezhda's consequential kidnapping used to prove that.

In fact, due to the many, many witnesses and victims from the Anti-Volkov group who had been through kidnapping and unlawful imprisonment, these charges were levelled against the group as a whole, though most of the evidence, in this case, was against Diana.

It seemed she was the family's usual representative when they carried out their 'arrests'.

The charges went on getting increasingly serious, with Maria's statement from when she had had to arrest Vasily bringing charges of him harassing, stalking, and threatening Nadezhda, attacking her family members and turning abusive in general. Other witnesses from the group could easily back that up.

In addition, the evidence that they had brought to the court, which it was now considered they had been right, despite their unorthodox methods, to acquire, showed that Vladimir possessed many unlawful, dangerous items and had created them with the intention of breaking laws and forming his cult-ish mafia gang of clones.

The technology, of course, had to be seized by the correct authorities, who would decide how to handle it from there, according to the court.

Each of these decisions, charges and pieces of evidence took a long time to consider, but now that they genuinely seemed to be making progress, Nadezhda didn't mind so much.

Things were definitely looking up. For one thing, the existence of this gang, which local authorities had overlooked for years, according to Sof and other locals, had been brought to the light.

The judge had recognised their activities as both gang-like and cult-like, meaning that, from her limited legal knowledge, their crimes would be considered worse and Vladimir, as one of their leaders, could face a very severe sentence.

On top of that, all of their crimes were being brought to light. Sadly, they hadn't any evidence to prove murders that had been committed, but the kidnapping, imprisonment, violence...

It had all been laid bare before the court, and if they were considering that the Anti-Volkov group's actions had been justified, then it was likely that they were considering them as serious and possibly even as true accounts.

At least, she hoped so.

So, as they were finally dismissed to wait for the judge and the jury to come to a conclusion, she crowded back into the waiting room with a little less anxiety and a little more hope in her heart.

It looked like they were beginning to make progress. The decision could well be in their favour.

Judging by emerging pockets of conversation in the group, this was a sentiment shared by others. Sof slapped Nikolina on the back and grinned.

"Hey, all that legal jargon seems to be getting us somewhere!" she cheered.

The lawyer tried to maintain her serious demeanour, though her daughter thought she could see hints of a smile tugging at her mother's lips as she answered:

"Well, yes, it does. I knew it would be more successful than some of those... awful words you wished to use."

Sof giggled, a sure sign that she was in a more positive mood than before.

"I'm just glad that they seem to be taking us more seriously now," Sasha commented.

Maria smiled at him as she joined in.

"I told you that you had a legitimate case, Honey. And I think it should be a clear-cut one. Whatever police person you spoke to before was either mad or didn't listen to any of your facts," she pointed out.

"Yeah, but you have to understand, that was before we had all our evidence together, Babe," Sasha answered.

Katya's sniggering interrupted this discussion. "'Honey?' 'Babe?'" she questioned. "I had no idea you two were getting so serious!"

This sisterly teasing made Sasha blush, and that prompted Nikolina to elbow her little sister firmly in the ribs.

"Now is hardly the time or place for this discussion!" She hissed. "Anyway, you are making things uncomfortable."

"It's fine," Sasha insisted, "I guess she's right; we've been spending more time together and..." he trailed off.

"It's just naturally progressed," his smiling girlfriend interjected.

"Well... congratulations." Nikolina nodded at this information, giving the still rather giggly Katya a hard glare all the same.

Nadezhda shook her head, grinning and took a seat.

It was nice that that morning's tension had gone, or least lessened enough for her family to return to their favourite bonding activity - arguing and embarrassing one another.

It meant things were probably back on track. Or they thought they were... They wouldn't know for sure until they were called back to hear the verdict.

Justice And Future

The wait didn't seem so long this time. Perhaps it was because they were all more hopeful than before.

Either way, they were soon summoned back into the courtroom by an official. They filed back in just as the jury returned to their seats too.

There was some more banging and shouting as the prison officers escorted the Volkovs back into the room as well, then the judge reappeared, walking to his seat, and sitting down as everyone stood and waited for him.

Once they were all back in place, the court resumed. As soon as it began again, Nadezhda felt the tension return, a knot forming in her stomach.

 She didn't know why. Perhaps it was just the atmosphere of the courtroom. Or perhaps it was because she knew that this was the crucial part, and the part they had nothing to do with.

All the work they had done building up to this day, and everything they had had to relive before the court today, could mean nothing, depending on the decisions the jurors had reached and the judge's view.

It was all so solemn now too.

It always had been, of course, but listening to the judge carefully question the foreperson of the jury as regards to every single charge they had brought against each of the Volkovs was even more serious and slightly depressing.

She found herself dismayed by how long the list was and wishing they could get through it faster. It just felt insane now.

Well, in many ways, it was.

She was a sixteen-year-old schoolgirl, sitting in a courtroom listening as an old man and two young adults, barely older than her, were accused of serious crime after serious crime.

She was out of place, this was wrong...

No one in her life could have ever imagined that this would have happened to her.

Apart from possibly her mother, who had lived in fear for sixteen years...

She glanced over at Nikolina, whose face was expressionless in the set, determined way of someone doing everything they could to hide their emotions.

Suddenly it was a moment of hope again. No, it wasn't normal, or even right, but it was necessary.

Necessary so that thousands of people like them could finally have lives that were normal.

She smiled slightly to herself and turned her attention back to the verdicts being declared.

Diana was found guilty of stealing Nadezhda's father's journal and of endangering Nadezhda, as well as kidnapping multiple victims of Volkov family and falsely imprisoning them.

Vasily was found guilty of stalking, harassment, threatening behaviour, and assault, charges she hoped would be enough to keep him away from her for a long, long time.

He had been staring at her again today... It made her flesh crawl.

Vladimir was found guilty of illegal possession of deadly weapons, assault, and inciting violence.

On top of this, it had been decided that they were guilty of being a part of a gang when they carried out these crimes, thus increasing the sentence.

And Nadezhda realised she had been correct, seeing as Vladimir was apparently guilty as a leader of a gang.

According to the judge, he was also guilty of contempt of court for his shouting and protesting when he had first arrived in the courtroom.

With all these charges against the main leaders of the Volkov family, it was all she could do to hide her excitement and sit quietly in the court.

After all, it was clear at this point that they had won, and she was overtaken by an amazing sense of relief.

They didn't have to be afraid anymore or wonder if it had all been worth it. But best of all, this was going to mean that soon, it would all be over. She could go home and try to be normal again.

Of course, the lesser gang members arrested in the family would have to be tried for their involvement, though the evidence she had fought so hard to get didn't pertain to them very much.

But that wasn't the point.

The point was, once they knew the justice system had finally acknowledged the Volkov family's dirty little secrets and all the crimes they had done in the dark, they could relax.

They could go back to being ordinary citizens, letting the courts handle it without having to fear that it would all go horribly wrong.

And the people of Yaroslavl, thanks to this court case, Sof's leadership, and the help of Maria's police unit, could breathe easily again.

There would be no more need for fear and mistrust.

So, there would be no more need for them to do the things they had done, to fight and fight and never give up. It would be over, and they could stand down without it being giving up.

And without being afraid of the consequences, of the idea that the Volkovs would return seeking revenge as they had done to her poor father.

That made Nadezhda's day, but of course, she had to keep her happiness bottled up inside as they sat through the sentencing.

Diana had a sixteen-year prison sentence ahead of her, most of it being for the kidnapping charges, particularly the kidnappings of Sof, Sasha and Nadezhda, for which there was the most evidence.

Vasily's sentence worried her slightly, as it was a lot lower. Apparently, assault and stalking weren't 'that serious'...

But she tried not to let that bother her too much. At least he would be locked up for 8 years, keeping him far away from her and unable to continue his grandfather's gang for him.

Vladimir was facing the most serious sentence, as a gang leader, he faced a thirty-five-year sentence, though a condition of his release was an apology to the judge for his contempt of court charge.

With the case finally closed, the family were hauled away from the court again.

As they were dragged out, Nadezhda heard Vasily scream something, a garbled sentence that contained her name, but intentionally looked away from him, determined to bear Maria's advice in mind and have nothing more to do with him.

He was nothing but trouble.

The three angry mafia members continued with their struggling and shouting as they were taken away, even once those in the courtroom could no longer hear them.

They were soon riding in the back of a prisoner transport van, muttering irritably to themselves and one another.

"I told you that Moroz girl was nothing but trouble! They're all nothing but trouble!" Diana insisted to the scowling Vasily, looking over at Vladimir for back-up here.

He was, after all, the one who had frequently insisted on telling the whole family the 'legend' of the Moroz family, the police officer involved with them and how they were a good sign that they should trust nobody.

But also, that they could rest assured that anyone who stood against them would be taken down...

The old man was silent and expressionless as he sat between his grandchildren.

It was more than slightly disconcerting. He usually had something to say about everything...

The effect was so weird that the sulking Vasily decided to humour his annoying and annoyed sister just to have some conversation going on and distract from the deathly quiet inside the back of the van.

"You say that about everyone I like," he answered coldly.

"It's not my fault you have bad taste," Diana retorted petulantly.

She finally got the raise from her brother that she had been seeking, sniggering to herself as he snapped back at her;

"I don't have bad taste! She was — is - special... Those others are just influencing her too much. One day, I'll get out of here and find her. Then I'll prove you and them wrong and marry her. We're meant to be! I knew that ever since I watched her sleeping in my car that first night..."

When he had finished this little rant about his current obsession or at least trailed off as he started to recall everything they had been through together, his sister responded by rolling her eyes with a dramatic sigh.

"You say that about every girl... Anyway, when I get out, I'll beat you to it, find her and slit her throat for landing us in this mess." she told him, her voice fading to a dark mutter as she trailed off into threats against Nadezhda and any other members of the Anti-Volkov group she managed to track down.

"I'll get out before you!" Vasily argued back.

"You won't, because I'm going to break out..." Diana revealed, before trailing off into mutters again as she started to make a plan.

Someone banged on the wall separating them from the cab of the vehicle and shouted, "Alright, you lot! Quieten down in there!"

Silence fell again.

Vladimir still hadn't moved but was simply staring at the back doors of the van with a look of hatred in his eyes, while Diana was scowling viciously and would still occasionally mutter something to do with her scheme under her breath.

Vasily sat quietly, trying to block out the other two completely, a task made difficult by the tiny van.

Instead, he decided he would focus on his own plan. He had to find a way to break out of the prison too, before Diana did, and hunt Nadezhda down.

Of course, some of their members would slip through the cracks and others would be out much earlier than they did...

So, he would gather them together, start his own gang, free from other interference.

Then, once he had stolen Nadezhda away from whoever those brainwashers of hers were, they could lead it together.

He could still have the happily ever after he had planned out.

He had started making these plans when he and Nadezhda had been separated.

Of course, he had liked her before then, when he had asked her out, but he had missed her when they had been apart.

From then on, he had become increasingly curious about their possibilities together, and he had read over their families' shared history over and over again in his mother's diaries in the hopes of knowing more about her.

Perhaps he, in his curiosity, had become a little obsessed. He was vaguely aware that that was a possibility. But he didn't care.

At this point, he had made up his mind. He wanted her.

And now he had a plan in his mind. He smiled to himself. He would get what he wanted, eventually.

It might take him a lot of time and a lot of challenging work, but one way or another, despite his current situation, Nadezhda would be *his*.

And so would the greatest, most powerful crime family ever.

The future was looking up.

Return To Normality?

The sun was just beginning to set, high above Yaroslavl.

The Anti-Volkov group walked away from the court building together, yet in stunned silence, still overwhelmed by their victory.

After everything they had been through, all the struggles and all the lives affected by this, it was over.

And all they could do was bask in the feelings of tired, numb, but somehow still brilliant triumphant.

It was like a beautiful end to a long, exhausting day. But multiplied thousands of times over.

And no one wanted to be the first to speak, lest they ruined that feeling and this moment.

They walked down the steps and along the drive without a sound, Sof wandering in front, Nadezhda hanging off her mother's arm behind her, with Katya walking on the other side of Nikolina.

Somewhere off to the side of them, Sasha and Maria walked along, hand in hand.

Others spilt past the family and gathered around them, a silent crowd made up of those citizens of Yaroslavl who had been abused, imprisoned and hopeless for so long, but now, finally free, didn't know what to say or do next.

Eventually, the still, soundless evening was broken by a small chirp. Sof stopped, people crashing into her or swerving around her.

Her hand flew to her pocket, and she pulled out her phone, the source of the sound. After a few moments, a grin spread across her face, then she broke into laughter.

"This is the second-best news I've heard today!" She announced joyfully.

"What?" Nadezhda peered over her shoulder curiously.

"I got into engineering school!" The other young girl told her, practically bursting with happiness.

"That's great!" Nadezhda congratulated her friend, genuinely pleased that, now the whole Volkov business was behind them, Sof would have something else to dedicate her energy to.

She had been a great leader for them, she had such energy in everything she did, always giving it a hundred per cent, so Nadezhda knew she simply wouldn't be happy doing nothing.

Some small part of her felt a little sad then, though.

Despite this day being a great victory for them and a step forward in her friend's life, she had just realised that she wouldn't be around anymore to see Sof take that step.

Now that everything was resolved, surely, she and her family would be returning home?

She would have to find a way to keep in touch. In school and in general, she had been more or less on the outside, without close friendships.

She had acquaintances and people who were sort of friends, but she had never made friends as she had on this trip.

Nothing like risking your lives together to bring you closer, she guessed.

Then Sof interrupted her thoughts again.

"I know! And the best part is... It's in Moscow! I don't have to stay here anymore; I can move on properly now and put all this behind me."

She smiled, glad that she could finally say she felt truly ready to do this.

Nadezhda's face lit up, though she could scarcely believe it. She wouldn't have to leave her friend after all if Sof was moving to her home city!

"Wow, that's awesome! We could be neighbours." She grinned.

"Yeah!" Sof nodded. "I've got to sell my house and get some money for somewhere else to live first though. But soon, I'll be moving," she told her.

Sasha wandered over at this point to join in with their conversation.

"Well... If you don't need your house anymore, I'll buy it off you," he offered.

A surprised Nikolina cut in before Sof had a chance to answer.

"You're moving out here?" She questioned.

Her brother blushed slightly, glancing over at the watching Maria.

"Ah, well, I've... *We've* been talking about it. The law enforcement out here could use some help, so I'll have plenty of work and..."

He left that sentence hanging, but it was clear what he meant.

Ekaterina stepped in first. "That sounds great for you, bro, go for it!" She encouraged.

Nikolina nodded. "Yes... Well, why not? Do what is best for you," She agreed, though she sounded a little more subdued.

Sasha smiled. "Thanks, you two. And don't worry, I'll still get out to visit!" He assured them, getting a smile from Nikolina for his trouble.

Then her smile faded. "You drove us out here though, how are we getting back without you?" she asked.

"The house sale, if Sof's fine with that," Sasha began, pausing and looking over at Sof, who nodded in agreement, "won't be instant, so I can still drive you back. And I'll need to sell my house..." he added, starting to consider the details.

Sof paid attention here too. "You have a house in Moscow? Couldn't we just swap?" she suggested.

Sasha considered this. "Well...I don't see why not." He nodded.

"That makes things easier for you two to be where you want to be," Nikolina nodded. "Today really has been productive in the best possible way," she declared, "but we ought to get on and leave."

There were some agreeing nods from the crowd, and they set off again, starting to disperse as they reached the end of the driveway.

The Moroz family, with Sof and Maria in tow, set off back in the direction of Sof's house.

A gaggle of journalists intercepted them, suddenly emerging from the car park of the courthouse with cameras at the ready, but Sof barged past them, still too high on all the day's successes to give them a second thought, and the others simply followed after her.

Soon, Maria broke away from them and headed to her own home for the night.

The others made their way to Sof's place, and everyone just fell straight into their beds that night, having spent a long day defeating the Volkovs and busily planning the aftermath.

The next day, however, they were straight back to planning for their future.

Nikolina sat down with Sof and Sasha to draw up the legal details pertaining to the house swap. Ekaterina was visited by Maria, with whom she spent some time whispering in a corner.

A mystified and slightly lost Nadezhda decided to satisfy herself with packing, ready to leave.

There wasn't much to pack, but that didn't matter, because before she was even half-way done, Katya and Maria appeared.

She looked up at them curiously, "What are you two up to?" she asked.

The two women traded glances, then Maria stepped forward and handed her a box.

"Here. Your Aunt told me you lost these. So, during the raids... I had a look for them. I hope everything's there," she told her.

Nadezhda took the box carefully and opened it. Inside, Daria's diaries, the music books and her father's journal were neatly stacked together.

On top of the books, the photo of her parents' wedding was resting neatly. She blinked away tears, moved by what they had done for her.

Seeing all these things, all she had of her father after she had closed the book of his legacy behind her, finally got justice for him...

She looked back up at the two women and smiled.

"It's perfect...Thank you."

"Hey, I'm your Aunt, it's my job to get you whatever you want. Even if your mother would say no," Katya commented with a grin.

Maria just settled for a "You're welcome."

But both made Nadezhda smile, grateful for the family she had always had but never deeply appreciated and the new friends she had made along the way and looked forward to spending more time with.

It wasn't until a few days later that they finally returned to normality again.

With the house-swap completed, Sasha gave Maria his new keys and access to the hotel room he had had during his time helping Sof since the policewoman had agreed to help him move in.

While she was moving his things, he drove his sisters and his niece home, with Sof hitching a ride as well.

It was just as well that the others had little other luggage, as she crammed his car full of everything that she was moving into her new house with her.

Consequently, the long drive wasn't very comfortable, but once they got there, there were happy moments, sad moments, but overall, normal moments, finally.

Happily, they got to see Sof run up the drive to her new home, dragging luggage behind her, and unlock the door for the first time, ready to move in.

She stood in the doorway with a grin a mile wide, wearing the brand-new Moscow engineering school hoodie they had sent her as a gift when she had been accepted.

On a sadder note, the family gathered in Nikolina's apartment to say goodbye to Sasha, who had another long drive ahead of him.

There were a lot of hugs exchanged, Nadezhda witnessed the rare event of seeing her mother cry, and Sasha hesitated about leaving for as long as he thought he could get away with.

But ultimately, this had its happy moments too, with promised visits and admissions of love pointing out that finally, the family were truly back together.

And they were 'reassured' by Ekaterina's comment that Maria would 'look after' Sasha for them.

And then he was gone, and since Katya had disappeared home as well, silence reigned in Nikolina's apartment again.

Nadezhda went to her room and sat quietly, just like she had on all those lonely afternoons before when her mother had been at work, and it had seemed like there was just her.

This time, it was still the same room, and the same silence.

But it was different somehow.

Different because she knew her mother genuinely cared, different because she had her family and friends so much closer to her now, and perhaps different because they had won.

Well, of course it was different because they had won.

If now, she probably wouldn't even be here to appreciate it. But she didn't dwell on that thought.

Instead, she took the picture that had changed her life out of the box and set it on her bedside table, vowing to frame it one day, to keep the memories alive.

Then she opened her drawers and slipped the diaries that had told her the true story of her life into them.

Finally, she took the song her father had written for her mother out of the music book and smiled, getting up to go and give it to Nikolina.

She wasn't sure her mother had ever really had a chance to read and appreciate it, after all.

It had simply lain in her father's old book for years, on the off chance that she looked there after his death...

With those thoughts in mind, she paused in the doorway, looking back over her shoulder at her bedroom...

Perhaps, most of all, it was different because she wasn't nobody anymore.

She knew something about her family, legacy, and her own identity that she hadn't before.

And there were no more hidden little family secrets to get between her and her loved ones.

End of Book 2

Secrets in The Flames

By

Ellie Jay

Nikolina
Katya
Sasha and Maria
Nadezhda
Sof

Dariya
Diana
Vasily

New Developments

"Dearly beloved..."

Nadezhda let the gentle tones of the priest wash over her, relaxing as she did so.

The last few weeks had been stressful, with ghosts from her past popping up all over the place and a thousand preparations to deal with. But that was over.

Today was going to be a perfect day, she told herself, with as much optimism as she could manage.

Her police training, her past experiences and her general lack of recent sleep had sucked most of her positivity out of her, but she tried.

She tried for her family, more than anything. They were the reason she had done all of this, after all.

She was tired because she had driven her mother, aunt, and best friend 173 miles just to be here for her uncle's big day.

She was anxious because, five years ago, she had risked everything, charging into the arms of a sinister mob, because of her family. They were easily the most important part of her life.

So, Nadezhda let the words of the ceremony relax her, focusing on what was happening in front of her instead of on the recent chaos. She smiled, and hoped it looked genuine.

Today was going to be a joyful day. Today, all her family members were in one place, and no one was fighting, arguing or in any other way distressed. They should celebrate this.

She glanced slightly to one side. Her mother was stood there, looking very neat and formal in her deep blue silk suit.

The other woman was watching the ceremony with an intense, difficult to read expression, but the way she had fiercely inserted herself into the wedding planning and talked of little else for months made clear that her mother was pleased.

Beside her mother, her aunt stood. It was good to see the two sisters together. Years ago, they had fought a lot.

But since the incident five years ago, they had managed to make up, despite their differences.

And there were many differences. It was easy to see that, just looking at them. To start with, Auntie Katya's attempt at formal wear was much brighter and less subtle.

Her happiness was also far more obvious.

She was practically beaming from ear to ear. It was infectious, and Nadezhda's smile became a little more genuine as she met her aunt's gleaming emerald eyes.

"Hey, you know you're meant to look at the ceremony!"

An elbow hit her ribs as someone hissed in her ear.

As it happened, this made her grin worse, because she instantly recognised the voice and the tone that told her this was a joke.

She turned to the other side, where her best friend, Sof, stood.

Sof was easily her closest friend who wasn't related to her. They had been through life and death situations together.

And Sof knew her uncle and soon-to-be aunt too, she had a lot of respect for them. What she didn't care for was formality.

"So are you, *stop!*"

Her protest was feeble and Nadezhda knew it, but at least her family and friends were making her smile for real. Even if it was for all the wrong reasons.

Nikolina, as everyone knew Nadezhda's mother, glowered at them, obviously a little more serious about the idea that they should be focused on the ceremony.

'Serious' was Nikolina all over, and this wedding meant a lot to her.

Her baby brother, to whom she had always been close, was getting married. Aware of this, Nadezhda suppressed her laughter and faced the front, feeling like a child again.

She was twenty-one, but her mother's glare never failed to have an effect.

She could imagine Sof grinning beside her and planning some new witticism. But she blocked out the image and directed her gaze to the altar at last.

There, in front of the gathered crowd, a middle-aged woman in white was beaming at a tall, dark-suited man, her hands clutched in his.

The priest stood there too, talking to them in a low tone. Then he stopped, letting the groom take over.

Holding onto his fiancée's hands as if his life depended on it, her Uncle intoned:

"I, Alexander Moroz, take you, Maria Sobachkina, to be my..."

A hand tapped Nadezhda's shoulder. She resisted the temptation to look around, assuming this was Sof fooling about again.

When this wedding was over, she was going to have some *words* with her friend.

Though, an attempt to do so would probably leave them both falling around laughing while Nikolina tutted at them. But that would be okay then.

Now, she would pay attention, for her family's sake, as the ceremony drew to a close before her eyes. The couple kissed and people began to file out of the church.

Walking back down the aisle, Nadezhda smiled. It had gone well, thank God. It had been too long since her family had been able to gather and enjoy themselves like this.

But after the week she had had, she had been wondering how smoothly things would go. She could see now that she had been paranoid, but that was hardly a surprise, she decided as she reflected on the past week.

It had been nothing but stress. She had just been getting to grips with her intense training as a police cadet, when Maria, her new Aunt, had called her with some frightening news.

She had expected the call to be something to do with the wedding plans and had prepared to deal with the bride's anxious chatter then hand her off to her equally excited mother so they could compare notes while she returned to work.

That had been how the last few calls had gone. On this occasion, however, things were quite different.

There was no greeting and no small talk, to begin with.

"You remember the Volkovs, of course," was the first thing the older woman said.

Of course, she remembered them. She was certain she would never forget the gang who had torn her family apart, killed her father and forced her into severe danger.

It had only been five years since her, her mother, her aunts, and uncles and Sof, who had recruited some fellow vigilantes, had managed to get them imprisoned.

In fact, that was how her family had met Maria, how she had met Sof... It had changed everything, for better or for worse.

"Of course. Why?"

Nadezhda had been quick to respond, despite her reminiscence. Something must have happened for Maria to call her like this, after all.

"Vladimir's dead, and Diana's on the run." Maria revealed abruptly.

Many, many words whizzed through the young woman's head. None of them were polite. Vladimir was the leader of the Volkov gang.

He was completely insane and had tried to kill her. Had had her father killed. She wouldn't be mourning his death, but this was still a terrible situation.

Because Diana, his granddaughter, was his right-hand woman who had a grudge against Nadezhda in particular. She recalled specific threats yelled in the courtroom...

"Good riddance to him," she replied, getting that out of the way first.

"But Diana's on the loose? How did that happen? And are your lot anywhere near catching her?"

Her next flurry of questions was more urgent. Vladimir had been behind all the past trouble, but Diana was now the immediate problem.

She hoped Maria would have some answers. Maria was a police officer in Yaroslavl, where the group had lived, terrorising the local population until they had later been imprisoned.

She was nearest to the scene, after all.

"That's where it gets difficult. He was murdered. Strangled. Prison staff and local police were responding to his death, and that was when she vanished."

"So, she wasn't free when he died, and they were in separate prisons, so she's not responsible. But a murder of a prisoner nearby would distract the staff..."

This couldn't be coincidence, but Nadezhda couldn't piece together a connection.

"Exactly."

It sounded as though Maria had been through all of this before.

"Did she know he was dead?" Nadezhda pressed.

They had to figure something out, both as police officers and as people who would be high up on Diana's hitlist.

They had both been involved in the Anti-Volkov group that had ended their reign of terror over the city of Yaroslavl, and besides, the Volkov family were notorious for hating the police.

It was imperative that they figure out what was going on before Diana became a serious threat.

"We can't tell. She vanished around his time of death, according to our calculations," Maria reminded her.

"So, whatever's happening is still--- Oh, blast, I'm sorry, I have to go, the lady's here to make adjustments to my dress."

After that last comment, she had to rush off. This must be so weird for her, Nadezhda mused.

Planning a wedding amidst a massive case like this. It was odd enough for her, her head was still reeling.

What had happened and how were they going to stop Diana before something terrible happened?

Because she was sure it would. Wherever the Volkovs were, sinister plans followed.

But she had had no time to figure out the answers to all these important questions, because she had to work, and to plan her family's route to Yaroslavl, and a whole lot of driving to do.

There was no wonder she had spent the week tired and stressed.

But now, she was standing outside the church in the fresh spring air, and it seemed as though she had worried too soon, over too little.

The wedding had been flawless. She could push aside her anxiety now and celebrate with her family instead.

She stood against the wall with her mother and Ekaterina as they waited for the couple to finish signing the register and join them for the photos.

A few moments later, Sof bounced over to them, all smiles.

"Wasn't that *adorable?* Well, the bits I saw were," she giggled and elbowed Nadezhda in the ribs.

The more reserved young woman flushed and shook her head.

"You are the limit." She responded, with a small smile.

Nikolina was nodding, but without the accompanying smile. A rant was quickly incoming. Ekaterina nudged her sister.

"It's a happy day, lighten up."

Sof nodded.

"Exactly, fun for all the family, right? Speaking of which, don't be mad at me! I wasn't the only one poking you, that lady was up to it as well," she pointed out.

Her best friend blinked.

"*What* lady?"

Perhaps she had accidentally misattributed the random tapping.

"The goth one, y'know, couple of rows back, all in black, great big hat over her face…"

Sof's description didn't really sound like a wedding guest, and Nadezhda couldn't recall seeing this woman, but then she had tried to spend most of her time actually facing the front.

"Are you having a laugh?" She checked.

"She must be. Why would she know who was behind her when she was supposed to be watching the ceremony?" Nikolina cut in sternly.

Katya rolled her eyes. "You *never* let up, do you?"

As the sisters bickered in the background, Sof shook her head.

"I swear it's true! In fact, look, she's over there, gawping at us!"

Subtle as ever, Sof pointed directly at the woman.

She was leaning against a tree, away from all the other guests, but facing towards the wedding party. Specifically, directly to towards Nadezhda.

Her wide-brimmed, floppy black hat hung over her face, but it wasn't hard to tell that she was staring at them. Her dress was also black and swept down to the floor.

She stood out among the colourfully dressed crowd. Around this dark apparel, Nadezhda could make out bare, brown arms with bouncing black curls around the slender shoulders.

She didn't recognise any of these vague features, and in any case, she didn't have much in the way of extended family. Perhaps she was a friend or relative of Maria.

She shrugged. "I don't know her. Maybe she mistook me for someone else."

Sof wasn't convinced.

"She's really staring. And tapping your shoulder during a wedding ceremony? Who does that anyway?" She ignored the fact that she had been a distraction too.

Nadezhda sighed. Her friend was a bit fiery, and if she thought anyone was giving them trouble, she'd like to confront them.

Personally, she preferred a quieter, more subtle approach where possible. But now her rather paranoid mother had finished bickering with Katya and chimed in.

"She *is* behaving oddly, is she not? Hm..." Now the older woman was also scrutinising the stranger too, making no attempt to hide it.

Nikolina was often more reserved too, but when it came to protecting her daughter, she had some unorthodox ideas.

In fact, this frequently made Nadezhda uncomfortable. Now was one of those times.

"Forget it! She's not doing any harm. This is a wedding! A happy occasion!" Nadezhda protested.

"I still don't trust her. Let's go and ask what her deal is," Sof decided, already striding across the way.

Nadezhda grabbed at her arm. *"Don't!"* She protested.

Sof hesitated for a moment, realising she might be going too far and distressing her friend.

But it didn't help. The woman in black had noticed them anyway, and she was coming over.

Dariya

The group muttered anxiously amongst themselves as the topic of their recent conversation glided calmly towards them.

She reached them, pushed the brim of her hat back from her eyes and fixed a piercing grey gaze upon Nadezhda.

"You're Antonin Jelennski's daughter, aren't you?"

This lady clearly didn't bother with small talk, but it was certainly a weird question to open with. And, in the circumstances, a downright threatening one.

After all, Nadezhda recalled, the whole reason that she had become anything more than an average person with an average life was because of her father. Never knowing him had driven her to find out more about him.

Doing so had revealed a sinister secret. Her father had been killed before her birth for investigating a mafia family called the Volkovs.

And, she recalled, flushing at the memory, she had quarrelled with her mother and stormed away, determined to deal with this family secret herself. In the process, she had nearly joined him.

So, now, they rarely spoke of him. She and her mother remembered him in their own way, of course, but there was extraordinarily little mention of him. His name was associated too closely with the grisly crime that had ended his life.

Which made a random stranger bringing him up not merely odd, but potentially dangerous. Especially as she was now beginning to recognise some things about her interrogator.

The steely grey eyes that looked right into her soul and the dark slash that marred the woman's left cheek were features she had become awfully familiar with during her time struggling against the Volkovs.

Their family were eerily alike, and, she had learnt later, were actually cloned from the same DNA. She didn't understand how that was possible, but the knowledge only made them creepier.

It also meant that she hadn't been paranoid after all. She should have worried more, paid more attention... Now what would she do? She could deny it, but she highly doubted that she would be believed.

As it turned out, she didn't have to handle it herself. Sof stepped in.

"What's it to you, *freak?*"

Nadezhda cringed. Sof must have recognised her too. After her cousin had been exploited and murdered by them, Sof carried a lot of hatred for the Volkov family.

And she wasn't the only one. Nadezhda glanced to the side and saw that her mother was as white as a sheet and staring straight through the woman.

She had noticed too, and while she might be in shock now, when she had processed this sudden encounter, it might become heated. Nikolina was a peaceful person, but that family had murdered her husband and kidnapped her daughter.

Katya still seemed oblivious to the situation and was cheerfully babbling away in the background. Given the state of the others, Nadezhda supposed she should be grateful for small mercies.

The strange woman shook her head.

"Forgive me, I'm intruding. I just wanted a word... I'm a friend of Antonin's," she tried to explain.

It sounded as though she was struggling to piece her words together.

Sof snorted derisively.

"Yeah, *right!* We know you're with them. Go con someone else." Venom laced her tone and there was a hint of things turning nasty if the other woman failed to leave.

"I understand why you would think like that, but really... I don't mean your friend any harm.," the woman tried to persuade her.

Her words seemed flat and empty, but then she spoke up again, before Sof could push her away. This time, a sense of urgency clung to her tone.

"Please, it's important. I have news."

Unconvinced, Sof stepped between the woman and Nadezhda defensively.

Retreating slightly, the woman nevertheless peeked around Sof's shoulder to shout a few final words.

"Please, listen to me! If... If now's an inconvenient time, find me later! My name is Dariya Volk—"

The woman's words were cut off by Sof shouting at her to get out.

But her name struck a chord in Nadezhda's mind. Yet it only served to convince her that this little scene had to be a trick or trap. If she had had any doubt, she didn't anymore.

This woman couldn't be Dariya Volkova, for she distinctly remembered attending that woman's funeral five years ago.

Dariya had been a friend of her father's. She had gone seeking the truth about his death from her, only to find that she had perished herself.

And, she recalled with a shiver, that was how she had ended up in the company of Dariya's less than charming daughter, Diana, and the ringleader of the group, Vladimir.

She made her way forward to help Sof make sure the trickster left, and to thank her for her support and protection, but her mother ran forward instead.

Nikolina raced in front of Sof and hurried towards the other woman.

Nadezhda cringed. Great, her mother had snapped out of her shock just in time to start a fight. This should be something to see, the middle-aged lawyer in her smart suit fighting against a sinister mafia member.

The trouble was, she didn't see her mother coming off best.

To her surprise, though, Nikolina didn't attack the woman when she reached her. Instead, she seized her arm.

"Wait! Did you say *Dariya?*"

The woman seemed more shaken by being chased down and grabbed then she had by Sof's anger.

"Well... Well, yes, I did. Because that's my name." She struggled to recompose herself, then peered at Nikolina from under the brim of her huge hat.

"Ah... Wait a minute, you're *her*, aren't you? Antonin's bride? The police officer's daughter? I'm so sorry."

She laid her hand on Nikolina's, which was still clinging to her arm.

Sof turned to Nadezhda. "What the hell's going on here?" She asked.

She shrugged. "No idea. But I'm pretty sure we've abandoned the photo shoot. I don't know why my mother wants to talk to this chick though. She's clearly lying. Dariya is dead."

"So, who's this bozo?" Her best friend retorted. "And don't you think we should tell her?"

"Do you know we can hear you, girls?" Dariya asked them politely, before grinning. "It's okay, I get it. I turned up out of the blue and freaked everyone out. But I have a good explanation."

"It had better be something special." Sof folded her arms.

Nikolina shook her head at the two younger women. "Just hear her out, please. She was… She helped Antonin."

By this point, she let go of Dariya, but she was still watching her curiously. She didn't normally speak of her husband, but she had a million questions for this woman. The woman he had spent his deadly mission with.

The diaries her daughter had discovered years ago had indicated that they had been as close as siblings.

It was a strange feeling to meet someone else who had known Antonin back then and had lived through his death, someone who could understand her pain. And from Dariya's initial gesture, she seemed to.

So, she needed to hear her out. Even if it was just for selfish reasons.

Nadezhda sighed. She didn't trust this woman at all, but her mother did, and she didn't want to ruin this for Nikolina unless she had to.

The two had only fixed their relationship recently, after Nadezhda had learnt about her father's death. They were still careful about upsetting one another in case they couldn't come back from another fight.

"Alright. I'm listening," she conceded.

Sof tossed her head. *"Huh!"* She scoffed but didn't walk away.

Nadezhda supposed that meant she'd listen too, even if she was only doing so to appease her. She smiled at her friend gratefully.

In the background, Sasha emerged from the church with his wife holding onto his arm and looked baffled to find that his family had mostly disappeared.

Katya was still waiting, looking equally confused. It had taken her a few moments to realise that her sister, to whom she had been talking, had left halfway through their 'conversation.'

The wedding didn't seem to be the main event anymore.

Instead, Dariya had an intently listening audience, all hoping for some explanation as to why she was back from the dead and gate-crashing a wedding to speak to the sworn enemies of her mafia family.

After all, hearing a story from beyond the grave is a one-of-a-kind situation, whereas people get married every day.

Besides, given recent developments, it could have a detrimental impact on all their lives.

War

Now that she had a captive audience, Dariya began to speak.

"I suppose this really began with my death. And yes, I know my being 'dead' is the part that has you confused."

She looked over at Nadezhda as she spoke, seemingly aware that the other had knowledge of her death.

Perhaps her hearing really was that good, or perhaps it was something else entirely that had given her this information. Her family, maybe?

Or perhaps she had been at the funeral, secretly watching, laughing at everyone in attendance.

Nadezhda still didn't understand and still didn't trust the woman, but she was talking again, so she waited for an answer that made sense.

"Here's the thing, I had to survive for years as an outsider in my own family. A sane person in a lunatic asylum," she went on.

"When I first met Antonin, I thought about leaving. He gave me hope…" Here, she paused, looking down.

Nikolina rested a hand on her arm, and suddenly Nadezhda realised that the memories of her father bonded these two women together.

The memories that had been too painful for her mother, had taken her years to finally acknowledge…

They somehow lived in Dariya, making her instantly trusting of someone who should be her enemy, who was from the family who had killed her husband.

Finally, Dariya glanced up, her hands moist, and gently touched Nikolina's hand before letting it fall away and beginning to speak again.

"But when he died, I knew I couldn't really get away with leaving, not without arousing suspicion and then probably being hunted down myself. But I wouldn't be suspected of caring about him if I stayed and lied."

"Besides, before long, I had my children to think about. They were so young then, and I had to lie for them. Because I thought I could make life a little better for them. I didn't want to leave them with my father."

They all nodded.

Nikolina and Nadezhda had Antonin's legacy to tell them that Vladimir Volkov was a vile human being, the leader of the deranged family, and no person to care for children.

And Sof's own experiences with the Volkovs had taught her that, too.

In front of them, the evil mob boss's daughter continued to get things off her chest.

"So, I stayed. I stayed and even though I lost hope for myself, I thought things would be better for the children. Especially Vasily, my youngest son. I had high hopes for him. He was always such a good child; I didn't think he could be a criminal. I'm sorry to say that I could see it in Diana's case. She was so keen to be close to her grandfather and didn't like other people very much…"

She trailed off again, and Nadezhda tried to imagine how that must have felt.

Having to watch her own children, judging them all the time on what they would grow up to be and ultimately, watching her daughter slip away from her.

And her son had, too. *Hadn't* he? Certainly, Nadezhda reflected with some embarrassment, when she had met him, he had been… Manipulative and clever.

He was never openly mean like Diana, but he had plans of his own.

Did Dariya know that, though? She had been… Well, allegedly dead, but at least missing, before all that had begun. And she had just suggested that Vasily was the better of the two.

The woman wasted no time in answering that unvoiced question.

"I was wrong, though. As they got older, Vasily changed. I nearly missed it, at first. He was always close to me, and I thought I could trust him. I thought he could be my ally, help me against the others. So, I confided in him, and he listened to everything I had to say... Then he started to become closer to his grandfather. And I realised just in time what was going to happen."

"What did he do?" Nadezhda asked, wondering how far Vasily would betray his mother.

"He had learnt everything he wanted to from me, so he planned to get rid of me and move onto the next target. He was playing us both, telling my father I was suspicious, then trying to lure me away so he could arrange for me to have an accident..."

"He was 'working away' and wanted me to go with him. Said we would get away and have a normal life, but I wasn't that stupid. Nearly, but not quite."

"He was playing you *both?*"

Nadezhda had to question that. Vasily was clever, sure, but he was a teenage boy, how could he have been playing the two most experienced members of a gang?

Dariya must have picked up on her incredulity because she gave her a sharp look.

"You must know that my son is an expert manipulator. He pulled the wool over my eyes, he duped my father, a so-called master criminal and genius, and he nearly seduced you."

That last part caught everyone off-guard.

"You nearly went off with *one of them?*" Nikolina gasped.

"Isn't he that bastard who wanted you to kill me off and marry him?" Sof questioned.

Her memories of Vasily were of him pointing a gun at her and her best friend.

Nadezhda sighed. She hadn't told the others everything.

"Yes. I made a mistake with Vasily," she admitted, blushing.

She had been sixteen then, naïve, inexperienced, taken in by promises that had quickly turned sinister.

"The important question," she added, turning back to Dariya, "is *how the hell did you know that?!*"

"Because the only way to get away from my mad son was to pretend to die, and the only safe place to hide when you have a distinctive scar is in a family full of clones," Dariya pointed out.

"I was never far away, I simply changed just enough to pass for a different family member. None of us were ever close enough for anyone to pay attention. But once the ringleaders were in prison, the rest of us could disappear. I finally got out and started my own life."

"But you... You *watched* everything that was going on?"

Nadezhda wasn't sure how to feel about having been watched as she dealt with the Volkovs before.

It had been a trying time in her life, and she wasn't even sure she had handled it well. She had just done what she had to do to keep herself and her loved ones alive.

"Of course, I did. I had to know what happened. And I was impressed. You're clever enough to see through him and quick enough to act when you had to. You are a credit to your father, and your allies were a credit to you."

Dariya gave her a motherly smile, far sweeter than any her own mother had ever shown her, full of pride and happiness that she had succeeded.

Blushing, she didn't know how to respond. The woman was somehow a stranger and almost a family member, through her connection to her father, at the same time.

"But it isn't over." Dariya saved her the awkwardness of replying by pulling her mind back to the present.

"I've wanted to help you all for a long time," she turned to Nikolina.

"I saw you briefly at Antonin's funeral. I just… didn't know what to say and I didn't want to approach you. I couldn't be sure how much he had told you about us and if I would alarm you or not."

The other woman opened her mouth to reassure her, but Dariya shook her head.

"Please. It's in the past now. So is the time I thought about helping you, Nadya," she nodded to the younger woman.

"I couldn't do it without giving away my identity and complicating the threat to you. But now I have to come forward and help you all. Because this time, things are more serious and harder to contain. A new threat is coming."

"A *new* threat?" Nadezhda questioned.

The Volkovs had been around for longer than she had, so surely, they were old news?

"I'm not stupid, my dear, I know that the legal authorities throughout the land will have heard of my father's death. This marks the end of an era for our family. And I'm sorry to say, the beginning of one. Vasily murdered his grandfather. Don't *ask* me how I know, because it will make no sense, but rest assured I do know how my family operates."

"To Vasily, my father was the last person in his way. He had manipulated him into believing they were on the same side, but it was only a matter of time before one of them decided the other was in his way. Now, my son has found new allies in prison. He's making a new powerbase, a new gang. This time, he is the leader, and he will be worse than my father ever was, because my father was stupid. He thought he was clever and let himself be blinded. But Vasily really *is* clever. In a dangerous way."

This sinister revelation out of the way, Dariya took a breath and laid a hand on Nadezhda's shoulder.

"Knowing what has passed between you two, it stands to reason that whenever he puts into operation whatever plan he has, you will be his first target beyond the prison walls. But I know what the next one will be. *Power.*"

"Power in Yaroslavl, like my father had, perhaps, but that won't be enough for him in the end. He will want all the power he can get."

Nadezhda stared past Dariya's shoulder, out at the gaggles of guests milling around. She didn't want to look at Dariya, nor at her friends and family.

The Volkova woman's words alone, without considering her deathly serious tone, had made her blood run cold.

They could be facing a threat against the world, and she could tell that Dariya was calling upon them, the last people to fight the Volkovs, to stop her son.

Nadezhda felt responsible, of course, given her connection to Vasily, a connection his mother had taken pains to highlight, but was there no alternative but another life-threatening battle that plunged her whole family into danger?

Here, on this beautiful day, in the middle of this gathering, family was at the front of her mind. Last time, her reckless actions had forced them to come to her aid.

Could she ask them to do it again?

Scrambling for another way, she remembered something that distanced her from the threat of Vasily.

"But he's still in prison!" She pointed out.

"Only because that serves his purpose now. Believe me, I know how he thinks. When he... Gets 'bored' there, he will arrange for his allies and himself to escape. Then who knows what he'll do? Gather the missing family members into another army, greater than the one he can amass in prison, or focus on hunting you down first? Either way, it will be dangerous."

The girl sighed, her head dropping to her hands. So, she would have to face this crisis that had been budding for weeks after all.

What about the other puzzle piece?

She suddenly remembered that there was one and wondered how that would further worsen her life.

"What about Diana? Is she working for him, now she's free?" She asked, not sure she wanted to know, but nevertheless needing to.

Dariya's laugh was melodic and surprisingly sweet for the situation.

"Of course not. She'd never work for him; they've always been rivals. In fact, when he wrote to her in prison, she was the one who broke out and came to find help in the family."

Nadezhda looked up, shocked. She had had Diana down as bad news since they met, and the woman had betrayed her to the family. Why would she stand against her brother now? Sibling rivalry, or something more?

"She... She knew you were alive and decided to use you to stop him? Why?”

The older woman shook her head.

"She didn't know. She was just looking for missing relatives who didn't want Vasily in power. He wasn't exactly popular, especially not when he got to be Papa's second-in-command. My family are a jealous lot,” she admitted.

"But she found me. I told her the truth and she agreed to help me. She told me what he had been up to in prison since he foolishly let her know in his letters. I don't know why. Perhaps she has her own agenda, but I wouldn't worry about her right now."

With the Diana mystery solved, Nadezhda had just one question left.

"What can we actually do about Vasily?”

Nikolina jumped in here.

“My question exactly. Unless he tries something, there's no new legal case to answer.”

"You won't survive if he tries something. Forget the law, gather your forces. I'll gather mine. We're going to war."

“Now you're talking!”

Sof hadn't spoken much in front of Dariya, who she still doubted, but war against the Volkovs? She could always support that idea.

Nadezhda, on the other hand, wasn't sure where to begin. What allies did she have? Who did she know who was prepared to fight a war?

Gathering Allies

"Here's the thing…" Nadezhda finally surfaced from her confusion and faced Dariya, "we don't have a lot of allies. The group we had before dispersed after we dealt with Vladimir, and I don't know where they are now. There's just us," she gestured to Sof first, automatically.

Sof had organised the group they had had before. She was one of the most ardent fighters against the Volkovs.

Besides her, the only 'allies' Nadezhda could think of were her family, who were supposed to be enjoying a happy event, not going to war.

Besides, even if she counted her mother, Ekaterina, Sasha, and Maria all in, there were still only six of them. And Dariya, who claimed to have forces of her own.

But all they truly had from Dariya were claims, mere words, and the shadowy bond provided by her relationship with Antonin, a man who had been murdered more than twenty years ago.

Something told her they would need more than that.

But Dariya didn't seem too fazed.

"Well, I can bring more. But I will need help. Your allies are part of the legal system, correct?"

Nikolina, who was still so convinced that this friend of her dead husband could be trusted, even as she dragged them towards war, stepped in as Nadezhda tried to think of a response.

"Yes. I am a lawyer, Nadezhda and Maria are police officers. Whatever you need from us, we can arrange."

Her mother's rash reply came as a shock to Nadezhda. Nikolina wouldn't normally promise aid unless she was sure it was within the rules.

And she wasn't sure they should be doing this... No matter what Dariya had told them, the fact remained that her family hated the police and the legal system above all their other enemies.

Getting involved on a personal level was dangerous enough, especially given their past with the family. Bringing their work into this only pushed their names further up the hitlist. And she was apparently number one, anyway.

But the older women were already planning, and she had to shove her fears aside to try and focus. She needed to keep up.

"Right. I'll need some strings pulling, I'm afraid. Most of my allies are persona non-grata now. My family members… If I can rally them before Vasily does and bring them here, they will help. Even if it's just to spite him. I just need something doing to make sure they're not arrested when they arrive."

Nikolina nodded. "I am sure Nadya can check if there are any outstanding warrants on them before they arrive."

They were both looking at her. She nodded reluctantly. Helping the Volkovs sat wrong, but she would do it, because who else did they have? And there was the catch.

If they couldn't trust Dariya, even with her dubious reasons for being her and her information coming through the devious Diana, then who could they trust?

They certainly couldn't do anything about a Volkov threat on their own.

Sof shifted beside her. "Is this wise?"

It was obvious that her friend was uneasy, too.

"I… I don't have anyone else. But I think I can more or less control them."

Dariya's answer wasn't reassuring. But that seemed to be how that family operated, always controlling one another, fighting to be the leader. Nadezhda thought of Vasily and Diana.

They had been... Nice to one another, in a strange way. Diana had wanted to protect Vasily from her.

And yet... Diana had trapped her, and Vasily had claimed not to have anything to do with it. He had said that he shouldn't trust his sister and that she didn't trust him. Their mother described them as rivals...

A family where they were always fighting would be prepared for war, at least. But would they take Dariya's side, or Vasily's?

Could Dariya really control them? And would she get there first, for that matter? What if Vasily had already found a way to reach out to his family members?

Nadezhda's mind was full of questions, but she wasn't alone. Sof spoke up again.

"Sure. And what if that doesn't work? Where are we then?"

Dariya sighed. "Look, I'll, I'll make it work!" She seemed flustered. "I *have* to. My son needs to be stopped. Give me some time."

"How much time do we have?" Nadezhda asked.

There was a pause, and the older woman bit her lip.

"Not much, I must admit. It's running short. In his letter to Diana, he said he would be reunited with you within a month. And Di's already been out of prison for two weeks."

Great. So, she was part of his nasty little plan, again. And she had a matter of weeks to prepare.

While her head was still spinning, Sof interjected.

"So, let me get this straight, we have to trust you on this, let you assemble a crime family you only 'think' you can control and start a war against your own son within two weeks, or this psycho is coming after Nadya?"

Nikolina glared. "We can trust Dariya. I am sure of it. She was Antonin's friend. She would never put Nadezhda in danger."

She had developed a strange loyalty to this woman, who she hadn't met before. But a heart-breaking memory linked them, and she couldn't ignore that.

But Dariya shook her head.

"No, she has every right not to trust me. I don't know this woman, but my family have wronged a lot of people and asking those people to trust me is... *Difficult.* But I promised twenty-one years ago to do everything I could to protect Nadezhda,"

"I was… Unable to act before. Now I have no choice. All I can offer is an army, and all I can do is my best to lead them. I know where to find them, and I think they'll join me, even if they only do so out of spite for Vasily."

Nadezhda looked around her group. Nikolina looked determined, Sof looked anxious, and now, even Ekaterina was paying attention.

She didn't look very sure of what was happening, but she was staring at Dariya. For her part, the Volkova woman looked hopeful, waiting for their response.

Sighing, Nadezhda nodded.

"It's looking like our only shot then, isn't it? We'll wait for you to gather them, but please be as quick as you can and…" She hesitated, "how are you going to contact us again?"

She wasn't sure what kind of answer she expected.

Dariya's approach here had been sudden and unexpected. The woman just seemed to turn up and lurk in the shadows until her moment came.

Perhaps she expected some enigmatic smile or some secret code, but what she got was a look of confusion that told her that, for all her mysterious ways, Dariya hadn't thought this far ahead.

Her mother stepped into the breech calmly, whipping a business card out of her clutch as though it was the most normal thing in the world and pressing it into the other woman's hand.

"Call me," she instructed.

"You brought *business cards* to our brother's *wedding?*"

This was Ekaterina's first contribution to the conversation.

She didn't seem to have processed all the doom and gloom about war with mobsters, but she was still capable of judging her sister.

"You never know when you might need them," Nikolina defended herself.

And, in the circumstances, there was no way to argue with that.

They hadn't been expecting to need to hand out a lawyer's business card to a mob boss's daughter to prevent her son from carrying out a sinister plan, after all.

The worst they could have possibly expected was bad taste in wedding outfits and late caterers.

Dariya looked down at the card in her hand and nodded.

"Thank you. Here," she fumbled up a sleeve and pulled out a scrap of paper.

"This is how you can reach me, if something else comes up before I'm ready," she handed it to Nikolina, then turned away. "Now… I should go. I wasn't invited."

Before anyone could respond to that, she had walked away, leaving them all with a lot to think about. Before she had swept into their lives and shook everything up, this had been a peaceful family event.

Now, they all had war on their minds, one way or another.

Whether they were considering how this would work, what it would do to their futures, or whether it was all true, it was still dominating their thoughts when Sasha and Maria finally came over.

"Hey, sorry we took so long. The priest was a talker…" Sasha began to explain before he caught sight of their expressions.

"Well, I was going to suggest getting on with the photos, but you hardly look up to it. Is everything okay?"

"Um…" Nadezhda surfaced from her thoughts first and glanced around at the others.

Was it fair to answer that right now? Even if they would need Sasha and Maria to help eventually, she still didn't want to ruin their wedding day.

She was on the verge of slapping on a big fake smile and facing the photographer, when Sof bluntly answered; "well, everything was going swimmingly then some creepy Volkov woman gate-crashed your wedding to tell us how screwed we all are."

She saw the panic on the previously happy couple's faces and felt her heart sink.

"It wasn't like *that!*" She jumped in quickly.

"Well, not exactly. The woman was on our side..." she still wasn't entirely convinced of that, but she hoped Dariya was on their side, and they weren't being tricked, "and she came to try and warn us that Vasily Volkov is back."

"But he's in prison! He's the only one we've still got!"

Maria's answer was rather desperate, but the Volkovs had been causing her a lot of stress recently, and this news on her big day was the last thing she needed.

"He's still there. But apparently, he's plotting something *big.* And I'm his number one target, so we *must* stop him."

Nadezhda explained. "The police aren't going to act without evidence and he's about to… I'm not sure…" She sighed.

That sounded lame, in the middle of her big explanation, but Dariya hadn't known the details of Vasily's scheme either.

Was that because it wasn't true, or had he not spilled everything to Diana, just in case his sister betrayed him?

Either way, she didn't have details. But she could give some information. She started again.

"He's about to do something that'll flip things and suddenly he'll have power over us, even if he's still in prison. We don't have much time. This could mean *war.*"

She repeated the word Dariya had used.

It was one that scared her, looming in the future like a threat. A threat that next time, it would be worse than the last time.

Last time, it hadn't lasted long, and it had ended in a court case, not a battle.

The word 'war' conjured worse images, images of death, bloodshed, and ongoing chaos. But it made things clear, at least. It was a word that couldn't be misinterpreted or ignored.

"How can we do that? We can't! Look around, Nadya, there's *six* of us!" Sasha gasped.

Nikolina took over now, and Nadezhda was glad she had done. Her faith in Dariya meant that she could speak with confidence, whereas Nadezhda still didn't know what to believe.

Addressing her brother, the lawyer shook her head.

"We'll have more. Dariya – The lady who came here – was standing against her son, who's behind all of this. She was Antonin's friend and she's bringing allies here to help us. All we need to do is wait."

Sasha didn't look ever so reassured. Perhaps he had realised, like his niece had, that it was less 'all we have to do' and more 'all we *can* do.'

They had no other options but to sit and wait for the mother of their sworn enemy to come to their aid.

Dariya's Allies

After the shocking announcement and the anti-climactic revelation that there was nothing that they could do, everyone felt as though they were in limbo.

Unable to truly focus on the wedding, but unable to progress in their war preparation, they made a lack-lustre attempt at finish the wedding.

They took photos, in which the main wedding party looked surprisingly sombre and hastily retired to the reception venue.

While the rest of the guests tried to party and felt confused at the fact that not even the wedding couple were joining in, those who knew of the Volkov situation were gathered around their own table in the corner.

Nothing was said for a while.

Then Maria tentatively asked; "is there *really* nothing we can do but wait?"

Nadezhda sighed. Hearing the fed-up tone in her new Aunt's voice was upsetting.

This was her wedding day, and she hadn't wanted to ruin it. But it was too late to take back the explanation, so she searched for an answer.

Nikolina's promise to Dariya sprang into her mind.

"Well, we still need to check up on the allies Dariya's going to bring. She's hoping to bring her family back here, but given their history..."

This was Yaroslavl, the city the Volkovs had taken over, after all.

"We need to check that there aren't any warrants out for them and that they aren't on record as wanted."

"Right. I can do that."

Maria seemed pleased to have something to do.

"I did tell my colleagues I wouldn't be in work at the moment, but I can always pop in to 'pick up a file'." She came up with a plan on the spot.

They all nodded, then fell into silence again. What else would they do? Waiting was clearly bothering them all. Where did they go from here?

The rest of the evening passed awkwardly, with small talk and drinks.

They didn't seem to know what to do with themselves, so they retired as soon as the guests had dispersed and returned to their hotels or houses.

The next morning found Nadezhda struggling to sleep. It was still early, but she had realised something about this war.

If it was real, if it was all happening after all, then what mattered most wasn't whether they could trust her father's mysterious old friend, or whether their uncomfortable alliance with the Volkovs came through, or whether this led to bloodshed.

For her, there was a deeper issue that came first.

She would have to face her feelings on Vasily Volkov, the first boyfriend and first betrayal she thought she had put behind her, for good.

Their relationship was a complicated subject.

They had, in some strange way, become engaged. Partly, it was because he had helped her, told her about her father...

And to some extent, it had also been because he had threatened her. But it had also been down to attraction too.

Even when she had hated him, there had been a part of her that wanted him. She was still deeply confused by that past attraction to him. It had been instant, and confusing.

He had put her through Hell, though. His family had betrayed her, locked up and tried to kill her.

After her escape, he had pulled a gun on her during his 'proposal', then tried to manipulate her into some horrid scheme to create an army of mutant children.

Because, just like his twisted grandfather, he had wanted to take over the world.

For some reason, he had decided she should join him in that venture.

Of course, that had been out of the question. She had her principles. And it was thanks to his family that her family had died.

She could never betray his memory and her own ideals in joining Vasily's sick scheme.

But... There had been moments of tenderness when he had seemed to want to help her.

Even five years on, she couldn't figure out if they had been pure manipulation or a sign of something more.

All in all, it had been a rollercoaster ride. She wasn't sure how she was going to deal with facing him again. Especially not because apparently, she was his 'priority.'

He wanted to be 'reunited' with her. To attack her? For something else?

She didn't have that information and that would make facing him again even harder. It didn't seem like she had much choice though. He was going to come after her, one way or another.

She sighed and swung herself out of her uncomfortable hotel bed. She couldn't get away from him, or her past feelings for him, or whatever she did or didn't feel now.

She could just try and prepare herself and hope that, when they met, there wasn't any lingering, confused attraction, so that she would be entirely ready to kick his ass.

Because this had to end somewhere. Her family and his had been entangled for decades. He couldn't keep popping back up and keeping this going. There had to be an end to the war.

The sooner they heard from Dariya, the better, she told herself. Then they could have this battle underway.

There would be no more sitting and waiting. No more stupid musings about feelings that shouldn't exist.

Should she go and help Maria? She had agreed that she would check up on Dariya's allies, even though she wasn't a part of the police department here, and she was awake with nothing else to do right now.

It would be a distraction, and it might help things get underway faster.

Freshening up as briefly as she could, she double-checked that she was presentable and then slipped out of her room. The other rooms near her own contained her mother, her Aunt Ekaterina and Sof.

She hoped they were all sleeping better than she had managed to and wouldn't wake up until after she had returned.

They didn't need to be bothered right now. Yesterday had been bad enough. It was meant to be a nice, family day and it had turned into a mess.

And, since she had a feeling that the days to come would be messy as well, they deserved to have some rest now.

As quietly as she could, she made her way through the hotel. It was still and sleeping. Hardly any other guests were around and even the staff were few and far between. In the streets, it was the same.

Yaroslavl was quiet. It had been quiet when she was there before, too, but that was because everyone was living under the shadow of the Volkovs.

Now, it was just peaceful, a town that was resting.

Sasha and Maria's shared home wasn't far away. Coming back here, however, was a little surreal. It was every time, though she had visited a fair bit. But this was where it had begun.

She could still picture Sof jumping onto the table and shouting out for justice. She wondered if they had begun a war that day. But no, they hadn't.

They had probably begun a battle. Perhaps all these moments, from her father's murder over two decades ago to this moment, right here, right now, had been battles, not wars, mere building blocks in something bigger.

But now, they were facing something bigger. Standing in front of the wall built from their past moments.

She knocked on the door and only thought about the timing after she had done so.

It wasn't even six am on the night after their wedding, and she was waking them up so she could tell Maria to go to work right now.

Because she couldn't sleep. I'm such an idiot, she thought to herself, as she turned to leave. She was a nicer person than this. How did crises like this always make her turn into a horrible person?

The door opened behind her. Sasha blinked at her, and she realised, as she faced him again, that he didn't look like he had got much sleep either.

"Morning… Sorry to interrupt," she tried to be polite and not bring that observation up.

He shrugged.

"Eh, don't worry about it. There's not been much of a 'honeymoon' since yesterday's bombshell. Maria and I spent most of the night, and a bit of the morning, talking about it," he admitted.

"It's crazy that these people still won't leave our family alone."

She couldn't quite remember how much she had told him about Vasily, so she kept quiet. She'd rather he thought they were all crazy than reveal that there was some personal connection here, too.

Besides, they were crazy. It wasn't deceitful. She supposed technically she should be thinking of Vasily as the crazy one and discounting the others, since they were meant to be her allies, but she wasn't sure she could manage that, either.

"Right, then I'm not barging in if I come and see if Maria needs some help with those background checks."

She thought it was best to get her intentions out there as soon as she could.

Maria appeared behind Sasha, looking slightly amused.

"Well, you can come in and 'see,' but I haven't got them yet. I was going to wait until nine, so I didn't give the night crew a heart attack by randomly showing up at the station," she pointed out.

"At least at nine it'll be my regular colleagues, who might not even have been paying enough attention to remember I'm on leave."

Nadezhda nodded. "Yeah, that makes sense. Just wishful thinking on my part. I thought if we got something done, that'd speed things up," she sighed.

"On the bright side, we can kill time with a coffee," Sasha suggested, as casually as he could.

If he was trying to lighten the mood, it failed. They were all still tense and frustrated. But with nothing else to do, Nadezhda agreed to wander inside.

After a few awkward hours in which they ran out of things to say, she and Sasha drank far too much coffee and Maria kept reading the same newspaper repeatedly, they finally decided to head to the Yaroslavl Police Station.

Maria strode in unnoticed, part of the scenery, and Nadezhda followed her, mostly out of a need to do something to help.

Sasha had decided that the three of them would be obvious going into together, and lurked around outside, as though that was any better.

With no specific names to search, the two women simply clustered around Maria's computer and hunted through all the Volkovs that were on record.

Most of these were people Nadezhda had never heard of getting caught for smaller things like breaking into places.

She supposed the nameless, faceless members of the mob getting themselves into trouble wasn't important. Perhaps it even helped, perhaps it kept attention away from the more dramatic things.

But really, those cases were all finished. On the record, yes, but not likely to prompt re-arrest. The only fugitive among them was Diana, and she had proved elusive so far, anyway.

It felt wrong to be relieved that there wasn't too much there, but at least it would mean they had more allies.

Nadezhda supposed that she ought to get back to the hotel before her mother sent out the search parties and pass the information on so that it could reach Dariya.

Then perhaps this information on a screen would translate into actual support in their perilous question, instead of feeling like a wasted morning.

She still wasn't sure how she felt about that support coming from the Volkov family, formerly sworn enemies of her own family and relatives of the man they were trying to stop, but it wasn't as though they had any choice.

They would just have to hope Dariya was actually in control. And, for that matter, that she was on their side.

Sof And Choices

It turned out that communicating with the mysterious Dariya wasn't going to be that easy.

Nadezhda said goodbye to her Aunt and Uncle and hurried back to the hotel, only to find her mother waiting impatiently in the foyer.

"Where did you go? You should have left a note! Five more minutes and I was calling Maria!"

She began to rant, in that typical parental way, not waiting for an explanation.

The younger woman sighed and let her mother vent before she answered.

"Relax. I was helping Maria out. I guess I forgot to leave a note."

She wondered how Nikolina had noticed.

She had probably banged on all the doors, woken Sof and Katya up and then stood around panicking when her daughter failed to show up.

It was a scene she could easily imagine, and she cringed.

"Sorry. Anyway, the background checks Dariya wanted are sorted. So, I thought we could let her know. It might get our 'allies' here sooner. Then we can be one step ahead of Vasily," she added, wanting to be ready if some surprise attack was coming.

"Right."

Nikolina dug into her pockets and rummaged for the scrap of paper Dariya had given her. She eventually found it and pulled it out.

"Oh. It's her address... That *is* a little odd. I expected a phone number or something like that. I guess we will have to pop in and see her."

It was probably an over-reaction, but Nadezhda felt her stomach churn.

Why? Why an address? Why make something this small and simple into a big, face-to-face issue?

They could have done this in less than a minute on the phone. It would be that easy. Making it a physical thing made it feel like a trap.

Maybe Dariya just hadn't thought of this part. Maybe she had assumed they would only need to contact her in an emergency and had forgotten about the background checks. She tried to reassure herself.

But even as she thought reassuring thoughts, she asked her mother; "are you sure that's safe?"

"Of course it is. She knew your father, she will not betray us," her mother's voice was cool and level with blind faith, "besides, what other options do we have?"

Once again, she put her finger on the all-important question, the hopeless answer to which had propelled Nadezhda this far into her uncertain quest.

And so, it was that, in the early morning sunlight, three women approached Dariya's house. It was on the outskirts of the town, quiet and almost entirely secluded.

Perhaps, with her family's local notoriety, it needed to be. It was unassuming too. A small, lonely cottage on the slope of a hill.

Nadezhda walked slowly down the remnants of a chipped stone path, still hesitant.

Nikolina was striding ahead of her, seemingly confident even now, as the decisive moment approached.

Sof, less certain, still close behind Nadezhda. She could practically feel her friend's tension. Even though the usually out-spoken woman wasn't speaking, it hung in the air.

Sof thought this was a trap, that the only reason any Volkov would want them in their home would be to slit their throats.

Nadezhda had to admit she had a point. She still wasn't as sure as her mother was. She *wanted* to trust Dariya.

In strange circumstances, some years before, she had read the woman's diaries and been compelled by the tale of her strange friendship with Nadya's own father, of her desperation to escape the mad life she lived...

At the same time, couldn't someone who had faked their own death fake anything? And the big, bad villain they were facing was her own son.

They said a mother would do anything for her child. Though, the Volkovs hardly seemed like a happy family.

But the doubt was there, and it was part of the reason she had brought Sof. Brilliant, brave, fearless Sof. Sof, the woman who could take anyone in a fight, who Nadezhda knew for a fact always had a knife on her.

If it came to a fight, Sof would be the one to defend her and Nikolina.

Her mother, normally so lawful, wasn't likely to be an effective fighter if she did raise her hand to someone, and she might be a trainee cop, but a part of her still flinched when the real battles arose.

She hoped Sof would snap out of the surliness and become her brilliant self if they needed her.

But she was also here because she had needed someone other than her mother to rely on. Nikolina was great in many ways, but she did nothing to help her daughter's stress levels.

So, to help her, she had decided they would go in a group of three. And Ekaterina wasn't an early riser, even with a war facing her and an impatient sister knocking on her bedroom door.

Besides, she would be too relaxed, bound to make silly quips every five minutes, ignoring the lives on the line.

Sof was the more reliable option. She was relaxed and fun to be around, something Nadezhda would no doubt need to calm her own nerves on this trip.

But the Volkov family had been responsible for the death of Sof's cousin, so she knew that the other woman would still take the situation as seriously as was necessary.

Anyway, she liked Sof's company. A lot. Well, that should be obvious, they had managed to build a bond like no other over the past five years.

There was nothing like fighting side by side to make you inseparable.

But there was more to it than that. Recently, she had had her best friend on her mind a lot. She kept thinking back to when they first met and everything that she had admired about Sof back then. Her leadership skills, for one.

She had jumped up on her table without a second thought and rallied a bunch of tired, abused, and miserable people to fight against a mob of violent psychopaths.

Then there had been her engineering skills, something she had excelled in even at sixteen.

Now, she had just graduated from engineering school.

And she was street smart too, feeding them inside knowledge of the way the Volkov family had operated on their home territory.

Nadezhda looked over at the woman she was privately admiring. There are things she had started to notice more recently too, like how Sof's new hairstyle stood out instantly.

Something about the combination of her natural strawberry blonde against her new purple highlights was able to brighten Nadezhda's day straight away.

Not that her bright, energetic smile and big blue eyes couldn't do that alone... And that was without hearing her strong, fruity voice whispering in her ear.

Perhaps this had been a bad decision after all. She suspected she was starting to develop a crush on the other woman, and it was clearly bad if just her voice could distract her from her mission.

Her mother cleared her throat, breaking through her thoughts and making her blush.

Nikolina made her feel as though mind reading was possible sometimes. But the older woman was merely standing on Dariya's doorstep, her arms folded, staring back at her entourage.

"Are you girls *coming?*"

Nadezhda sighed, and Sof sighed with her. She knew her friend was here on sufferance because she had begged her to come. And she was beginning to feel just as reluctant.

But her mother was already waiting for them, and they could hardly turn back now.

Pushing all her craziest thoughts about this mission to the back of her mind, she made her way to the door, slightly sluggish as reluctance slowed her down.

Once Sof had joined them, Nikolina turned and knocked firmly on the little cottage's door.

They didn't have to wait long before Dariya opened the door and gave them a welcoming smile.

"Ah, you found me! Is there something you need?"

Now it felt silly to be here in numbers, or at all. Once again, Nadezhda was reminded that this could have been a phone call.

Nikolina rolled her eyes at the two silent, tense girls behind her.

Children, these days. Or at least, young people. In their twenties, they should have better manners.

"Yes. We came to let you know that the background checks are all clear. Apart from your daughter, Diana. I am told she is still wanted. Is there anything else you need?" She spoke up.

Dariya looked hesitant for a moment. Her eyes flickered over her assembled visitors. Then the warm smile was back.

"Thank you for that! But I'm sure things will be fine for Di… Speaking of how things will be, why don't you come in?

We have a lot to plan, and now that this is out of the way, we can truly get started."

Even Nikolina paused for a moment then. She glanced at the girls. They had never wanted to come here, was it fair to drag them inside?

Even if her own curiosity about the woman with whom her beloved, long-lost husband had spent many of his last days was eating away at her?

Nadezhda, unable to deny her mother's gaze, though it carefully avoided crossing the line from searching to pleading, gave the barest of nods, and thought of Sof's hidden knives.

She glanced over her shoulder to her friend.

Sof's pause was the longest. Eventually, she nodded.

"Fine, but I'm doing this for you. And if she double-crosses us, I've still got my knife on me," she muttered darkly into Nadezhda's ear.

Her best friend shook her head.

"We'll be fine," she assured her, her voice carrying far more confidence than her heart.

Planning and Vasily's Scheme

The three women almost tiptoed into Dariya's living room. It was a small room, papered in cream coloured wallpaper that bore a floral pattern. Beneath their feet, a soft white carpet lay, their shoes leaving muddy stains.

Nikolina looked down awkwardly, and Nadezhda tried to be careful as she stepped in, but Sof strode on through, not caring.

The rest of the room was even more unexpected, given that they were dealing with a woman from an infamous mob.

There was a small coffee table, a half-read newspaper resting on it, with the TV remote beside it.

The TV itself was placed on a stand nearby. Floral armchairs were clustered around the coffee table.

And a young woman was slouched in one of them, glaring at the newcomers. She was slender and tanned, with incredibly short black hair and piercing grey eyes. Nadezhda bit back a groan upon seeing her.

Dariya had somehow failed to mention that Diana, her fugitive daughter, would be here.

Nikolina seemed oblivious as she took a seat, but Sof tensed, and Nadezhda wondered if they were getting close to knife territory.

The presence of the other woman was starting to make this seem more like a trap.

The younger girls traded glances and eventually sat down, perching on the edge of the cushions.

Sof swung her leg across the opposite knee and rested her hand on top of her boot, where she always hid her weapons.

Dariya strolled into the room just behind them, took a seat beside her daughter and gave her audience a nervous but optimistic smile.

"Well, here we all are again. Thank you for calling. I'm glad my family will be able to visit. And don't worry about Di, she's been here for ages, and she's doing just fine," she gestured to her daughter.

"I guess she's just great at coping with these things, aren't you, love?"

Silence answered her. She laughed.

"Sorry, she's not a people person. But I think it's important to include her in our plans, since she's the one Vasily contacted."

Nadezhda's curiosity managed to defeat her nerves.

"I still don't understand why he would do that."

To her surprise, this brought her old enemy out of her stony silence.

"Well, for some reason I could never see, Vaska's completely *mental* about you. He was raving about finding you when they took us away. Then just before I escaped, he sent me this... *Stupid letter!*" She paused at this point, clearly still angry about it all.

"He told me he wanted to find you again, and that he had a plan. He wanted my 'help'..." Now, Diana was fading away into a rant.

Nadezhda would have preferred the continued silence.

This announcement was hard to process. Dariya had said Vasily wanted her dead.

But Diana seemed to believe he was still besotted with her... What *exactly* was he planning?

Sof jumped into the gap while she sat there silently, deep in thought.

"I don't suppose *'Brother Dearest'* thought to spill all the juicy details of his plan to you? Could be kind of handy, y'know," she pointed out, somewhat sarcastically.

Flippancy and silence were the only non-violent ways she knew of to handle the Volkovs, and she didn't seem able to keep quiet any longer.

Diana glared at her, livid at the way she was speaking to her.

"You really think I didn't consider that?! If I knew what the little *slimeball* was up to, I would have mentioned that a tad earlier. Besides, we were both in prison, our mail was being monitored. He couldn't say too much," she explained.

"Would you really have mentioned it? You *were* on his side, weren't you?" Sof fired back.

Nadezhda gave her a stern look. She didn't want any trouble stirring up. Things were bleak enough as it was.

But Sof had a point. Diana had been very protective of her brother in the past... At least, she had appeared to disapprove of their relationship at the time.

Diana rolled her eyes.

"The only reason I ever gave a toss about him was because I didn't want anyone else to kill him before I got a chance. All he ever did was make my life harder, and then he had the nerve to come crawling to me, *begging* for my help!"

Sof couldn't take a hint, ignoring the anger in the other woman's voice and demanding to know: "Did you give him any?"

Dariya must have picked up on the tension in the room. Well, she would have to be deaf and blind to miss it.

"Now, girls, play nicely," she cooed at them, chuckling when the only response was her daughter turning her angry expression on her.

"Anyway, Ms..." she paused, unsure of Sof's name.

"Sof..." The woman reluctantly supplied, after Nadezhda nudged her in the ribs impatiently.

"Thank you. Ms. Sof did make one good point there, dear... The letter might say something, something we missed before, perhaps. Could you fetch it?" She finished, practically shooing her daughter away with her suggestion before another argument could start up.

Diana got up and trudged out, obviously irritated by this, but nevertheless following her mother's directions.

"Sorry about that," Dariya tried to smooth over the mood of the room after the argument.

Nikolina, who had been sitting very quietly and primly in her chair, giving Nadezhda and Sof hard, stern glares, sighed.

"So am I. *Children.*" She shook her head.

A small laugh escaped Dariya.

"I suppose they can be a handful. Not that I mind. My family and yours have been enemies for a long time. It's understandable that things would be awkward now."

"Nonsense. Some members of our families were enemies. Some were great friends. Nadezhda showed me your diaries, and Antonin's letters. He never had the chance to tell me about you, but I can tell that there is a precedent that means it is only right for us to help one another again."

The other woman smiled at her, more warmly than her stoic nature usually allowed.

Listening to her mother, Nadezhda felt bad. She ought to trust Dariya more, knowing how she had helped her father.

But it was hard, seeing Sof in such distress, seeing Diana, who clearly didn't like her any better now they were on the same side, again...

It was a hard contrast to Nikolina and Dariya's determined alliance. Her loyalties were being tugged in two.

She supposed she should speak.

"My mother's right. I'm sorry, this has all been a lot to process, but if you helped my father, I'm sure you can help us now."

Dariya's face lit up.

"Thank you, both of you! Antonin was like a brother to me; it's because of his memory that I must help you. That, and the fact that my own son is too twisted up for me to ignore..." She sighed and turned to Nikolina.

"I don't know you, and I'm sorry I didn't try to back then. Antonin didn't talk about your relationship a whole lot. He never had time. But he told me enough to let me know that he loved you more than anything. And I like to think he would have been proud of his daughter, too."

Nikolina looked away, and Nadezhda knew instinctively that she was crying, something she hardly ever did.

She couldn't help but feel teary-eyed over the memory of the father she had never known as well.

She had run into the Volkovs because she had tried to find some connection to him, after all.

Now, the woman she had searched for, the woman who knew his story, was sat in front of her, telling her he would be proud of her.

She cleared her throat, coughing away the lump in it, and tried to focus again.

"Well, I'm glad you think so. But even if our families have worked together before, it's not going to be easy. My father was apparently public enemy number one when Vladimir was still around. And from what I know of your family so far, they don't like me much…"

Dariya laughed at that remark, though it was no joke.

"You mean Di? She's not exactly subtle, is she? Still, better the blunt one than the manipulator. Now he *did* like you, and see how that's going?"

The shrewd yet sympathetic, motherly look she gave Nadezhda made her blush and turn her gaze away.

Her own experience of 'the manipulator' was still a touchy subject. One that his games had unfortunately dragged up again.

She was saved from having to respond to that in any way by Diana's return. She never thought she would be glad to see her, but it meant they could get back to business, and away from any awkward comments about Vasily.

Diana dumped a piece of tattered paper on her mother's coffee table and flopped down in her armchair again, without bothering to utter a word.

Dariya picked it up and started to read through it. Aloud.

"Dear Di,

It's about time we got back in touch, right? I'm *shocked* you didn't write to me sooner," from his sister's scowl and the smug tone that his mother could, surprisingly, imitate perfectly, that was sarcasm.

The letter continued.

"Anyway, I have good news to share this time. I'm sure you've been waiting, as I have, for *Dear Old Grandpa* to get out of the way, and now it's happened, I've got a plan formed. As you well know, I've been waiting *so* patiently to see my Nadya again..."

Here, Nadezhda squirmed uncomfortably. She didn't want to listen anymore, but it could be of use, so she let Dariya continue:

"I promise you; I will be with her again within a month. Well, I'll see her again, anyway... That may be short-lived. I want to make good on your promise to her as well, just for you, Dear Sister."

There was the sarcasm again. But what was he saying?

"What promise?" Nadezhda asked, a little nervous about hearing the undoubtedly dreadful answer.

Diana squirmed as well now. It was one thing hating someone but admitting something like this to the person in question was a whole different scenario.

Especially with your mother looking over your shoulder and said person's protective friend watching you like a shopping mall security guard watches a teenager.

"When we were taken away, I said I would kill you..." She admitted, looking down at the floor uncomfortably.

"So, he wants to find me sometime in the next few weeks and kill me? Or get you to kill me? Or something about killing me, anyway?!" Nadezhda questioned, frightened and a little confused.

Wasn't he besotted with her? Not that she *wanted* him to be, but... It didn't add up.

One moment he was talking about his 'love' for her, the next, he was proclaiming that he wanted her dead.

"I'm not sure what he's on about, there's more, and even for him, it's seriously weird." Diana rolled her eyes.

"None of these psychos are killing you, anyway!" Sof interjected angrily.

"No need for that, we are allies now, and we are beginning to make progress," Nikolina tutted.

Just as she and her daughter had begun to build a relationship with Dariya, the volatile Sof and the resentful Diana had to come along and complicate it.

"Relax. I don't know Ms. Sof's story, but I'm not going to be offended if she hates our family." Dariya stepped in again.

"Yeah, *I* hate our family, and I'm part of it," Diana was typically bitter, but at least the potential fight had been stopped, "speaking of hating family, there's more to my *lovely* brother's tale."

On that note, they all turned back to Dariya expectantly.

She began to read again:

"A friend has rigged me up a nice little machine I can have once I'm a free man, and I'll lure her into it. It'll be perfect, carry out all our wishes in one."

"That's where he signed off," Dariya blinked, confused. "What a weird and blunt ending. What's he up to?"

"And if your mail was meant to be monitored, how the hell did that get past?!" Sof questioned, shocked, "it's *full* of threats."

"He didn't actually say anything *threatening...*" Diana muttered grumpily, "not outright, in plain enough words for the dumb legal people to understand it."

Nadezhda might have felt insulted by that, but her mind was racing, because she could remember some of Vasily's 'promises' and was trying to work out his little plot before he got to her.

"If he's had another machine made... Is he planning to clone me, then murder the real me? Wasn't cloning something he was obsessed with?"

"And he wanted to marry me... So, what's he going to do? Clone some mutant version of me to marry and then... Get rid of me so I'm not in his way?"

She mused aloud as some of the insane stuff he had told her drifted back into her mind.

Vasily had certainly seemed obsessed with the weird cloning machine that his grandfather had created.

It had spawned his family, and he had had bigger plans for it. This was how he planned to create his army of mutants.

A bizarre and terrifying thought that she remembered him describing as though it was his greatest wish. But that may have only been the start of his sick ideas after all.

He might have a far darker plan up his sleeves.

One that specifically involved his obsession with marrying her, and his apparently conflicting desire to kill her.

The others stared at her as though she was the insane one just for mentioning it.

But she could see the flickers in his relatives' eyes, and knew they knew it was entirely possible, coming from a mind like his.

Then Sof growled. "We're *not* letting that happen. *Right?"*

She glared at the others, edging closer to her best friend protectively. Nadezhda wondered how they would respond and if Sof was reaching for her knife to get the right answers.

Her mother looked almost as protective.

"Of course not. We are going to stop him," her voice was determined, as unbending as iron.

Dariya nodded. "We're certainly going to try. I'll contact my relatives as soon as I can, and once they're here, we'll prepare a counterattack so we're ready when he comes for Nadezhda."

Great, just great. Nadezhda groaned inwardly again. This 'planning session' had made her feel *much* better.

At least she was feeling more trusting towards Dariya now. But Diana's involvement wasn't helping, and the other Volkovs were pretty much unknown quantities.

So, all she had gained from this session was an emotional incident concerning her dead father, the knowledge that at least one of her new allies hated her guts, and a feeling that Sof and Diana, still both occupied with their own issues, would fight for the whole of this trip.

Oh, and now she was involved in an enterprise to try and stop her insane ex-boyfriend murdering her, so that he could marry a 'perfect' cloned version of her.

And here they sat, planning a counterattack, because with no way of predicting his attack, no way of convincing the police or prison authorities that a pre-emptive strike was needed, and no more hints, beyond Diana's letter, as to how the attack would come, or when.

Vasily's Creation

The women weren't the only ones who were planning. Vasily's secret contact was waiting for him in the corner of the courtyard where they always arranged to meet. But this time, he hoped, it would be the last time. Everything else was ready, after all.

He walked over to the other man as casually as he could, hoping his excitement didn't show. They were so close now.

Glancing over his shoulder, he checked that they weren't been watched. But his friends had done their jobs well, and there were no guards around. Or anyone else for that matter. They had the little grey square all to themselves.

Time to get down to business.

"You have what I need?" He demanded to know.

"Of course." The man nodded.

Vasily gritted his teeth. If he didn't need this idiot, he would have killed him by now. His arrogance had always been frustrating.

But that didn't matter. Soon he would be in control, and the need for all this sneaking around in the shadows and acting nicely would be over.

And then he would be able to see his Nadya again. That was how he thought of her, and he had thought of her every day since they had been cruelly separated.

She had become the focus of all his plans.

That, of course, was never the intention. All he had wanted, growing up, was to take absolute power for himself. That was why his mother had had to die, why his grandfather had had to die...

But in between all that, just when his plans seemed to be coming together, she had waltzed into his life and made him fall in love with her.

That was a cruel trick because then she had turned on him and left him here to rot.

Fortunately, he was too clever for that to be the end of it. He had made it his mission to find her again.

And then... Well, he would both be reunited with his love *and* have his revenge upon her for her cold-hearted betrayal.

After that, he could return to his original goal of taking power for himself.

And her, of course, because after his revenge she would see things differently and be persuaded to stay by his side. They would rule the world together, but for now...

For now, he had to focus on getting there. He snapped out of his private musing and turned to his associate again.

"Hand it over then." He stuck his hand out and waited expectedly.

The man took a long, thin silver cylinder and lay it in his hand wordlessly.

Vasily's fingers closed around it triumphantly. This was the last piece. Now it could begin in earnest.

"Send out the word. We're going to war," he announced coolly.

For once, the wretched man looked slightly fazed, and he took some smug pleasure from that.

"*War?* I thought we were just getting out..."

Vasily looked up at the towering building above him. "No, we're taking over."

"The prison?"

"First, sure. Then the world."

He smiled and started to walk away, leaving the confused and distressed man behind him. The fool had never even realised what he was helping to build, or all the power he held.

He had neither vision nor ambition. But that didn't matter now because everything was about to change.

He sauntered back to his cell innocently, attracting no attention. He had got the hang of pretending he wasn't up to anything a long, long time ago, after all.

Once he was inside, he pulled the bed out of the way and pushed on the wall carefully. It swung aside.

That little mechanism had taken quite some time to perfect. The creation had taken far, far longer. Finding someone to design it had taken long enough.

He might have more ambition than his grandfather, but he didn't have the technical genius that had led Vladimir to possess a cloning machine.

He had had to resort to keeping an eye on new arrivals, trying to suss out who might have the knowledge he had needed.

When a man who was accused of building a bomb had been brought in, he had… interrogated him personally. He had explained his vision to him.

The word 'insane' had been used. But after a few threats, in conjunction with a makeshift weapon to the man's throat, they had reached an agreement.

The exact plans for the… thing he had dreamt up had landed in his lap just days later.

Parts had been harder. This had been the hardest piece to find. Now, it would be complete.

Eager, he stepped into the opening, moving towards his creation, and ran his hands over the cold metal rim.

The device sat there, reaching nearly to his waist. It was large, round, and open-topped, almost like a paddling pool.

But it was made of solid metal, smuggled in piece by piece, and bolted together with brute force. The bottom of it was filled with a vivid blue liquid.

It was thick, like jelly. That had taken some mixing to get it right, and had had to be concocted with great care, because if he had got the right quantities of the right chemicals, spilling any would have been, well... Fatal, to start with.

But even that toxic mixture wasn't as important as this final piece.

He leant down, carefully avoiding the liquid as he placed his hand on the cold, metal wall of the device and pushed the cylinder into a small hole he had left there. There was a click, and lights came on, flashing bright white light throughout the cell. He grinned to himself.

So, the electricity supply in this place was up to powering a motor. Perfect, then his creation would get hotter... Hot enough to work. It was ready.

That meant it was time to begin, and already, he could hear the rioters getting started outside. His associate had put the message out, just as he had ordered. Soon, they would be unstoppable.

He knew that because he had taken great pains to train and arm the other inmates, so that they would work for him.

Some had to be bullied, some simply promised weapons and freedom, but they had all joined him eventually. They would be more than rioters this time, they would be an army.

And the guards weren't prepared for something this carefully planned. The usual riots were chaos. Not this time. This time he had plans. And they were about to be set in motion. First, they would take the prison.

During this, of course, there would be a perfect opportunity to test the device. And so, his army would grow. Even the guards, those who survived the first wave, would join them.

And of course, by the time they were truly in control, word would get out about this.

And Nadya, *Dear* little Nadya with her naïve ideas about helping others, would not be able to stay away. She would come home to him.

After that, it was a matter setting the device on her, the target he had dreamt it up for.

The ideals that she had betrayed him for would lead her into his trap. Then she would be indisputably his, and they could focus on taking the world. Together.

He smiled. Finally, the future was beginning to look more and more perfect. Because the future was theirs to create.

And he was already buzzing with ideas of what their future, their world, would look like whirled around his head excitedly. Because it would be happening very shortly.

There was, of course, no way they could fail. Not this time. Of that, he was very sure. They were unstoppable now that his creation was ready.

The prison would be his and after that, the world would only be a few steps away. So would Nadya.

She would belong to him. And this time she would be unable to resist, even if she claimed she would rather die than marry him and aid in his plans. Even if she had to die first.

Because, and he was rather proud of this, he had exceeded his allegedly brilliant grandfather already.

Vladimir might have found a way to create life with his cloning machine, which, annoyingly, he had not managed to replicate, but a far greater idea had occurred to him.

What if he could do what people had strived to do for hundreds of years and overcome the obstacles death presented?

Then, instead of an army of mutated children, he could have the undead, immortal army so often feared in films.

And he could fix the apparent... Conflict of interest that was stalling his relationship with Nadezhda, because there would be a way of granting his own wish, to be with her, the wish of his family, to kill her, and her self-proclaimed desire to escape him by any means.

One simple thing was all it took.

Her death.

He looked down into the vivid ocean in his machine and his own smile was reflected at him. How had he never thought of this before?

It could all be so easy. It *would* all be so easy.

Revelations

With the dubiously reassuring knowledge that Dariya would soon summon her Volkov army to help them, there was little more that Nadezhda and her allies could do.

And, as the atmosphere grew increasingly uncomfortable, thanks to Diana, they decided to leave.

As they were walking back, Nikolina spoke.

"Well? Do you see that she wants to help us now?"

"It seems she does."

Nadezhda commented with a thoughtful nod, a little more trusting of Dariya and her support now that she had heard the woman sharing memories of her father.

Sof interjected. "Sure, *she* seems okay. What about the one who hates your guts?"

"Diana?" Nadezhda questioned, though she knew exactly who Sof meant.

She was stalling. Truth be told, she wasn't too sure about Diana.

The woman had no explanation for her sudden change of heart, except possibly some element of hatred for her brother.

The two had definitely had an odd kind of relationship, but Nadezhda couldn't be totally sure that the letter was genuine, and Diana's hatred of her brother was enough for her to put aside her dislike of her.

"Yeah... Where do you think she stands on this?" Sof pressed, not letting her back out of this conversation.

Nadezhda shrugged. "No idea. But at least she won't try anything with her mother around."

Sof looked unconvinced. "Look, maybe we can trust Dariya, but I don't like the fact that our only allies seem to be Volkovs. We know what they're like..." She pulled a face.

"Dariya will organise them and keep them under control," Nadezhda said hopefully. She was trying to be optimistic here, though she had doubts of her own.

Sof pressed on.

"But she's not in control of them, is she? She's just using their factional hatred of one other to get them to take Vasily down..."

"What happens if they decide they would rather fight one another again? Or that she's the enemy? Or that we are, for that matter? We're 'outsiders,' after all."

Nadezhda sighed. She wasn't too sure about that either. The Volkovs weren't people she wanted to be around at all, let alone if they decided to start a fight.

But at least Dariya had allies to offer. They didn't, so they couldn't do this on their own.

"I trust Dariya. As for the others... Maybe we can't trust them, but we don't have a choice, do we? What else have we got?" She replied.

Sof looked over at her and for a moment, Nadezhda felt her face flush and her heart speed up.

There was an unusually tender look in her friend's eyes as she murmured: "We have each other."

The moment of gentleness passed suddenly and sharply, though, leaving her with tears bubbling up in her eyes.

Because since she had first noticed her feelings towards Sof developing, she had wanted something like this to happen.

But it was so bittersweet it was painful because she knew that, however precious those sweet words were, it wouldn't be enough to save them in this terrible situation.

The tears rushed over her cheeks before she could stop them.

"I know, and *I love you!* But that's not going to stop Vasily, is it? I wish it was enough; I wish that you and I could take on all the world's evil together and win, just like that, but that's not how it works!" She cried out desperately, losing all sense of restraint and speaking from her heart.

Sof stopped in her tracks, turning to her with an expression of total shock.

"What did you just say?"

Nadezhda came to a sharp halt too and her world seemed to stop around her. What had she said?

It was suddenly hard to remember, her emotions had taken over completely for a moment. Now that she had calmed down, she stood stock-still, staring at her friend.

"At the start, what was the *first* thing you said?" Sof prompted her.

She started to breathe again as it came back to her.

"I love you. I said I love you," she whispered.

Sof didn't answer her immediately but simply threw her arms around her and pulled her in close, hugging her tightly.

"I knew it!" She cried at last. "I knew when I met you that we were meant to be more than friends."

Her words made Nadezhda blush again.

She had taken all this time to work out her personal feelings and hadn't realised that all these years, her best friend had been in love with her.

She rested against Sof for a second, enjoying the moment and letting their current situation fade into the background.

It couldn't last, of course. Sof pulled back slightly and raised a hand to wipe her tears away gently, then spoke again.

"I love you too. And I promise I will stand by your side throughout this. I know it won't be enough. I know this will be hard. And I'll be here for you all the way anyway. I'll even let them into my life again if they're the best way to help you, "she vowed.

Nadezhda smiled, knowing Sof's words were sincere. She hated the Volkov family in all shapes and forms, so tolerating them was an act of love for her. As for things being hard.

They had met in the midst of her first struggle against the Volkovs, and she knew from that that Sof understood what they might have to go through to survive this.

She knew that they might not survive this.

"Thank you," she replied softly, planting a small kiss on the other's lips.

"You don't need to thank me for loving you," Sof answered, before moving away, "but we should get back," she added.

"Ahem. Yes. We should. Did you two forget I was here?"

Nikolina stepped into the silence. Seeing the younger women blush, she chuckled uncharacteristically.

"Do not worry, I realised what was going on and hung back a bit. You deserved your moment," and indeed, she had been walking a little further behind them. "But time is of the essence now. Let us head back."

Even with that warning tacked on the end, the walk back was a lighter moment, compared to recent times.

The young couple talked about their feelings for one another, and all three women joked about old times together.

There finally seemed to be some respite from the stress that had stalked Nadezhda through the recent days.

But when they reached the hotel, there was no time for jokes and suddenly the stress came rushing back.

Because as they drew near to the hotel, Maria was standing outside, looking around with a worried frown on her face.

Nadezhda realised, with a sense of dread taking over her sinking heart, that her Aunt was standing there, waiting for them.

Why? Because she was supposed to be home, with Sasha, at least trying to enjoy a honeymoon. But she was here instead, looking desperate and miserable.

Something had happened. Something was very, very wrong. The familiar knot of tension in her stomach returned, hard and cold inside her.

She dropped Sof's hand and ran towards Maria, shouting out to her in a panic.

"What? *What's wrong?*"

"Nadya!" Maria looked up as she came running towards her and set off as well, meeting her in the middle.

"You haven't seen the news, have you? They've shut down Yaroslavl main prison! There's a riot going on there and now the prison officers are going missing..."

Nadezhda's blood ran cold as she met her Aunt's gaze. "It's Vasily, isn't it?"

It wasn't a question. She knew what he was doing.

He was putting hundreds of people in danger to lure her in, knowing, as she did, that if there were officers and prisoners dying there, it was her fault.

And that if she went to save them, she was walking into a trap.

He had vowed to kill her. Diana had said he had a plan to find her again. This must be it. That was exactly how his manipulative mind worked.

He would come for her by turning her own personality against her, finding weaknesses to target until she cracked and went to him.

Then she would have to face him, to find out who was stronger. And he always seemed to be a step ahead of her.

What could she do? She couldn't leave people to suffer for her, she couldn't sacrifice them to Vasily's madness.

But even with Dariya's support, there was extraordinarily little chance that she could walk into and take on a whole prison full of desperate, angry rioters.

She looked at Maria's pale face as she nodded, glanced over to Sof's expression of anger, and felt complete helplessness set in.

What the hell could they do now?

She sighed and looked over at her new Aunt. Perhaps she knew something that would help them work this out. Though she found that unlikely. The future was looking hopeless.

"Anything else you can tell me about what he's doing?" She asked desperately.

Maria shook her head. "I'm trying to get in touch with my friend, Olga. She works in the prison; she might know something. But it's not going to be easy to contact her in this situation..."

"We don't exactly have a choice though, do we?" Sof chimed in as she walked over to join them.

And that was the trouble. They didn't have a choice. They never seemed to have a choice when they were up against Vasily.

Even from prison, he was slowly cutting off her options, driving her towards him again.

Every moment of happiness that she found in this bleak situation, he destroyed. Every step she made; he dragged her back.

And now, people she knew, like Maria, were losing contact with loved ones because of Vasily. Because of her.

And there was nothing she could do.

A Plan of Attack

Time seemed to be standing still as they all sat around a table in the hotel's bar and stared at Maria's phone.

It sat in the middle of the table, in the process of trying to call Olga. This was the fourth attempt, and so far, she hadn't picked up.

Everyone was impatient. Nikolina looked angry, Sasha had arrived with Maria and sat tensely by her side.

Ekaterina looked confused but was beginning to realise something quite serious was happening to her family members, as her expression was devoid of its usual cheer.

Nadezhda found herself gripping Sof's hand for comfort. It was an indication of the others' worry that no one commented on this.

Maria watched her phone intently and almost leapt out of her seat when there was a click. The sound of someone picking up the phone. She grabbed it hastily.

"Olga? Are you there?"

"Masha? I'm here. I'm okay... But I can't talk," her friend's voice came to her in a panicked whisper.

"Do you know what's going on?" She questioned anxiously.

There was a brief, frightening pause, and some distant crashing on the other end of the phone.

"I... I'm not *sure,*" Olga spoke at last, "some *psycho's* organising a huge riot and now some of the other guards are disappearing..." She sounded terrified now, and Maria was shocked.

She remembered her old friend as a fearless and determined woman.

"Are you alright? What are you doing?" She asked nervously.

"I've found a supply cupboard; I'm hiding here until I find some more resources. Then... I'm going to take them down. Somehow, if I can find a way."

Now she sounded more like her old self, dead set on stopping them, even though she had no idea what was happening.

"Be careful," Maria cautioned.

"I wi-"

BANG!

The phone line crackled. Someone screamed loudly, and Maria heard her name briefly shouted another sharp crash rang out and the line went dead.

Maria gasped as though she had been hit, and the others looked at her in concern.

"Olga? *Olga?* Are you there?" She asked, her words coming out in a garbled flurry as panic kicked in.

After a few moments of this desperation, Nadezhda tentatively interrupted.

"Is everything alright? What's *happening?*" She asked.

"I don't know. She's gone... They're doing *something* to the guards, and I think they've taken her," Maria explained grimly.

There was a terrible silence while this sank in. Then Nadezhda spoke up again.

"What can we do now...?" She asked.

Olga had been their hope of a solution, by gaining some kind of inside information from the prison. What hope did they have now?

"Well... We could wait for it to be enough of an emergency for the army to be sent in. However long that would take..."

Maria looked around at the ring of grim faces. Clearly no one wanted to wait that long, leaving Vasily time to make things worse.

"Dariya said we should act fast..." Nadezhda reiterated, though she knew they had already failed to do that.

They were too late, but they should still try and make sure Vasily didn't get too far ahead of them.

"Then our other choice is to storm the prison, rescue the guards and take him on," her newest Aunt suggested.

They all glanced around the table, looking at one another. There were only the six of them, here and now. Sof looked determined and angry that they had to go through all this again.

The light in her eye burned. Nadezhda smiled. She knew her friend.... Well, girlfriend, would stand by her.

And personally, despite the risks... She wanted to go in there and stop Vasily once and for all. But she had her own, deeply private reasons for that.

Would the others follow? Maria had made the suggestion, and Sasha was, by now, no stranger to danger. His life as a detective threw him into all sorts of situations.

Nikolina, on the other hand, was normally a strait-laced lawyer and surely wouldn't want to get involved in this... And Ekaterina looked nervous.

She faltered. She needed everyone's support to do this. Her other 'allies,' relatives of the very man they had to fight, weren't ready yet.

And even when Dariya had successfully rallied them... They were still outnumbered if it was true that Vasily had the whole prison on his side.

"Do you think we should?" She inquired, leaving it open to anyone who wasn't sure.

"They need to be stopped!" Sof was first to decide.

Maria nodded. "We need to get in there, it sounds serious," she commented, still worrying for her friend.

She saw Sasha nod too and watched her mother hesitate, then nod.

"If we can stop them, we should act now. A proper response is likely to be a long time coming. *Too* long, I fear," Nikolina replied, rather long-windedly as always.

Ekaterina looked unsure. "I don't know about this..." She told them.

Nadezhda was a little surprised. Her Aunt was normally energetic, in an insuppressible way, and down to try anything she thought stood half a chance of working out.

This was where she and Nikolina often clashed. For her mother to be in favour of something this dangerous was odd enough.

Ekaterina's hesitation was downright strange.

"Well... It should be okay if we can get Dariya to hurry up her side. We'd only need to wait a few hours."

Nadezhda had been trying to reassure her Aunt, but now she bit her lip. How long would it take for the Volkovs to arrive? Where were they even coming from?

"Perhaps someone should go back and ask this Dariya then?" The nervous Ekaterina suggested.

Hearing the tentative tone to her voice, Nadezhda remembered that the rest of them were used to action.

She and Maria had their police training, Sasha his detective's past and Nikolina the life she had cultivated to survive since her husband's murder.

Then there was Sof and her... questionable experience leading what could be called either a revolt or a riot against the Volkovs in this city, last time they had 'needed stopping.'

She took pity on the inexperienced Katya and nodded.

"You go. We'll try and find a way into the prison without attracting too much attention. Then at least we can help Maria's friend."

She thought of the screaming they had heard through the phone.

A group this small couldn't tackle Vasily but they might be able to free the distressed guards.

She continued to advise Katya. "if you take a message to Dariya, she can organise her family and when they arrive, you can all meet us as reinforcements."

"A message? *Just* a message? Right, sure, I can do that. Where do I go to find her?" Ekaterina babbled a response, trying to be useful despite her steadily increasing panic at this whole situation.

Nikolina passed her the piece of paper bearing the address. Ekaterina hastily pocketed it and got up.

She seemed almost relieved to be leaving the others with their insane plot of breaking into the prison. But she did hesitate.

"Oh, well, I... I'm fairly sure what you're doing is mental, but good luck," she made a tactless attempt to be supportive.

"Oh, it definitely is. But it's necessary. So, thanks, Auntie Katya, but we'll have to remain mental," Nadezhda responded, waving her away.

When Katya had left, Nadezhda turned to Maria.

"Is there any way we can get in without being instantly slaughtered? I know you said 'storm' the gates, but it might be worth considering that there's *five* of us," she pointed out.

Maria didn't speak for such a long time that her niece was beginning to think it was because she had asked such a stupid question there was no way to answer it, but eventually, she nodded.

"I think we have a chance. Just one little chance," she spoke up at last.

"Right. We'll take it. Now... To business."

'Business,' in this case, meant some kind of plan for storming the prison, the most dangerous task of all.

They would be charging right into a riot, and, Nadezhda suspected, right into Vasily's trap.

The Break-In

The planning meeting dragged on through the night. Somehow, they worked out a way that had a slim chance of working. A nerve-rackingly slim chance.

Ekaterina wanted no part in it, but she owed it to her family, always the rock in her chaotic life.

Nikolina and Sasha had been second parents to her, helped her figure her life out, helped her settle down after a wild youth. The least she could do was summon help for them in their hour of need.

Sasha's wife had lost a dear friend, the first potential causality of this war. Nikolina's daughter was in grave danger, the most wanted person on this villain's list, from what she had heard.

So, she rose early, washed, dressed, and unfolded the paper she had been given.

She read the address several times before she shoved it into her pocket and stepped out, hoping she wasn't as shaky and nervous as she felt.

It was a short distance to walk and in crisp, cool morning air, she should have been motivated to walk quickly, but she dawdled along, looking around the streets of this unfamiliar town, acting like a normal tourist.

Not for fear of suspicion. She was doing nothing wrong, however odd her errand was.

No, simply because she had grown used to putting off the things that she found uncomfortable or difficult.

Dodging hard conversations with humour, playing college student over and over until she decided on a career path.

Her life had been built differently to her siblings' lives. Nikolina was ruthlessly ambitious, as any good lawyer must be sometimes. She dived in headfirst.

And Sasha didn't appear to care about throwing himself into the path of criminals, either. He positively enjoyed his strange job.

She wasn't ready. She wanted to put this off, even though there was no way to put off the war itself, already brewing inside the prison.

A sudden image of her siblings trying to charge into a captured, gang-controlled prison, just with their tiny band of allies, spurred her on.

She wasn't ready, but hell, who had been?

Even Lina, as she affectionately called her sister, had been shocked. But they had to face it, and even if she was terrified, they would face it together.

She had just about got this motivational speech straight in her head and was beginning to feel some confidence when she stopped, pulled out the address and checked it.

Blinking, she looked up at the path stretching up to the nearby door. She was practically on the doorstep of a mobster.

Could she really do this?

Nadezhda had also risen early, unable to sleep properly. She planned to check on Maria and see if she had secured the support she had promised, but there was something else on her mind as well.

She had spent the sleepless night thinking of Sof and the sudden change in their relationship. Of course, she was pleased that her friend returned her feelings.

Now, the burden of worrying about her crush being discovered and ruining their friendship was gone, destroyed in an instant by their emotional confessions.

Yet, her worries weren't over. She knew in her heart that it wasn't fair for her to start a relationship with Sof.

Not now, with the threat of Vasily looming over them.

He had been her first crush, and even now, she wasn't entirely sure how she felt about him.

Besides, the man was obsessed with her. Taking Sof as her girlfriend would only make her a target to him.

As if their mission wasn't going to place her loved ones in enough danger.

The trouble was that these things seemed to make sense while she was lying in bed, staring at the peeling paint on the ceiling. In the dim light of her hotel room, she had reasoned it all out and convinced herself that Sof would understand.

But in the cold, hard light of day, she felt sick with nerves. What if this conversation destroyed any glimmer of a relationship between her and her love?

Knowing that she had to take that risk, for Sof's safety as much as any other reason, she reluctantly knocked on the door to the other's hotel room.

The wait for an answer seemed to take forever.

She wondered if it was a sign that she should give up and slink back to her room, hating herself for overthinking everything.

Before she could, the door was tugged open by a dishevelled looking Sof.

Multi-coloured hair was strewn all over her face and she was still wearing her raggedy blue pyjamas.

The way she was squinting at Nadezhda gave her the impression that, despite all the stress in their lives at the moment, the other woman had somehow managed to sleep.

"Have you got a minute? We need to talk," she began, kind of hoping that Sof would need some time to wake up, giving her a few minutes to work out how she was going to bring this up.

Or just stalling in general. She really didn't want to do this. But she knew it was important.

Sof rubbed her eyes, then nodded.

"Sure, come in. Must be important if you're up this early, after all," she observed.

"We do have a 'war' to get ready for," Nadezhda pointed out, making an excuse.

"Yeah, true, but I can have some proper beauty sleep and still be ready to kick that idiot's sorry ass," she retorted, "so what's kept you up?"

Apparently, Sof had noticed the bags under her eyes. Or she just knew Nadezhda too well by now and was aware of when she had and hadn't slept.

Nadezhda gave a bittersweet smile. Of course, Sof would know, she had seen her, frantically waiting for the response to her application to join the Police Force.

She had watched her go through sleepless nights, chew on her nails and fiddle with her hair... She knew when something was wrong.

"Ah, well, there was one other thing I wanted to talk to you about," she confessed.

"Go on then." Sof nodded encouragingly.

"So, after yesterday... What does that make *us* now?" Nadezhda began tentatively, raising the subject of their relationship instead of diving straight into the issues with it.

"Depends on what you want," Sof replied simply, shrugging as though it didn't matter to her.

Nadezhda could have kissed her. She was so laid-back and casual. Of course, this would as easy as she had imagined. Sof wouldn't make a scene.

But after Vasily's possessiveness, it was hard to get used to having normal conversations with her partner.

And there it was again. Thoughts of him wouldn't leave her alone. She shook herself slightly and looked over at Sof as she thought of how best to express her feelings.

"You're what I want. I want to be your girlfriend. Hell, I'd be your wife if only the law allowed it," she assured her love.

Watching Sof light up at her words felt like a kick in the stomach, knowing what she had to do next.

But she had wanted it to be clear that, no matter what else they went through, she loved her.

"The thing is, we can't always have what we want. At least, not straight away. I think if we start something now, we'd be making a mistake. This will be hard enough without risking having Vasily turn on you..." She began to explain, leaving the hardest part, her complicated feelings for Vasily, out of it for now.

Even without that, there was a moment of silence. Her own heartbeat filled it, pounding as though it was in her ears. She wondered if she had blown it.

But then Sof was at her side, taking into her arms. For someone so strong and full of life, her touch was curiously tender and her grip feather-light.

Her fingers, calloused and care-worn from her practical work, tangled in Nadezhda's long, mousey hair.

"It's okay, it's *okay*. Don't worry about me. I'll be fine. But if it makes you feel better, we don't have to tell anyone about our feelings. Nothing has to change right now. I can wait, until you feel safe, until we're ready... Okay?"

Her girlfriend's words held nothing but love and overwhelmed with emotions, Nadezhda lay her face against Sof's shoulder and let her tears fall.

"Thank you," she whispered.

"Hey, you don't have to thank me for loving you." She smiled softly, before gently pulling away and flashing her usual energetic grin instead.

"But we *do* have a war to get ready for, right?"

And so, emotionally reassured, Nadezhda had to face up to the physical challenge ahead of her.

She started by meeting Maria in the foyer. Having taken a moment to dry her tears and compose herself, she pulled her Aunt aside, checking her watch as she did so.

"Dariya called last night and told me that she had just spoken to her allies. She told them to get the first train."

"The first arrival here is at 8:30. Give them half an hour to get to here, another half an hour for the briefing. Fifteen minutes to reach the prison... We should get our reinforcements by quarter-past nine," she tried to set out a timeline.

Maria looked doubtful, glancing at her watch too.

"It's only five now. That's a long time to hold out, just the five of us."

"We'll find the guards, right? Get to your friend? Then I'm sure we'll be able to last a few hours," Nadezhda tried to remind her of their own chance.

"I sure hope so. Oh well, let's get the others and move in, then."

Fifteen minutes later, the group were standing outside the prison gates.

"Ready?" Nadezhda asked them, as she peeked through the gates.

Some rather unpleasant looking men were prowling through the courtyard.

Nerves kicked in. Okay, so they had a plan, but Vasily had a lot of thugs on his side, by the looks of it.

And she still wasn't sure how she was going to react to seeing him again. He had a nasty little habit of getting under her skin and messing with her head...

Sof's voice managed to pull her back to reality. Her boundless energy and determination not to take any crap always managed to make her feel like anything was possible.

"Of course, we're ready, let's go kick their asses!"

Somewhere behind Sof, Nikolina cleared her throat.

"There is no need to be crass about it, but in principle, I agree. We should go in and kick... Well, kick whatever we can."

Nadezhda stifled a grin at that. Of course, her mother was still taking the moral high ground at a time like this. But not entirely, because her hatred of the Volkovs got in the way.

Sasha looked at his elder sister and laughed, shaking his head.

"Yeah, Sis, sure, let's kick them if it'll work. There's not much else we can do, is there?"

Everyone seemed to agree that this was their best - and only - plan. So Nadezhda turned her attention to Maria.

"Well, let's see if you're right about how we can get in here, then."

The older woman nodded.

"Alright, follow me."

She beckoned to them as she slipped along the side of the wall and around the back.

There was a smaller gate around the back. She pointed to it triumphantly.

"I knew this would still be here. I used to meet Olga here after work."

"Won't it be locked?" Nadezhda looked doubtful.

She had expected the secret entrance to be a bit more secretive than this.

"It'll be locked, but the point is, it's smaller. We can climb over. The prisoners won't be watching around here because they don't know it's here," Maria explained.

"I hope you're right..." Nadezhda commented, eying the gate nervously.

"It'll be fine," Maria assured her.

Sof walked over to the gate. "Well, let's get to it, then."

She jumped up and caught on to a metal bar, using it to swing herself further up. Looking down, she surveyed the other side.

"It's clear. We're in."

Her sudden, bold movement shocked them all, and Nadezhda remembered, with a wave of admiration, how brave she was.

But still, she didn't move until they had heard her jump down, her feet hitting the ground. Only then, one by one, did they begin to follow her in.

Once they were all on the other side, they looked at one another.

"Alright, where to?" Sof asked.

"We need to head inside. That's where everyone is. And then we'll find the missing guards." Maria ran over the plan again.

"Follow me."

She took the lead. They scurried through the unguarded back area of the courtyard and found a door.

Yanking it revealed that it wasn't even locked.

"Your ex is getting rather sloppy," Sof commented to Nadezhda.

"That's because he's an idiot," she retorted.

But was it? She wondered anxiously. He was normally pretty clever. Dariya had told her he was dangerously clever.

Why was he overlooking such obvious things as doors and gates?

It was a trap, wasn't it? He was playing some kind of game with her again. He seemed to like doing that.

But she was on his territory now, and he didn't know. So, the game was on, and she was, temporarily at least, one step ahead of him.

Olga And The Deal

Creeping through the corridors of the captured prison was a grim and disturbing experience, but not in the way Nadezhda had expected.

After hearing that Vasily had taken over and seeing the courtyard teeming with guards, she had expected to be faced with armed thugs on the inside too, to be in constant danger and have to fight through, all the time worrying for her friends and family as well.

Instead, there was... No one. The corridors were deserted.

That had clearly not been the case earlier. There were broken doors, piles of rubble and twisted bars from the windows littering the floor.

Blood stained the walls in places, doubtlessly a relic from the struggle, before the takeover had been completed.

But where were the inmates now? They had destroyed everything in the place, then... Vanished.

Maria was clearly thinking along the same lines.

"Where *is* everyone...?" She asked, looking around anxiously.

She had been motivated to take on this mission by the possibility of finding her missing friend, but there was no sign of anyone, let alone Olga.

"I don't know," Nadezhda admitted. "Apart from the guards outside, there's no one here. I don't like it. Something must have... *Happened* to them."

"What could have happened to them in here?" Sof asked.

It was, after all, a prison. It was supposed to be secure. The only threat here was meant to be the people they were looking for.

Nadezhda had her own sickening suspicions about how and why that wasn't the case though.

Vasily might have been allied with these people, but he wasn't exactly known for his loyalty. He wanted power, and he used people. His grandfather had given him power, and he had told her of his nasty scheme to kill off the old man.

Come to think of it, he was probably responsible for Vladimir's death. But there was no time to dwell on whether one crime lord murdered another.

Not if her grim train of thought was right.

"It's Vasily, he must be doing something to do them. Maybe he's got some kind of horrible contraption again, like his 'modified' cloning machine."

She thought of his last creepy plan, making mutated clone-children with her, and using their 'powers' to destroy his grandfather and take over the world.

A shudder ran through her.

"He can't have built something like that in this place, surely?" Sasha put in doubtfully.

Sof sighed.

"He could. If he found someone with the right knowledge, inventions like that can take shape anywhere."

Her wisdom was accepted here. She had watched her cousin build the all-important component that Vasily had needed for his first scheme.

She, herself, had been through engineering school. She knew what she was talking about.

"If that is the case, we may need to act fast. If he has some sort of... Device, we had better find this girl before he uses it," Nikolina chimed in, stating the obvious thought that had jumped into all their minds.

Yes, they all knew they had to find Olga right now, but no one knew how.

Meanwhile, Vasily had closed off part of the building. His cell had become his office, and the surrounding area was the only populated part of the prison.

Guards filled the corridor outside. Inside, he was preparing. The room where his device waited had been opened, and two of his guards had brought him another test subject.

This one was apparently troublesome though. He had issues to address first. He turned to face the woman as she stood between the two men, glowering at him defiantly.

"So, one of the guards found somewhere to hide? A pity it did nothing to help you, or your friends. However, my men did find this…" He held him her cracked mobile phone in his hand.

"What were you doing with it when they found you? Tell me who you were contacting," he demanded.

This could be important, after all…

"No," Olga insisted.

She wouldn't give in to this man. His guards were thugs and had attacked her, but she wouldn't be afraid. Not even when he looked right through her with his cold, grey eyes.

His jaw tightened. "You *will* tell me."

"No."

"I am not a patient man, my dear. Tell me what I want to know now, and we will let you live. Continuing to stall my plans will not help anyone. And you will die..." He smiled at that thought.

She paused, telling herself not to be afraid of him, or of death. She should protect everyone who was at risk from his plans.

But... Could she not protect them better alive? And what advantage could the knowledge that she had taken a call from Maria possibly give him?

"...Maria. I was talking to Maria."

"Maria *who?"*

He had his suspicions, of course, but he needed to know. If it was wrong, then his plans would have to change.

"My friend, Maria Sobachkina," she explained, hoping he didn't recognize the other woman's name.

"Ah, of course..." His grin widened and she mentally cursed. He remembered. "Your delightful police officer friend. Good. I need to speak to her again. She is, after all, the reason I'm here..."

"You're here because of your own stupidity, nothing else," she informed him coolly.

His hand connected sharply with her face.

"Shut up. You're only still alive for one thing..."

Suddenly, he pressed her phone into her hand.

"Your friend Maria knows Nadya. Tell her to bring the girl to me if she wants to see you again."

Dazed from his blow, Olga looked down at the phone in her hand.

"Your thugs smashed it," she pointed out.

"You *dropped* it. But the damage is only to the screen. It's superficial. Now make the call."

He wouldn't allow any distraction. Not when he was this close...

The intruders were still searching for any trace of Olga, but it was fruitless. All they were doing was getting lost inside the huge prison.

"This is ridiculous! Where can they have taken everyone?" Sof sighed, getting grumpy as the hunt seemed to drag on forever.

"I don-" Nadezhda opened her mouth to respond and was cut off abruptly as music blared.

"That's my ringtone..." Maria looked baffled and pulled her phone from her pocket, "Huh? It's Olga."

She frowned, surprised that her 'missing' friend was phoning her.

"Perhaps she's escaped from them," Sasha tried to be optimistic, "she could help us if we meet up."

"Good thinking, honey," Maria smiled. She took the call and held her phone to her ear, "Olga? Where are you? *Are you okay?*"

"I'm... I'm fine for now, but I have to tell you something." Her friend's tone was urgent now.

"What is it?"

"You need to bring..." She hesitated, turning away from her phone and back to Vasily. "Who?"

"Nadya!" He snapped, growing impatient.

"You need to bring some girl called Nadya here, apparently. Otherwise, I'm going to die."

"You're going to die? Olga, what's happening?" Maria started to question her friend, but Vasily grew fed up and snatched the phone.

"Enough talk! Bring the girl if you want to see your friend again!" He ordered.

Maria sighed, lowering her phone, and switching it off. Her face was pale, and she looked shaken.

"Bad news?" Sasha asked, sounding concerned.

"Some bad, some good. The good news is Olga is alive. The bad news is she's been captured." She revealed, taking things a step at a time.

This was a shock, and she had no idea how to handle this. One friend for another. One she had been at school with, the other, her niece...

What could she do? She tried to process it as she told it to the others.

"There's more good news; we're being offered a deal to get her back."

"Well, why not get to it and save her? And maybe in the process, they'll reveal their location!" Sof suggested.

"The deal is this: they want us to give them Nadya," Maria managed, feeling sick as she did so.

She was saying this to the girl herself, one of her closest friends and her family. How could they possibly consider this?

Sof's reaction was instant.

"What the hell? They can't have her. Tell them to *screw off!*" She yelled, forgetting herself and grabbing at Nadezhda's hand.

Fortunately, in the circumstances, this gesture went unnoticed.

The others began to clamour, all putting forward their own reasons why Nadezhda would not go, in different ways.

Then a small voice interrupted them.

They turned.

"What?" Sasha questioned.

"I'll go," Nadezhda repeated.

She knew they would try to talk her out of this and raised a hand.

"Please don't. I have to go. More people will die if I don't. Besides, Vasily is... He behaves oddly towards me. I may be able to make him slip up and tell me his plan. Then we can take him down."

"That is very brave of you, darling.”

Nikolina smiled at her, though there were tears in her eyes at the idea of her daughter walking into this obvious trap.

“But there is just one problem. We still do not know where to go."

"Olga will tell us," Maria said with a sigh, "I suppose if you're determined to do this,” here, Nadezhda nodded, "I'll call her back and make the arrangements."

Nadezhda sat back and let her do so, wondering what the 'arrangements' would be.

She had known that this was a trap for her when she had come here, and it seemed like the only way to stop Vasily was to play along and hope there was a point in the game where she could change the rules.

There must be something he had overlooked, some weakness he had left exposed. She suspected she was his main weakness. But she had to find out what he was up to in order to stop him.

That meant pressing on and heading deeper into his trap, hoping that she was right and could stop him.

If not, she would probably die. And she wouldn't be the only victim, knowing him.

An Escalating Situation

A quick phone call to Maria revealed that Nadezhda should 'meet' the guards outside. They didn't look like they were the sort of people she wanted to have any dealings with, but at this point, she didn't think she had much choice.

Especially not if she wanted to get to Vasily...

There was, though, one little advantage to this. Now that he was contacting them through Olga, information was slipping through.

"At least a meeting outside confirms one thing; They don't know we're here," Maria pointed out after the call.

"True. That should mean if I go, you can still stay here and continue with the plan," Nadezhda agreed.

Sof looked confused, wrinkling her nose.

"How can we continue with the plan? We were going to find the prison officers and free them. If they won't tell anyone but you where they are..." She trailed off, leaving the obvious contradictions hanging in the air.

"I meant the part of the plan where we wait for our allies to arrive then take over. If they're not guarding this bit, we should be able to establish a base quickly, then take them on, right?"

"And rescue me, I'm hoping. By that point, I hope I'll have some inside information to help you out as well," she explained.

"Ah." Her friend nodded.

"Good idea. In that case, best of luck! And don't worry, we'll get a good foothold here and when the others get here, we'll come and kick Volkov's stupid head in!" She told her enthusiastically.

"...Something like that, anyway," Nikolina added, a little disturbed by the violence, "hopefully Katya will get them back here soon and we can come and rescue you. And your friend, right Maria?"

Maria nodded slowly "You will have to take it from there..." She murmured.

There was general agreement, then, after a small pause, Sasha noticed something unnerving in his wife's words.

"...You didn't include yourself in that. What are you going to be doing?" He asked her.

"I'm going with Nadya." She told him.

"Are you sure?! You'll be in their headquarters; you could be in serious danger..." He looked panicked at the suggestion.

His niece going into the heart of their enemy's camp didn't sit well with him, let alone his wife.

She smiled and went over to him, pulling him into a hug. Holding him, she spoke softly.

"I'm no stranger to danger, Sasha. I've always been okay before," she tried to assure him, "I *promise* this time will be the same."

He pulled back and met her gaze, tears welling up his baby blue eyes as they rested on her dancing hazel orbs.

"But you're..."

"I know."

Mystified, but nevertheless wanting to reassure her poor, panicking uncle, Nadezhda stepped in.

"We'll have each other. I'll do what I can to keep her safe."

The moment broke and Maria stepped away from her husband, surveying the family instead. Nikolina was masking her concern with a set expression but was still clearly worried, her brow furrowed.

"And I'll keep Nadya safe. I promise," she told them, "but I have to go with her. I need to see Olga…"

She turned back to Sasha now, trying to justify leaving him, though it tugged at her heart to walk away. Especially so soon after their wedding, and knowing what they did…

Nadezhda nodded.

"We should go now," she said, almost reluctant to say so, knowing she was breaking her uncle's heart by dragging Maria away.

But it did, in some small, childish way that she was ashamed of, offer her some comfort to know she would have her Aunt with her.

Vasily had a nasty habit of making her uncomfortable and facing him alone would be worse.

"We should." Maria nodded.

She hugged Sasha again and leaned in to kiss him.

"I'll be back soon," she reiterated her promise when she finally pulled away from him.

"Good luck," he gave her a somewhat shaky smile, "be careful, both of you," he added.

Nikolina nodded. "Yes, be careful." She urged, giving her daughter a worried look.

"I'll be fine, Mama," Nadezhda assured her.

"You *better* be, or he's a dead man. Well, he is anyway, but..." Sof's angry, protective muttering faded as Nadezhda laughed and gave her a hug.

"I appreciate it. See you later." She smiled as she stepped away, Maria hot on her heels.

Unaware of this drama, Ekaterina was waiting on Dariya's doorstep. She had tapped on the door tentatively, still unsure about this.

Now, impatience and nerves had mixed inside her, and she felt as though she was five minutes from snapping.

Not that she would do anything if she 'snapped.' She would just feel her spirit quiver and twang like an elastic band as it breaks.

Then she would run, or scream, or break down. She had none of the certainty or stoicism of her sister, none of her brother's easy ability to get along with people.

She just had two layers, humour, and raw emotion. Stress was chipping away her sense of humour, and she didn't want to bare her soul for ... whatever kind of monsters these 'Volkov' people were.

Just as her legs began to shake, the door was opened. She looked into the soft, smiling face of... Dariya, wasn't it? The woman who had gate-crashed her brother's wedding.

"Yes? Can I help you?"

The woman's voice was polite but there was a hint of distrust there. Perhaps she was like this with every visitor. She was of a questionable legal status, after all.

That thought didn't help. The last thing she needed to do was remind herself that she was face-to-face with a member of an infamous crime family.

"Um..."

Words died in her throat, and she stood, frozen, hating herself, waiting for the woman to shoo her away and her chance to help her loved ones to shrivel up.

But slowly, uncertainly, a look of recognition crossed Dariya's face.

"Aren't you something to do with Nadya? I saw you at the wedding," she voiced her thoughts.

Mutely, Katya nodded. She still didn't feel like she could speak, but a second chance was being offered, and she had to seize it.

"Ah… Then come in. We can speak freely inside." She pushed the door further open, standing aside.

The doormat bore the word 'welcome,' and the hall was covered in floral wallpaper, but this place didn't feel remotely cheerful.

The sickening nervousness within her growing, Katya stepped into what felt like the most innocent-looking trap ever.

Nadezhda and Maria were also nervously heading for a trap, but in their case, they knew trouble was right around the corner, rather than merely suspecting it.

They had slipped back out of the prison at the back and looped around to the front. Now, they were inches from the gates.

"Ready?" Maria asked.

Nadezhda nodded uncertainly.

"Let's do this." She tried to sound confident, nervous that she wasn't ready to do this and face Vasily.

She reached out and tapped against the gate. All the guards instantly swung around and glared daggers at her.

One approached the gate and growled at them. *"Get lost!"*

"We're here for a meeting with Vasily. My name's Nadezhda Moroz, this is Maria Sobachkina," she began to explain, hoping her nervousness didn't show in her voice.

He looked them both up and down, then gave a reluctant nod.

"Fine." He opened the gate.

As soon as they stepped through it, they were surrounded by the other men.

The guards started to push them, and the two women moved reluctantly through the courtyard, in through the front doors and through a maze of deserted corridors, not unlike the ones they had visited earlier.

Eventually, though, they arrived in the shut-off wing Vasily was using as a base. Here, it was a completely different story to the other corridors. They were crammed full of guards.

Somehow, this was equally disturbing.

They didn't have time to dwell on it though. They were shoved through and into a cell.

Well, it had been a cell. Now it was expanded and... Odd. Nadezhda couldn't quite put her finger on it, but there was something very weird about the room, despite it being more or less empty.

There was just a strange sort of boxy... Thing in the corner. Apart from that, there was nothing. Well, no furniture...

She saw four people. There were two more guards, holding a red-haired woman in a prison officer's uniform between them.

She guessed, from their deal and from the way Maria suddenly tensed beside her, that this was Olga. Maria had probably tagged along in hopes of seeing her again, after all, and it made sense to assume that she had recognised her straight away.

The other person was instantly recognisable. Vasily hadn't changed much.

He could still stare right through her with his cold grey eyes. And he was doing, right now, with that horrible smirk that made her stomach tighten and churn plastered all over his face.

"Nadya! I knew you would come. Are you still playing at being Ms. Morals or did you just want to see me again?"

She glared at him, flushing. He always did this.

Just... Said stupid things that made her all confused and flustered.

"Let her go and leave me alone," she told him, aware that it was a lame retort, but had no idea what to say.

She never did when he was around. She didn't know how to deal with him. Perhaps it was a mistake to think she could stop him, after all. She might be his weakness, but he was hers as well.

He tutted at her.

"Let's not rush things here, my dear. I still have plenty to show you and your friends."

He turned his glare on Maria. "Your friends who are *forever* getting in my way."

"You mean protecting her?" Maria lashed out at him.

He snorted, rolling his eyes. Then turned back to Nadezhda.

"Do you still think you need these people?"

"I don't *need* anyone. But unlike *you,* I care about others. *Especially* my friends and family!" She hit back, hating his constant negativity towards anyone else she happened to care about.

"I *see.* Then I think it's about time to introduce you to my cure for you," he told her, a grin spreading across his face as he spoke.

"Cure? There's nothing wrong with caring for people!" She spat at him.

"You'll see things differently after I kill you. You see, the cure is death, Nadya, dear."

Maria instantly stepped in front of her.

"Don't you try laying a *hand* on her!" She snapped.

"Oh, I wasn't going to. You see... I need to demonstrate first," he told her, stepping towards Olga.

He motioned to the guards, and they moved aside, letting him grab the woman himself.

She struggled, swinging at him, but he dodged her blow and caught hold of her anyway. He pushed her back, shoving her towards the contraption behind her.

Nadezhda looked at Maria with rising panic. What *was* it? What would it do to kill Olga?!

The thought seemed to be too much for Maria, and she lunged forward, throwing herself between her friend and the device.

"Maria!" Olga gasped.

"Olya..." She panted, clinging to her. *"You're safe, you're safe..."*

"You really think so?" Vasily snorted. "A valiant effort, Ms. Sobachkina, but you've got my way enough now."

He stepped forward and shoved them both.

Maria screamed, letting go of Olga and seeing her fall to the floor. That was the safest outcome though, for she herself was hurtling back towards the machine.

She tipped back, falling over its edge and disappearing inside with an unpleasant squelching sound.

The First Casualties

"*Maria!!* Damn you, Vasily, you, you, *you...*"

Nadezhda's words were barely coherent, and she even couldn't think of something suitably insulting to call him.

Rage had taken over. He had murdered her Aunt, in cold blood, in front of her.

Of all the horrible things he had done to her, this was the first time he had taken someone she loved away from her, while she stood helplessly by, watching.

His creepy little invention was designed to kill, after all, so... So, Maria was dead. And after she had promised her Uncle that she would keep her safe, as well. How could he do this?

Just when it was all getting better, he came along and tore her family apart again. And this time, it was her fault.

He chuckled. "Relax, Nadya. Everything will be fine. Better than before, in fact."

Olga stood up now, angry as well.

"*Better?* You *killed* Masha!"

He sighed. "She's really starting to get on my nerves. Ruslan?"

"Yes?" One of the guards looked up.

"Kill her."

'Kill her.'

The words seemed to be bouncing off the walls, all around Maria, but they had no meaning to her, her head was swimming.

She lay on the ground, a strange, blue jelly-like substance covering her body.

Yet she could open her eyes and see straight up to the white of the ceiling. She could breathe fine and easily hear the whirring of a generator somewhere nearby. Yet she couldn't move at all, her whole body felt heavy and slow.

Her head was really starting to hurt. She wanted to fall asleep, to give in and rest her heavy body and her aching head, she wanted to...

Olya. Nadya.

The words came at her out of nowhere and for a few minutes, they meant nothing, nothing at all. The memories tried to push through.

The pain grew worse and worse every time they did, but if she focused, she could remember.

It was unbearable though. She tried to scream, her mouth filling up with jelly. It tasted foul and she spat, struggling.

Kill. That word again. And now it had meaning. *Kill... Who?*

'Her' must be one of the women. One of her... *Friends?*

Her mind was full of confusion.

The headache was fighting the memories, and the desire to sleep was growing overpowering now.

But the voice of memory was persistent. *Someone is trying to kill Olya and Nadya. Get out of here and help them, it pushed.*

She tried again to move. This time, she pulled an arm slowly from the jelly and lifted it. Holding it up was almost too much effort, but there was a spike up above her legs.

She stretched forward and felt her fingers graze it. Reaching desperately for its support, she grabbed and just managed to close her hand around the end.

Pulling, she felt it twist upwards a little with the pressure but managed to haul herself forward.

Her upper body ripped through the jelly, and she managed to stand, pulling her legs free slowly.

She was just in time to see Ruslan plunge a knife into Olga's chest.

The room suddenly seemed to be full of screams. Olga's scream was cut off by her desperate struggles for breath, pain coughs and gasps.

Nadezhda's was one of fury, directed at Vasily because he knew was doing this just to spite her and it sent fires of hatred through her.

Maria's scream was a desperate cry for her friend. She knew she was too late.

Vasily laughed.

"Oh, deary me, what a *fuss*. Oh well, at least she's out of the way. Now we can get back to business. I need to finish my demonstration, don't I, Nadya?"

He turned to Maria with a menacing smirk.

Nadezhda followed his gaze. A wave of hope ran through her as she saw her Aunt still standing, still alive.

But it was soon replaced by a horrible chill. Something was wrong. Maria's skin, normally tanned, was deathly pale and had an unsettling blue tint to it. She was swaying gently.

"Maria...?" She questioned tentatively.

But the older woman was focused on her friend's dead body, laying on the ground in front of her.

Her eyes, still heavy and tired, were barely open, but through slits, she could see Olga lying there.

Tears began to ooze down her cheeks.

"Olya..." She managed to murmur softly.

Vasily rolled his eyes.

"I *really* need to find a way to speed this process up... but I suppose leaving you for a while will suffice. Because some of this really is *too* boring. It only gets interesting after she goes to sleep."

He grinned. "Enjoy finding that out..." He strolled towards the door.

"Later, Nadya, Dearest," he winked at her.

She pulled a face, disgusted by him.

As the door clicked shut behind him, she turned back to her Aunt, hesitantly approaching the weeping woman.

"Maria? Are you okay...?" There was no reply.

Her Aunt took a slow step forward, exiting the device she had been so unceremoniously shoved into and approaching Olga's body.

She crouched down beside her, still crying.

"I'm sorry..." She murmured to her friend.

Guilt set in and Nadezhda felt tears welling up in her own eyes. She had come here hoping to save her Aunt's friend and promising to protect Maria.

"I'm sorry too," she whispered.

Only now did her Aunt manage to look up at her.

"Nadya... *He's killing us*. You have to... You *have to* get out of here!"

She tried to compel her to escape, not wanting her to suffer as she and Olga had. But now it was an effort just to keep her eyes open.

The headache was getting worse. She slumped forward, her head in her hands.

Nadezhda edged towards the door.

One of the guards grabbed her.

"You're not going *anywhere!*" He snapped.

She looked back at her Aunt desperately, wishing she could follow her advice and flee.

And desperately wishing there was a way to take Maria with her, to safety and to their loved ones.

"I can't go. Anyway, I can't leave you," she replied, guilt raging within her.

Maria had come here to help her, and she had been hurt instead. She couldn't leave her to suffer further.

But her Aunt's eyelids flickered shut, and she couldn't hear her anymore.

The Attacks Begin

Walking down the hall, Ekaterina was painfully conscious of Dariya's footsteps behind her. This still felt like a trap.

She reached the door at the other hand of the hall, at last, and placed her hand on the door handle.

"Through here?" She turned back to check with Dariya.

Since her voice had returned, she had been acutely polite to the other woman. She might be on their side now, but the reputation of her family alone was enough to terrify Katya.

As Dariya opened her mouth to reply, there was a clatter on the other side of the door. Jumping away from it as if she had been stung, Katya gasped.

"It's okay, it's okay!" Dariya rushed to reassure her.

"Look, I can see you're nervous, and I get it. If you're a friend of Nadya, you'll have heard nothing good about my family, but I promise, this time we're here to help. That was probably just Di dropping something. Please, do go in and take a seat."

There was a pause while Katya tried to calm her heartbeat and privately judge how much truth there was in that statement.

Certainly, her sister seemed to trust Dariya, and right now, the woman's tone was pleading. She seemed nervous too.

"I'm sorry. It's just… Nikolina's my sister, so… Like you said, my impression of your family hasn't been great. And I'm not really used to being involved in the action like this. I leave that to my family…"

She tried to explain away the tension between them.

"But now you want to help them. You must be very worried about them all."

These words were accompanied by a nod of understanding.

Relaxing a little, Katya nodded.

"Nadya stumbled into something dangerous so young, and we're just trying to help her fix it. You know, they all say young adulthood is when kids get into real trouble, but none of us expected this."

The return of her ability to quip showed her relief.

As she pushed open the door, Dariya was chuckling at her joke, and it seemed as though things would be okay.

On the other side of the door, though, she was met with a hard, suspicious glare.

The young woman, who she guessed was 'Di,' turned straight to her host.

"Who is this?"

"Nadya's Aunt. She needs to talk to us about… Actually, you never did tell me why you were here." Dariya's explanation was cut short by this discovery.

They were both staring at her now and Katya had to fight to keep the nerves from creeping back in. Instead, she blurted out the news.

"Nadya's storming the prison. *Right now.* How soon can your family get here to back her up?"

"Woah! I know I asked her to take action but… Well, does she at least have people with her?"

Dariya's less than supportive reaction did nothing to help Katya. She grabbed the other woman's shoulders in a panic.

"No! There's *five* of them! That's why they need the allies you promised *right now!"*

She stared into Dariya's stunned eyes and began to realise what she had done. Was this what snapping really felt like?

She hadn't expected to do anything, and yet here she was, yelling in the face of one of the notorious Volkovs.

Before she could truly process this, there was a whistling sound and a knife shot past her, embedding itself in the wall.

"Let. My. Mother. Go." Diana's words came out as a growl.

Slowly, Katya removed her hands from her host and stepped back shakily.

"I'm sorry, I'm ju—"

"It's fine," Dariya shook her head, brushing the incident off, "obviously, this is more serious than I thought. It's just as well they're arriving today. My brother sent me a message and said he'd met up with the others on the train."

"What train?" Katya asked.

"There's a train due to arrive at 9:20. They should all be on it."

"Not a moment too soon. Are you going to meet them? Then you can send them to help Nadya."

Relieved that their allies were nearly here, and her stressful task was nearly over, Katya urged Dariya on.

Turning to pull the knife out of her wall, Dariya glanced at the clock near it.

"I suppose we had better." She nodded.

"We?"

This had been the part where Katya had planned to back out of the action, return to her hotel room and pray it would all work out.

Dariya nodded. "I'm glad you came on time. They don't trust me, I'm not sure they even believe I have any allies. But if you come, they'll know. And they'll be more likely to support us."

A sharp spike of fear shot through Katya. Was this a trap? She was just starting to trust this woman but there was something odd about this.

Why did she have to convince their promised allies to help them?

Then the initial panic faded, and she remembered Nadezhda's uncertain recollection of Dariya saying that she might not be able to control the other Volkovs.

She sighed. If that was the case, she was obliged to help, wasn't she?

"Fine. I'll come along," she agreed reluctantly.

The journey to the train station was short but uncomfortable.

For starters, Diana trailed after the older women and her silence almost had a physical presence of its own.

Then there was Katya's mounting nerves, coupled with Dariya's attempt to compensate for the awkwardness by talking all the time.

It was a relief to arrive. They stood for a few moments but soon spotted their quarry.

A gaggle of people were heading towards them. Dressed in uniform black, with tanned skin and dark hair, they were otherwise nothing alike.

Their ages, genders and body types encompassed a vast range, as did the style of their clothes.

One member of the group bounced cheerfully ahead of the others, running towards Dariya.

He reached them and flung his arms around her. "Sis! We made it!"

Dariya embraced him in return. "Hi Dima."

'Dima' released her and looked over at her companions.

"Is this Di? Wow! She's so grown up!" He moved to embrace his niece too, only to be put off by the intensity of her scowl.

"She always was grumpy..." He muttered.

Trying to lighten the mood, his sister laughed tentatively.

"Sure, sure, she was. But we're not just here to catch up, Dima," she reminded him.

"Oh. Oh yeah, Vasily..." He paused awkwardly. "He's causing trouble again, isn't he?"

"He's trying to take over the local prison. And threatening a young girl... Katya's niece."

Dariya touched her ally's arm for support, but, feeling overwhelmed, Ekaterina didn't manage to say anything.

Instead, the crowd of Volkovs closed in around them, and instantly jumped into the conversation.

"Yeah, and it's hardly a surprise. You and your psycho kids," someone put in sharply.

Diana glared at them and opened her mouth to speak, but her mother laid a hand on her arm.

"You're right. I made a mistake with him. But now it's time to put it right," she conceded.

"And we're with you, Sis!" Dmitri assured her with a smile. "Let's go!"

He turned and was about to charge off into the distance, enthusiastic to begin the mission.

The woman who had spoken out earlier, a tall, angry-looking woman with grey roots in her black hair, stopped him abruptly with a single comment.

"Who put you in charge?"

He looked flustered. "Well, no one, but I'm trying to help here..."

"But no one asked!" A large man in a black tracksuit argued.

Dariya sighed, "Guys, now's hardly the time..." She tried to calm them down.

"Oh, so *Papa's little favourite* thinks she's the boss now?" Her angry older sister turned on her again.

The voices faded into one and Katya couldn't hear herself think.

"What's happening?" She managed to shout desperately above the din.

"Oh, someone always starts an argument about who's in charge. It's how we were raised, to compete. It's worse now Papa's gone, and we don't have a leader, after so many years," Dmitri explained with a remarkably casual shrug almost commentating on his family's argument.

"But I try to stay out of it, it's easier. And I never saw the point in all this anyway. I wish we could just live our own lives."

Blinking, Katya tried to focus on his words.

Something in them managed to pull her back to reality. She shook her head sadly, moved by the implications.

"That's not a family. It's not even *living*."

She hadn't realised how much she took her basic freedom, along with her undyingly supportive siblings, for granted until now.

"That's our way." He shrugged again, dismissing the issue.

"Well, it has to stop!" She raised her voice again. "You all sound like the father you hate so much when you argue about who's in charge!"

Her words brought silence. It was an angry silence though, accompanied by several cold, steely glares.

For once, she didn't let her fear silence her.

"I mean it. You're thinking the way he wanted you to think. You don't need to think like that anymore. You can all be equals. A *real* family. The only one trying to undermine that and take things over is Vasily."

Dariya nodded. "He is. I know him. He won't stop at the prison. And when he has more power, you can bet he'll come to find us. Either for our help or to get rid of us."

The members of the crowd exchanged glances. Then the angry-faced lady shouted out: "let's kick his ass before he can!"

The ensuing whoop made the station guards turn in their direction, and Katya broke into a run, sensing that this was the moment to race to the prison.

This news, had they been aware of it, would have probably been a comfort to those inside the prison. Nikolina was pacing nervously up and now.

"Sis, I know this is scary and all, but you need to calm down or we'll get caught," Sasha tried to tell her.

"I know, I know. But I do not like sitting here waiting for our former enemies to rescue us. *Especially* not while my daughter is in there with that *awful* man!" Nikolina fired back.

"Nadya's strong, she'll pull through," Sof commented optimistically.

She didn't look too convinced though.

And she wasn't. But she was trying to keep her worries to herself in case she said too much. She had promises to keep to her love.

Even if she might never see her again. Even if they had to take the secret of their feelings for one another to their graves.

"I hope so. They've been gone a long time."

Sasha frowned, thinking of his wife's promise to return soon as well.

He sighed. This was a great situation. His wife and niece were missing in this prison full of feral criminals.

He was stuck here with only his increasingly anxious sister and Nadya's hothead of a friend for company, and they were just sitting here, waiting to find out if their enemies or allies got to them first.

Nadezhda sat on the floor, watching over her Aunt.

Maria was laying on the floor where she had collapsed, muttering, and rolling around.

Every time she did so, Nadezhda's panic grew. The woman was muttering about killing... Someone.

Every now and again she would pause thoughtfully, as though listening to some inner voice, then start up again.

Her tossing and turning was growing more vigorous now and occasionally she would hit out. Nadezhda had got the hang of when to duck now, after a few vicious swipes.

She had never realised how strong Maria's attacks were... Suspicions were beginning to assail her. Maria wasn't normally this aggressive.

Was this a part of Vasily's scheme? But what had he done to her? He had claimed it would begin when she fell asleep, and that it would kill her...

Well, she seemed to be alive, but in her sleep, she had become something so far removed from her true self that Nadezhda edged away from her collapsed form anxiously, wondering what she would be like when, or if, she finally awoke.

Her eyelids flickered and she gave a low groan that almost sounded like a growl.

Nadezhda backed away a little further, tentatively calling out.

"Maria? Can you hear me?"

Behind her, the door creaked open slowly and she heard Vasily chuckle.

"She can hear you, but I'm afraid she'll only be listening to me from now on," he informed her smugly.

Maria sat up.

A few moments later, Ekaterina skidded to a holt outside the prison walls. She was breathless, and still unable to believe what she was doing, but she was here.

"Ow! Seriously, bad timing!" Diana grumbled from behind her as she slammed into her back and bounced off.

"Di, chill. And look where you're going," Dariya told her off.

There was a moment's angry silence, broken by someone sniggering.

"Oh, she always was an angry little one, even as a baby. Cute though," Dmitri commented.

Diana glared at him. "And your timing's even worse. *Can it!"* She scowled.

Dariya tried to keep the peace.

"Yeah... Sweet as the memories are, maybe we could do that another time, Bro?" She encouraged.

"I just meant that there's no need to give Katya a hard time, she's trying to help us..." She pointed out.

"Yeah, yeah, I'm trying to help, so maybe we should use that anger for something useful? Like, I dunno... the fact we have to break into a heavily guarded prison?"

It was obvious from her voice that Katya was still terrified. But she was trying.

Diana sighed and gave her mother a slight nod. Their watching family members tensed at that moment.

If even Diana was abandoning other battles for this, then It was a sign.

Now was the time to attack.

Dangerous Setbacks

A roar went up as the mob poured around the walls of the prison and charged at the main gates.

Katya, caught in the middle of the shouting crowd, was pulled with them into something she wasn't even sure if she was capable of.

The confused guards inside the compound looked up, hearing the battle cries, only to see a crowd running at them, which naturally caused panic.

Bodies hit the metal gets and shook them, sending clanging sounds ringing through the courtyard. Their sceptical leader tried to keep control.

"Hah, *idiots,* ignore them. They can't open the gates." He rolled his eyes.

Brute force having failed them for the first time in their lives, the Volkovs changed tactic and began hoisting themselves up the gateposts.

Agile Diana went first, pulling her way up and slashing the barbed wire along the top of the wall. It had cut her hands and torn her clothes, but she always carried a knife and soon had a section removed.

Now the way was clear, her relatives followed her.

"Uh..." One of the guards tried to attract their leader's attention back to the threat.

"Leave it, there's no way they can get through." He shrugged, not even turning around.

Diana dropped down behind him with a thud. A satisfied smile spread across her face. Their break-in had been successful.

And this was important because it was for a worthy cause - really annoying her brother.

Hearing her, the guard spun around and was met with a sudden blow to the nose, staggering back with his hands clutched across his bleeding face.

The guards looked at one another, unsure now.

Obviously, they were hardened criminals with weapons, and they weren't just going to let this random woman assault their boss...

But how should they handle this without a sudden, vicious attack?

While they paused to consider this, Diana attacked again. She grabbed her previous victim, who was still stunned and brought her knee sharply into his stomach.

As he fell to his knees, something dropped from his belt, and she seized it triumphantly.

It was the keys to the gate, which had been carefully stolen from the prison officers earlier.

The criminals-turned-guards looked on, horrified, then sprang into action as she moved to let her less bold allies in.

Katya and Dariya hadn't opted for the climb, but now they could get in. Dariya ran to join her family. Katya trailed timidly behind them.

She didn't have a weapon and the thugs inside did. How much help could she be here?

No sooner had she thought that than a man rushed at her with a knife. She ducked under his arm, and he stumbled straight into Diana.

Angry, the younger woman turned on him and jabbed a key into his eye.

His screams echoed around the courtyard and his fellow guards hesitated again. This woman was clearly insane and had already taken out two of them, what could they do now?

Suddenly, the courtyard was full of people brawling.

The Volkovs were former mob members and had therefore picked up some clear ideas about how to deal with and take out enemies.

They met with some resistance, of course, but having never quite adapted to life outside of their father's mob, the Volkovs were as heavily armed and as vicious as their enemies.

Katya managed to keep herself behind them most of the time. Before long, she found herself standing in a pile of bloodied bodies.

There were a few groans that indicated some had survived.

But those who had wouldn't be in any position to stop them.

"Right. Now for the next lot."

Diana rubbed her hands together smugly and approached the nearest door, brandishing her knife in one hand and her newly acquired keys in the other.

As soon as she had opened the door, her incensed family members stormed into the building and found... nobody.

Just a load of empty corridors. And of course, they had absolutely no clue which ones to follow to find their allies.

They crashed into one another again in their shock, suddenly drawing to a halt.

"Where is he, then? Where's Vasily?!" Diana burst out.

Dariya shook his head.

"I'm guessing he's not just going to stand around waiting for us. He'll have a plan and he'll be putting it into operation so he'll be as strong as he can when anyone comes against him."

She knew how her son thought.

"Great. So, you brought us here for *what*, exactly? If we can't get him right now and *beat the snot out of him*, what's the point?" One of the Volkov men scoffed.

"Um... To find and help Nadya?" Katya put in tentatively.

Diana rolled her eyes irritably. "We're not search and rescue! *Especially* not for his little---"

"Di." Her mother cautioned.

"I know, I know..." She sighed, her rage fading to hopelessness.

"Well, whatever. The point is we don't have to hunt for anyone, and we certainly don't have to stand around arguing, because I happen to have a *plan.*"

She looked around at this point, a smug smirk plastered all over her face.

The other Volkovs began to bicker.

"Oh, so you come up with the *plans* now? *Just* like your brother!"

Even Dariya looked unsure.

"Well, dear, maybe we should just try doing what we originally came here to do."

"No. I want to hear her plan."

Katya's comment shocked even her, but she realised it was probably for the best.

She was the one who had originally brought them here, and God knew she didn't have a plan. She was totally out of her comfort zone here, and she had no idea where to find her niece.

To her surprise, the young woman faltered, stunned.

"Wait, really? You're all willing to follow *my* plan?"

For someone so bitter and sarcastic, she sounded almost vulnerable now and Katya flinched.

Was that her problem? That no one ever validated or believed in her?

Now she felt bad for her, so she doubled down on her decision. "Yeah, we are."

"But--" Someone began to object and was silenced by glares from Dariya.

Dariya turned to her daughter.

"We're listening, go ahead," she encouraged gently.

"Right, yeah..." Diana looked embarrassed by her slip-up and tried to regain her usual fierce composure.

"The plan's pretty simple, we find the nearest guard and beat him up until he tells us where everything important in this place is, then we take over!"

"How... violent of you, dear..." Dariya commented nervously.

"Ha, that's typical, remember when she used to bite me all the time?" Dmitri's timing for inappropriate comments was impeccable.

"Not now, Dima!" Dariya scolded him again, before turning to her daughter. "There's another flaw... How much do the guards know?"

Diana sighed. "I don't know. I was just trying to help..."

"I mean... We don't have a better plan. So, go ahead." Katya stuck to her original reason for supporting the girl.

A slow, grudging smile crept across Diana's face.

"Great... Uh, I mean, it'll be great to finally find out where we need to be. *Let's go!*"

That said, she charged off down a corridor with a mad scream.

The others traded glances and, with varying degrees of enthusiasm, followed her. After all, she had at least found a way around their setback, albeit a dangerous and violent one.

Blissfully unaware of the attack on his fort, Vasily was feeling on top of the world. He had won; he had finally won.

Last time things had gone wrong. But that had been his grandfather's fault. Not this time.

He was cleverer and stronger than he had ever been with his family's 'help'.

Besides, he was clearly making progress. He had taken over a major building in the city, which was apparently spreading panic.

The idea that he could make the silly little law-abiding people panic amused him.

But more importantly, it was a key step. If the people were panicking, they would try to stop him.

And once it became apparent that they couldn't, they would have to negotiate.

Then, he could have whatever he wanted... He already knew what he was going to ask for. It wouldn't be much, not at first. A city wasn't much when you could take the world, after all.

The world, however, would have to wait until his bride was ready... And right now, she seemed a little distressed.

Nadezhda was yelling frantically.

"Maria!"

She tried to get through to her Aunt, shaking as she stared at the other woman's drained blue skin and the blank look in her hazel eyes.

He laughed. She was *so* interesting to watch, he couldn't help but enjoy all her emotions. It was such a pity, what he would have to do to get her by his side.

But the price was worth paying. For their children, and the future of the world. The world that would belong to them.

When her cries seemed unable to reach her Aunt, she swung around and glared at him.

"What have you done to her?!" She demanded to know.

"Ah, so *finally* you take interest in my little demonstration."

He smiled.

"Let me explain. Well, to be quite honest, I did as I said I would. I killed her. At least, the part of her that feels emotions. Instead, I replaced it with a few things..."

"Basic strength stims, of course, and a complete inability to respond to anyone they don't recognise as me. Rather handy, don't you think? Strong, emotionless, and mine to command. Perfect soldiers to help us gain anything we want."

"And you think for a second that I want something like *this?*" She gasped, feeling sick.

"Of course not. I know how difficult you can be my love. Which is why, as I said earlier, I intend to do the same to you before our wedding. Then you'll be on my side."

She backed away from him.

"I'll never marry you, you sicko!!" She screamed, horrified.

He chuckled.

"Oh, but you will. You see, I already have several soldiers, both modified and otherwise, serving me. I'm the only one in a position to make decisions here," he told her smugly.

"Maria?" He added, waving a hand.

Her Aunt's hands closed around her arms and held her tightly as she tried to struggle.

But the other woman was too strong for her to fight, and she sagged, despairing.

If he had several soldiers this strong, what chance did she stand? Or her allies, for that matter?

Even when back-up arrived, it would be futile. They had already lost.

And what would that mean for her loved ones? Death, or something far worse, no doubt.

Growing Tension

Diana charged through the corridors of the prison, adrenaline pounding through her veins and her supporters hot on her heels.

Now she was in charge, she was alive, and the first person she crashed into was going to regret ever being born.

She was going to make this plan work if it was the last thing she did.

Around the corner just ahead of her, there was a sound, small, subtle, and distant, but there, all the same.

She stopped sharply and held up a hand for the others, signalling to them. They drew to a stop.

She pulled her stolen knife out and crept closer, waiting to catch a glimpse of her target, listening intently for more signs of life, so that she could be ready to attack as soon as she rounded the corner.

"I *do* wish they would hurry up," someone was saying. It was a woman's voice, sharp with irritation and worry.

Diana hesitated for a second. This was a male prison, the 'guards' her brother was using were ex-inmates... Had her plan failed already? Or had they finally found their allies?

That second thought excited her again and she threw caution to the wind, racing around the corner.

She almost crashed into Nikolina, stopping just in time. Her allies were right behind her.

Nikolina looked up, stunned, then smiled as it dawned on her who they were and what was happening.

"Thank goodness you are finally here," she said gratefully.

"Yeah, yeah, you're welcome and all, but where's everyone else? I was looking forward to kicking butt and taking this place back," Diana told her, shrugging it off and getting back on track.

Ekaterina hurried after her Volkov accomplices, reassured by hearing her siblings.

"Lina! Sasha! You're okay? Where's Nadya? Where's Maria?" She checked up on them all in one breath, her worry coming rushing back now the adrenaline from the break-up was wearing off.

Sasha looked pained.

"Maria went with Nadya. They're not back yet. It's been…"
He glanced at Nikolina.

"Half an hour," she supplied.

"Nadya? Is she in some kind of trouble?" Dariya asked.

Sof rolled her eyes.

"Yeah, she's in trouble. Your psycho son demanded she went to him, and she just took off! Haven't seen her since," she explained.

Dariya paled.

"I was worried Vasily might... try something," she sighed.

"Well, now we're here, why don't we go and find them? You want her back and I've just been *dying* to see my little brother again..." Diana smiled dangerously at her own suggestion, twirling her knife.

Sasha sighed. "We don't know where they are..." He admitted.

"You didn't get his location?" Diana sounded incredulous at this laxity.

Sof felt she ought to defend their group.

"He wasn't exactly volunteering information, you know!" She pointed out.

"Well… Don't you have your phones on you? I could probably use one to find them."

A tall, lean man in a dark suit stepped forward.

"Great!" Sasha lit up at the idea of finding his wife again.

He pulled out his phone and handed it over to a member of the Volkov family without a second thought. Maria and Nadezhda were more important.

"Why didn't you say so earlier, Vadim?" Diana glowered at him.

"Slipped my mind. Can't imagine what was distracting me." He made stabbing gestures at her.

"Enough. We do not have time for squabbling. We must go and rescue the others," Nikolina urged.

Dariya nodded hastily before her family got started again.

Vadim fiddled with the phone.

"And we're looking for this… Maria, right? The one with three hearts next to her name?" His disdain was apparent.

Sasha looked a little sheepish. "Well, she is my wife… And yes, yes, she's one of the people we need to find."

"Then let's go."

The man set off, leading the army of vigilantes after him.

While her allies came together, Nadezhda felt more alone than ever. She didn't know what to do now, unable to reach Maria or to escape from Vasily.

And now she was afraid of what might come next... Was her own Aunt going to murder her?

She looked up at Vasily and tried to keep the fear from her face, glaring at him angrily instead.

"Well? What now, are you going to kill me? Or get Maria to do it for you because you're too afraid?"

He laughed.

"You're ridiculous, Nadya. Don't try to act tough. And of course not, I need to save you for later, my dear," he smirked at her in a way that made her feel sick to her stomach, before continuing, "I suppose I should have Maria demonstrate what she's capable of though..."

There was a moment's pause while he considered this, letting the dread set into Nadezhda's mind as she wondered how he intended to do that.

Then he gestured to his guards.

"Go and fetch some of the officers we captured," he demanded.

As they left, he looked down at Olga's fallen body.

"In hindsight, perhaps I should have kept her little friend alive for this moment, but she really was insufferable," he commented.

"You're insufferable!" Nadezhda threw back at him, feeling slightly childish for repeating his insults, but sure that if she didn't cultivate her anger, she'd burst into tears instead.

He shook his head, leaning closer to her. He was right in her face now and one of his hands grabbed her chin.

The movement was sudden but surprisingly gentle. She would almost prefer him to hurt her at this point.

His touch made her feel disgusting either way.

He smiled and she watched the lights dancing in his steely eyes. He was enjoying this far too much.

"You'll learn to suffer me, I think, my dear," he assured her smugly.

And at that moment, she hated him more than she had ever done before. How had she ever thought he might help her and be her friend?

How had she ever been attracted to him? All she wanted to do now was punch him as hard as she could.

But Maria's grip on her arms was unyielding, so she could do nothing but stand there, burning with anger.

She was soon distracted again though, as the door opened once more and the guards half-pushed, half-dragged a couple of the prison officers into the room.

She saw the fear on their faces and her stomach churned again.

Vasily grinned.

"Let's finish this little demonstration, shall we? Maria," he clicked his fingers, then pointed to the prison officers, *"kill them."*

And suddenly Nadezhda was released. She tumbled to the floor abruptly.

Maria stepped over her as though she no longer existed and fell upon the officers instantly, her hands grabbing at them wildly, until she caught one of them around the throat and squeezed with such a frightening voice that Nadezhda thought her hands would tear through the man's crushed neck.

She watched in fascinated horror as Maria shook him a few times, checking him for signs of life, then tossed him aside like he was a ragdoll.

The body hit the cell wall with a horrible thump. She wasn't sure she would ever get that sound out of her mind.

Unmoved by the destruction she was causing, Maria simply seized her next victim and began again. Even with the officer's best attempts at struggling, it was over before it had even begun.

"You see?" Vasily turned to her smugly. "Such *power.*"

Suddenly, the anger was back, hotter, and harder than before.

She shook off her sickening fear and sprang up, jumping off the ground with her fist out and putting all the force of her leap into her punch.

Her fist caught Vasily across the cheek and his head snapped sideways with the impact.

It only lasted a moment, but it was deeply satisfying to see the pained expression on his face as it did so, then the look of shock, as though he didn't believe she had hit him.

She only wished she could cause him as much pain as he had caused her.

But that wouldn't be right, then she would be as bad... She started to tell herself as she calmed down, sticking to her morals.

It was probably unwise to suddenly become focused again just as he recovered from the blow, because without her red-hot anger urging her forward, she was defenceless and now he was angry.

He turned his head back to face her, a red mark growing on his cheek and his features set in a furious scowl, all his shock and pain replaced with pure anger.

"You stupid, ungrateful girl!" He spat at her, lashing out and grabbing her.

"You're always making things difficult, aren't you? Just learn to co-operate with me and we can be *great!*"

"Never!"

His grip on her tightened and he stared down at her.

"Yes. Yes, you will!" He growled determinedly.

The group of would-be rescuers had raced through the prison, weapons at the ready, but encountered little resistance.

This was a relief to Sasha, Nikolina and Ekaterina, who followed the Volkovs sedately, whispering worriedly among themselves.

Sof had somehow got a knife of her own and was gripping it determinedly. She had shoved her way to the front.

"You're sure about this little trick of yours?" She demanded of Vadim.

"I'm the best hacker in this family. I can handle it, little girl."

He assured her without even taking his eyes off Sasha's phone.

A growl rose in Sof's throat. *Condescending ass.*

"Forgive me for not trusting a family full of *murderous scum!*" She snapped.

"Why the hell did you bring us here if all you want is to insult us? Got a *Deathwish?*" Diana cut in sharply.

"*Stop!* We're all allies here. And we're here to save people," Dariya reminded them.

"Speak for yourself, Mama. I'm just here to kick Vaska where the sun doesn't shine," Diana commented.

"Now you know why we brought you here," Sof answered back.

"Getting close, now," Vadim called out.

The Battle

Almost as soon as Vadim had spoken, the group rounded a corner and crashed into guards.

Shocked and outraged, the thugs turned on them, and the battle for the prison began in earnest.

Diana stood at the front of the group and swung aggressively at the guards, only the most daring approaching her.

Some of the other guards crept around her and attacked the 'weaker' targets instead.

The Moroz siblings hung back, unarmed, and afraid.

Sof saw them and rolled her eyes at them.

"C'mon, do you want to rescue Nadya and Maria or not? 'Cause they're not going to hand them over without a fight!" She told them.

“Well, what are we supposed to use? I don’t see any spare bars around here, and it’d take too long to get them out of the windows,” Sasha argued back.

He was remembering that last time he had fought by Sof's side, she had pulled some metal bars out of a cell window, and they had used them against their enemies.

The young woman sighed and ducked behind some of the Volkovs for a second of protection while she lowered her own guard.

Then she stooped and pulled some knives out of the side of her boots. She handed them out.

"Now let's get our friends back," she urged them.

The siblings traded glances, then Sasha surged forward. He had learned last time he had had to follow Sof's lead that sometimes, you had to fight.

And he was fighting for his wife this time.

Nikolina sighed, glancing at the furious brawl ahead of her. Could she do this? The image of her daughter's face rose in her mind.

She gripped the knife tightly. Of course, she could, Nadya needed her. She had let her down too much in the past. This time, she would save her!

She pushed forward into the battle, brandishing her knife, only to realise that they had run out of targets. She turned and stared at her allies, shocked.

Diana was standing there, bloody but triumphant. Sof and Sasha stood side by side with set looks of determination on their faces.

The guards' bodies were scattered around them.

Dariya emerged from the group of allies and looked around.

"Well... I think we got rid of most of Vasily's thugs," she commented as she surveyed the chaos.

It seemed to have an effect as well. They all traded glances and smiles, pleased with what they had achieved together.

Then Diana spoke up. "Where to now then?" She asked.

Vadim pointed down the corridor, and, still fired up from their fight, they wasted no time in charging on.

Vasily was completely unaware of this.

He was still locked in a more personal battle, with the woman he was determined to marry, who hated his guts.

At the sound of yells outside, he let go of her hastily, spinning around.

"What was that?!" He demanded to know.

His guards gave him blank looks.

"No idea, sir," one of them helpfully volunteered.

Nadezhda risked a small smile, despite the circumstances. Her friends were finally coming to her aid.

She only hoped that the screams were Vasily's men, not her allies. They had to be winning, or she was stuck here with this madman, and they were in grave danger.

Vasily must have noticed the change in her attitude because he turned back to her abruptly.

"You know something about this, *don't* you, Nadya?"

She glared at him, masking the strange mix of hope and fear she was really feeling behind her contempt for him.

"What makes you say that?"

"It's obvious. I invite you and your friend to come and visit me here and your freaky little crew decides to intervene. It was them the last time, wasn't it?"

"The bouncy blonde with the anger issues and the sneaky little detective, then your stuck-up mother and her law degree..."

He rolled his eyes.

"They were all rather tedious and incredibly persistent when it came to getting in my way. So, I assume they're back for round two."

Nadezhda considered this.

By 'bouncy blonde with anger issues', she guessed he meant Sof, who had strawberry blonde hair and when she had last met Vasily, an intense desire to stab him.

'Sneaky little detective' - That would be Sasha, who had encountered the Volkovs while helping Sof investigate her cousin's murder.

His job as a private detective tended to get him into situations like this.

And finally, there was her mother, the one who had been responsible for putting together the legal case and eventually prosecuting the Volkov family.

Clearly Vasily remembered her team who had helped her before. That only added to her fervent hope that he didn't get his hands on them this time.

If they were captured, no doubt he would exact revenge.

She couldn't bear the idea of seeing her closest family members hurt. At least he didn't appear to know any of her other supporters.

In fact, she had a secret weapon: she was using his own family against him.

He didn't even know Dariya was alive, and yet she had been the greatest help in all of this. She had been the one to arrange it, after all.

So, he was right, she did know something about it, and she couldn't keep that from her face as she thought it over.

So, she admitted it.

"Well, that much is true, but at least I have friends who support me, not just a bunch of brainwashed cons!" She spat at him defiantly, "and they'll take you down for a second time!"

He snorted derisively. "Rubbish, I have loyal soldiers, and you have a band of crazies. They won't succeed."

The noise from outside seemed to be drawing closer.

There was a flicker of doubt on his face, and he changed tactic slightly.

"Now, you must know I care for you more than *they* do. I planned all *this* just for *you.* I spent every day thinking of you... They're just mindless thugs."

"Come with me, we can move to another part of our base together and be safe," he urged, stretching out his hand towards her invitingly.

Someone hammered on the door desperately. "Sir, Sir, please let me in, they're *coming!*"

Vasily ignored his pleading guard, focused on Nadezhda.

"Are you coming or not?" He asked her.

She remembered the last time he had made her an offer like this. He had proposed to her... While holding her at gunpoint. She slapped his hand away from her.

"I'd rather die."

"So be it," he shrugged, "we'll leave you here then. A casualty of the battle is all you'll be."

He turned his back on her and gestured for the guards to follow him. He had bigger things to worry about right now than this blip in his plan, after all...

Opening the door, he grabbed the man who had desperately collapsed against it and dragged him off too, followed by the soldiers from the cell and finally Maria.

Seeing her Aunt walk away, Nadezhda was overwhelmed with the urge to reach out to her and pull her back, but in her mind's eye, she saw the bodies of Maria's victims again and hung back, frightened of what the other woman had become.

Instead, she pulled the cell door shut and crouched in a corner in case the retreating guards came looking for her.

Though she hoped if anyone would find her, it would be her allies, and soon. She didn't know how long she could stay trapped here with three dead bodies for company and a raging battle approaching her.

Footsteps clattered towards her. There was a final scream, then a pause.

Through the bars, she glimpsed Sof demanding information from a man who was leading a dishevelled group.

Most of the group appeared to be Volkovs, and the rest were her family. She smiled. Dariya had pulled through and they had all made it.

Pushing open the door, she sprang forward to greet them, only to have a knife suddenly pointed at her.

"Stop right... *Nadya!*" Sof lowered her weapon and threw her arms around her without another care in the world.

Everyone turned to face her abruptly.

"Oh, thank goodness, you are safe!" She heard her mother gasp.

Sof hastily let her go, as though she had suddenly remembered her promise and thought the gasp was about their embrace.

But Nadezhda didn't care right now.

She would have happily spent hours in Sof's arms after everything they had just been through.

Yet, there was always something else they had to do, something more important to focus on.

"I'm safe." She nodded as Nikolina came over and hugged her as well.

"Good." Dariya appeared next to Nikolina, looking just as concerned. "Did he hurt you?"

"He had a good go, but he seemed more interested in making menacing speeches and messing with my emotions than actually attacking me," she assured her sarcastically.

Behind her sarcasm, she hid the truth. She had been deeply hurt by his emotional attacks.

But that probably hadn't been what Dariya was asking about.

Besides, she hardly needed two mothers fussing over her and demanding to know about all her emotional weaknesses so they could 'help.' Not right now.

Diana interjected with a roll of her eyes.

"Huh, typical Vaska." She couldn't resist an opportunity to moan about her brother.

This comment was largely ignored since a reunion appeared to be taking place instead.

Sasha ran over to his niece.

"Are you okay?" He asked her.

Make that two mothers and an uncle who was almost as bad, she thought as she shrugged it off again.

"I'm fine."

"And Maria?" He pressed eagerly. "Where's Maria?"

"She's not here." Vadim interrupted, "I thought she was, but her location's changed..."

Sasha looked at Nadezhda in confusion. "But... She was with you..."

She looked away, tears springing to her eyes.

How could she explain this? How could she break her uncle's heart with the news of his wife's terrible fate?

They had come here on a high, expecting victory and a perfect reunion and she had to ruin it.

"Vasily... He..."

She managed to choke out a couple of words before the tears took over and she buried her head in her uncle's chest.

He stood there for a moment, stunned. Then the implications of her reaction dawned on him.

"No..." He gasped, paling as tears came to his eyes as well.

Nadezhda was in no state to tell him that it was even worse than he thought, so a heavy, miserable silence took over.

Mourning for Maria's death was an easier burden to bear than revealing that her fate was far darker than death.

Further along the corridor, Vasily's retreat was in full swing. He had re-grouped with several of his guards and they were well away from the attacking forces, who had been stalled by Nadezhda.

There was, however, general panic beginning to spread through his group.

"What are we going to do now, sir? We're losing control!"
One of his guards pointed out, hoping that he had a plan.

Fear of what would happen if this went wrong had
vanished when they had first overwhelmed the prison
guards, but it was now steadily returning.

"Shut up!" Vasily snapped.

He couldn't have panic now, or he may really lose control.
Not just of the prison, but of his allies. He couldn't have
that, not now, when he had been so close to total power.

"We are *not* losing control!" He reiterated.

"But... But we can't fight them off," His uncertain ally
responded.

"Quiet!" His temper was really fraying now.

"Of course we can! *We're* in control here, not them.
Besides," he pulled some keys from his belt and grinned,
"we have one weapon they are powerless against..."

As one, the group turned to look at a group of cells at the
far end of the corridor.

As he held up the keys, Vasily's unnerving grin reflected in
the glinting metal. He wasn't defeated; he was merely
preparing a counterattack.

His first plan may have failed, but he was quickly adapting it so that there was no way it could fail again.

The silence of the mourning group was suddenly broken as shuffling footsteps echoed down the corridor towards them.

"Uh, anyone else hearing that?" Dariya suddenly asked, nervous.

She knew that her son was a schemer and that he probably had a plan. So, anyone approaching them right now was probably a bad sign.

"Yeah, what *is* that?" Ekaterina seconded, nervousness in her voice.

Diana raised her knife again.

"Hopefully it's Vaska. I've been looking forward to kicking his butt..." She grinned.

Her grin faded again rather sharply as a pale blue arm shot around the corner and tried to grab her.

The others watched in alarm and Nadezhda raised her tear-streaked face.

"Run!" She instructed as she spotted the approaching creatures.

The Mutants

Nadezhda's desperate cry was enough to send the allies fleeing back down the corridor they had just charged into.

The mutated warriors kept coming though, shuffling towards them with surprising speed.

They walked over the bodies of the fallen guards blankly, barely acknowledging they were there.

"What the hell are those things?" Sof demanded to know as she ran alongside Nadezhda.

She could hardly think of them as human, even if the outline was. They were a strange blue colour, and their bodies moved ... wrongly. It was disturbing just to glance back at them.

"Vasily's latest weapon... He's changing people with it. Turning them into emotionless super-warriors who only take commands from him," she explained.

"That's insane!" Sof gasped.

Diana appeared beside them and rolled her eyes. "Yeah? Only just noticed that he's a little short on sanity?"

"Like you can talk." Sof shot back. "Your whole famil-"

"Less arguing, more running!"

"Definitely more running!" Dariya agreed, sounding frightened.

She had been prepared for murder, mayhem, and insanity, knowing her son well. But she hadn't quite been ready for his latest weapon.

So, everyone sped on, trying to keep their focus on running. There was a sudden curse from behind them and some mix of fear and curiosity made them glance back over their shoulders.

Someone had fallen, tripping on the body of a deceased guard. The mutants were closing in.

"Vladlena!" Dariya cried out, half-turning back.

"Leave her!" Nadezhda grabbed the woman's arm and pulled her away.

"Leave her? She's my *sister!"* She protested.

"Huh, didn't know you lot were big on playing happy families," Sof muttered under breath.

"Sof, please!" Nadezhda protested.

She sighed and her arguments faded to a mutter. She was trying her best to tolerate the Volkovs.

After all, Dariya seemed trustworthy, and the others were helping... But she couldn't exactly put aside all her feelings on them in one go. Not after everything that they had done.

After hushing the bickerers, Nadezhda focused on Dariya.

"I know, and I'm sorry! But I've seen what these things do... There's no way you can help her. There's no way to save her," she told her.

"Just keep running. *Please!*" She implored her.

It was bittersweet to say. She remembered the feeling of helplessness all too well. There hadn't been any way to save Maria either.

Dariya nodded tearfully and continued to run, risking the occasional glance back.

All that gained her was the sight of a mutant grabbed her sister by the head and snapping her neck as though it was a twig, then dropping her to the ground carelessly and marching forward, its eyes still blankly staring at them.

"Holy..." She gasped.

"I know, these things are pretty serious..." Nadezhda nodded miserably.

By some unspoken agreement, everyone sped up again, motivated by the haunting scene behind them.

For a few minutes, everyone ran on in silence, and then her sharp-minded mother asked the question Nadezhda had been desperately praying that nobody thought of.

"And how exactly did you learn about these awful creatures? Did he set them on you?" She demanded to know.

Nadezhda sighed. She was running out of ways to put this off, but at the same, she couldn't bring herself to share the full details.

"Not *exactly...*" She began tentatively.

"I... I think we should discuss this another time, right? When we've got to safety somehow," she deflected again, too anxious to tell the truth and reveal her Aunt's fate.

"Very well." Nikolina nodded in agreement.

After all, escaping from these monsters was their priority, they could probably all agree on that.

Besides, it was obvious that her daughter didn't want to talk right now.

Sof looked up ahead and pointed.

"We should be fine if we can get through there, right?"

She gestured to a large set of double doors up ahead that should lead them back into a different wing of the prison.

Nadezhda glanced behind her doubtfully.

"I'm not sure doors are going to keep these things at bay. Then again... *Anything's* worth a try right now."

"Really? Why not just try stabbing them then?" Diana cut in.

"They're already dead, in a way. Besides, they'll probably rip your head straight off! Just aim for the doors!" Nadezhda responded.

So, everyone hurtled towards the doors and threw themselves through them in a desperate attempt to reach safety.

Sasha grabbed the heavy doors and slammed them shut behind the group.

"Did... Did we make it?" Sof panted, tired from running but hoping that her plan had saved them from the mutants.

"I-I *think* so." An equally out-of-breath Nadezhda managed to nod.

"Great. So now what do we do? Because we're basically trapped in here with Vaska's latest creepy toys trying to get in and rip our heads off or whatever," Diana pointed out dramatically.

"Is she *ever* happy?" Sof quipped, looking around at the Volkov crowd with a roll of her eyes.

"Not really, not since she was a kid--" Dmitri began, before his niece's fiery glare shut him down instantly.

Nadezhda cleared her throat to try to get the conversation back on track.

"She has a point though. We do need a plan."

"Well, you seem to know the most about them. What do you suggest?" Nikolina quizzed her.

She stared blankly at her mother's expectant face, her mind racing desperately. What could they do?

Vasily was very clever and hadn't left any clear weakness. He had specified that they answered only when they could see his fa---

Something slowly dawned on her as she looked at the other expectant faces watching her. He wasn't *that* clever, was he?

A clone who had set his secret weapon to rely on recognising him.

The room was pretty much *full* of his look-alikes right now.

She gestured to the assembled Volkovs.

"You can stop them! Vasily said they only take orders when they recognise him... They don't look that bright to me, and you all share features." She explained excitedly.

"If only you had remembered that a little sooner, no one would have died out there," Diana snapped.

Nadezhda sighed. She got the feeling she was never going to be able to win with this girl, even when they were working together.

Diana had hated her from day one and she still seemed determined to argue with her at every opportunity.

Dariya stepped in instead. "What matters is that we know now," she pointed out. "We have to get out there and stop them."

Sasha sighed and grabbed the door again.

"Well... If you're sure about this, are you guys ready to try?" He asked.

Dariya surveyed her family members.

There were a surprising number of nods, though some were more enthusiastic than others.

The doors were yanked back by Sasha, who proceeded to let out a whimper and let go of the door again. It slammed shut with a bang.

"What the hell? We were about to stop them!" Diana protested.

"Maria..." Sasha groaned, shutting his eyes.

The image of his wife, pale as a corpse, lurching towards him murderously attacked him again through the darkness.

Nadezhda looked up at her pale, trembling uncle guiltily.

"Vasily did it to her... I-I'm so sorry, I wanted to protect her, but..."

"What's the problem?" Diana, not remotely considerate of the current emotional situation, cut in bluntly, "we're going to free them anyway."

Sasha slowly opened his eyes. Despite his usual calm demeanour, he fixed the young woman with a glare.

"I'm sorry for being upset at seeing my *wife* as an undead monster trying to rip my head off my shoulders!" He snapped sarcastically.

She had the decency to look a little sheepish.

"I didn't realise..." She murmured.

He took a deep breath and fought to calm down.

"Alright. Not your fault..." He nodded, then turned to Nadezhda, "nor is it yours, Nadya. Now, let's do this."

He motivated himself again, hoping this would work so he would be reunited with his wife again, without the danger that she might snap his neck.

The doors were pulled open one last time and the mutated army shuffled closer, almost upon them now.

"Quickly, please!" Nadezhda urged.

She was ignored. The Volkovs were focused on their task. They lined up in front of the attackers and joined forces, following Dariya's count-in.

"STOP!!"

Their yell seemed to fill the whole building.

The warriors stopped in their tracks.

Diana stepped forward.

"From now on, no matter what happens, you follow us, okay?" She commanded.

The assembled warriors nodded slowly.

"Wait, no," Dariya put in.

Her daughter turned on her. "Why not? We can use his weapons against him!"

"*Or* we can give these people their own minds back," Dariya pointed out, "that would be better, and then they would surely join us against him anyway," she argued.

Diana shrugged. "Whatever."

She stepped aside, letting her mother take over.

Dariya approached the mutants. "You're free now. Think for yourselves once more," she encouraged.

There was no discernible response whatsoever.

"I'm not sure that's going to help," Sof pointed out, "if he's created some device to get into their heads, the only way to fully free them is to make a counter-device. But look at it this way, at least they're no longer murderous."

"That's something," Dariya sighed, "but I hoped to help them."

"I'll see what I can do." Sof promised, thinking to see if she could make up a device of her own.

Her cousin had invented the cloning machine that had spawned the Volkovs, after all.

And between his inventions and her time at engineering school, she'd learnt a few tricks of her own.

Sasha wandered over to Maria, who was still staring blankly through him.

"I hope you can help..." He murmured sadly as he looked at his wife's empty, emotionless face, before sighing and turning away, unable to bear seeing her like this anymore.

"I hope so too. But while I'm working on that, what's our next plan?" Sof replied.

"Catching up with Vaska, hopefully." Diana insisted, still carrying her personal vendetta against her brother with her.

But she wasn't alone in that. Nadezhda nodded in agreement.

"It's about time he paid for all this. And after the destruction you lot caused on your way to me, I think he's just about all that's left to deal with, right?"

"In that case, finding him is definitely imperative," Nikolina agreed.

"I believe this development calls for a planning session," she added, always insisting on organisation and discussion, even in the depths of a battle with a psychotic ex-mob member in the middle of a prison.

She had a point though, so the group retreated to work out their next steps.

They were going to need a surprisingly good plan to end this brutal battle once and for all.

Putting The Plan Into Operation

The planning meeting got underway, minus Sof.

Instead, she began a crude design of something that she supposed she could make with her limited resources that would help free the mutants from the control of the Volkovs.

Her ideas came together from what she guessed he had done. They were stone cold and 'dead,' she needed to find some way to reanimate them, to warm them up and breathe no life into them.

She couldn't think of a way to create super-strength, so she couldn't concoct an antidote for it, but that was a secondary problem. Giving them life came first.

Dariya opened the conversation. "What should our main priority be from now on?" She asked.

"As we discussed, we need to get to Vasily." Nadezhda reiterated their earlier agreement.

"I've got to agree with her there." Diana nodded. "And it shouldn't be too difficult. All he did was run off around the corner, right?" She snorted. *"Wimp!"*

Sof sighed and got up, abandoning her plan for the time being.

"Look, I don't want to throw a spanner in the works, but there's something else we need to do first. It's more important."

She glanced over at the mutants, standing numbly on the edge of their group.

Nadezhda followed her gaze.

"Right. The machine. We need to stop him from making more mutants," she agreed.

The others nodded thoughtfully.

"Let's smash it up!" Diana encouraged.

"That should stop him," Nadezhda agreed.

"Well then, why don't you girls go and smash his toy while I go and find him? It's about time he and I were reunited." Dariya suggested, clearly having a lot to say to her son-turned-enemy.

Five years of pretending to be dead just to avoid his attacks had given her plenty of time to think on how this conversation would go.

Diana scowled.

"I was looking forward to seeing him too. Besides, you're not to go off on your own," she told her mother sharply, suddenly protective.

"You would go too far, too soon. I want to talk to him before you try to gut him," Dariya retorted.

"Well, that's true," Dmitri grinned, "and before you scold me, I was just going to offer to help you, Sis, so I do have something useful to say this time."

Dariya smiled. "You always do; no matter how much Di complains. And I'm sure she'll be glad if I have some help. So, feel free to come along."

"May I come too? I feel you and I have a lot to discuss. And if I stay here, I'll be worrying to death about Nadezhda," Nikolina said.

Nadezhda shook her head. "You really don't need to."

"But any mother would." Dariya was understanding. "You're very welcome."

"Are we ready then? We seem to have two teams and two plans, so the rest of us can hold the fort here and you might as well get to it," Nikolina suggested.

"One mo…" Sof jumped up from her work. "I'll come along with you, Nadya."

She gave her secret love a sweet smile, before shooting a look of deep distrust towards Diana.

"What about your... Thing?" Nadezhda answered, gesturing to a strange heap of contorted metal laying on the floor.

It was a series of twisted up cell bars, forced into something resembling a badly woven basket.

In it, there was a pool of deep black liquid. A fuel of sorts, probably coal based. Sof had found barrels of it hidden in a side room.

Now, she looked over it critically, then shrugged.

"I'm nearly done, I just need to heat it up, but we can do that when we get back."

"In that case, you're definitely welcome to come!" Nadezhda grinned, glad to spend some time with Sof, and know that she had her back on their mission.

Even though they hadn't made their relationship official, Sof was the one she trusted most, as well as the one she had missed the most.

"Time to go then," Diana interrupted as the two gazed at one another.

She stepped between them and wandered off, heading for the door.

"Coming?" She demanded to know, turning back to glower at them.

The two women sighed and followed her, exchanging brief, hidden glances as they did so.

"Well," Dariya spoke up as she watched them walk away, "I suppose we had better go too."

They headed back to where Vasily had last been seen, retracing their steps.

As they walked, Nikolina sighed.

"This hardly seems real, does it? I have spent so many years of life in the shadow of Antonin's death and now the man responsible is gone. Now all I must do is protect my daughter. And when Vasily is gone, that will be done too. What happens when all this is over?" She mused aloud.

Dariya shrugged her shoulders.

"I don't know. So far, I've only known life under my father's regime and life in hiding..."

"We all have," Dmitri put in, "but once we've got Vasily out of the way, I suppose it's up to us...”

That was a strange idea, and he fell into a deep silence as he mulled over it.

“Of course.” Nikolina nodded.

That, too, was unreal too. She wasn't used to thinking of the Volkovs, seeing things from their point of view.

But Dariya's sudden appearance in her life had changed that. The strange bond the other woman had had with her dead husband made them the only people true to his memory.

But her newfound friend sighed. “I don't know how we'll manage.”

“You need to learn to help one another,” Nikolina spoke up.

“I had to learn to trust my siblings again after I shut them out. You can learn to trust one another; I am sure of it. And I will stay in touch, so that... If there's ever anything I can do to help...” She trailed off.

"You want to help us? After all this?" Dmitri's voice was incredulous.

"Why would I not? You are not bad people because your father was. Dariya was a devoted friend to my Antonin, and you have all risked so much by coming here today, just to help us. In fact, is that not your first step? You claim to be always fighting, but when it came to it, you were willing to all come together," she pointed out.

Dariya smiled. "I was, Antonin gave me hope for a future without my father. I'll never forget him. Nor you, and your daughter. For his sake, we're a kind of family now."

She took the other woman's hand in hers.

"And you're right. We can do this."

In her other hand, she clasped her brother's, squeezing his fingers gently, "will you help me? Like you did back then?"

"Of course." Dmitri was a little choked up, but he responded warmly.

Now it was Nikolina's turn to be surprised.

"You helped Antonin too? I thought he was alone, except for Dariya."

"Dima watched over him when he came back to you. He didn't know. I couldn't tell anyone, but I had to try and do something, and Dima has always been the only brother I could trust," Dariya explained.

"Tell me about those times."

The words came slowly and uncertainly. Nikolina had shut out thoughts of her youth, those days with her husband, before his murder, for so long.

But now, amongst friends who remembered him, it wouldn't hurt so much.

They began to reminisce about one of the hardest, yet most hopeful times of all their lives.

Further along the corridor, another conversation had broken out. The girls' discussion wasn't quite as friendly or heartfelt though.

Diana had decided it was about time to air some of the unspoken issues between them and went straight for confrontation with Sof.

"So," she had begun, "why did you decide to tag along? Don't trust me with your precious little friend?"

The sarcasm riled Sof a little, and she glowered at her.

"No, I don't trust a backstabber alone with my *girlfriend!*" She hit back, forgetting about their secret in the face of Diana's withering scorn.

The other woman's behaviour annoyed her far too much for her to be subtle.

Nadezhda sighed. "Can we not have this conversation right now?" She pleaded.

No one listened.

"Seriously? I don't know why you think you need to lie to us all, but it's quite obvious you have some cutesy little thing going on…" Diana rolled her eyes at Sof's indignance.

They hadn't exactly acted like 'just friends' from the start, hence her sarcasm.

Though it was her chief form of communication anyway.

"See? She keeps mocking us! She's *starting* it!" Sof protested.

"Yeah, I am. And we *are* having this conversation. You know why?" Diana was no longer sarcastic.

She was spitting with anger now.

The others exchanged shocked glances and mutely shook their heads, nervous of what was to come.

The rant continued, now Diana finally felt able to unleash her irritation.

"Because you two are waltzing around pretending you're better than me! So, I made mistakes in the past. You think it was easy for me, that I had a *choice?* I was trying to impress my grandfather because that's how people in our family *survived!*"

There was a hot, shocked pause, a silence full of tension.

When she spoke up again, her voice was softer than they had ever heard it before, far more human and tinged with grief.

"I had a sister, once. A twin. Her name was Vera, and she gave me hope. Because she didn't want to be a part of that world. When my grandfather found out... He made me shoot her in cold blood.

"If I didn't, I would have died too. We were twelve. Perhaps I did become a backstabber then, perhaps it messed me up, because I was 'the strong one', the one he chose, and I had to fill the role."

Silence fell again. The other girls were reeling. How could anyone have done something so horrible?

And how had someone survived that? Badly, that was how. Diana was the angry, messed up person she was today because of Vladimir's legacy of pure evil.

Diana wasn't finished.

"So, I learnt to. And apparently, I did it well," she sneered with contempt here, contempt for her grandfather's praise and for her own actions, "then Vaska came along and suddenly he had a new favourite. I had to compete with him to get anywhere, even though I gave my heart and soul for that role!"

Finally, Nadezhda found the courage to speak up again.

"So, is that why you attacked me? Because you wanted to impress him and get one over on Vasily?"

The other woman nodded in response.

"Those are two reasons. The third... Well, at the time, I *hated* you. You seemed to have life so easy. I guess I was wrong about that."

The final sentence came grudgingly, but it came all the same.

"Damn right, you were!" Sof gloated on Nadezhda's behalf.

"No, you weren't. I thought I was so hard done to at the time, just because my mother wanted to protect me. And I didn't think about people who had it worse than me..." Nadezhda cut in, interrupting before a fight could start.

Diana still didn't meet her gaze, reluctant.

"I guess we're both messed up because of our families then."

Nadezhda nodded, giving a little smile. It had been hard to start working with Diana, the woman who had betrayed her before, but finding some common ground and understanding the other's - albeit warped - reasoning made her feel a little better.

Sof seemed a little reassured that the others were getting on - her main reason for distrusting Diana was Nadezhda's safety.

But she still wasn't one hundred percent happy with the idea, so she changed the subject, re-focusing on their current goal.

"Well, now we're all messed up in some way, because of your stupid brother. So, let's go and smash his little plaything up!" She urged them on.

This time, for once, the three women all agreed, and they continued their charge along the corridor.

Finally, they came to the door of Vasily's old cell, where his machine rested in the corner.

At the same time, Dariya, Nikolina and Dmitri approached their destination as well. They had found the next wing of the building, where Vasily was hiding now.

They lapsed into silence, dropping one another's hands, and reaching for their weapons, getting ready to face him. He must be close.

It became obvious that they were right when he opened a door up ahead of them and stared at them in shock.

He had just concocted a new plan and regained his confidence.

But as soon as he stepped out to put it into operation, he was met by the ghostly sight of his apparently deceased mother bearing down on him.

For Dariya, it was finally time to confront her evil son.

The Beginning Of The End

Vasily froze as he saw Dariya approaching.

"Yes, I'm here, and I'm real. I know you thought I was gone. But I heard about your little plan to get rid of me ahead of time. My death was faked," she explained, knowing he was in shock.

He thought he had killed her five years ago.

She remembered his smug smile as he threw her from a balcony at their family home...

"So, you tricked me and lied to everyone about it? Oh, and I thought you were meant to be the *nice* one, mother dear."

Sarcasm dripped from Vasily's voice.

"You tried to kill me. I'm sorry, Vasily, I hoped you were better than this, but if you keep acting this way, you'll have to pay for it."

Dariya seemed genuinely saddened by this, even after all he had put her through.

He laughed.

"You really think so? You're still as stupid as you were back then! We're done here," he scoffed at them and turned his back on them, moving away.

The door was forced open again and they were able to run through in pursuit, but the guards inside moved to block their way, closing in around them.

Dariya drew her knife and attacked, stabbing into one man's chest.

He went stumbling across the room, with an ear-splitting scream.

While his would-be-attackers fought off the guards, Vasily fled from his hideout and looped back around through the maze of corridors that made up the prison.

He had to get in a position to put his brand-new plan into operation, after all.

He had had a rethink, and he knew what to do, he just had to start doing it.

So, he needed to head to his former headquarters, the cell that had both imprisoned and freed him. He hoped his guards could be relied on to keep the people chasing him at bay while he got back there.

The last thing he named was his irritatingly moral mother breathing down his neck about how terrible he was, with her stupid goons in tow.

Thankfully, his guards seemed to be doing their jobs - that was, dying so he didn't have to - and it didn't take him very long to find his cell again.

He hurtled back in and stopped sharply, cursing. Just when he thought he had got away from them, there were more meddlers here!

The annoying blonde with the anger issues was holding a knife over his precious creation, inches away from ramming the blade into it.

That would cause who knew what kind of catastrophic damage!

Without even thinking about it, he released a deafening roar.

"STOP!!"

Sof's knife clattered to the floor, and she spun around.

"Ugh..." She groaned at the mere sight of him.

He opened his mouth to retort and was interrupted.

"Ah, Vaska. We finally meet again." His sister was standing nearby with a knife in her hand and a glint in her eye.

"Di!" He gasped.

Okay, so she had escaped from prison, of course he had heard about that.

But why was she *here?* Unless she had come to join him! Yes, of course, she would want to be his second-in-command now he held all the power.

"Di, help me! Get this crazy woman," he gestured at Sof, "out of here. The other one's mine..." He turned his attention back to Nadezhda.

She glared at him. "What makes you think I'd want to do that?"

The look she was giving him was horrible.

He was beginning to suspect she was serious about not helping. Which meant...

"You're with them!" He gasped.

"Wow, aren't you the clever one?" She retorted. "Yeah, I'm with them, because even when I've been stupid towards them, they treat me better than you, my own brother, ever did!"

"Fine, fine, be foolish if you wish. But I warn you, betraying me now, when I'm gaining power, is only going to get you hurt," he rolled his eyes.

"Speaking of which, Nadya, Dear, changed your mind about the wedding yet?"

"There's not going to *be* a wedding!" Nadezhda snapped back at him insistently.

He laughed.

"Of course there will be, you'll come around. Of course, you'll come around, after I..." He glanced over at his machine, "change your mind." He smirked.

"You stay away from her!" Sof growled, suddenly furious as she darted forward, stepping in front of Nadezhda protectively.

To see someone speaking to her love like that made her blood boil.

"But she's mine." Vasily countered. "Aren't you? Tell her, Nadya."

"I'm not yours. I never was. As soon as we even considered getting together, you turned on me." Nadezhda pointed out.

Vasily shook his head. *"Diana* betrayed you, not me. And you seem quite content to pal up with her again."

"She had her reasons." Nadezhda stated calmly as she saw Diana open her mouth to scream at her brother.

She didn't want her to get upset again, after everything she had revealed before.

"Besides, if you really cared, you would have defended me. You didn't even *try!"* She turned it back on Vasily.

"Oh, come now, that wasn't that serious. I knew you would handle it in your own way, and you clearly did, because we got together again after that. I helped you in your little quest or whatever it was..."

He sounded scathing now, "and then it was *you* who betrayed *me!* You led me into a trap!" He accused her.

Sof couldn't resist arguing back at this point.

"No, you stalked her, barged into my house and then you got what you deserved!" She told him.

"What I deserve? But what I deserve is only the best! I'm clever, talented, and the best part is I'm not afraid to take what I want, however ruthless I have to be to get it. So, I think you'll find you're all wrong and *Nadya will be mine!"*

Vasily threw his head back and laughed dramatically, making the women exchange uncertain glances, wondering just how insane he had become since he had been imprisoned.

Then Diana rolled her eyes.

"Oh, I've had enough of this. Your stupid little villain act has gone on far too long, and I certainly didn't come here to talk about whether or not some girl will marry you!" She protested.

Vasily took a step towards her, glowering at her as he stood over her.

"So, what are you planning to do about it, Sis? You can't whine to *Grandfather* like you used to if you didn't get your own way. Or *Mama*. So now what?"

Diana looked at the knife in her hand, sorely tempted to stab him.

But a better idea surfaced from somewhere deep her memories of her brother's flaws, and she smiled.

"I know. You always did make the stupid mistake of putting a self-destruct button on all your favourite 'I'm a big bad villain' toys..." she taunted.

There was a brief flicker of fear on Vasily's face.

His self-control was good enough for it to be gone in a second, but a second was all she needed to tell her that she was onto him now.

"You *have*, haven't you? I wonder where you put it..." She stepped towards the machine and examined it carefully.

He lunged at her, trying to pull her away, but she had been expecting an attack and neatly side-stepped away from him, sending him crashing into the wall with a bump.

She giggled, then turned her attention back to the machine.

"Hmm..." She walked around it a little way and looked down, seeing the red switch at the back of it.

"Ah, there it is!" She grinned triumphantly.

Vasily sprang up off the ground and tried to grab hold of her, yelling, *"no, don't touch that!"*

It was too late. Diana leant down and flicked the switch with one easy movement.

She stood up and turned her grin of victory on her brother, who stood there staring, shell-shocked.

The flames rose behind her and the sudden, intense heat on her back made her glance around, her smug smile fading fast.

Already, the fire was winding itself around the machine, and rogue, outlying flames climbed steadily up the cell walls.

Horrified, Diana broke into a run. Sof and Nadezhda were seconds behind her.

But Vasily snapped out of his horrified state just fast enough to grab Nadezhda's arm as she hurtled past.

Sof and Diana were already in the corridor, and so Nadezhda's desperate attempt to grab at them and free herself failed.

Vasily pulled her back into the cell and held her in his arms while he shoved the door shut with his foot, trapping them both in the raging inferno.

Outside, Sof and Diana cannoned down the corridors, focused on getting away from the fire. They crashed into Dariya and her group coming the other way.

"What's going on, where's Vasily?" Dariya questioned breathlessly.

"Never mind that, we have to get out of here! There's a fire, this whole place could go up!" Diana told her hurriedly.

Nikolina looked around fearfully for the flames. Then she thought of something else, something noticeably missing.

"And where is Nadezhda? Did she go to warn the others?!" She asked.

"Nadya!" Sof gasped. "She must have stayed behind!"

It dawned on her that the other woman hadn't been running with them.

"We have to go back and get her out of there!" Diana pointed out, uncharacteristically determined to help.

Despite the tense situation, Dariya risked a smile.

"You guys bonded then," she commented.

Diana looked sheepish. "I guess."

"Great, because you'll have to go and get her. I have something else to do!" Sof told her.

"What? She's your girlfriend!" Diana gasped, apparently oblivious to the idea that that was meant to be a secret. Or just too shocked to care.

"I know..." Sof looked torn for a second, "but this is important for all of us."

"What is?"

The girl gave a mysterious smile.

"Oh, just warning the others, of course."

She obviously avoided a true answer, then shot off in the direction of the others before she could be subject to further interrogation.

Dariya turned to her daughter. "It's up to us to save Nadya then."

"I'll go. You get to safety," Diana insisted, worried for her mother.

"You're sure?" Dariya lingered, equally concerned about her daughter.

"Positive, now go! I'll take care of the rescue," she told her firmly.

"I'm so proud of you," Dariya whispered as she turned to leave, emotional at seeing how her daughter had changed from the vicious, angry young woman she had been to someone willing to risk her life rescuing another.

Diana blinked the tears from her eyes as she watched them go.

She hadn't been ready to hear that. But it was motivation, after all.

She had to make her mother proud and get Nadezhda out of the fire before anything worse could happen.

She turned and began to retrace her steps, back along the corridor, growing hotter and hotter as she did so.

The smell and the heat of the fire were obvious now, making her feel as though it was closing in around her.

Fire

Sof ran back to the wing of the prison that Vasily's enemies were using as their headquarters and threw open the doors.

People turned to stare at her, curious as to what was going on now.

"Everybody, get out of here! There's a fire!"

Immediately, panic broke out and people scrambled for the exit.

She moved aside and let most of them pass, hoping they would make it to the exit before the fire spread.

But she stuck out her arm as one of the Volkovs passed, determined to stop someone.

"I need your help!" She insisted urgently.

"What now?" Vadim sighed.

She pointed to the mutants, standing idly by the wall with no idea that they were in grave danger.

"We can't just leave them here!"

"Fine," he groaned, "shall I tell them to move their sorry butts out of here?"

"No, just get them to follow me, then go on your way," she told him, a little sharply because of his reluctant attitude.

She picked up her contraption and nodded to him to go ahead.

"Alright, follow her," he ordered them, pointing to her.

They began their march towards Sof, and she set off determinedly ahead of them.

Her reluctant assistant turned his back on them and fled the building with the others.

A dishevelled and anxious crowd was gathering outside, glancing at one another to check who else had escaped and whether they were hurt.

Nikolina pushed her way through the crowd in a panic, searching desperately. She grabbed her brother's arm.

"Sasha! Are you okay?"

He was in tears. "I left Maria in there!"

"Nadya isn't with us!" His sister added, tears welling up in her own eyes as well. She had failed her daughter again!

Ekaterina rushed over to join them. "Is she still in there?"

Nikolina shook her head tearfully. "She's with Vasily. Diana went back for her," she explained.

As one, the three siblings turned to look at the burning building, their eyes were drawn to the flame-filled window where Nadezhda was trapped.

Her fate was in the hands of the Volkovs now.

The room was almost entirely surrounded in flames now, and the couple stood in the middle of the raging fire, on the small patch of ground that wasn't burning.

The heat was unbearable, making Nadezhda feel as though she had already been engulfed by the flames.

She looked up at Vasily pleadingly.

"What on *earth* are you doing? *Trying to kill us both?* Let's just get out of here!" She tried to persuade him to leave with her.

Yes, they were enemies, yes, he had endangered her, but it might be her only way out of the fire.

And she could always arrest him after they had escaped.

He laughed in her face.

"We're not going anywhere. If death's the price I pay for this, so be it. But I *will* have my way," he told her stubbornly.

Nervousness kicked in now, and Nadezhda wished she could back away from him.

But the fire was pressing closer, giving her the choice between his arms and the inferno. She reluctantly stayed close to him as she questioned what came next.

"What way? What are you planning now?"

"Really? You've forgotten already. Oh, Dear Nadya, how foolish. What I'm planning is our wedding and our future together, of course. The whole point of all *this...*" he reminded her.

Nadezhda did take a step back now, changing her mind.

The burning heat in her back was better than dealing with his constant advances, not to mention his horrible little plan to change her own life and make her into some evil queen for himself, some jewel in his crown, some prize...

His grip on her arms redoubled.

"No, don't start with this again. We are going to this, even if it's the last thing we do. I will die knowing *you're all mine...*"

His hands on her were like a vice and she couldn't tug herself away from him.

He held on tight and jumped into the air suddenly, pulling her up with him, over the blazing fire and somehow onto another patch of free ground.

"There, we're married now. Jumping over the fire is an ancient tradition, surely you can't argue with it," he told her with a smug smirk.

"if only I had my knife, I could mark you as part of my family..." He added, slightly disappointed.

"What *are* you on about?!" She blinked, confused.

He pointed to the scar on his cheek. "Our family mark."

"*I'm* not one of your little clones!" She spat at him.

He shook his head.

"That's nothing to do with it. It's a loyalty mark. We all put it there on purpose, to show our true nature. And now you're mine, my true nature and yours are the same..." He smiled.

"That's sick and insane! A little flame doesn't make me yours!" She retorted.

"Really?" He rolled his eyes. "You're even more difficult than I realised. Why are you so determined to make this hard, when we could be some happy and so powerful together?"

"Because your idea of happiness involves *killing* people," she pointed out.

He gave a deep sigh, looking away from her for a moment.

"You know, even after all my hard work, I had considered not doing this to you. Out of love. But I'm afraid your nasty little 'morality' problem really has to go. It's holding us back."

He turned back to her, the flames reflecting in his glinting eyes.

The rest of his face was suddenly completely impassive.

This was almost as freaky as his usual insane grins.

He advanced on Nadezhda, and again, she was without anyone to back away from. His grip on her grew tighter as he pressed himself closer.

She squirmed against him, trying to pull away, but he held her tightly and spun her around, turning her towards the heart of the fire, his dying invention.

He leant down and kissed her, his lips against her making her stomach churn. After a second, he pulled away again.

"Goodbye, Nadya, darling. Until you wake up."

Before she could even process that, he put his hands on her shoulders and pushed her backwards with all his strength.

She shot backwards through the flames and shut her eyes, bracing herself for the stinging burns.

They never came. Instead, she plummeted to the ground, crashing against it hard. There was a sticky splash.

The machine's weird jelloid liquid seemed to have saved her from the flames, leaving her too submerged to be burnt.

But at what cost? She waited numbly to experience whatever the others had been through.

At least she would find out what had happened to Maria... And she wouldn't even be able to be upset over it if Vasily's explanation of the machine was truthful.

Nothing seemed to be happening, apart from a growing pain in her legs.

She glanced up, through the jelly, at the blue-tinted world. A twisted lump of metal was sticking out of the side of the machine.

Her legs were caught on it, suspended in the air.

The fire soared higher around the machine, flickering against her legs.

Her screams never came out, they were drowned by the jelloid liquid.

Again, the machine was choosing between two terrible fates. It was too broken to turn her but had left her more exposed to the fire than she had realised.

Vasily appeared over the side of the machine and peered down at her curiously.

She saw him smirk again as he looked at her, stuck in this stupid position, her fate swinging between two awful options.

Rage boiled up inside her and she managed to pull one leg free, kicking at him.

He grabbed at her leg and twisted it, but the unexpected blow had knocked him, and he couldn't regain his balance, stumbling into the blaze behind him with a scream.

She allowed that thought to satisfy her a little, knowing that she had got some kind of revenge upon him.

It wasn't what she would normally do, preferring justice to revenge, but after the lives he had ruined, perhaps inflicting similar pain on him was a kind of justice for his victims.

Besides, feeling better about hurting him at least distracted her from the excruciating pain in her legs.

One leg was caught on the spike of metal, and she couldn't shake it loose, the flames were assailing it.

The other was twisted at a nasty angle from Vasily's desperate counterattack and was also sticking into the raging fire.

She couldn't move either of them now. The suspicion that she was about to die was creeping into her mind.

After all, there didn't seem to be any way that she could get out of the machine, and even if she could, the fire would claim her.

So, this was the end. Vasily had been right, they would die together, trapped in the blazing prison as the fire spread throughout the building.

She wondered faintly if they would be dead before the structure of the prison began to crumble in on them as well, or if it was too much to ask that she was spared another kind of pain on top of everything else.

Then, as everything grew blurry and distant, she thought of her family and friends, wondering if they had cleared the building yet.

Of course, they had, Sof went back for them. *Sof... Sof would help them.*

They had to have got out, otherwise, it wasn't even worth it to get rid of Vasily. It would have been too great a sacrifice.

And now she couldn't think straight anymore, so she lay back and listened to Vasily's screams and the crackling of the rising flames.

There was a distant creak, like the sound of an opening door somewhere. But that was the last thing she heard before she passed out.

Vasily was going through a similar thought process. Agonising pain was attacking his skin, but he was trying hard to concentrate on these last moments.

Because he knew it was over, and that he was going to die.

So, he hadn't succeeded in taking over the world, as he had always planned. But he had, at least, got Nadya to himself.

Despite all her resistance, she had endured the same fate as he had at the same time. And before that fate arrived, they had been joined together in marriage.

He smiled to himself, though just that small movement hurt his burning flesh. In that way, at least, he had won because he had got his own way there.

He had won over his mother too because he had easily escaped from her pathetic attempt at revenge by lecture.

The only annoying niggle left was that Diana had finally beaten him.

His sister had always longed to kill him, he knew that. And he had considered doing the same to her.

She seemed to have beaten him to it. But the others, the weaker ones, they had lost.

It was only someone with the same set of beliefs tattooed - forcibly, by their shared past - on her heart that was able to beat it.

Didn't that just prove him right?

Oh, their mother had shared the strength of their blood and some of the same features of their upbringing, but she had shunned it and changed herself, becoming weaker. So, she had been unable to stop him.

Whereas when he had changed, it was only to grow stronger, to throw off the shackles of his grandfather's ways and make something of himself.

And Diana... *Had* she changed? She couldn't have because she had known how to beat him. And yet... She had been with those...

Ahh, the concentration was slipping, and the pain was growing. He couldn't go on this way. The fire was going to claim him.

His sister. His sister, backstabbing as ever and... helping.

The thought seemed insane.

He wondered if the pain was messing with his mind, but he seemed to be wondering that through a deep, intense fog in his head. Something somewhere moved.

A mere breeze passing by him, a sound somewhere that appeared to be very far off.

He tried to open his eyes and see what was going on, to check if someone had come back to rescue him or if Nadya was trying to escape the fire.

His eyelids wouldn't move. Instead, the deep blackness that lay behind them surged towards him and engulfed his whole being, leaving him lying on the burning ground, completely unconscious.

The flames danced across his form, covering him more and more as time marched on uncaringly.

A Happy Ending?

Diana pushed through the pain as she stepped into the furnace of a room. The flames lashed out at her, but she pressed on.

She stepped over the fallen, burning body of her brother and stopped, looking down.

Was he alive and merely in such pain that he had passed out? Or had she killed him?

Perhaps it was stupid to pause here, but she had to be sure. If he found some way, any way at all, - however slim the chance was - then he would be back to haunt them all, she was sure.

She crouched down and grabbed his wrist, smacking the sparks off her hand before it could set her alight as well. She felt for a pulse.

Nothing. He was gone.

Dropping his wrist, she stood up, feeling guilty for feeling as though a great weight had lifted from her shoulders.

Vasily was her brother; she should cry for him or something. But all he had ever done was make her life much harder.

She walked away from his smouldering corpse and pushed onwards through the fire, biting her lip against the pain.

She had to find Nadezhda. Her sharp eyes scanned quickly for any sight of her, a strand of brown hair, a splash of the blue of her dress, anything that would tell her where the girl was.

In the end, it wasn't her eyes that came to her aid but her knowledge of her brother's twisted mind, again.

Nadezhda had been trapped alone with him, and so there was only one place where she would be.

She approached the blazing machine nervously, afraid of what she would find.

A dead burnt, mutilated body, perhaps... Or Nadezhda might just be alive. There was only one way to know for certain. She peered over the edge.

Nadezhda was lying on the bottom of the machine, half engulfed in jelly. That, at least, had protected her.

And the machine was also broken, thank goodness. So at least she wouldn't be transformed.

Her legs were burnt beyond recognition though, twisted up as well.

Her heart in her mouth, Diana leant forward and dipped her hand into the machine, searching through the jelly until she could find Nadezhda's wrist and grasping it, feeling for a sign of life.

For a moment, nothing happened. Then she felt it, the faint, feeble beat beneath her fingers.

She was alive, *just.*

Just was enough. Enough for Diana to spring into action, pulling on her arm hard until she managed to tug the girl free from the substance with a squelch.

Then she lifted her onto her shoulders, stumbling under her weight for a moment until she adjusted and straightened up.

Carrying Nadezhda's weight across her shoulders, she staggered through the flames, her eyes blurring over with the pain and smoke filling her lungs, making her splutter.

She held her breath as tightly as she could and pushed on, knowing she had to get herself and Nadezhda to safety but unsure of how far the fire had spread and much further she had to go.

She ducked down, keeping low to avoid the rising smog and heat and pushed forward.

The corridor had filled up with heat as well now, and there was thick smoke everywhere. How was she going to get out now?

There was only one way, and that was to persevere, so she forced her way forward.

The stinging burns on her skin and the lack of fresh air to breathe were beginning to make her feel lightheaded, but she kept going.

She had come so far; she couldn't stand the idea of failing now!

Besides, she had promised her mother. Earlier, when she had volunteered to save Nadezhda, it felt like the first time that her mother had been proud of her, and she didn't want to give up now, ruining it all.

Her whole life had been a competition for her grandfather's approval, by doing horrible things to innocent people.

All her mother wanted was for her to save a life.

It would be so typical of life and yet so unfair if this was the first task for her family's approval that she cared about, and the first that she would fail to complete.

These bitter thoughts filled her head and urged on, although the rest of her body was begging her to give up, telling her there was no way out of here alive.

Somewhere up ahead of her, she heard a voice.

A distant whisper at first, seeming as though it was a mere figment of her imagination. Then it began to grow louder and clearer as she stumbled forward.

There was still someone else in the building. Who had been insane enough to not run away when they had the chance?

This raging inferno was surely too dangerous for someone to have stayed behind...

Perhaps they had come back for her. No, who would throw away their lives to save hers?

Maybe one of Vasily's men had become trapped in the building. That seemed far more likely than a sudden, unexpected rescue attempt from her allies.

The voice was getting louder, even as the rest of the world seemed to grow more distant as her blood pressure plummeted.

She staggered onwards shakily, hoping she found the other person before her legs gave out completely and desperately praying that they were on her side.

If she reached them, only to realise they hated her and would leave her to die, then everything would have been in vain.

Sof's desperate mission was growing harder.

Against all odds, she had managed to make something - even in this dump, with no real resources - that would reverse the curse Vasily had been inflicting on his prisoners and victims.

But now, to activate it, she had to wait for the heat to spread to it.

And as she stood in the corridor with hundreds of the mutated people watching her blindly, she wondered how many lives would end here and now if it didn't work.

The device lit up, glowing bright orange as a flame caught on it.

Knowing the next part would be the hardest, she took off her jacket and beat the flame with it, extinguishing it.

The metal was still glowing with the heat. She wrapped the jacket around her hand tightly, protecting it, before bending down and grabbing the device.

Straightening up, she aimed it at the blankly staring, glassy-eyed crowd and took a deep breath.

"Well…" She said to herself, "this had better work, or we're all screwed. So, I guess it's now or never."

She pushed a button through the layers of fabric coiled around her hand and waited.

Slowly, humanity began to return to the gathered people.

The light came back into their eyes, and they were suddenly free of the controlling voices in their heads and the intense headaches the mind-altering had brought about.

Maria shook herself and blinked. It felt amazing and yet surreal to be back to normal, as though she was lucid dreaming or something.

Around her, others shook their heads and looked around hazily, as confused as she was.

Then she froze up as the memories poured back into her head.

The feeling of crushing a man's throat with her bare hands assailed her and she stared down at her blood-stained fingers in pure horror.

Her head swam with the enormity of that thought. She had killed them in cold blood, in front of her stunned, helpless niece.

And then... She remembered chasing her allies down, reaching out to try to grab her own dear husband with murder in her heart.

Sof could see the distress in the eyes of the newly restored people and the penny finally dropped as she remembered what Vasily had forced them all to do for him.

"It... It wasn't your fault," she tried to reassure them, "the stuff he's been using is a powerful mind-altering drug. There was nothing you could do to fight it."

"And that makes it *better?*" Maria questioned when she finally managed to find her voice, still incredulous about the whole affair.

"It doesn't make it better. The only thing that would make it better would be if I could undo it. I can't do that. All I can do is tell you it doesn't define you, to try to take away the guilt," Sof did her best to explain.

Maria managed a feeble nod as she processed that.

"It doesn't define us..." She repeated in a stunned whisper.

"Not at all. Now, this building is burning down, so let's get out of here first and discuss it all later!" Sof added as she noted the fire, still spreading.

She dropped the device she was holding on the ground and unravelled her jacket, scowling at the scorch mark.

Still, ruining her best hoodie was better than burning herself.

She threw the jacket over her shoulder and broke into a run.

The others, still emerging from their dazed state, looked at one another, at the flames, and then at Sof's running shape.

Then they bolted as well.

A dishevelled Diana stumbled around the corner, charred in various places, and struggling just to walk. Nadezhda kay across her shoulders, dead weight at this point as she was still unconscious.

She was just in time to see that the voices had belonged to her allies, but they were just leaving. Sof had nearly reached the prison doors. Soon, they would leave her behind completely.

She couldn't stay here to die, not when she had been this close. There was no way she would make it alone.

She swallowed her pride for the first time in her life and tried to find her voice, coughing to clear her throat of smoke.

"Wait!" She called out to them desperately.

Everyone ground to a halt. They turned and looked back.

Sof saw her standing there, looking as though she was barely alive, with another figure slumped over her shoulders.

The flames blazed up behind her, close enough to singe her back.

"Everyone, keep going," Sof told the freed mutants.

Diana felt her heart sink. So, this was it, she had been abandoned to her fate.

She knew Sof didn't like her much, but she thought her help might count for *something.*

Especially since she had done all this to carry the other's girlfriend to safety on her shoulders.

Some of the others gave her doubting looks.

"Are you sure?" Maria asked.

"Yeah, you lot get yourselves out. I'll go back," she told them, turning around, though she was the closest to the door, just inches from her freedom now.

She began to run back along the corridor as the others fled towards the door instead.

By the time Sof reached her, a stunned Diana was swaying on her feet. Sof's arm slid around her waist, catching her, and pulling her up.

"I got you, it's okay..." She heard the other girl reassure her.

"I thought you were leaving me..." She mumbled faintly, drips of water cutting through the hot ash that was caked to her cheeks.

Was she really crying about this?! No, of course not, her guard was just down because it had been so hard, she tried to tell herself.

"Let's just concentrate on walking, right?" Sof told her, picking up on her lowered guard and fierce pride enough to brush over the incident.

Side by side, the two women walked down the corridor towards safety.

Someone pushed the door open from the other side. An anxious Nikolina stood in the doorway.

"Nadya?" She called as she saw figures in the smog.

Dariya appeared at her side.

"Diana?!" She called out.

The two concerned mothers watched, united in their prayers for their lost daughters, as the figures limped towards them, growing clearer as they did.

Diana and Sof reached them in the doorway and Sof pulled her arm away, letting Diana fall into her mother's embrace.

As she did so, Sof reached up and lifted the unconscious Nadezhda down from her shoulders, laying her in her arms gently.

She heard Nikolina gasp.

"Nadya!" The older woman covered her face and turned away, grieving for her daughter, who looked, to her at least, like a broken China doll as she lay in the other's embrace.

Nikolina turned into the comforting embrace of her two siblings, who felt her pain and rushed to grieve with her.

But Sof just knelt on the courtyard's stony ground with her girlfriend in her arms, feeling empty.

They could have been so great, have done so much, and they had spent so little time together as a couple.

Had they ever even *been* a couple? It seemed that Vasily had snatched that experience from her, and yet, they had loved one another enough to take him down...

How cruel of the world to let her say 'I love you', but never live out the love?

She had been robbed by fate, and it seemed she could do nothing. Nadezhda showed no sign of waking up.

Slowly, Sof lay her down on the ground and reached up one hand, running it along her cheekbone gently in a loving caress.

"Nadya..." She whispered as tears began to blur her vision.

"Sof..." It was a gentle murmur, barely there. But it was enough.

She blinked away her tears and looked down. Nadezhda's eyes were open, just barely. The merest flicker of blue watched her lovingly.

"Nadya!" She gasped again, this time feeling a rush of joy.

Nikolina turned back to look at her daughter and her heart leapt. She had been sure that she had lost her daughter for good. Now, she was awake again.

Nadezhda looked past her grinning girlfriend and saw her.

"Mama, don't cry..." She whispered. "Just... Call me an ambulance, please," she added, the pain in her legs becoming too much to bear again.

Ekaterina pulled out her phone. "I'm on it, Sis. You guys have some time."

Nikolina gave her a grateful smile.

"Diana might need the ambulance too," Dariya chipped it to tell her in a concerned tone as she propped up her daughter.

Diana scowled. "I'm fine!" She snapped.

"You don't look fine, missy," Dariya scolded.

Diana sighed. Well, she didn't have a choice now, did she? Her mother was the only member of her family she was sure loved her.

"Fine." She shrugged, playing it off.

"There." Dariya smiled. "By the way, I'm very proud of you, honey!" She gave her another hug.

"You're embarrassing me!"

"But you deserve something," Nikolina put in, from where she was sat, on the ground beside Sof and Nadezhda.

"For saving my daughter. Thank you." She smiled, taking Nadezhda's hand gently.

"You saved me? Yeah... Thanks..." Nadezhda managed to speak up as well.

Diana shrugged. "Don't thank me, thank Sof. She saved me."

She gave the other a grateful look. "Thanks..." She managed sheepishly.

"You went back for my girlfriend when I couldn't. I wasn't gonna turn around and leave you both to die, was I?" She retorted.

"Wait, your *girlfriend?*" Ekaterina cut in, lowering her phone, and giving Sof a hard stare.

Nadezhda sighed. She still wasn't ready to have this conversation.

"Katya, not now, please..." She implored.

Nikolina raised her head, smirking at her out-of-touch sister.

"You did not notice?" She asked. "Seriously? They've been joined at the hip…"

"Thank you! I'm not the only one who noticed!" Diana agreed.

"Katya, the ambulance, please?" Nadezhda reminded her Aunt, hoping to end the interrogation for now.

Her Aunt sighed and turned back to her call, letting the chatter lapse into silent moments of reunion.

Questions gave way to gratitude that they had even made it this far.

Families shared their first moments of peaceful appreciation for one another…

"There, are we all caught up?" Sasha suddenly interrupted, having felt a little lost in the sea of conversation about who did what.

"Not quite," a familiar voice said, falling on his ears like music.

"Maria!" He gasped, spinning around.

The couple flew into one another's arms.

"Maria." He repeated. *"You're back!"*

"Not exactly." She inspected her own arm. "I'm still a little blue, but otherwise, I'm okay. And I'm so sorry!" She added, hugging him tighter.

"For what, telling me you'd be okay then not being?" He quipped.

She swiped at him playfully. *"No!* For trying to hurt you!"

He rubbed his arm. *"Ow, that hurt!* But seriously, that wasn't your fault!" He insisted.

Maria glanced at Sof, expecting an 'I told you so', but the other seemed too busy with her girlfriend.

She turned back to Sasha. "I'm glad you can forgive me. Wait, did I really hurt you? I barely touched you!"

"Super strength, remember?" One of the other ex-mutants interrupted.

"We kept that? *Wow...*" Maria's tone was thoughtful, as though she was considering the implications of her new ability.

An Almost Perfect Day

It wasn't until much later, at the hospital, that Nadezhda started to recall everything that had happened.

Slowly, she gathered her memories of the events and considered them.

She had been injured badly in her fight with Vasily. But his plan to change her into a mutant had failed, and he was dead.

So ultimately, she and her allies had won, finally managing to stop his sinister plans. She had made her peace with death knowing that, then someone had come back and rescued her.

She didn't know who, she just remembered the door opening and then waking up outside the burning prison. Later, she had come to the surprising realisation that her rescuer was Diana.

But that had only made what had followed sweeter. Not only had she been reunited with her loved ones, but her old enemies were on her side now.

Everyone, excepting their enemies, had escaped from the blaze. Maria and the other mutants were free from the mind-control Vasily had inflicted on them, and the Volkov family had been freed from the shadow of Vladimir's evils.

His grandson's attempts to follow in his footsteps were truly over.

The rest of the information about the aftermath of their quest came to her via visits.

After she had had her broken legs reset and her burns had been carefully treated, a gaggle of her allies turned up to visit her. Her mother seemed to be leading them.

She told her that Yaroslavl prison had completely burnt down now and would have to be rebuilt.

They had made the news apparently, and there had been a big party.

Nadezhda was a little saddened that she had missed the celebration, but more than happy to see her allies get the recognition they deserved.

It wasn't until later in the week when the partying had died down and Nadezhda's doctor had okayed more people at a time, that the rest of the group crowded into her room to see her.

A smiling Dariya had plenty to say. She greeted her softly.

"Hi, sweetie. How are you feeling?"

"I'm okay, thanks. I mean, I can't walk, but I'm okay." Nadezhda's answer was a convoluted attempt to reassure her.

"Well, I have some good news to make you feel better," she told her.

"I'm all ears."

"There'll be no more attempts to live up to our family's legacy of evil. My father and my son are dead, and no one else is going to try. The last of my siblings have left today, gone to make their own lives. I gave them what I could to help them. I've had more experience, after all. Since I faked my death, I've been doing things my way. But even I'm free now. I don't have to look over my shoulder."

This did get a smile out of Nadezhda.

"I'm glad to hear it. I hope it goes well for them. And that you can build a better life now. I suppose Diana can too, now she's not a fugitive."

Diana, who had only needed the one day in hospital but was still looking a bit sore, rolled her eyes.

"I guess. I have no idea how to though. I guess I have to hang around and bug my mother."

Nadezhda saw her give a small smile at that. She was glad to see Diana was recovering, not to mention developing a slightly easier-going personality now that her family had some peace.

"We'll figure something out," Dariya assured her.

"In fact, I kind of have a plan. I thought of setting up a little community centre, especially for people like us. I got the idea when I was helping my siblings. There's nothing for us, so we have to look out for one another. I thought you and I can run it. Maybe we can work with some of the local authorities that don't hate us. Maria seems nice, she might help."

"I'm sure she would," Nadezhda assured her.

Diana hesitated. "Nice idea, but working with the cops? Hah, yeah right. They don't care about people like us."

"That's what your grandfather tried to tell us," Dariya cut in sternly.

Nadezhda hauled herself upright and nodded.

"It's not the truth. My father helped Dariya when he was here. I would help if I was closer. I'm sure Maria will do what she can, even if some of her colleagues aren't supportive."

"Oh, that's what this thing with Nadya's father connecting you was about? He *helped* you?" Diana, wanting rid of the subject, teased her mother instead, her voice dripping with sarcasm.

Dariya turned red. "He was like a *brother* to me!"

"So that makes you my Aunt. I'm glad of that." Nadya smiled.

Grinning at another distraction, Diana poked her.

"That makes *me* your cousin, which gives me free licence to torment you."

The subject wouldn't be dropped that easily.

"Look at you two getting along! And Nadya's a cop, so…" Dariya folded her arms pointedly.

"*Fine.* We'll try it," Diana conceded.

"And I'll do my best to help," Maria finally spoke, stepping forward to join the Volkova women by her niece's crowded bedside.

Sasha was hanging onto her arm.

"Can we share some news of our own, now that deal's made?" He asked.

Mother and daughter shrugged in unison, so Nadezhda nodded. "Go ahead."

Everyone turned their expectant eyes on him.

"I guess you haven't shared this with anyone else yet, either, huh?" She commented as she saw him shift a little nervously under their sudden, intense gaze.

He shook his head.

"I wanted everyone to come together so I could say this. We didn't want to detract from the wedding, when we were last all together, so we were planning to have a party just to announce it after our honeymoon, but thanks to Vasily we didn't exactly have one, so... Babe?" He looked over at Maria.

She rested one hand on her slightly swollen stomach and gave them all a smile.

"I'm pregna-!"

Someone instantly grabbed Sasha and hugged him tightly.

"*Yay!* Can I babysit?" His youngest sister asked him as she crushed him in her arms.

"Katya, I live in Yaroslavl, you live in Moscow. There are 173 miles between us. It's a bit far for babysitting," he explained patiently, shaking his head at her.

"Are you at least gonna name it after me?"

"If it's a girl, sure…" He agreed, not wanting to upset his child-loving sister too much.

He knew she was just overly excited to be an Aunt. Ekaterina loved kids and missed babysitting for Nikolina when Nadezhda was small.

Nikolina had a calmer approach, hugging her sister-in-law and brother as she congratulated them in a much more relaxed way.

Something dawned on Nadezhda.

"Wait, is that why you were so worried, in the corridor before Maria and I went on our mission?" She asked Sasha.

He nodded. "Of course! I didn't want to lose any of you, my niece, my wife, or my future child…"

"I didn't realise it was going to be that serious…" She admitted.

It was a sobering thought, but not as much as the idea that crept up on her next.

"*Wait!* Have you checked that the baby *is* okay? After everything that happened…"

Suddenly the congratulations halted, and everyone looked pale and serious for a moment. But Maria soon reassured them.

"Don't worry, I got checked over. The only risk is that the baby might inherit some of my super strength," she explained, "and possibly blue skin."

Everyone gave a collective sigh of relief.

"Well, the worst that'll do is people might call them 'bluey' or stuff at school, it won't have hurt them like it could have. And if they're real strong, they can probably handle that," Ekaterina commented, sniggering at her own joke.

Nikolina shook her head. "That is not funny!"

Before a debate could break out between the sisters about whether the joke was funny, Sof pushed her way through the crowd of visitors.

She looked very serious and Nadezhda felt a flutter of nerves. Was there more news to come? Would it be good or bad?

"Is that all the family news?" She asked. After a number of nods, she spoke up again.

"Great, because I really need to say this," she paused, taking a breath, and taking hold of Nadezhda's hand.

"Nadya, look, I'm really sorry to do this, I know you asked me not to make a big deal out of our relationship. But I figured, since all this stuff with Vasily is over, I should tell you the full truth. I love you *so much*. And I'll be honest, I was so *freaking terrified* that I was gonna lose you as soon as I had had the courage to make you mine! When you were laying in my arms like that..." She faltered, her voice betraying the fact that she was on the verge of tears.

Nadezhda clasped her hand tightly.

"Sof, I..." She began, upset at seeing her this distressed.

Sof held up her other hand.

"No, please, let me say what I have to say," she begged her, even though she was in tears now, "I don't ever want to think I'm losing you again, okay? I want to know that you're mine, and you're always going to be by my side...

"So ... Let's call this what it is. Let me tell everyone you're my girlfriend. Because I want to shout it from the rooftops. Let's be together. You can move in with me, or I'll move in with you. We can start a life together, while we still have the chance."

Nadezhda held on to Sof's hand tightly, tears in her eyes as she realised that her love was right. They had nearly lost each other, just like her parents had.

They needed to make the most of what they had and celebrate their love while they still could.

Somewhere behind them, Diana pretended to throw up.

But despite all the joking around from her newly adopted cousin, Nadezhda concluded that the day had been as perfect as it could be for a day spent in the hospital with two broken legs.

And then, in one swift, simple movement, it was ruined.

As the excitement died down, Maria pulled something from her pocket.

"Oh, I almost forgot! This was delivered to the police station. It's from your branch, Nadezhda. I said since I know you, I'd pass it on." She plonked an envelope in her lap.

"Thanks."

She nodded to her and picked it up, turning it over to check the return address. It was indeed from the unit where she was training as a police cadet.

"I wonder what it's about..." She pondered aloud as she tore it open.

"Probably want to tell you you're a hero." Maria shrugged.

Nadezhda tugged the letter from the envelope and unfolded it, her eyes scanning over lines of text. She visibly paled.

"No, it's not..." She murmured.

"What is it then?" Nikolina asked, a little worried by her daughter's odd reaction to the letter.

"The chief of police there has heard about everything we did, but he doesn't approve because we didn't follow procedure and wait for the police to tackle the situation legally. So, he's firing me..." She explained.

Nikolina snatched the letter from her daughter's fingers and read over it.

"He cannot do that!" She protested.

"He *is* doing..." Nadezhda replied numbly.

It had been an emotional rollercoaster ride of a day, and she just lay back in the hospital bed, wondering what the hell she was supposed to do now!

Fixing The Problem

As soon as the news was out, the room became a buzz with anger. This seemed like a major injustice, especially after everything Nadezhda had already been through.

She had done it to save others, only to be turned on when it was all over. Protests came from all corners.

Sof resorted to using some very choice language. Diana started making some very nasty threats towards the police officers responsible for the decision.

Maria shook her head.

"I could talk to my higher ups, but I really don't think they'd do anything..." She sounded miserable.

Sasha's brow furrowed at his wife's comments. He had hoped she might be able to help his niece, but she made it sound impossible.

"Why not?" He asked.

"I've been losing confidence in the systems within the force lately. It just doesn't seem as though anyone cares anymore," she admitted sadly.

Diana rolled her eyes.

"Seems pretty obvious to me. No compassion for anyone who really needs help, either," she muttered bitterly. "Knew we trusted those asses too soon."

The police force had been her grandfather's number one enemy for a long time, despite the fact that they never truly threatened him.

For a while, they had taken bribes from him, then they had simply ignored the Volkovs, afraid and embarrassed to deal with the source of that old scandal.

And when they had eventually caught him - only due to external work - they had labelled the whole family criminals instead of helping them.

Sof wasn't enthusiastic about them either, having witnessed their lack of care first-hand when her cousin was killed.

"Yeah, exactly. Why don't you just quit? They're clearly failing you all together, not to mention the way they're treating Nadezhda..." She pointed out, more than a little irritably.

Maria looked stunned by the suggestion that she quit.

"Do you not know what else to do?" Sasha asked her tentatively, "because you can always help me with my private detective work..." He offered.

"Thanks, but there's actually something else I was already considering," she admitted.

"I got talking to a few of the other..." she hesitated, unsure of the correct word, before settling on, "people who were affected by Vasily's machine. We're planning to put together a specialised unit of prison guards. All of us will be extra-strong and able to make sure nothing like this happens again. Since no one else came to help when the riot got out of control..." She mused on that for a moment.

"So, I guess we're not gonna try and find other idiot cops to work with..." Diana turned on her mother.

Dariya shook her head.

"I think this is a sign that we need to figure it out for ourselves, don't you? And we will." She sounded determined now.

"That's great for you and all, but we're getting distracted here. How are we going to help Nadya? 'Cause we can't just lie down and take this!" Sof butted in indignantly.

"I don't really think there's anything else we can do..." Nadezhda objected wearily.

She was still devastated, but she had more or less accepted the news now, too tired to fight it and worn down into resignation by her Aunt's complete lack of faith in the idea of help from within the system.

"Of course, there is." Nikolina tried to cheer up her daughter. "There is always something that can be done. Even when it really does not seem like it."

"Oh, yeah? What do you suggest then?" Sof questioned, without a great deal of confidence.

This just seemed like a typical motivational lecture, full of empty proverbs about hope and believing in yourself.

"What I suggest is that we go and pay this chief man a visit and talk it over with him," Nikolina told her.

Sof sighed. Of course, the old 'just talk it out' solution, which had probably never solved anything.

"And what happens when he tells you to get lost?" She asked sharply, scowling at the older woman for her useless advice.

Nikolina stared her down calmly.

"If that happens, then we can sue him for every penny of his department's precious state funding for unfair dismissal," she announced triumphantly.

This got a much better reaction.

"*Damn right we will!*" Sof cheered, brightening up.

Nadezhda even managed a smile as well, and the others nodded and shouted out their support.

And so, a few weeks later, Nadezhda was finally discharged and allowed to begin the trip back to Moscow for a meeting with her ex-boss.

She was still struggling to move her legs and so was taken from the hospital in a wheelchair.

They were also given crutches, which Sof forcibly wrestled into the back of Nadezhda's car before she lifted her girlfriend from her wheelchair and into the car.

Others squashed in.

Sof had taken over driving, and Nikolina sat beside her with a notebook on her lap, already furiously planning out her argument.

The journey was long and uncomfortable as always, but once they arrived at the other end, Sof located the local police station's car park and pulled into it aggressively.

It was only Nadezhda's cautionary comments that dissuaded her from doing a handbrake turn.

With that attitude in mind, Nadezhda refused to tell her suddenly overly interested girlfriend which vehicle belonged to the chief.

Instead, she allowed her mother to help her from the car and hand her her crutches.

She hobbled inside, accompanied by Nikolina.

Sof had decided to stay in the car, which was probably a good thing, given her attitude towards Nadezhda's sudden termination.

Nikolina strode inside like she owned the place, her daughter hobbling along behind her, and stepped straight up to the desk.

"Yes? What can I do for you?" The man behind the desk demanded to know haughtily.

Nikolina glared at him for a second, then adopted an even worse tone herself, determined to win this.

"We would like to see the chief here. As soon as possible please, as it concerns a pressing legal issue."

The man scowled at her but gave a reluctant nod and disappeared into the maze of back rooms behind his desk.

A few moments later, he returned and beckoned for them to follow him, before leading them through the back into the chief's office.

Nikolina pulled up a chair and directed Nadezhda to sit down.

She was too tired from the effort of moving herself with crutches to protest about her mother's bossiness, so she simply staggered to the chair and collapsed over it.

The chief, a large jovial-seeming man, watched from behind his desk with apparent amusement.

Once she was settled, he turned his attention to Nikolina and finally spoke up.

"Well? What seems to be the issue here, Ma'am?" He questioned her.

"The issue, *Sir,* is your treatment of my daughter," she gestured to Nadezhda. "A former employee of yours."

She dropped the letter he had sent Nadezhda onto his desk and stood back, her arms folded, as she waited for an answer.

He picked up the letter and skimmed it, his ever-present grin vanishing as he did.

"Seriously? What's your problem with this?" He demanded to know.

"Is that not obvious? The reason you allegedly dismissed her for would be completely unfair. She saved a city and possibly more than that." Nikolina pointed out.

"She didn't follow procedure," he said bluntly, "besides, look at the state of her! How could I take her seriously and train her like that?"

He pointed to Nadezhda's crutches dismissively.

"She handled a genuine emergency. And as far as I am aware, it is not legally sound to refuse to employ someone based on their injury or disability. But if that is your final answer, I will quite happily relay it to a judge," Nikolina told him icily.

"Whatever, woman, just get out of here!" He snapped at her, waving her away.

Nikolina helped Nadezhda to her feet and swept out. All the way home, she sat quietly, scheming, and plotting for their day in court.

The day soon arrived and Nikolina did what she did best, brought the case calmly, despite her personal involvement, and efficiently.

The judge didn't take that much convincing, seeing as Nikolina had the letter and a recording of her altercation with the chief.

Nadezhda walked, as well as she could, away with some monetary compensation and a satisfied feeling.

She had also been offered her job back but had come to the conclusion that she didn't want to work for that man ever again.

Granted, she had no idea what she was going to do instead, but she would just have to cross that bridge when it arrived.

"Excuse me, Ma'am?" Someone spoke up behind her as she was leaving the court.

With some difficulty, she spun herself around on her crutches.

"I'm sorry to bother you," the woman she had turned to face began, "but my name's Elena Davydova, I'm a reporter for Justice magazine."

"We've been following your case, and we wondered if you'd like to come and work with us. We report on injustices and offer legal advice to those in need. Given your work with the police, you should be in an advantageous position to help us. What do you think?"

She finished her offer with an open question and a friendly smile.

Nadezhda smiled. That was pretty much perfect timing, a new job opportunity was just what she needed, and this way she would be able to go on helping others.

"When can I start?" She asked.

Happily, Ever After

Months ticked by without any more trouble starting and everything had been quiet in Nadezhda's life.

She had eventually recovered from her injuries and returned to her everyday life, getting on with her new job in peace.

But now she was back in Yaroslavl for an especially important reason.

She strolled into the hospital, arm in arm with Sof. Nikolina followed behind, they followed the signs through the building and located the maternity ward.

Once they were there, it wasn't too difficult to find Maria's bed.

A crowd had formed around it. Dariya and Diana were there, bearing gifts to help the new arrival get a good start in life.

There was also a small group of blue-skinned people in prison officer uniforms, presumably Maria's co-workers.

They were a strange-looking bunch, but the gathering nevertheless seemed incredibly happy. At the centre of it,

Maria was lying in bed, with Sasha standing by her side, holding a bundle in his arms.

Ekaterina immediately broke away from her family and ran over.

"Let me see!" She begged.

Sasha smiled and handed her the bundle.

"You're lucky, he's just stopped yelling his head off," he told her.

"See? He likes me already!" She responded with a grin as she took the baby in her arms, rocking her new-born nephew happily.

The others reached them as well. Nikolina gave her brother a hug, congratulating him on being a father now, then turned to her sister-in-law.

"And how are you feeling?" She asked, remembering what it was like to give birth and hoping Maria was starting to feel better.

"Much better now my son's here," Maria replied, "but thanks for checking," she added gratefully.

It wasn't a question she had heard a lot from her visitors, who mostly got carried away by the joy of seeing the new baby.

Nadezhda peeked past Ekaterina's arm and took a little look at her new cousin.

"What's his name?" She asked curiously.

"Alexei," Sasha replied.

"Nice name, Katya would have been better," his sister quipped, unable to resist the opportunity to joke around, as usual.

"Maybe if he gets a sister someday." Sasha laughed along with her.

"Well, while we are here, I suppose we should catch up a little," Nikolina suggested, partly out of a genuine desire to catch up and partly to distract from her sister's jokes before they got worse.

"How have you been since we were last here?"

Sasha nodded. "We probably should. Well, we've been good, just preparing for the baby coming. And Maria's been settling into her new job," he began to explain.

Maria joined in.

"Yeah, it's going really well. We've started a new security scheme now that they've rebuilt the prison and coupled with the rehabilitation programmes the community centre volunteers have started up, things are going great. There haven't been any disturbances in months."

She seemed very enthusiastic as she explained the progress they were making.

"Oh?" Nadezhda looked over at Dariya.

"You got your community centre started then? I didn't realise you planned on starting rehab schemes there as well."

"It was Di's idea," Dariya told her, "she thought it was one of the most important things to focus on, since the authorities are more concerned with justice than helping."

Diana looked away, seeming flustered.

But she got a smile from Nadezhda.

"She's right. Justice is one thing. And it is especially important, but most people still deserve second chances." She agreed.

Her adopted cousin glanced up and there was a brief hint of a smile on her face before she looked away again.

That was probably as close as she was going to get to gratitude and friendship.

Dariya nodded.

"They do. Which is why I'm so glad that I've heard a little from some of my other family members. They all seem to have taken the chance at a new life seriously and have found various jobs." She smiled.

Nadezhda let all the heart-warming news wash over her as she stood in a room full of her closest friends and family members, gently rocking her little cousin in her arms and thinking.

She reflected on everything they had been through just to get here. It wasn't so long since people in this very room, who were now happily chatting together, had hated one another's guts.

It was even less time since she had lain in that same hospital, not knowing if she'd ever walk again, with her family and friends weeping over her.

Or since she had learnt she had lost her job for doing it too well, pretty much. For responding too quickly to a dire emergency.

Or since her uncle had shared the news of little Alexei's arrival and she had wondered if he would make it, and if he would be normal. And here he lay, in her arms, a normal baby.

And a symbol that they had moved on from those not-that-distant times, into a new and brighter future, a future in which he would grow up safe, without having to worry about the dark secrets that had plagued her throughout the last few years of her life.

"Hey, Nadya, when's the wedding? I take it we're all invited?" Katya's voice cut through her thoughts.

She smiled at her Aunt's little jest.

"It'll happen one day, I'm sure," was her vague reply.

After all, that was another thing to do for the future; marry Sof and finally get the fairy-tale happily ever after.

But that might take a while, under the current marriage laws. One day, though, she quietly vowed that they would have their dream wedding.

She thought she had earned it by now, after everything they had been through lately.

It was about time for a happy ending. And, standing here with her future bride by her side, her little cousin in her arms and everyone she loved surrounding her, this seemed like that happily ever after moment to Nadezhda.

End of Book 3

Bonus Content

Never seen before short stories released to celebrate this new edition. All use the characters you know and love from The Secrets Series, but I've dabbled in all genres, from horror to romance.

Enjoy!

The Volkov Project

It was sheer coincidence that brought the hair-raising story into the spotlight. It just so happened that two journalists, travelling alone at night, were lured from the road and into the heart of evil.

They had been on a week-long trip to Belarus, where a conference for journalists in Eastern Europe had been hosted. Now, making the trek back through Russia, the women were tired and quiet.

At the wheel was Elena, the older and more experienced journalist who had been tasked with representing her company at the conference.

She was middle-aged and very thin, having missed a few too many meals. From the bags under her tired brown eyes, it was clear that she got by on coffee rather than sleep.

Elena was a workaholic who ran a small magazine and had paid over the odds to get herself and her companion into that conference.

She had worked for weeks to make it happen and had done all of the driving on the trip herself.

Now, though, she knew she was flagging and was beginning to wonder about pulling over for a quick rest. Or at least another cup of coffee.

With her was Nadezhda, her much younger assistant. The girl had joined the magazine after making headline news when she was abruptly fired from the police force for breaching protocol.

Though her actions had been rash, she had been fighting against an obsessive and insane mobster, so many had viewed her as a heroine.

Just twenty-two, Nadezhda was warming to her life as a journalist, but the long trip back to Moscow, where the magazine was based, had her distracted and anxious.

She was remembering her last long road trip, which had culminated in her breaking her legs, losing her job, and nearly dying in a fire.

Staring out of the window as the road whizzed by, she sighed. If only she had been stronger, smarter, more prepared... Perhaps it would never have happened.

But that was behind her now. The villain who had tried, so many times, to destroy her family was dead.

The people she had met along the way were rebuilding their lives, better than ever. She had to start moving on, too.

She turned back to Elena, trying to push her thoughts away. But as she opened her mouth to address the other woman, a piercing howl broke the silence of the night.

Elena rolled her eyes. "Damn wolves. I guess that puts pulling over here off the table."

Nadezhda shook her head. "Wolves can't open can't doors. We should be fine. Is there a motel or anything? I can't sleep in cars anymore." She shuddered at the thought.

The older woman slowed the car, pulling to the side of the road. "Let me check." She scrambled for her phone.

Another howl came, much closer.

Impatient, Elena tapped at the screen.

"Stupid thing… Why is it so slow…? O… Oh!" Suddenly, the car was bright with the light from the screen. "Here, we need to go… Huh… It's a little remote…" She frowned.

So far, they had stuck to main roads, but the map was suggesting they turn off down some distinctly rural looking tracks.

"I'm sure it'll be fine," Nadezhda mumbled, "I'm tired."

Her attitude would come back to her later, along with the realisation that she had learnt painfully little from her past horror stories.

But Elena dutifully followed her instructions and turned into a narrow, winding side road.

High hedges ran along each edge of the road, with occasional gaps giving brief flashes of green fields. Iced-over puddles glistened in the potholes… Of which there were many.

"Oh! Ow. It's a little… Ouch! Bumpy!" Elena grumbled as the little hatchback bounced from side to side.

She served to avoid another hole and brushed along the hedge. Branches pinged off the metallic shell.

"That better not have scratched my paintwork!" The tetchy driver muttered.

Nadezhda sighed, gripped the door for support, and closed her eyes.

The car swerved to the left, twisted with some vicious bends, and bounced over a few more dips and bumps.

 Then, finally, they juddered to a halt.

The young girl opened one eye. "We're here?"

"I guess so."

Elena indicated a dilapidated building that stood alone in one of the fields along the roadside. An old wooden sign read 'Motel: no parking.'

They were pulled up on the grass verge. At the thought of walking the distance from the car to the motel, across the mud and ice, Nadezhda groaned.

"Really? They could at least have put in a path."

Elena shrugged. "You said it'd be fine. Anyway, it's not that far. I have a torch in here somewhere…"

She reached over her companion and rummaged in the glovebox.

Moments later, they were standing at the side of the road. Elena was brandishing her touch like it was a weapon, and Nadezhda was viewing the car curiously.

"Should we bring our bags or anything?"

Her mentor shrugged. "We won't need much for one night."

"True. And lugging them across this field is the last thing I need."

The brunette gave a little yawn and set off over the frosty grass, guided by the beam of Elena's light.

Behind the two women, branches rustled in the hedge and twigs snapped underfoot.

These sounds, faint and subtle, passed unheard. But then, all of a sudden, a low growl filled the still, silent night air.

Nadezhda sprung around, her entire body tense.

Elena laughed.

"Don't worry. Probably just a random animal. Won't bother us. I forgot this was your first time out in the sticks at night."

She was still chuckling as she walked away, overtaking her assistant now.

But Nadezhda stayed rooted to the spot, even as the warmth of her friend's torchlight began to fade.

Something in her, some primal instinct maybe, warned her not to turn away from that chilling sound. The moment her back was turned, something would pounce.

The bushes twitched. Over the sound of her pounding heart, she could hear heavy breathing.

Again, instinct came to her aid. She threw herself to the ground and rolled to the side at the same moment that something sprang from the bushes.

Tumbling across the grass, she slipped down into a ditch and lay there, her stomach churning and her head spinning.

Heavy footsteps ran overhead. There was more deep breathing and some snuffling sounds, alongside grunts and growls.

She dared to raise her head. Mud was clinging to her face, hair, and clothes. She eased herself up on her elbows and crawled up the ditch's banks.

They seemed much steeper when adrenaline and gravity weren't rolling you abruptly down them.

When she managed to peek over the side, it took all her willpower to bite back a gasp.

Between herself and the edge at the field's edge, bathed in moonlight, stood a beast.

Another person may have simply called it a wolf, but Nadezhda, a born-and-raised city child, had only ever seen a wolf on nature documentaries.

Besides, this creature was quite unlike those dog-like animals.

It crouched on massive hind legs, its front paws – equipped with fearsome claws – held aloft by a barrel-like chest.

Like some cross between the hugest, most muscular man she could imagine and a feral, wild dog, it had a gigantic, albeit hairy, body but a canine snout that was twisted into a permanent snarl, saliva dripping from its jaws.

Her breath caught in her throat. She had heard of creatures like this, but only in stories.

Grim tales of horror and destruction always featured characters like these. Evil werewolves that tore people limb from limb.

But surely such a beast couldn't exist?

Unless… *No.* Surely not? But it *had* to be.

The only other time she had thought something couldn't exist; she had been thinking of the clones and mutants of Volkovs and their twisted experiments.

And as she stared, she could see a jet-black mane of fur and long scratch below the left eye of the creature.

Distinctive features that the cruel family had had in common.

Her chest tightened. It couldn't be… How? She had sworn she'd seen the last of—

With a mighty screech, the animal rounded and strode towards her.

It was all she could to scramble to her feet and race across the grass.

As she hurtled through the darkness, she could feel its breath on her back. It was so close. Growls and snarls burned in her ears.

She urged her legs to go faster, though every muscle and joint in her body was crying out after she had hastily flung herself on the frozen ground.

"ELENAAAAA! HELP!!" She screamed, knowing that, alone, she stood no chance.

But where was her mentor? Had she reached the motel already? Was she tucked up in bed, unsuspecting?

Oh, please, let her hear. Let someone hear. *Anyone.*

A claw caught her arm and tore the flesh, driving another yelp of anguish from her lips.

The force of the blow and the resulting dizziness made her stagger, but she managed to keep running. Somehow, she managed to keep just ahead of the monster.

Another, more distant howl rang out through the moonlit night. Nadezhda swore.

There were more of them. How many? Where? Was she to be surrounded and ripped limb from limb?

Blood dripped down her arm. Her breath was growing more ragged, and her heart felt as though it would explode.

There was a light glimmering in the motel.

But she wouldn't make it that far.

Something skimmed her cheek. She gasped, feeling her legs wobble beneath her.

Not another gash. Dare she raise her hand to her face and find out?

Wait... She didn't need to, did she? Whatever it was had come from in front of her, not behind. And the way ahead was clear.

She blinked, confused. Was the blood loss cracking her mind already?

Another sliver, barely visible, shot by her. There was a furious screech from the beast. Desperate to escape its wrath, she surged forward.

Her sudden burst of speed was just in time. Moments later, the creature collapsed, flattening foliage, and swirling up a huge cloud of dust around it.

At the deafening thump, she risked a glance over her shoulder. She skidded to an abrupt halt, nearly clattering to the ground herself as she did so.

The monster lay in a crumpled heap, bleeding. Around her, she could hear footsteps fleeing. Nothing else would attack her tonight.

But how had she been saved?

It took some time before Elena reached her, coming running across the field, torch still clutched in her hand.

The older woman wasn't alone, either. A stout, elderly man with a gun slung casually over his back trailed after her.

"Nadya! Are you okay?" The woman shook her head, answering her own question. "C'mon, let's get you an ambulance."

"Wh… What happened? How did you save me? How did you know?" Nadezhda was full of questions.

The man at Elena's side cackled.

"You're kidding. The whole village must have heard you squealing like a stabbed pig, girl. Anyway, your friend was worried about you, so I got my gun. Silencer, of course. People get a bit touchy about gunshot sounds in the middle of the night."

"So, you shot… It? Should we report it? Call the police?"

The man laughed again. "It's an animal. I'll come out and bury it in the morning."

But by morning, there was nothing to see.

And though she had escaped with her life, Nadezhda was left with the sickening fear that the Volkovs and their dark experiments were still out in the world, lurking in the darkness and hiding in quiet corners.

Who knew how many there may be? Or what each monster or mutant was capable of?

The Beginning Of A Promise

It was midsummer when they met. Not that you would have thought it from the weather.

Later, Nikolina would remember it as simultaneously the most miserable and the happiest day of her life.

College lectures had finished for the year, and she found herself at a loose end, no work to throw herself into, younger siblings mooching around the house, getting in her way and on her nerves.

So, she had agreed to do something stupid. Just to get herself out and about.

Katrina, a passing acquaintance from her law course, was having a party.

A busy, loud affair that celebrated, or, given the amount of alcohol involved, mocked the ancient festival of Kupala.

It wasn't remotely Nikolina's scene. Yet, that evening, she stood glaring into wilting flowers almost dropping from her silky blonde locks.

"Liiina!" A voice whined at the door, "Are you done? I need to go!"

"Hold it." Her tone was cold and unsympathetic as she considered her unsatisfying reflection.

"I can't! *Please!*"

With a sigh, she stepped out of the bathroom, giving way to her little sister, Yekaterina.

Katya hurried past. Nikolina made it to the top of the stairs before a new problem arose.

Sasha, her teenage brother, came dashing up the steps.

Upon seeing her, he exclaimed loudly, "*there* you are! I've been looking everywhere for you! It's storming like there's no tomorrow and all our laundry's still hanging out in the garden. It'll be soaked!"

"Well, go and get it in then!" She snapped.

"... Oh." He sounded genuinely shocked, as though that idea had never crossed his mind before.

Most likely, it hadn't. Nikolina loved the boy, but he was pretty helpless when left to his own devices.

But he dutifully scurried towards the back door. Then he turned and called over his shoulder.

"What's for dinner? I'm starving!"

When he had rushed outside into the pouring rain, Nikolina swore.

No matter how close she was to her siblings, their attitudes really did sum up everything she was sick of right now.

The whole… being a homemaker and second mother situation. Since her mother's passing, she had tried so hard to look out for the whole family.

But it was taking over her life. She was just twenty-two years old and could feel herself slipping into the routine of a middle-aged housewife.

So, for once, she had planned to do something fun, spontaneous, and entirely selfish. And it was being torn apart before it even got started.

No, not tonight. Her father would have to cook, just this once.

And… Where was Papa, anyway? He should have been home by now. She glanced at the clock again, nervously.

Actually, he should have been home half an hour ago. She had a bus to catch in 20 minutes. Sasha and Katya would be totally lost on their own.

She bit her lip. Should she give the station a ring? See if he was working late? But he was always so very good about letting her know…

Then again, his job was dangerous. Police chief in a bustling city. Her stomach flipped. What if…?

As she was beginning to think the unthinkable, to fear the worst, the front door banged as it swung open, then shut again.

She hurried to greet him, then froze as she realised that he was mid-argument with someone.

"No, no, I insist!"

"I really can't stop for long…"

"You must! Come in, come in!" Pushing the living room door aside with the same ease that he brushed off all concerns, her father ushered in his guest.

Ignoring the newcomer who stood awkwardly by her father's side, Nikolina demanded to know, "and where were you? I was worried!"

Though he was a grown man, and the Chief of Moscow's police force to boot, Ilya Moroz looked sheepish in the face of his daughter's wrath.

"I'm sorry, love. I've been having car trouble lately and when I got out of the station, the wretched thing wouldn't start. We were all locked up, so I didn't have a chance to call. I started to walk home but…"

"Walk home?!" The outraged girl couldn't help but interrupt. "In this weather?! It's at least 25 minutes without your coat! You'd have---!"

"Caught my death from a cold. Yes, yes, I'm quite sure." Ilya's tone was calm.

"Exactly what I told him! I saw him walking home and made him accept a lift!" Ilya's young companion spoke up at last, clearly enthusiastic about his good deed.

Ilya's kindly smile implied that the stranger couldn't 'make' him do anything, but would, for the time being, be permitted to think that he could.

Nikolina turned to regard the young man properly for the first time. He was around her age, tall with short, wavy brown hair and an ill-fitting, cheap suit.

His blue eyes twinkled as he caught her gaze and gave her a warm, welcoming smile.

But Ilya was shaking his head. "And yet, you refuse to accept a meal to return your favour!"

He was still grinning, but his tone was a touch indignant now.

Nikolina's lips twitched. That was so very typical of her father. Such a strict, almost transactional view of morality. And a hatred of being in any way indebted to anyone.

"You'd better say you'll stay for dinner. He'll be like a kicked puppy afterwards if you don't," her quip was light-hearted, even if it wasn't far from the truth.

Not catching her jocular tone, her father simply seized the opportunity. He pointed to her triumphantly.

"Yes! See? From the mouth of the cook herself! You must stay!"

"Oh. But… I can't stay tonight. Not even to cook…"

She glanced at her watch as she spoke, for some reason feeling a stab of guilt. In fact, she was almost saddened at the thought of leaving.

Even though she had almost certainly missed her bus and had been longing for a break all day. What had got into her?

It didn't seem as though she was alone in her feelings. The young man looked instantly crestfallen.

Ilya shook his head. "No need to look so disappointed, Antonin, I may not have the gourmet skills of my dear daughter, but I'm sure I can whip up something better than those awful frozen meals you exist on."

She felt a stab of sympathy for him. How sad, to be utterly alone, dependent on frozen, mass-produced rubbish and the kindness of strangers.

Maybe she was lucky, after all. Perhaps she should stay home and…

"Lina!" Her father's voice interrupted her thoughts.

"What?" She jumped slightly.

"I asked where you're off to. Can't be too far, not on a night like tonight. Remember, I can't give you a lift." His brow furrowed with concern.

"Katrina's having a party down at Bitsa Forest. It's a Kupala thing. Ish..." She gestured to her folk dress and the wilting wildflowers hanging from her hair by way of explanation.

Ilya looked stricken. "That's a long way! And there's no shelter out on the road. Don't tell me this party's outside? Dancing in the woods sort of thing?"

"It's fine." She shrugged. "There's buses. And I'll take a coat."

"You will *not!*" He exploded. "You'd be soaked after 5 minutes at the bus stop, let alone anything else! Honestly, you scold me about these things... Too busy looking out for everyone else, but what about yourself, hm?"

"I could say the same thing, you know." She crossed her arms as she spoke.

They stood, glowering at one another, each knowing the other had a point, each too stubborn to admit it.

"I'll drive her."

The squabbling duo turned on this intruder to their conversation. He smiled hopefully, his face full of innocence and charm.

"Aren't you dining with me?" Ilya raised an eyebrow, "I can't keep accepting favours from you with nothing in return. It looks like favouritism, especially after I just made you detective."

"Besides, I don't know you! I'm not getting into your car!" That sudden outburst made Nikolina flush.

She hadn't planned to say that. This man had been so sweet to her and her father, and her words were sharp and hurtful.

But Papa's job meant she had heard all the horror stories, seen the faces of the missing girls, the dead and the abused who had taken a simple favour from the wrong man.

But this man was a police officer, and her father's friend. Surely, she could trust him?

"I'm sorry, I didn't mean…"

He shook his head. "I understand. Safety first. Smart girl."

Ilya relented. "It's fine. You'll be safe with him, Lina. And Antonin… Dinner tomorrow night, yes? To thank you. Though I still don't understand your generosity."

Nikolina looked at her father with a stunned smile. She had just about given up on a night out.

"You mean it? We should go?"

"If you take care. So much as sneeze tomorrow and you'll never forget this."

Antonin laughed. "Right you are, sir. I'm happy to help. I miss family life, anyway. And don't worry," he turned to Nikolina, "I solemnly swear not to ruin your life or let you get sick. Now grab a coat."

Five minutes later, they were pulling away from the house at speed. His driving wasn't to Nikolina's taste, but she couldn't complain, after he'd done this for her. Instead, she searched for something polite to say.

"Thanks again for the lift. Are you sure you didn't want to go home? Won't your parents be waiting?"

He shook his head. "I don't see much of them these days. I live alone. Livens up my evening, see."

She lapsed into awkward silence. She really shouldn't have said that.

But he kept speaking as though nothing had happened. "So, Kupala, huh? Are you... into that?"

"Religiously? No. It just... seemed like a bit of fun." She shrugged her shoulders. It had been the only fun she could see in her life at the moment.

"Dancing in the rain? Sure does. Can I have a dance?" He was grinning. Was he teasing her? Probably.

It didn't matter. Her long-awaited break was here, and she was ready to let go and enjoy herself.

"You're on. But don't let me get sick." She flashed a playful smile of her own.

"I don't break my word, Lina."

It occurred to her that they hadn't been properly introduced, as he called her by her family's nickname. But she didn't correct him.

Within days, he felt like family anyway. They had laughed as they spun around in the forest, as she threw her pathetic excuse for a flower crown in the river, as they sat in the car, eating picnic food and sheltering from the rain.

Okay, so it hadn't been a wild college party, but she had had a far better time than she had ever expected to.

And, true to his word, he was at her home the next evening, brightening up their repetitive, dutiful dinners with his warm smile and sparkling eyes.

He could talk shop with her father, make childish faces with her little sister and keep her brother amused. And he could make her heart sing.

That was enough to make her life feel full again. Now all she had to do was hope he'd keep his promise.

'I solemnly swear not to ruin your life.'

Professor Volkov's Sob Story

He was a brilliant man. Brilliant like a diamond, with sharp edges and a soul as hard as rock, but brilliant, nevertheless.

And he must have worked hard to achieve anything at all, because his life had been one long misery.

When he was very young, his family immigrated from Kazakhstan to Russia. This move, supposed to improve their fortunes, did little for young Vladimir.

He was one of many children in a family that could ill avoid him. There was no money and little love to spare in his childhood.

His thirst for knowledge, which began at an early age, was never encouraged.

In fact, at fourteen years old, he was given the delightful birthday gift of a suitcase and told not to come back until he'd earned some money and made something of himself.

As he'd longed for parental support through higher education, this cut deep. But it wasn't as hard as coming to terms with his sudden homelessness.

A bright child, top of his class and full of complex ideas on how to make the world a better place, but neither practical nor streetwise, he wasn't cut out for this new life.

That, he explained, was how he ended up in trouble in the first place. The way he told it, it was inevitable.

By sixteen, he was running 'errands' for a small gang of low lives in the bustling criminal underbelly of Moscow. But he still had dreams.

Occasionally, one of the 'clients' he had to attend to would be some young-down-and-out wanting whatever drug was cheapest dropped off in some remote, forgotten corner of a school or college campus.

It always made him bristle when these orders came in. How dare they have what he burned for and still throw it all away?

Regardless of his feelings, he still delivered. He had little choice in that.

His current employer didn't take kindly to disappointment and Vladimir had seen at least one of his 'colleagues' splattered against the wall for arguing with higher-ups.

Besides, these visits provided an excellent opportunity to sneak around the places he so desperately wanted to attend.

It was easy to blend in with other teenagers, just by wearing nondescript black clothes and nonchalantly following the crowds.

Every now and then, he'd get into a class or a lecture and sit at the back of the room, silent and tense, hoping that no one would notice one extra student.

At Bauman Moscow State University, he even managed to slip into the central library and stood there, overwhelmed in front of the endless bookshelves until a librarian appeared.

The smart, stern-faced woman in the tweed suit cleared her throat. "Can I help you?"

Her tone was cold. Vladimir froze. She must know somehow that he didn't belong here. She didn't want to help him; she wanted to chase him away.

"I... Uh... I... I'm very sorry, I..." He stumbled over his words.

What should he say? Anything? Or should he save himself the pain and just bolt now, before she could have him arrested or thrown out?

The woman rolled her eyes. "Look, it's not that hard. What course are you on?"

"What?"

"What are you studying?" Now, the tone was patronising, as though she was speaking to a small and particularly unintelligent child.

He blinked. He hadn't expected to get this far. But of course, if he was in the library, he was a student here.

He straightened his back, held his head a little higher. Yes. He had a right to be here. Or at least she believed that he did. Now all he needed was one convincing lie.

What would he love to know more about?

So much. Oh, so very much. But she was already frowning at him, and he doubted he'd get away with this for much longer if he wasn't extremely fast.

"Science?" He felt his voice raise, that traitorous inflection creeping in and making him sound uncertain.

Another eyeroll. "Which kind?"

He blinked, like a rabbit in the headlights. *There are different kinds?*

That astonished remark was halfway to his lips when his brain caught up.

He hastily bit it back and swallowed, searching for something better to say. But he was well and truly stuck this time.

How could he convincingly lie about something he wouldn't recognise if this rather stern woman beat him over the head with it?

Which, looking at her face, she may well do.

Instead, she vented her impatience by folding her arms, glaring at him as though he was on thin ice, and beginning to list options.

"Biology? Physics? What is it? I do not have all day."

"Biology!" Relieved, he seized the first vaguely familiar word to sweep by.

In his painfully short-lived school days, he'd loved a good dissection.

When she dumped a tower of huge, plain-covered textbooks in front of him and stalked off through the library shelves with a disapproving sniff, it was clear that this was going to be different.

For one thing, that hatchet-faced madam would never allow anything as fun or messy as that. Besides, the first three books were all on human biology.

Aside from the assumption that it was probably different from a frog, he had never wondered what made a human tick before.

The books were all pretty bulky, but in the last few years, Vladimir had become adept at concealing certain packages.

Fortunately, he also had his backpack, intended for this very purpose, with him. Only four could be crammed in, and their weight was considerable.

He shoved another two under his jacket and, heart thudding with excitement, slipped through the doors of the library.

Heading for home, he considered the idea that this moment could be the beginning of all of his dreams coming true.

Not that his 'home' really looked like the location of success and happiness.

It was, in fact, a run-down rental property on the outskirts of Moscow. He shared it with six other young men of invariably charmless personality.

His delightful bosses at the mob hadn't put them up here out of the kindness of their hearts, after all.

They were here to watch the 'crop' in the attic, keep a low profile when it came to the neighbours and if the worst came to the worst, take the fall with the local police department.

But it hadn't come to that, as long as the landlord never dropped in for a surprise spot check, it was unlikely to.

So, the accommodation was free, relatively low-risk and a big improvement on the streets.

When he arrived, he flopped onto the sagging, ancient couch and opened up one of the books.

Its contents were a fascinating blend of medical knowledge – that could be carefully applied to … he preferred to call it self-defence – and sneak peaks at what made humans work.

To get more depth on that, he needed another kind of 'ology,' a funny word that he doubted he could pronounce but craved more of.

Next time he was on a campus, he decided he'd find out more. Hopefully from someone a little more cheerful.

"Get your nose out of that book, creep!" A huge hand swiped his remaining pile of books to the floor.

"Just because you can't read, Boris, there's no need to be bitter." He responded, barely glancing up.

Boris was one of his roommates, a hulking great man whose biceps were considerably bigger than his brain.

His response to being insulted was predictable. He lunged.

Vladimir smirked as he ducked. This was a dance they had done many times. He was no physical match for Boris, but he was faster, lighter and could generally wait until the other tripped over furniture or simply tired of chasing him.

Not today.

One of his newly acquired books caught him a glancing blow on the shoulder. The big man had learnt how to throw.

Biting back a swear word because he liked to think he had maintained some standards while in this god-forsaken hovel, he rolled off the couch and onto the floor. Crouching for cover, he rubbed his bruised arm.

Boris loomed into view over the back of the couch. Vladimir scrambled for an escape plan.

And found one. Something in his brain latched onto a piece of new knowledge. He sprung to his feet; arm outstretched.

His fingers jabbed into his roommate's solar plexus, the power of his leap still behind them.

It may tell you something about our subject that his pleasure upon seeing his roommate staggering backwards, coughing horrifically, far outweighed the sense of joy he'd felt when he had first pilfered those books.

He didn't share the aftermath of this altercation with me, except to say that he wasn't troubled by Boris going forward.

But he did delight in repeating his little library escapade at any and every campus he could gain access to. When his dubious job didn't take him there, he found some free time.

He discovered the joy of University libraries that were open all hours, tired students pulling all-nighters to plough through overdue assignments paid him no heed.

He took illegal crash courses in anthropology, psychology, anything that he thought could get him power over people.

Oh, and a misguided physics course that led to a small explosion or two. But he glossed over that one quite hastily.

As he got bolder, he did sneak into classrooms, workshops, and laboratories on campuses too.

One slightly ditzy professor did give him a decent grade because, though he had never done an assignment in his life, he did have the best attendance in the class.

He was rather insufferably smug about this, and so the label 'Professor Volkov' began, as a self-congratulatory joke that he eventually stopped explaining and simply let everyone believe.

His educational journey gave him the knowledge to do some incredible things. But incredible does not always mean good.

I think what I've learnt about the 'professor's' early life suggests that he was always a deeply twisted man.

I don't doubt that his family's rejection of him and the way his adolescence was spent only added to this; but his motives, his thoughts, the way he chose to achieve his goal of knowledge and what he did with it...

You see, when he was 19, after some time studying people both through science and low-level involvement in the fast-moving criminal underworld of Moscow, he disappeared.

Around the same time, several members of one of Moscow's many infamous gangs, including the esteemed Boris, were found to have been poisoned by a strange, obscure substance.

Few in the general populace knew of it. But those who had studied medicine did.

A short while later, an unfortunate explosion demolished the slum Vladimir Volkov was born in. His parents and six of his siblings were instantly killed.

After that? It's difficult to say.

A string of bizarre crimes probably. But what we do know is that he surfaced sometime later, already in his late forties with a set of sinister family members and dark schemes.

He was nothing if not ambitious, dragging himself out of his beginnings… Only to become something much, much worse.

Of course, we're supposed to believe in second chances for everyone. Everyone's redeemable.

But that man... Ah, well, I was only his prison counsellor, what do I know?

All I can say is that I wasn't sad when he met his end here.

Charity Work

"Do you do gay people?" had to be the strangest question Diana Volkova had ever been asked.

And she was no stranger to oddness.

"Uh… Well… This is a charity hotline… What exactly was it you were hoping we did for the LGBT Community?" She managed to stammer a semi-professional answer in response, though some of her co-workers glanced at her questioningly.

"Your website says you deal with unwanted people. 'Freaks of nature' with 'toxic family situations'."

Diana's heart sank. She recognised the words. They were her own.

Putting together a website for the small charity she and some family members had founded had been completely beyond her usual realm of experience.

An ex-cultist whose previous skillset had primarily been violence; she had wanted to make a positive difference instead.

It had been her mother's idea to draw on her own feelings in order to write the webpage. She had definitely felt like a freak enough times.

But this call... How was she supposed to take this?

The shifting tone, the heavy implication of air quotes... Was this a person in need of help?

Or someone trying to say something more sinister?

She felt a bubble of old anger. The rage she had used against her enemies, once upon a time.

If *that* was what they were saying, she'd gut them like a fish. Her adoptive cousin was in love with another woman. And they were *not* freaks.

But the phone line was crackling. "Hello? Are you still there?"

She exhaled slowly, remembering the counselling she'd been through. She wasn't supposed to let her anger get the better of her. Or jump to conclusions.

"Those are our aims, yes. How do they apply to your situation?"

"I don't know what to do. My family says I'm a freak. Especially my grandfather…"

Diana tensed. *Grandfather*. The very reason she had been a mess herself. The very reason she was here, now, trying to turn everything around.

"You are not a freak."

She tried to keep her tone calming, reassuring. Tried to push down the anger. She wasn't speaking to the man himself. Just a traumatised, rejected child.

After a deep breath, she started over.

"You're not a freak. This isn't your fault. All you can do is be yourself and ignore everyone who tries to push you down."

Was she doing this right? Those words felt cheap, empty, copied from her therapist.

But they had been true enough for her. They had helped her to start a new life. One she had never thought was possible.

The phone crackled. The voice on the other end came through shakily.

"I... I can't ignore it. Not now. Not after everything..."

Her stomach tightened into a knot. Months had passed, and it never got easier to hear the real moments of pain. The sobbing, the fear.

Had she ever sounded like that? No. She had just been angry and closed off, until she couldn't be any longer.

"What happened?" She heard herself ask.

"He kicked me out. There was this awful screaming match between him and dad because I told them I was seeing my boyfriend this weekend and..." A pause. A hiccup. Or perhaps just a stifled sob.

Screw professional. The rage was back now. Burning bright and hot in her chest.

"Where are they?"

"Wha?? Well, *I'm...*"

"Right. Yes. Where are you? That's what I meant..."

"I'm in the college library. They have free wi-fi and they're open 24/7. I thought I might… Be able to figure something out…"

"Right. And is there anywhere you can go? A friend's house?"

Another pause. "I messaged Ivan. My boyfriend. But I haven't heard back…"

"A back-up option?"

"I could go to Izabella's… She's always good to me."

"Go somewhere safe. What do you have with you? Anything?"

"A few clothes. My phone. Some change."

Diana nodded, to herself more than anything. Then she glanced to the side. The other on-call girl today was deep in conversation.

A clatter from the back room alerted her to the fact that her mother was making tea. Good. That should take some time, and the kettle made all kinds of hellish noises.

That should cover her. She didn't like to do this, after all.

And her mother, paragon of virtue and founder of this charity, would hate her for it. But sometimes there was only so much she could take.

Only so long that she could keep the rage down for.

"Okay, that should be all the immediate concerns. Our website also has numbers for therapy and legal advice at affordable rates, if you need some extra counselling, or want to recover specific belongings."

This spiel was standard. Now it was time to mix things up.

"Now, would you mind answering a few questions? It's just for our... demographic survey..."

And that sounded professional enough, too. Enough for the young man to kindly provide his former address.

He probably thought nothing of it. It was sandwiched between other personal questions, like age and race.

But for Diana, it was all she needed to know to implement her bespoke survey. If she was going to do charity work, she'd do it her way.

With violence.

As soon as she had hung up, she slipped her personal phone from her pocket and scrolled through her contacts.

When her family had finally been freed from her grandfather's twisted little cult, they had dispersed around the country.

Many had found their own jobs, hobbies, and skills. But some still fell back on what they knew best.

And some of her nastiest Uncles didn't live far from her recent caller's location.

It wasn't evil. It was *justice.*

She'd never had faith in the conventional justice system.

And this way, when the anger came close to choking her, when she realised just how awful people could be, she had a way to make a real difference.

Her mother had good intentions, but talking did nothing.

And this wasn't the first time she had taken matters into her own hands.

It had started with a late-night call. A woman's trembling voice, desperate. She begged them to let her have a room.

She had the wrong number. But Diana couldn't find the words to say that. So, she kept quiet and listened.

The story – the messy, bloody story that she couldn't get out of her head, even now – had come tumbling out in a rush.

The man who was trying to kill her had been her husband. The father of her child.

And Diana hadn't been able to keep the rage down. She had screamed and shouted at the woman to call the damn police.

She wouldn't. She *couldn't*.

So, Diana had dragged her location from her. As she had done so, she had remembered all the advice she had been given.

When you're fucked up, everyone wants to give you advice.

Mama said: *We must help people. It's our duty, after everything that happened.*

Her adopted cousin, Nadya, had shown her that sometimes, the law was stupid, pointless, and downright dangerous.

If you followed it to the letter. If you waited around to see if the police or the murderer got there first.

Her therapist, in the midst of one of Diana's angst-filled rants about her family and how they were broken now, had said that maybe they didn't need to completely start over.

Maybe they already had skills that could make the world a better place.

That first, fateful night, she had done the deed herself. A description of the man, a location. That had been all she had needed.

She found him in an alleyway, and though he was armed, he wasn't ready for her.

After she had sunk the knife deep into his stomach, she had thrown up. The smell of blood had never bothered her before.

Perhaps she had changed. But somehow, she got away with what she had done. And vowed not to do it again.

But the world always had another scumbag. Kill one, another one comes around the corner.

So, she had spoken to her family. Those of them who had changed the least.

And, for once, the Volkovs had agreed to make the world a better place.

She still had that bloody knife. Sealed in a bag under her bed to remind her that, even when the phone calls didn't feel significant, she could make a big difference to someone's world.

There had been many others.

The abused, the downtrodden, the frightened and the rejected.

Some were very intimate, personal issues she learnt about. The bullies who threw the word 'freak' into the face of a vulnerable child.

The vicious women who would tell their husbands that they were broken because they couldn't give them children.

The father whose daughter was starving because a fat girl was disgusting and unnatural.

The ambiguous wording on their site brought in all sorts of people. And all sorts of evil.

Sometimes, she had bigger problems to address too. Someone would call, seeing they were thinking of hurting themselves. Or giving up on life.

Because of a decision some councillor had made. Some thoughtless, careless decision that would drive someone out of their home, would leave someone's family bankrupt.

That would be a fresh rage. A rage against the system.

And the way that the country she lived in would quietly kill its own people for the satisfaction of a fascist would-be emperor.

Of course, she wasn't going to get away with assassinating the President of Russia. Besides, she had more or less given up actually killing her targets herself.

But every now and again, she would be talked into taking out a mayor, councillor, or some other moronic politician with a pompous title.

Only the ones who were doing the cruellest, nastiest things. Who came closest to doing his bidding.

But whoever the target was, her own personal charity works always made her feel better than the long calls with people who had no problem but loneliness.

When the messages came through from her uncles, they made her grin.

They really were improving the world. One dead bastard at a time.

"Tea is ready… Who are you texting, Zvezdochka?"

At the sound of the old pet name her mother called her, she jumped, nearly throwing her phone across the room.

"No one, Mama. No one at all."

Family Dinner

It was Nadezhda's idea. Now that they had all reconnected, put old differences aside. Now that they had something to celebrate.

Perhaps if she had ever actually eaten out with her family, she would have known better. Poor, naïve Nadya.

The evening began with tired, stressed Nikolina bursting through the door after work.

Her hair was beginning to unwind itself from the tight bun she bullied it into every morning, her tie had gone AWOL, and she snapped at her daughter:

"Are you even ready to go to this God-forsaken meal?"

"In a moment, Mama. Why don't you take a breath in the meantime?" Nadya smiled as she pulled a brush through her hair.

Since they had come home, things had changed. She could call Nikolina 'Mama,' for one thing.

Though the word still felt strange on her tongue.

And she could call her out when she was being too cold and harsh. The older woman was trying to relax more. Now that she no longer had to hide from the world.

She heard her mother sigh.

"Sorry, sweetheart. Work. Again."

"I know, I know. Why are you still at that firm if all they do is drive you up the wall?" She adjusted her headband as she spoke, squinting critically at herself in the mirror.

Nikolina resisted the urge to roll her eyes. Try leaving the house on time with a teenage daughter.

"It is … easier than going somewhere new. I am too old for that nonsense."

Her daughter giggled. "Well, I guess I can't argue with that." She stepped away from the mirror. "Just need to find some shoes now…"

"Oh, I will take a seat then…" Nikolina drifted towards the sofa.

Nadya stopped in her tracks.

"Was that … *a joke?*"

"Yes."

"We really are making progress. Just look at us," she laughed again, then turned her mind back to current events.

"I'll just grab some trainers or something, won't be long."

In the ten minutes that she was out of the room, Nikolina's phone began its constant, irritating chime.

She groaned. Reached for her bag. Groaned again.

The first night in a lifetime that she had put aside to do things with her family, and it was being interrupted.

But conscientiously, she answered it anyway. After some deliberating.

"Hello?"

"Lina? Where are we meant to be going?"

At the sound of Sasha's voice, she sighed. Her little brother was as scatterbrained as ever.

"Smolenskaya Square Food Emporium," she explained. Suspicion made her add: "Why? Where are you?"

"Uh…" His voice was evidence enough of his guilt.

"Sasha. Where are you?"

Nadya appeared in the doorway in a pair of very sparkly trainers. With her teeth gritted, Nikolina gestured to the phone.

At the end of the line, Sasha began to speak.

"Well… Uh… You know the big roundabout that takes you out of Moscow?"

"It is called a ring road. Anyway, we are eating in the city. How are you there?"

"I'm sorry! It's been a while."

No. You moved 3 months ago, after living in Moscow your whole life. You're just a rubbish navigator.

Nikolina bit back her thoughts. Maybe there was another way out of this.

"Did you bring the GPS? Or failing that, Maria?"

Surely, fixing Sasha's terrible sense of direction was his girlfriend's problem now.

"Maria came in her own car. She doesn't like mine. Or the way I drive it..." He sounded sheepish.

"And you've never got the hang of technology for navigating, have you?" She predicted his next comment.

Nadya nodded knowingly and mouthed, 'Uncle Sasha.'

As her mother began to dictate directions over the phone like the world's most reluctant GSP service ever, the doorbell rang.

Her Aunt, Ekaterina, was on the doorstep. With blood on her face.

"What on *Earth* happened to you?"

"It's nothing. I just... I had a little fall earlier and my nose met my desk. It wasn't a friendly meeting."

Katya was still joking, even though she sounded like a cartoon character.

"You broke your nose?"

"It's fiiiinee. Where's Lina? Can I wash the blood off before she sees?"

"She's on the sofa, on the phone. Why didn't you just wash it at your house?" Katya was as baffling as ever.

"Builders are in. I was working in the library," Ekaterina stepped past her niece and pointed up the stairs. "So, she won't know if I head up there?"

"Uh… Sure. Go for it…"

Nikolina appeared in the doorway.

"Who is it?"

"Auntie Katya. But she had to … reapply her lipstick upstairs…" Nadya lied.

Nikolina rolled her eyes.

"Is no one ready? Our reservation is at 6:00 pm and it's now 5:30. Your Uncle Sasha has been swallowed up by the roads, Maria is travelling separately so who even knows where she is..."

"Mama. *Breathe.* It'll work out fine. I'm ready, you're ready, we'll wait for Katya, pick up Sof..."

Another groan. "I forgot we invited Sof..."

'We' meant Nadya. Apparently, she was now best of friends with this vigilante girl she had met in Yaroslavl.

At least she *had* friends her own age now.

Katya came hurrying down the stairs. "Great, that's done, she won't kn—"

At the sight of her sister, she froze.

Nikolina peered at her in confusion. "You're not wearing any lipstick..."

Ekaterina blinked. "Was I supposed to...?"

Both women turned to Nadezhda.

The truth, slowly, came out. And the argument continued out into Nikolina's car.

"And you call *me* a liar!" The oldest woman scolded her daughter.

"And *you!*" Her accusing finger narrowly missed her sister's already damaged nose.

"You should have called me straight away! I ought to be driving you to the hospital!"

"No way. I wasn't gonna miss this! Anyway, you can't lecture anyone on asking for help!"

"Next left." Nadezhda had Sof's address on her phone. "And what happened to putting the past behind us?"

There was a guilty silence.

"That does not change the fact that she is injured."

"She said she's fine. Let's just go."

When Sof crammed into the backseat beside Nadezhda, she winced.

"Sheesh, talk about cold. Why the silence?"

"Things didn't really get underway as we had hoped. But it's okay. We're all here now. All we have to do is make it to the restaurant and see if Uncle Sasha has escaped the clutches of the evil motorway yet," Nadya told her.

This lightened the mood, at long last. Katya snorted. "He got lost again?"

Even Nikolina's lips twitched. "Apparently so."

But it seemed that Sasha had eventually found the right place, because as they pulled into the car park, he and Maria were standing between their two cars, catching up.

"Finally. We're all here in one piece." Nadya gave a sigh of relief.

"More or less."

Nikolina glanced sideways at her injured sister, who tried to pull a face in response and ended up giving a little whimper instead.

Then Sof decided to put forth some truly famous last words.

"Don't worry. Nothing else can go wrong now."

Inside the restaurant, it was poorly lit, and the air smelt of someone burning their dinner.

"Where did you book us?" Sasha's brow wrinkled.

"It had good reviews online." Nikolina was defensive.

"Give it a chance," Maria advised her partner.

"Let's at least get our table before we make judgements," Katya agreed.

"Well, well, someone matured."

Her brother's joke earned him an elbow in the ribs.

Meanwhile, Nikolina had led them into the main dining area. But now she was standing, hands on hips, glaring about her.

"What is it?" Nadezhda asked.

"There is no one to show us to our seats..."

In fact, she could have halved her statement. There wasn't a solitary member of staff in sight. Just some rather bored-looking diners.

"What do we do now?"

Sof chimed in with a very typical attitude: "I don't see why we should have to wait for them. That's clearly our table..."

She pointed across the room to a family-sized table with a large 'reserved' sign in the centre.

"You do not know that! What if someone else reserved a seat? I would feel awful..." Nikolina shot the idea down.

"Can I *help* you?"

The voice that boomed from behind them strongly suggested that it did not wish to help them unless it was to the nearest exit.

Nadezhda laid a hand on her hot-headed best friend's arm. No need to retaliate. The man would surely seat them once the matter was explained.

Nikolina seemed to agree, as she turned around and began to explain the situation.

But the man shook his head firmly.

"I'm sorry. We're closed."

"You are… very clearly not."

Nikolina gestured to the assembled diners.

"Ma'am. I'm from the health board. I assure you; this establishment is closed."

The large man reached into his jacket and drew out a card.

"But our reservation… I…"

Nikolina was usually very composed, this stammering wasn't at all like her. But she was also very organised, and her plans didn't tend to go so catastrophically wrong. Certainly not so many times in a row.

It seemed that the health inspector had a kind streak, though. Even if the owner of the restaurant may have disagreed. The man sighed and drew something else from his pocket. A notebook.

As he scribbled, he spoke:

"I've no intention of ruining anyone's evening. I can see you have plans. Go to this place and give them my name.

We're friends, they'll give you a good meal. And you won't go home with food poisoning…"

He tore the page from the book and handed it to her. Then he looked around grimly.

"That reminds me. I better shut this place down and clear everyone out before something nasty happens."

As if on cue, a woman got up from the dining room and fled, clutching her stomach.

"Time to go," Katya decided almost instantly.

"Thanks!" She waved to the health inspector and pulled her stunned sister out of the way.

"Well, this is the last time I suggest we do anything nice…"

A despondent Nadezhda spoke up as they exited the building.

Sasha shook his head and put an arm around his niece's shoulders.

"Nonsense. This has been our family at its most… typical, after all."

Even Nikolina had to smile then because it was true.

"Yeah, we've made the memories. Now let's go get some real food!" Sof took her friend's arm from the other side.

And in spite of everything, they were all smiling as they walked away.

Praise for the Author

'The author did a great job keeping the story engaging and moving at a pace that wasn't boring allowing me to look forward to the next scene or the introduction of the next character.' - Stanley McCluskey

'Ellie Jay is a gifted writer and storyteller. What I loved about the author was the way she managed to hook the reader. I felt like I was a voyeur over hearing gossip, arguments, and conversations, knowing that I should not eavesdrop, but being unable to pull away. The dialogue was spot on and witty.' - OSBAuthor

'This author is a wonderful human being. Her wit and sass is what got me to try one of her books to begin with.'

- Peter McCollum

'It was an interesting and extremely well written tale by Ellie Jay. My favourite aspect is the author's excellent storytelling ability. She has a fluent and engaging writing style.' – Sophie Bowns

'Ellie Jay's unique style of transporting the reader to the scene and helping the reader go through the emotions of the characters, once again came through in this fast-paced story. Her art with sarcasm is sprinkled in throughout and I love her use of language as she takes the reader through the very imaginative story. The author

does not dwell too much on long descriptive boring scene

or character descriptions. Instead, she uses language and

the characters.' – Dr. Mansur Hasib

'I was sucked into the story from the start and kept

engaged till the last page, and I appreciated the clear and

vivid writing style. A recommended read for those who

enjoy suspense and interesting characters, and I'm

looking forward to reading more by Ellie Jay.' - Steph

'Ellie Jay expertly weaves together a complex plot filled

with unexpected twists and turns, keeping readers

guessing until the very end.' - ProMystic B.

Find More By Ellie Jay

Not had your fill yet? Craving more?

Follow me on Twitter @EllieJayWrites, Instagram

@elliejaywriter or search for Ellie Jay Author to find all

my links.

For more books, check my Amazon author page:

https://www.amazon.com/stores/Ellie-

Jay/author/B08XC1CVMG

Thanks for reading.

Don't forget to leave a review!

www.ingramcontent.com/pod-product-compliance
Lightning Source LLC
Chambersburg PA
CBHW070319140726
47910CB00015B/6